WISH UPON
A MATCHMAKER

BY
MARIE FERRARELLA

First published in Great Britain 2013
by Mills & Boon, an imprint of Harlequin (UK) Limited,
Eton House, 18-24 Paradise Road, Richmond, Surrey TW9 1SR

© Marie Rydzynski-Ferrarella 2013

ISBN: 978 0 263 90126 9
ebook ISBN: 978 1 472 00505 2

23-0713

Harlequin (UK) policy is to use papers that are natural, renewable and
recyclable products and made from wood grown in sustainable forests. The
logging and manufacturing processes conform to the legal environmental
regulations of the country of origin.

Printed and bound in Spain
by Blackprint CPI, Barcelona

USA TODAY bestselling and RITA® Award-winning author **Marie Ferrarella** has written more than two hundred books for Mills & Boon, some under the name Marie Nicole. Her romances are beloved by fans worldwide. Visit her website, www.marieferrarella.com.

To
Andrew Gallagher,
who mentioned
his daughter's name
to me
and inspired a story.

"Are you the lady who finds mommies?"

The high-pitched, rather intelligent little voice cut a hole in Maizie Sommers's mental haze. For the last half hour, the successful Realtor had been busy putting together an ad for her newest local real estate listing so that it could be entered on her website. Finding just the right words to place the proper emphasis on the twenty-year-old ranch house's best features had been nothing short of a challenge. The term *fixer-upper* carried such a negative connotation.

Absorbed in the task, Maizie had only vaguely heard the front door to her office opening and closing. It had registered as just so much background noise. Part of her thought she'd only imagined it.

Especially when she'd glanced in the direction of the door and hadn't seen anyone come in.

But there obviously was a reason for that. The person who had come in was only approximately half the size of an adult.

Maizie stopped working and after looking around, she half rose in her seat and looked over the edge of her desk. Ten small fingertips were firmly pressed against it. The little girl pushed herself up as far as she could go, standing on the very tiptoes of her black patent-leather shoes.

Maizie put down her pen and smiled at the child, judging her to be around four, or possibly a small five. Slight and a strawberry-blonde, her newest visitor had exceptionally intelligent-looking blue eyes. She was going to be a knockout in a dozen years, Maizie judged.

"Hello."

The girl, who more than anything resembled a perfect little doll, tossed her head—sending her curls bouncing—and paused only a moment to politely return the greeting, "Hello," before she got back down to business.

No doubt, she was a woman on a mission.

"Are you the lady who finds mommies?" the pint-size strawberry-blonde asked again. "My friend Greg said you found one for his dad and that she's really nice and now they're all very happy."

Maizie never forgot a name, especially not a child's name. The little girl was talking about Greg and Gary Muldare. After Sheila, Micah Muldare's aunt, had come to see her, lamenting the young widower's state, she and her two dearest friends had strategized and gotten the boys' father, Micah, together with a bright, up-and-coming dynamo of a lawyer, Tracy Ryan, who solved

Micah's legal problems and along the way wound up becoming Mrs. Micah Muldare.

Word was getting around faster and faster, Maizie mused with a smile. She'd had walk-in clients before— both for her professional services and for her unofficial ones, but none of her clients had ever come in the economy size.

"What happened to your mommy, dear?" Maizie asked the girl kindly.

And just what was the child doing here by herself? Had the little girl run away in order to come see her? Her own daughter had been precocious, but even *she* hadn't been this independent at such a young age.

There was just the slightest hint of sorrow in her voice as the girl said, "Mommy died before I could remember her, but Daddy remembers, and it makes him sad when he does. I want Daddy to be happy like Greg's daddy is." Her voice took on conviction as she said, "My daddy needs one. He needs a mommy," she clarified in case that had gotten lost in the shuffle of words. "Can you find him one? And make her pretty, because my daddy said he wants one as pretty as me. That's why he's with Elizabeth now," she confided. "She's pretty, but she's not a mommy, just a lady." Lowering her voice as she raised herself up as far as she could on her toes so that only Maizie could hear, she said in what amounted to a stage whisper, "I don't think she likes kids."

Before Maizie could recover or comment on either the little girl's request, or her summation of her father's current relationship, the door to her widely sought-after real estate agency opened a second time in the space of less than five minutes.

It wasn't that Maizie was unaccustomed to a lot of foot traffic, thanks to both her reputation and the popular shopping center location of her agency, she was more than used to a constant flow of humanity. However, the two people who worked for her were currently out showing properties, and she had no appointments on her calendar for at least an hour. She'd been promising herself a quick lunch now for the last ninety minutes—the second she finished writing the ad.

But something far more interesting had come up and her neglected stomach was pushed into second place.

Humor curved the corners of Maizie's mouth. She'd never had a walk-in who wasn't able to see over her desk before.

But just as Maizie had gotten her newest would-be client to tell her story, an utterly frazzled-looking woman suddenly burst into her real estate office. The second she did, the woman made a beeline for the tiny visitor who was standing on the other side of Maizie's desk.

"Virginia Ann Scarborough, are you trying to give me a heart attack?" the blonde demanded as she fell to her knees and smothered the little girl in a huge hug that utterly reeked of relief as well as panic.

"No," the little girl replied in a small, somewhat contrite voice. Her pained expression told Maizie that the girl was merely enduring the hug. Apparently, unlike the distraught woman who'd found her, she hadn't been at all afraid.

"I was trying to find a mommy for Daddy," the child

explained, as if that would clear everything up and exonerate her as well.

"You know you're not supposed to run off like that, Ginny," the woman chided.

Making a swift survey of the little girl, the woman appeared satisfied that the only thing worse for wear were her own nerves. She rose to her feet and only then turned her attention to the other person in the room.

"I'm very sorry about this," she apologized to Maizie. "I hope my niece didn't break anything."

"I wasn't in here long enough to break anything, Aunt Virginia," the girl protested indignantly.

Maizie rose from behind her desk, a little bemused. "Are you her guardian?" she asked the woman, nodding at the little girl.

"I'm her aunt." She slanted an exasperated look at the little girl that was nonetheless laced with love. "Her long-suffering aunt. I swear, Ginny, if you weren't named after me…" Ginny's aunt let her voice trail off, then flashed another apologetic smile at Maizie as she took a firm hold of Ginny's hand, her intent clear. She was taking the little girl out of the office. "I'm sorry about all this—"

"No, please, wait," Maizie coaxed in her best maternal, nurturing voice. "You look a little frazzled. Let me get you a nice cup of tea." She glanced down at Ginny. "And I think I might have some lemonade for you if you like."

"Yes, please," Ginny said with restrained enthusiasm.

"No, really, we've been enough trouble already," Virginia protested.

"Nonsense. You're no trouble at all and I must say my curiosity has been piqued," Maizie admitted as she went to the small island against the wall that housed an all-in-one unit, combining a small refrigerator, a stove with microwave features and a sink on one side. With a minimum of movements, she made a hot Chai tea for Virginia and poured a glass of lemonade for the small whirling dervish who'd been named after her.

"Now then, Ginny," Maizie began, addressing Ginny as she handed her the glass of lemonade, "you said something about your daddy needing a wife."

Hearing that, Virginia's eyes widened in stunned amazement. "Ginny, you didn't—why would you do that?" the woman demanded of her niece.

"Because she finds them," Ginny told her aunt, nodding at Maizie. "Greg said so," she said with the conviction of the very young.

"This lady runs a real estate agency," Virginia pointed out, her nerves beginning to fray no doubt.

"Perhaps I should explain," Maizie interjected, coming to Ginny's rescue. "My friends and I dabble in matchmaking on the side—there's no charge," she said quickly in case the other woman thought this was some sort of a scam, "just the satisfaction of bringing together two people who were meant for each other but who might never—without the proper intervention— come together," she said. Her eyes shifted to Ginny. "Like your friend Greg's father and Tracy Ryan. My friends and I supply the 'intervention,' so to speak," she told Virginia.

"Is that why you begged me to bring you here, to the ice cream parlor?" she asked her niece.

"They have very good ice cream," Ginny piped up innocently.

"See what I'm up against?" Virginia asked Maizie wearily.

Maizie did her best to appear sympathetic. In her line of work, she'd had a great deal of practice. "Are you her father's sister?" she asked.

Virginia nodded. "His name is Stone Scarborough. I'm his younger sister. I moved in with him to help out after Eva—Ginny's mother—died. That was a year and a half ago. I'm still helping," she added.

And you want to move on with your life, Maizie surmised from the other woman's choice of words and her tone.

Maizie sat back in her chair, her mouth curving in a smile of anticipation. She could sense the thrill of a challenge taking hold. Nothing she loved more than being challenged.

"So, tell me about your brother," she coaxed Virginia.

"I don't know where to start," Virginia said with a sigh.

"At the beginning is always a good place," Maizie encouraged.

"I guess it is." Taking a deep breath, the other woman began to talk, with frequent interjections coming from Ginny.

Maizie listened attentively to both.

And a plan began to form.

Chapter One

Stone Scarborough stared at his younger sister, trying to make sense out of what she had, rather breathlessly, just told him.

Whatever it was, Virginia seemed very animated about it and he'd managed to glean that it had something to do with the business card she had just pressed into his hand. But her narrative came out so disjointed he found himself feeling the way he had back in the days when he'd walk into the middle of a movie with his late wife—Eva never managed to be on time for anything no matter how hard she tried—and he was forced to try to make heads or tails out of what he was subsequently watching.

In addition to Virginia's overwhelming flow of words, his daughter, Ginny, seemed to have caught the fever and was fairly bouncing up and down right in front of him. It was as if both were experiencing a massive sugar attack.

In an attempt to sort out the verbiage, Stone held his hand up to get Virginia to stop talking for a moment, regroup and begin at the beginning.

"Run this by me one more time," Stone urged his sister. "From the top," he added.

His sister Virginia shook her head, her light blond ponytail swishing from side to side. "You know, for a brilliant man, you can be so slow sometimes."

"Must be in comparison to the company I keep," he said drolly. If he practiced for a year, he'd never be able to talk as fast as his sister—or his daughter. "Humor me," he instructed, looking down at the card in his hand. "Why am I calling this woman?"

Taking a breath, Virginia recited the facts. "The number belongs to Maizie Sommers. She's a Realtor who owns her own company. She said she needs the name of a good general contractor to recommend to her clients."

He had never believed in coincidences or good fortune without there being strings of some sort, no matter how invisible, attached.

Consequently, Stone regarded the card in his hand with more than a smattering of suspicion. "And she just walked up to you and said, 'Hmm, you look like you probably know a good general contractor,' as she handed her card to you?"

"No."

Virginia closed her eyes, doing her best to get herself under control. She knew she'd gotten too excited, but the picture that Maizie Sommers had painted for her earlier today had filled her with hope. It had been a very long time since she'd seen her brother with more than an obligatory smile on his lips.

And, like her niece, she really didn't care for the woman he was currently seeing. Try as she might, she couldn't get herself to warm up to Elizabeth Wells—and she definitely didn't see the woman as being Ginny's stepmother. For one thing, the woman was not the patient sort.

"Okay, from the top," Virginia announced. "And this time," she told her brother, "try to pay attention, all right?"

"Yes, ma'am," Stone replied, executing a mock salute and doing his best to be patient.

Stone had just been on the receiving end of disappointing news. The owners of a house he was scheduled to begin work on had just changed their minds and canceled the project on him. That didn't exactly put him in the best of moods.

He didn't have time to waste like this. There were cages he needed to rattle in order to replace the work he'd lost. But Virginia had gotten right in his face and insisted that he listen to her.

"Well?" Stone prodded.

Virginia took a deep breath. She decided that she would stay as close to the truth as possible without coming right out and telling her brother that he was being set up—not to take a fall, but to fall in love. If he even *suspected* that, he would never agree to any of this. And he needed to agree because, at the very least, he would wind up earning some money doing what he did best these days—working with his hands.

Five years ago, he'd been an aerospace engineer. But that industry was all but dead in Southern California, so he had fallen back on what he'd done while working his way through college. He'd worked in construction.

But now *that* was on shaky grounds. The economy had taken a bite out of everyone's livelihood and his line of work was seeing a definite downturn. Remodeling was a luxury people felt they could put off until later without any major consequences. Virginia was confident that her brother wouldn't turn down work.

She just had to sell him on how this had all come about.

"Okay, from the top," Virginia said, echoing his words, then started with her narrative. "I took Ginny out for some ice cream."

Stone looked a wee bit exasperated. "Just what she needs, more sugar." He loved his daughter more than life itself, but there were times when getting her to behave was a challenge—one that wore him out. Stone slanted a glance toward his only child. Ginny had been in constant motion since she and Virginia had walked in. "Is that why she's bouncing five inches off the ground?" he asked.

"You're interrupting," Virginia accused, frowning at him.

He suppressed a sigh and waved his sister on. "Sorry, continue."

"Anyway, we went to that old-fashioned ice cream parlor at the Brubaker Mall, and I got her an ice cream cone. They had so many wonderful flavors to choose from, I couldn't resist so I decided that I'd get one, too—it's been a while since I just indulged in a treat," she explained by way of a sidebar.

"The point, Virginia, Get to the point," Stone directed. Ever since they were children, the shortest distance between two points for Virginia had never *once* been a straight line; it always wound up being an elaborate journey—a very pronounced squiggly line if he didn't adamantly put his foot down about it.

"Okay. While I was getting myself a cone, Ginny decided to go exploring—" Catching her lower lip between her teeth, Virginia slanted a side glance in her brother's direction. She was waiting to get the inevitable explosion out of the way.

Stone was looking sharply at his daughter. "Ginny, you know better than to go running off like that."

Rather than protest, Ginny surprised him by looking down contritely at her shoes and murmuring, "Yes, Daddy."

It wasn't that his only child was willful. She was just extremely exuberant and given to incredibly energetic enthusiasm. This apparent remorse, however, was a whole different side of her he'd never seen before.

Had something put the fear of consequences into his little girl?

Concerned, Stone glanced back at his sister for a further explanation.

Virginia instantly obliged. "I caught up with Ginny just next door. She'd wandered into a real estate office," she told him.

Stone could only stare at his sister. Ginny in a toy store he could understand, but what could have possibly attracted his precocious child to walk into a real estate office?

"Why?" he asked, looking from Ginny to his sister and then back again, waiting for one of them to give him a satisfactory answer.

Virginia was at a loss as to how to explain this part and was about to say she had no idea why Ginny did half the things she did when Ginny suddenly said, "I heard you say that you didn't know if you could find enough work to pay the bills, so I asked the lady if any of the houses in the pictures needed fixing—'cause you could do it."

Virginia was as stunned as her brother with her niece's creative explanation. It took her a beat to pick up the lifeline that had just been thrown her way.

"As it turned out, she did," Virginia confirmed belatedly. "Your daughter charmed her," Virginia said, putting her arm around Ginny's small shoulders, "and instead of just ushering us out, the woman said that as a matter of fact, she was currently looking for a good general contractor for her reference file. Naturally, Ginny and I told her you were the best, so she gave me her card and said that you should call her when you had the time."

It sounded like a fairy tale, but in there somewhere Stone assumed was the truth, otherwise, why had the woman given his sister her card? And, since he suddenly found himself unexpectedly free, what did he have to lose by calling?

"Well," Stone said slowly, looking the card over again,

"I could always use another contact but…" He glanced at his daughter, concerned and reading his own interpretation into what she'd just said. "Honey, we're going to be just fine," he assured her. "I don't want you worrying about things like bills for a long time to come. I'll take care of us," he promised.

"Yes, Daddy." Ginny smiled at him. It was the same smile he'd seen on her mother's face, Stone thought with a pang. A smile he missed seeing. "I just wanted to help," she told him.

"You do, honey, just by being you, you do," Stone assured her. He regarded the card again. No time like the present, he decided. "Okay, let's see what this Maizie Sommers has to say."

Ginny crossed her index finger and middle finger on both hands and held them up for him to see as he took out his cell phone.

We've got a great little girl, Eva. God but I wish you were here to see her, Stone couldn't help thinking as he called the number on the card.

He had no way of knowing that his daughter wasn't crossing her fingers because she was hoping he'd wind up with a job. Ginny was hoping that the "nice lady at the agency" would do for her father what she'd already done for Greg's father and that was to find her father someone who would be her new mommy.

Stone returned his daughter's hopeful smile as he heard the phone ringing on the other end.

It rang a total of two times and then he could hear the other end pick up. A sunny voice was saying, "This is Maizie Sommers, how can I help you?"

Stone turned away from his daughter and his sister, focusing his attention on the person on the other end of the call.

"Ms. Sommers, this is Stone Scarborough—" He got no further than that.

"Ah, yes," Maizie said warmly, "the general contractor. I've been waiting for your call."

Her admission caught him off guard. "You have?" Was business on her end bad, too? And if so, then what sort of work could she possibly have for him? Still, he'd called so he might as well see where this actually wound up leading.

"Absolutely," she replied. "Are you by any chance available tonight?"

"Tonight?" he echoed, wondering if he'd just made a big mistake.

Something didn't seem right. Maybe this woman wasn't looking for a general contractor but for something else entirely. Granted this Maizie Sommers didn't sound as eager and excited as Virginia had when she'd told him about this, but the woman was incredibly cheerful. Too cheerful to be talking strictly about work.

Several possibilities ran through his head, but he tamped them down until he had more to go on. No point in thinking the worst—yet.

"Yes. Or if that's too short a notice for you, then perhaps tomorrow evening might be better for you."

She kept specifying evenings, which made it sound way too much like making arrangements for a date. "Why not in the daytime?" he asked suspiciously.

The woman took the question in stride, making it

sound as if she was already prepared for it. Maybe he was being too suspicious, Stone told himself.

"I'm afraid the woman I'm giving your name to isn't available during the daytime," Maizie told him. "At least, not until the weekend. She's busy taping her program during the day," Maizie explained.

"Her program?" Stone repeated, confused.

This was a lot like talking to Virginia, he thought, wondering if vague obscurity was a gender thing or if he was just slow, the way Virginia had accused him of being. Either way, he was in need of either a further explanation—or subtitles.

"Yes, she has a daily cooking show broadcast on a cable network and right now, her weekdays are taken up taping the program before a studio audience. When she first came out here and signed her contract," Maizie continued proudly, "I sold her this lovely house. That was about six months ago.

"I got her a really good deal on the house, but that was because the owner was in a hurry to sell. The house needed a lot of work and it was sold as is. She didn't have the time then, or, I suspect, the money, for repairs. The poor dear was just starting out. But the program's doing really well and she feels that she can finally afford to have the house fixed up the way she'd like." Maizie paused for a moment, letting that all sink in before she asked him, "Are you interested, Mr. Scarborough?"

It was work. He was *more* than interested. "Yes, of course I am." But he had a question of his own. "Don't you want to see some of my work before you refer me to someone?"

She liked the fact that he was cautious and that he wasn't trying to rush her into any sort of an agreement. For her part, she had already researched his background and had seen all she needed to. Virginia Scarborough had shown her a photograph of her brother and given her enough background information to get her started in the right direction.

She felt she had the perfect match for Ginny's father. Matches usually didn't present themselves *this* quickly. They ordinarily took a little time. However, this time she'd thought of Danni almost immediately.

That, to her, was a very good sign.

"Your sister and daughter speak quite highly of you, Mr. Scarborough."

"And that's enough?" he asked rather skeptically.

"Yes," Maizie told him with feeling, and then added with a slight chuckle, "of course, what I saw on your webpage didn't exactly hurt, either."

"My webpage?" Stone echoed, confused. He turned to look quizzically at his sister as he said it. This was all news to him.

"Yes, your sister very kindly gave me the URL address. I must say it was very impressive, Mr. Scarborough," Maizie said warmly. "If my house was in need of work, I would hire you in a minute."

He supposed that was good news, but he was still a little confused. "Thanks," he murmured belatedly.

Poor man was probably still trying to figure out what hit him, Maizie thought, amused.

"So, do I have your permission to pass your name on to my client?" she asked. Maizie had learned that it never paid to appear to take things for granted. People liked the illusion of being in charge of their own fate—even when they weren't.

"Yes, of course," Stone said with feeling. If this was on the level—and it was beginning to sound that way—he definitely wanted the work. He made a point of never turning anything down.

"Wonderful," Maizie said, enthused. "I'm sure you'll be hearing from her shortly," she promised. "Just so you know, her name is Danni Everett."

"Danni Everett," he repeated.

Despite what the woman on the other end of the line had said about a cooking program on one of the cable channels, the name was not familiar to him. But then, he didn't exactly spend his days watching cable channels or any other channels for that matter. When he wasn't working—or trying to land work—he spent time with Ginny. That meant being outdoors, not locked in some room with the TV on, tuned to some brain-crushing program.

Stone politely ended the call and then turned to look at his sister again.

"My webpage?" he asked. "I thought we were going to discuss that." The last he remembered, he'd told Virginia he'd get back to her. She'd obviously decided to go on without him.

"We did discuss it," Virginia told him innocently. "You said we'd talk about it when you had time. I decided that would take too long so I just put a few simple things together. You can change it any way you want."

"Oh, thanks," he said sarcastically.

Virginia sighed. Stone had to be dragged, kicking and

screaming, into the present century for his own good. "Look, I do your accounting for you. I've got access to all your old jobs and the before-and-after photos you always take."

Photos, he thought, that his sister had insisted he take before and after undertaking each job that came his way in order to keep an accurate record of the work that he did do. He was a detail man only insofar as the actual construction work that he did. The other details, organizing the before-and-after photographs, keeping them readily accessible, well, he wasn't so good at that. But luckily, he now had to admit, Virginia was.

And apparently, she'd put that talent to work. But Stone didn't want her thinking she was off the hook just yet.

"Just how long has this webpage been up?" he asked.

"About a week," Virginia answered. However, she avoided looking at him when she said it.

"No, it's longer than that, Aunt Virginia," Ginny piped up. "You told Maizie it was up for two months."

Virginia offered her brother a forced smile. "I exaggerated," she told him.

"To whom?" he asked. "Her or me?"

"Um…"

The time didn't matter as much as the actual deed. "The point is, Virginia, you put up the webpage without telling me."

"I was waiting for the right time to tell you," she answered. It looked as if she had waited too long. With a sigh of surrender, she said, "I guess this is it."

Virginia took her netbook out of her purse, turned it

on and then typed in the appropriate address. Once the
website was up, she turned the computer around so that
the screen faced him.

"What do you think?"

Stone took in the various photographs he'd taken of
his work, work he was very proud of and with good reason. Still, he shrugged carelessly. "Not bad."

That sounded like typical Stone, Virginia thought. He
wasn't exactly heavy-handed with his praise. Nonetheless, she splayed a hand over her chest, tilting her head
back dramatically as she cried, "Oh, be still my heart. I
don't know if I can handle such heady praise."

Stone got the message. And, in all honesty, the website did look rather impressive. She'd done a commendable job.

"Okay, good." He paused. "Better than good," he
amended.

Virginia did a rapid movement with her hand, urging
him on. "Keep going," she coaxed.

The phone rang just then. "Later," he told his sister.
Taking his cell out again, he answered the call. "Hello?"

"Is this Scarborough Construction?" an exceedingly
melodic voice on the other end of the call asked.

He thought he detected just a trace of a Southern accent in the woman's voice. He caught himself trying to
place it.

"Yes," he replied, wondering if this was the woman
the Realtor had just told him about. Could she have gotten back to them so quickly?

He was all set to doubt it, but then he heard the woman
with the melodic voice say, "Maizie Sommers gave me

your phone number. I was wondering if we could get together tomorrow evening...if you're free, that is. I'd like to show you around my home and explain to you what I'd like to have done."

He felt as if he were standing in the direct path of a city-owned snowplow. "Sure. What time?"

"Any time after four would be fine."

"Four-thirty?" he suggested.

"Perfect." She rattled off her address, then said, "I'll see you then."

"Four-thirty," he repeated, confirming the time just before he hung up. Turning around, he saw both his sister and his daughter smiling at him. Widely. "What?" he asked uncertainly.

"Nothing," Virginia replied quickly.

But she knew if she didn't say something, he might grow suspicious. Her brother was the type who, upon finding a pot of gold at the end of the rainbow would look around to see if there was a group of leprechauns somewhere, having fun at his expense.

"I can just hear the sound of bills getting paid," she answered cheerfully.

"Well, don't count your checks before they're written," he cautioned, thinking of the job that had just fallen through earlier. "You never know how these things can turn out."

"Sorry," Virginia murmured. "Don't know what came over me." There was a time, Virginia couldn't help remembering, when her brother was just as optimistic as she was. She missed those times.

I hope you're as good as Ginny thinks you are, Mai-

zie Sommers, Virginia said silently. *I can't wait for my brother to fall in love again and become human, like he was with Eva.*

Chapter Two

Sometimes, when Danielle Everett thought about it, it *still* took her breath away.

Three years ago, she was living in Atlanta, struggling to pay off not just her student loans but also the mountain of medical bills her father had left in his wake. At the time, she was working at an insurance company, living on a shoestring and feeling her soul being sucked away, bit by bit, with every passing day.

Back then, Danni was vainly trying to keep her head above water and wondering if her utterly unfounded optimism would eventually erode because from any angle she looked at it, her optimism had absolutely nothing to hook on to.

All she wanted back then was to wake up in the morning and not feel as if she were struggling against an oppressive feeling. She didn't want to feel that if she ever let her guard down, she'd be a victim of the dark, bottomless depression whispering along the perimeter of her very being.

Back then she'd never dreamed that she could actually wake up grinning from ear to ear—the way she did these days.

Granted she was as exhausted now as she had been back then, but then the exhaustion had come from trying to keep her footing on the treadmill she was running on—the treadmill that threatened, at any moment, to pull her under. Now she was exhausted from trying to do ten things at once. The difference being was that these were ten things she *loved* doing.

Back then she'd been a company drone, an anonymous, tiny cog in a huge machine, expected to perform and make no waves. These days she was her own person. And, in many ways, her own boss as well. She took suggestions, not orders. Which made a world of difference to her everyday existence.

And all because of a skill, a talent she'd never even thought twice about.

Danni cooked like a dream and baked like a celestial being.

It all started innocently enough. She began by cooking for friends, then for friends of friends. Friends of friends who insisted on paying her for her time and skill. Before Danni knew it, she had branched out to catering full-time. There was no room left to squeeze in her day job.

The happiest day of her life was the day Danni handed in her resignation to Roosevelt Life Insurance's actuarial department. Her second-happiest day was the day she paid off the last of her late father's medical bills. Her last student loan payment followed a year later.

She was finally solvent and didn't owe anyone anything!

By then Danni realized that she was doing far more baking than cooking. A few heady connections later and she found herself being courted to star in a brand-new cooking show.

Initially, Danni had some serious doubts about going in that direction and she hesitated about making the commitment, which also meant relocating cross-country. After all, weren't there more than enough cooking shows already all over the airwaves? Their life expectancy was projected to be somewhere a little longer than that of a common fruit fly—but not by all that much.

By then Danni had become too successful catering parties for an established clientele to want to set herself up for failure again.

She had no gimmick, she protested to the agent who had approached her with the idea of cooking before a live audience. She had nothing to set her apart from all the other chefs on TV.

"I think you're selling yourself short, Danielle," the agent, a thin, diminutive man named Baxter Warren told her with more than a little conviction. "A lot of people—the *right* people," he emphasized dramatically, "think you make desserts to die for."

As the words came out of his mouth, the agent paused for a moment, looking as if he had just had a world-altering epiphany. And then his thin lips split into a wide smile.

"That's what we'll call the show. *Danielle's Desserts to Die For.*"

"Most people call me Danni," she'd told him.

"Danni's Desserts to Die For," he amended, then nodded his head. "Even better." Baxter gave her a penetrating, almost mesmerizing look. It was easy to see that he was exceedingly pleased with himself. "You *can't* say no."

She didn't.

Danni had packed up her pots—Baxter told her she could buy a complete designer set of new ones once she landed in Southern California, but she'd insisted on bringing the ones that she'd been using. The ones her father had given her before she'd even hit her teens. They had belonged to her grandmother and to Danni the pots were the very embodiment of family history. They represented who and what she was.

She'd also brought along a box full of recipes. Recipes that she habitually—and unconsciously—augmented each time she prepared them.

With her prized possessions safely packed away, Danni had flown from Atlanta to begin a new life in the land of endless summers and endless beaches: Southern California. The cable station where her half-hour program was scheduled to be filmed was located in Burbank. Baxter had encouraged her to find either an apartment or a house in the area.

But the pace in Burbank was too frantic for her and she longed for something a little more sedate and laid-back, as well as a town that was a little less populated. What she was looking for was something to remind her of the Atlanta suburb that she'd left behind.

She was searching for a little bit of home in a completely unfamiliar environment.

She found what she was looking for in Bedford, with the help of a Realtor one of the cameramen working on her new show had recommended.

Maizie Sommers.

Moreover, Maizie, with her low key approach, her soft voice and especially her kind smile, reminded her a great deal of the mother she'd lost years ago.

What Danni appreciated most of all was that her association with Maizie was *not* terminated when escrow closed. When the woman urged her to call if she ever had a problem or needed anything—or just to talk, Danni believed her.

As a matter of fact, they'd talked several times since Danni had sent out her change-of-address postcards to the people back in Atlanta and Danni had even dropped by the woman's office a couple of times, always bearing some sort of new dessert she was currently trying out.

For her part, Maizie never put her off or told her she'd come at a bad time. On the contrary, she'd greeted her like a long-lost, beloved family member—like a daughter.

"You do realize that just the pleasure of your company would be more than enough," Maizie told her when she'd dropped by a week ago. "You really don't need to bribe me—although, I must say, you really outdid yourself this time with these little glazed Bundt cakes." Maizie had sat at her desk, examining the mini cake in her hand from all angles. It appeared perfect from all sides. "Have you thought about either writing a cookbook or marketing these? You'll make a fortune," Maizie prophesized.

Danni had modestly demurred, but the idea about writing a cookbook remained in the recesses of her brain. *Maybe someday.*

Each time she reflected on the changes that had come into her life in such a short amount of time, it always astounded her. She could hardly believe that at long last, there was enough money in both her savings and her checking account for her to be a little—hell, a *lot* extravagant if she wanted to be, instead of always having to count pennies, constantly be vigilant and deny herself even the smallest of indulgences.

Danni almost gave in to the cliché to pinch herself. Life was *that* perfect. For the first time in her life, she was living in her own house, a house she'd paid for, not a house she was merely renting and that belonged to someone else.

The rush she felt when she put the key into the lock of her own front door for the very first time was one she couldn't even begin to describe. It was unequal to anything else she'd ever felt.

But Danni wasn't so enamored with the idea of ownership that she was blind to the house's flaws. She wasn't. She was very aware that the house came with warts. Quite a few warts.

The two-story building, built somewhere around the early 1970s, was in need of a new roof, new windows that kept the air out, not invited it in, and the three bathrooms were all but literally begging to be remodeled.

The kitchen, which to her had always been the heart of the house, needed a complete makeover as well. To anyone else, these might have been a deal breaker, but Danni had fallen in love with the layout and had bought the house for an exceptionally good price. So she'd signed on the dotted line, promising herself that if and when her show's option was picked up and renewed, and *if* it subsequently took off, she would give the house a much-needed facelift.

That day had come.

Her last visit to Maizie had been to tell the helpful Realtor that she was finally at a place where she could afford all those renovations they had talked about.

"What I need now," she'd said over an enticing small pyramid of a dozen glazed wine cupcakes, "is for you to recommend a reliable general contractor who can do it all. I really don't want to have to deal with a half a dozen or more men, all at odds with one another."

There'd been a slight problem with her request. The man Maizie had been sending people to for the last eight years had recently relocated to Nevada to be closer to his daughter and her family. Consequently, Maizie had told her she'd be on the look-out for someone reliable and that she would get back to her as quickly as she could.

Danni had no doubts that the woman would find someone.

And Maizie had.

When she came home yesterday, bone weary after a marathon taping session, the first thing she'd seen was the red light on her answering machine blinking rhythmically as if it was flirting with her. Danni had stopped only long enough to drop her purse and step out of her shoes before listening to the message.

She waited less than that to call Maizie back. Five minutes after that, she was on the phone, dialing the number that Maizie had given her.

Danni wanted to call while her lucky streak was still riding high. There was a part of her—a diminishing but still-present part—that expected she would wake from this wonderful dream, her alarm clock shattering the stillness and calling her to work at the insurance company back in Atlanta.

Before that happened, she wanted to take full advantage of this magic-carpet ride she found herself on.

The man who Maizie had recommended sounded nice on the phone. He had a deep, rich baritone voice that was made for long walks on the beach beneath velvety, dark, star-lit skies.

He looked even better, Danni thought as she brought her vehicle to a squealing stop in her driveway and all but leaped out of her car. He was on time, she noted ruefully. And she was not.

"Sorry," Danni declared, approaching the man who looked as if the stereotypical description of "tall, dark and handsome" had been coined exclusively for him. She put her hand out. "Traffic from Burbank was a bear," she apologized.

His fingers closed around her hand, his eyes never leaving hers.

Stone had been all set to leave.

He absolutely hated being kept waiting and felt that

the people who were late had no regard for anyone else's time and no respect for them, either.

But the attractive, bubbly blonde's apology sounded genuine enough rather than just perfunctory and it wasn't as if he were awash in projects and could turn his back and walk away from this one.

So far, it had been a very lean year for him and the savings he'd put aside to see himself and his daughter—and sister if need be—through were just about gone.

Danni suddenly paused just as she was about to unlock her door. She half turned and looked at him over her shoulder as a thought occurred to her that she had just taken his identity for granted.

"You are Mr. Scarborough, right?" she asked belatedly, punctuating her question with a warm, hopeful smile.

Even if he wasn't, Stone caught himself thinking, he would have temporarily changed his name just to be on the receiving end of that smile. But, with a clear conscience, he could nod and say his full name, just in case the woman had any lingering doubts.

"Call me Stone," he told her. There, that should set her mind at ease about his identity. After all, he reasoned, how many men were there with that first name?

"I'm Danni," she said, her smile all but branding him. "But then, you already know that." There was just the slightest hint of pink tint on her cheek as she turned away.

She opened the front door and despite the fact that it was July and the sun had yet to go down, the interior of the house was all but utterly enshrouded in darkness.

"The first thing I'm going to need is light," she told him.

"That usually happens when you turn up the switch," he pointed out dryly, indicating the one that was on the wall right next to the doorjamb.

Danni laughed then, even as she did exactly as he'd suggested. "I mean light from above." She pointed toward the roof, which was some eighteen feet up, thanks to cathedral ceilings. "Like a skylight. This room appears incredibly gloomy in the winter, even when the drapes are opened. And I'd really rather not have to leave the lights on all day long."

As she spoke, Danni dropped her purse near the front door and saw him looking. "I could use a small table there," she admitted. "Haven't gotten around to that, yet. Haven't gotten around to a lot of things yet," she admitted ruefully in a moment of truth. "They said the pace here in Southern California is laid-back." Danni just shook her head about that. "They lied."

"They?" he asked, curious.

"The people back East."

There it was again, that accent he couldn't quite pin down. This was probably his one chance to ask her the question.

"How far back East?" he asked.

"Atlanta." She saw the look that came over his face. He assumed a triumphant air, as if he was congratulating himself on a guess well played. "Is it that obvious?"

"No, not *that* obvious," he told her. "Just that you weren't from around here."

She laughed shortly, thinking of the people she'd been

interacting with since she'd transplanted herself. She had the kind of face and manner that drew people to her. Not only that, but it drew them out as well. People would find themselves telling her things they wouldn't even whisper into their priest's ear.

"Is anyone from around here?" It was meant to be a rhetorical question, but obviously, not for Stone.

"My wife was," he told her, then added, "and my daughter is."

Is and *was*.

Danni was instantly aware of the switch in tense.

He mentioned his daughter in the present tense, but not his wife. Did that mean he was divorced, or—?

She'd always been interested in people, in the way they felt, thought, what their background was, but she also knew that men didn't like having to answer too many questions at any given time, so she let the questions bubbling up within her all go for now.

Except for one.

"Are you hungry?" she asked Stone. "Can I get you anything?"

"No, I'm fine," he assured her.

Yes, you certainly are, she couldn't help thinking. But her Southern training couldn't accept no for an answer. It wasn't in her DNA.

"No coffee? Tea?" He shook his head at each suggestion. "How about water?" she coaxed. "Everyone likes water."

He laughed at her comment and decided he was waging a losing battle. The woman would obviously remain uneasy until she'd given him *something.*

"All right. I'll take some water," he told her, all but raising his hands over his head like a prisoner being taken into custody.

"Great," Danni declared. "Water it is. And dessert," she added in a lowered voice, talking quickly. So quickly that he had to replay the words in his head in order to realize what she'd just said. "Kitchen's this way," she told him, leading the way to the rear of the house.

"I don't need dessert," Stone told the back of her head. At the moment, it was the safest place to look. If he lowered his eyes for even a second, he knew he'd regret it. The view was far too tempting. Her hips were moving at a tempo that was all but synchronized with the beating of his heart.

"Sure you do. Everyone needs dessert," she assured him.

Reaching her final destination, Danni went straight for the refrigerator and the secret weapon she used to win everyone over.

Her dessert.

Chapter Three

This was obviously a man who did *not* like being told
what to do, Danni decided as she placed the large plate
of freshly made dessert on the table. When he was growing up, his mother probably had to *suggest* that he drink
his milk, otherwise, she was willing to bet, he went out
of his way not to touch it just to prove his independence.

In some ways, she supposed she could relate to that.
While she liked being polite, she was never anyone's
pushover.

Maizie Sommers had sung this man's praises, which
meant that in the Realtor's experience, the contractor got
an overall A rating for both the quality of his work *and*
the prices he charged. That was certainly more than good
enough for her, Danni thought. There was no way she
wanted to antagonize the man on top of already being
late for their appointment and having kept him waiting.

So Danni put on her very best smile and graciously accepted his refusal of her dessert.

"Don't worry, I won't force-feed you. But it'll be right there, waiting for you, just in case you wind up changing your mind," she told him, moving away from the table. "Okay, why don't I show you what needs doing?" she offered cheerfully.

Stone barely nodded. "That sounds like a good idea," he agreed.

Danni began to regret not wearing a sweater. Did this man take time to warm up, or was he always going to be a wee bit cooler than an artic breeze?

It wasn't that she required Stone Scarborough to ooze personality and charm, it was just that she knew the work she had in mind wasn't going to be something that could be accomplished in a day or a week—or a month, even if the man moved in to do it. Since this would be a long, drawn out process and they would be around each other for a long stretch of time—unless he had a magic wand in his arsenal or a squadron of eager elves at his disposal—she definitely didn't want to feel uncomfortable in her own home for the duration of the renovations.

That meant, quite simply, that they had to get along.

More than that, it required, in her opinion, that they liked each other, at least to a modest degree. She wasn't looking for a best friend, but neither was she looked for someone who behaved as if he might appear on the cover of *Grouches Inc., Monthly* some time in the very near future.

So, as she showed the general contractor around her two-story house, Danni did her best to break through what she viewed as his crusty outer shell, hoping against hope that she wouldn't wind up just coming up against a crusty inner shell.

"Have you been a general contractor long?" Danni asked, trying to draw him into a round of pleasant small-talk.

She actually knew the answer to her own question— she'd Googled Stone Scarborough during the very short lunch break she'd taken at the studio and found the contractor's website—but it was the first question that occurred to her. In her experience, people liked to talk about themselves. It tended to put them at ease.

"Long enough to get it right," Stone answered crisply. "I can give you references from former clients if you'd like," he offered.

It couldn't hurt, Danni thought. "I'd like," she echoed out loud.

More than his caliber of work—which, because Maizie had recommended him she assumed was top-drawer—Danni wanted to talk to the women whose houses Stone had worked on. She wanted to find out if he'd been as monotone with them as he was being with her. At least then, if his personality came across the same way with them as it did with her, she wouldn't feel as if she'd offended the man.

"Then I'll get them to you tomorrow morning," Stone promised her. "Do you want to wait until you've had a chance to look them over, or do you want to go ahead and tell me what you had in mind by way of changes for this house?"

Danni looked around for a moment, as if making up

her mind one final time before speaking. As it happened, she'd already decided and she wasn't seeking other's opinions on his work to see if he was equal to the project. She just wanted to know if he ever turned out to be a "real, live boy" or continued being as wooden as Pinocchio for the entire time he worked on their renovations.

Turning toward him, Danni summed up the answer to his question regarding the work she wanted done in one succinct word. "Everything."

Because he was waiting for an answer to the first part of his question first, her answer initially confused him. "Excuse me?"

"Everything," Danni cheerfully repeated. "I need a great many changes made to this house, from top to bottom."

Stone found that that made no practical sense at all to him. "If you want to change everything, why'd you buy the house in the first place, if you don't mind my asking?" He knew that in her position, he wouldn't have. But then, he'd come to realize that the female mind worked much differently from the male one.

For one thing, logic appeared to have little or no place in it, or in making final decisions.

"No, I don't mind," Danni replied.

From her tone, he felt she wasn't just putting on an act or pretending not to mind the personal question he'd just asked—God knew that he would have. So far, she sounded pretty guileless, considering her gender. Maybe she wasn't so typical, after all.

"I bought the place because it had a price range I could afford," she admitted honestly, "the front yard had a great orientation for my flower garden and, as they say in real estate, the house looked like it had 'a lot of potential.'"

Stone shook his head when she was finished. "That's usually real estate speak for 'the house is a real clunker.'"

"But it does have potential," Danni insisted. "I can see it." And she really could. When she walked through the fifty-year-old house, she could visualize the changes she wanted. The transformation would make the two-story house into a showplace.

Stone merely shrugged. It was her money. "If you say so," he conceded. And then he got back to something she'd said about the property's orientation. "You have a flower garden?" he asked. When he'd come up the front walk, he hadn't seen a single bud and when she'd brought him into the kitchen, he had a view of the backyard—which also barren. Where was this so-called flower garden of hers?

Her smile held promise rather than embarrassment. "Not yet. But I intend to."

Stone took a wild guess. "This is more of that 'potential' the property has, right?"

The woman practically beamed at him, as if to congratulate him that he was finally getting the hang of it. "Right."

Why did she feel as if she were on trial? Maybe he was just trying to see if she committed to this and wouldn't lose interest and send him on his way in the middle of the job. If that was what he thought, he didn't know her. Once she signed on to something, she remained committed for the duration.

For the time being, she decided to stop trying to make a personal connection with the man and just get his input on the house. Danni continued showing the contractor around.

Stone quietly followed the woman through the first floor, listening to the sound of her voice as she pointed out room after room, giving him a thumbnail summary of what she wanted changed or added or redone in each one.

The first floor was comprised of a living room, a dining room, a kitchen that fed into a family room and a slightly larger than closet-size bedroom that was located all the way in the rear, just off the family room. The entire floor had one bathroom.

The second floor, with its wide-open staircase and carved wooden banister, contained three more bedrooms, including the less-than-masterful "master suite." There was a bathroom between the two bedrooms and another bathroom within the master suite. The second floor also had a recreational room which, she discovered when he corrected her, was called a "bonus room" in Southern California.

Stone listened without comment as she pointed things out, saying things like "I'd like bookshelves all along that wall" when they were in the bonus room, and "a walk-in closet here would be nice," in the master bedroom. He neither nodded, nor said a word one way or another until the "tour" was over and they came back downstairs to the kitchen.

Unable to endure the man's silence any longer, Danni finally asked, "Well? What do you think? You haven't said a single word during the whole tour." Did that mean he wasn't going to take the job? Was she just wasting her time with him?

"You were right," he replied quietly.

She watched him, waiting for him to continue. Right? Right about what? She'd done a lot of talking in the last twenty minutes.

"Yes?" she asked.

"When you said 'everything.'" He'd thought she was kidding at the time, but it was obvious that she had to be serious. Every room needed to be redone in order to make it more useful, more pleasing to the eye and part of the twenty-first century.

He had one all-encompassing suggestion for her. "You just might be better off tearing everything down and starting from scratch."

"Not everything," Danni protested. "I actually do like the fireplace in the living room, and the staircase. And the balcony in the rec— The bonus room," she corrected herself.

In response, she saw what looked like a hint of a smile on his lips. At least she'd managed to make a very slight connection, Danni congratulated herself. It looked like the man *was* human, after all. And that meant that there *was* hope. Maybe they would be able to get along in the long run.

She crossed her fingers.

Stone watched her for a long moment. Just as she was going to ask what he was thinking, he said, "You like the balcony, huh?"

The feature, visible from the street, was what had attracted her to the house in the first place. That and the colors it'd been painted: gray and Wedgwood-blue. Like her parents' house had been, back in Atlanta. It made her a little homesick to see it, even though the actual structure looked nothing like her old home.

"Yes," she responded, then after a beat, asked, "You don't?"

He dismissed the appendage under discussion with a wave of his hand. "Well, since the balcony doesn't look out onto anything but the cul-de-sac and the house across the street, I was going to suggest you close that up and extend the bonus room by the balcony's square footage."

Danni rolled the idea over in her head, trying to picture a large window rather than the two sliding-glass doors currently there. The glass doors separated the bonus room from the balcony. The latter ran the width of the room, which in turn was the length of two of the three garages. Because the bonus room ended over the second garage, the third one had never been finished. Something else she wanted Stone to add to his list. She wanted the garage to be finished and to have an attic put in, complete with stairs that folded out onto the garage floor.

"It's worth considering," she told him. "I'll think about it."

The balcony would continue to thrive, he could see it in her eyes. He had one more suggestion for her. "It might be less expensive if you just sell this place and get something more to your liking."

She looked at him, confused. Didn't he *want* the

work? "Are you trying to talk your way out of a job, Mr. Scarborough?"

He didn't say yes, he didn't say no. "Just wanted you to be aware of all the possibilities." He paused, letting that sink in and then informed her, "All those suggestions you made during the tour, they're not going to come cheap."

How dumb did he think she was? "I didn't expect them to. That's why I waited before looking into having it done until my contract was renewed," she told him. "I wanted to be sure the money was there before I started to undertake all this."

That was commendable, Stone thought. He'd seen far too many people who harbored grandiose plans, only to allow themselves to get overextended and in over their heads when they neglected to take escalating prices and building costs into account.

He took another long look at her. The woman might look like one of those fluffy blondes who seemed to be almost everywhere you looked in Southern California—most of them would-be actresses—but she seemed to have a head on her shoulders.

Maybe they *would* be able to work things out, after all.

"When would you want me to get started?" Stone asked, then added a coda. "Provided, of course, that the estimate that I'm going to work up for you doesn't turn your hair gray."

As he talked, she subtly directed him back toward the kitchen table—where the coffee she'd made and the dessert she'd left were still waiting for them.

"I'm sure it won't," she told him. "And even if it did, there're enough hair-care products out there to restore my hair to its natural shade," she assured him with an easy, unself-conscious laugh. "Ms. Sommers seemed really sold on you and I trust her judgment implicitly. And I really liked what I saw on your website," she added for good measure. "Some of those before-and-after photos were absolutely incredible." That had really impressed her and confirmed the man's abilities.

Stone had always believed in doing the best possible job he could, bar none, but he'd never been very comfortable being on the receiving end of praise. Now was no different.

He shrugged off her words, and murmured, "My sister was the one who put together the website," as if that were enough to deflect the compliment and allow him to remain anonymously in the shadows.

"Your sister," Danni echoed. The information didn't diminish her response to his work and actually enhanced it slightly, expanding it in another direction. A direction she naturally followed.

"So, it's a family business?" Danni assumed.

"No" was his first response, but then he reconsidered. He had to admit that in the last couple of years or so, Virginia had become exceedingly involved in helping him run his construction company—in more ways than just one. "Well, actually, yes in a way," he amended. "Virginia put together that website and she handles the accounting end of the business."

Initially, Virginia had done freelance accounting for several small businesses in the area, his among them.

But of late, his business had been taking up more and more of his sister's time. It would be nice, he caught himself thinking, to be able to pay her accordingly.

If this woman was serious about two-thirds of the things she said she wanted done to her house, he could afford to pay Virginia more money—not that she ever asked for more. That wasn't her way—but he knew he'd be lost without her, not because of her accounting—or the fact that she had put together that website behind his back which, lucky for her, had turned out well—but because she was always there to help him with Ginny.

If not for Virginia, he would have had to resort to turning over Ginny's care to complete strangers and he didn't like the idea of people who weren't family or friends looking after his little girl. Especially since Ginny was not all that easy on some people's nerves. Strangers—even strangers who were paid for the job— were not always all that patient.

Virginia was.

"That sounds pretty much like a family business to me," Danni was saying, unaware that there was a wistful smile on her lips. She would have given anything to have a brother or sister around to work with, to be there for them—and have them be there for her. She had some cousins, a couple who had relocated here as a matter of fact, but it wasn't the same thing. "You have any other family?" she asked.

What was with all these non-work-related questions? "Why?" he asked.

"No reason," Danni replied with an innocent shrug.

"Just curious. I guess I just like knowing things about the people I'm dealing with."

Stone had momentarily been captivated by the movement of her shoulders as they rose and fell in an innocent shrug.

But he came to fast enough.

"All you need to know is that I take pride in my work and I stand behind everything I do," he informed her.

The woman nodded in response, then continued looking at him without saying a word. It was against his better judgment, but he decided there was no real harm in it, either. So he told her what she was obviously waiting to hear for reasons that completely escaped him.

"I have a daughter. Ginny. She's four," he added, "going on forty."

The smile he received in return made the surrender of this small piece of information oddly worth it.

"My father used to say the same thing about me," Danni recalled fondly. He'd always followed it up by telling her to slow down, that there was no hurry, the years would all be waiting for her no matter how long she would take to reach them.

"Well, my condolences to your father, then," Stone told her. There wasn't so much as a sliver of a smile as he said that.

Danni's own smile didn't appear to waver, but when he looked closer, Stone realized that what he was seeing was pain etched into the edges of that smile. She was far too young for that sort of pain.

"Too late for that," she told him. "He passed on a few years ago."

"Oh, sorry to hear that," Stone told her stiffly. Then, to his surprise and horror, he heard himself saying, "Ginny's mother did, too."

He had absolutely no idea what possessed him to share that with her. Only that it somehow seemed appropriate at the moment.

Rather than gush or give him empty platitudes the way he expected, the woman whose house he'd just finished touring and whose table he was currently sitting at, reached over and placed her hand on his. The soft, gentle, fleeting contact seemed to convey the level of her sorrow, their common *shared* sorrow, far better than a battalion of words ever could have.

"Are you raising her by yourself?" she asked. There was compassion in her voice.

Sometimes it felt that way, but that was unfair. Virginia dealt with Ginny far more than he did—unless he was between jobs and had the time to spend with Ginny. "My sister moved in to help when my wife died."

"Your sister the accountant who does your website?" she asked just to keep the details straight.

The smattering of a smile grew just for a moment before returning to a neutral expression. "That's her."

Danni smiled broadly again. "Then it really is a family business, isn't it?"

He considered the situation for a moment, then realized he had no idea why he was fighting the concept so stringently. He wouldn't have been able to take on any new jobs if it hadn't been for Virginia. At the same time, his sister had placed her life and her own business pretty much on hold because of him.

That needed to change.

Soon.

Just not yet.

Chapter Four

"What do you mean you can't watch Ginny for me?" Stone stared at his sister in utter disbelief. He'd been *counting* on Virginia. There *was* no back-up plan for him to turn to. "I'm supposed to be start working on that woman's house today. The one who cooks things," he added by way of a description in case Virginia didn't remember who he was referring to.

Virginia was caught between feeling guilty over lying to Stone and putting him through this—even if it *was* for his own good—and trying desperately to suppress the laugh bubbling up in her throat in response to what her brother assumed for an enlightening description. Leave it to Stone to reduce a notable, thriving career and identify it in such a way that it could fit just about every single woman both he and she knew—excluding herself since she had yet to learn how to successfully boil water without burning something.

But, for the sake of playacting—and the fact that Maizie thought that it would be in everyone's best interest to have Stone acquaint Danni with Ginny at the very outset of this relationship, Virginia pretended to be a little confused.

"Are you talking about the woman with the cable network cooking show?" she asked innocently.

"Yes, her. The one whose house is going to pay for Ginny's college education," he underscored. Stone was only half kidding.

Danni Everett had said yes to his estimate, but not until after asking some rather surprisingly intelligent questions. He'd been rather impressed by that. Truthfully, he preferred working for people who had some sort of understanding about what was involved in making the renovations they wanted and were aware that he couldn't just mumble some incantations under his breath and make their requested changes happen overnight. He also appreciated that she fully understood and accepted the fact that the house was going to look considerably worse before it looked better. A lot of people he'd done work for had taken exception to that.

But none of that was going to happen if he couldn't go over there and get started.

"I'm going to college?" Ginny asked in surprise.

Stone paused to kiss the top of Ginny's head. He kept forgetting that she listened to everything rather than tuned conversations out, the way that most kids Ginny's age did.

"Yes, someday," he told her. "It just might be a little harder without this new project coming through." He eyed Virginia accusingly. How could she let him down like this, without any warning? "I thought you said you'd be able to watch her for me."

They had an agreement. Since this was summer, Ginny wasn't in school—not that he considered kindergarten actually "school." But the teacher had been nice and Ginny had been with kids her own age, so that gave both of them time to conduct their business. Once the official school year started for Ginny, one of them would pick her up in the afternoon and look after the little girl.

If he was in between projects, he always made a point of being the one there for Ginny. Virginia was there the rest of the time, whenever he wasn't available. That, to him, was the beauty of his sister running her business out of the house.

With school out, Ginny had to be watched full time. For the most part, this last month, that responsibility had fallen to Virginia. There were two more months to get through and then Ginny would be going back to school, this time to first grade and that entailed longer hours, giving them both a little more time to attend to their own work.

But they weren't there just yet.

"I know and I'm sorry," Virginia apologized, doing her best to look properly contrite. "But that was before this thing came up."

"Thing?" he repeated, no more enlightened than he

had been a moment ago. "What 'thing' are we talking about?" Stone pressed.

His sister hadn't said anything to him about there being any possible snags when they'd discussed his taking on this latest job. Why had she waited until the last possible moment to throw this curve ball at him?

Virginia shrugged self-consciously. She really hadn't considered the possibility of getting the third degree when she'd begged off. She hadn't thought a plausible alibi properly through.

"A *thing*," she repeated more forcefully. "I've got this *thing*."

The annoyance over being broadsided like this by Virginia at the eleventh hour temporarily faded as Stone looked at his sister with growing concern.

"There's nothing wrong, is there, Virginia?" he asked, all sorts of horrible possibilities running through his mind. After all, Eva had been healthy and thriving until suddenly, her life ended. He knew firsthand how quickly fate could strike, canceling out a life. "You're not going to see a doctor or anything like that, are you, Virginia?" he asked, his voice pulsing with growing concern.

Virginia was exceedingly tempted to grab the excuse he'd just handed her on a silver platter, but she knew Stone. If he thought there was anything wrong with her, if he even *suspected* that she was ill, he'd put his own entire life on hold and insist on going with her to the doctor, or specialist, and he'd want to be right there, in the office to discuss her options and offer her his physical and emotional support.

He could be incredibly selfless at times, but she felt

he was letting that sterling quality go to waste on her. Somewhere out there—hopefully a lot closer to home—there was a woman who needed a man like Stone—and who could be the kind of woman that *he* needed as well.

What she needed right now, for both their sakes, was a plausible excuse he could accept, one that would cause him to back off.

The "thing" could be a new client, she suddenly thought. Quickly, her brain scrambled to come up with some details—*any* sort of details—to toss her brother's way.

Specifics continued to elude her.

She went with vague. "I've got this new client I'm trying to land. They said they wanted to meet with me for an early lunch. If things go well, it might turn out to be a very *long* lunch," she told him. "I just can't take the munchkin with me."

Stone nodded. "No, you can't," he agreed.

"Hey, I've got an idea," Virginia said brightly. "Why don't you take her with you?"

"As what?" Had Virginia lost her mind? "My assistant?" he asked with a touch of sarcasm.

"Sure, Daddy, I can be your assistant," Ginny piped up excitedly, enunciating the last word very carefully. "I can help. Like when you were fixing the leak in the kitchen. Remember?"

He remembered. The leak had taken him twice as long to stop, but he hadn't wanted to discourage Ginny's desire to be helpful. He couldn't afford to take that kind of time on a customer's house, otherwise, he'd be there until Ginny graduated high school.

"I remember, honey. But that was our leak and our kitchen," he pointed out.

Her eyebrows drew together in consternation. "The lady doesn't like little kids helping to fix leaks?" she asked him.

Stone looked at her, caught off guard by something she'd just said. "Ginny, how did you know my new client is a lady?" To the best of his recollection, he hadn't said anything to his daughter about the woman.

Unlike her aunt, Ginny seemed to have an answer for everything. "I heard you talking to Aunt Virginia about her," Ginny told him innocently.

"I really don't remember saying anything," Stone told his daughter as he tried to recall what Ginny could have overheard. Giving up, he shrugged. "Not important," he decided. "However, I'd better call to tell her I won't be able to get started today."

But as he reached into his pocket to extract his cell phone, Ginny caught his hand, pulling it toward her. "No, don't, Daddy. You can go see the lady. I'm a big girl. I can stay home alone until you get back. I'm brave," she added as a final convincing argument, lifting her chin up proudly.

Touched, Stone laughed as he ruffled her hair. "Nice try, kiddo—and don't think I don't appreciate this—but you're not quite old enough to be home alone." She began to protest, but he cut her off before she could say anything. "Besides, you get into trouble just being in a room alone, never mind a house."

"But Daddy—" Ginny began, this time sounding far

more urgent than the first time she'd attempted to convince him she could remain alone.

"Quiet, kiddo," he chided. "I'm dialing." Stone nodded at the card he had in front of him as he tapped out the numbers. The phone rang only once. And then he heard the phone on the other end of the line being picked up. He really hoped the woman was as reasonable as she looked. "Ms. Everett?" he asked once he heard the melodious greeting on the other end.

Danni recognized his voice immediately. She also recognized that tiny little flip her stomach had made. A tiny little flip it had no business making.

"Stone."

The way she said his name brought an instant feeling of warmth rushing over him. Since when had his imagination taken on this extra dimension? His imagination had always been restricted to envisioning projects, not anything else.

"Today's the day you're going to get started, isn't it?" he heard her saying. "I didn't get my dates confused, did I?" she asked him.

"No, you didn't, but about that," he began, taking advantage of the segue, each word weighing heavily on his tongue, "I'm afraid I'm going to have to cancel today."

"Oh." He heard genuine disappointment throbbing in her voice and he was sorry about that. Still, he wasn't prepared for what came next. She asked him "Why?" Ordinarily, when delays cropped up—and they did on rare occasions, usually involving a delay in the primary materials arriving—the people he was working for at the time never asked *why* he wasn't coming, they just accepted that he wasn't.

"My sitter canceled at the last minute," he told Danni, sparing Virginia a less than pleased glance, "and I've got no one to watch my daughter. It'll take me time to make other arrangements, so I thought it might be best if I just—"

"Bring her with you," Danni interjected the invitation before he could finish his sentence.

Stone halted abruptly, caught completely off guard. He was certain that he'd misheard the woman on the other end of the line.

"Excuse me?"

"Bring her with you," Danni repeated, then added, "Your daughter," so that there was no wiggle room for misunderstanding. "Look, I had my producer rework the taping schedule so I that could take the day off and be here—in case you had any concerns or questions that suddenly occurred to you when you got started on the house," she explained. "Since I'm going to be here for the day, you might as well take advantage of that."

For a second, it sounded like an invitation to him, but he knew she couldn't possibly mean what he thought she was saying. "Are you saying that you're volunteering to take care of my daughter for me today while I work on your house?"

"That's exactly what I'm saying."

He could have sworn he heard a smile in her voice. And he would have been lying if he pretended not to be tempted by what she was proposing. Still, he knew he couldn't agree to it. This arrangement would somehow bend the rules—wouldn't it?

"I can't ask you to do that," he told her.

"Well," she began slowly, "as I remember this conversation—you didn't. I'm volunteering," Danni pointed out. "I'm really pretty good with kids." Then, in case he needed convincing, she continued, "I've got a goddaughter who's just a little older than Ginny and I've taken her to the amusement park a few times without losing her or breaking her."

"How do you know how old my daughter is?" Stone asked, still somewhat stunned that his client was offering to help out like this.

"You told me," she reminded him. "The first time we met. You said she was four, going on forty," Danni repeated the phrase he'd used. "Remember?"

"Now I do."

He remembered the whole exchange. Remembered thinking that she had drawn the information out of him because he was talking more than he was accustomed to with a client. Stone found himself feeling rather awkward and foolish about the whole episode—and he wasn't altogether certain as to why.

"Then you'll bring her over?" Danni asked, clearly pleased by what she assumed his answer would be. "I would really love to have you get started on the house and I'm sure I can keep your daughter occupied for the duration that you're here."

Stone paused, giving her offer some genuine consideration. He knew he could ask Ginny to be on her very best behavior and she would promise him she would be and she'd actually mean it. But there was absolutely no denying that the diminutive girl was a live wire, one that couldn't readily be contained, or entertained in hopes that she would be mesmerized enough to actually remain still.

Still, he heard himself asking, "You're sure about this?"

He had no desire to wind up losing a client because he didn't want to postpone his starting date.

"Absolutely," Danni said with feeling. "I'd love to meet her."

Careful what you wish for, lady, he warned her silently. Out loud, he said with more than a trace of skepticism, "Okay, I'll bring Ginny with me. But at the first sign that my daughter's getting to be too much for you, I want you to let me know and I'll take her right home."

Danni sensed that protesting she was perfectly equal to anything a four-year-old had in her bag of tricks wouldn't convince the stoic contractor one bit and would just be a colossal waste of time, as well as her breath.

So instead, she replied complacently, "I'll let you know."

"All right. We'll be over soon," he said, ending the call.

The woman wasn't going to let him know if Ginny got to be too much for her, he thought, putting his cell phone away. He could just *feel* it in his bones. Something about the woman struck him as being much too stubborn to admit to being tired out by a four-year-old.

He looked at his daughter doubtfully, then glanced

over at his sister again. "You're absolutely certain that you can't—"

"Absolutely certain," Virginia echoed his words, cutting him off. "As a matter of fact, I should be getting ready to go right now." About to leave the room and run up the stairs to her bedroom, Virginia paused to kiss the top of Ginny's head and to issue the little girl a warning. "Remember, I want you to be on your best behavior, Munchkin."

"I will, Aunt Virginia," Ginny promised.

Virginia eyed her niece, not completely convinced she'd gotten through to her. Ginny was just too exuberant for anyone's own good.

"Remember what's at stake," she reminded the little girl. In response, Ginny nodded her head solemnly and vigorously.

"What's at stake?" Stone asked, wondering if his sister and his daughter had some sort of code worked out between them. It seemed like an odd choice of words to use.

"My college education," Ginny immediately piped up, then looked at him expectantly. "You said so, remember, Daddy?"

Virginia turned away so her brother wouldn't see her smile. Ginny had the makings of a great little spy someday, she couldn't help thinking.

"I remember," Stone answered.

He looked from his pint-size offspring to his sibling. Something was up, he could swear to it. But for the life of him, he had no idea what it could be, or how to even begin to frame his question so he could ask the two of

them what was going on. He knew they'd feign innocence and ask him what he meant—and he wouldn't be
able to tell them, or go into any sort of an explanation,
other than to say that something just felt...off.

So for now, Stone decided just let it go and hope for
the best.

"Okay, Gin, go pack up a few of your toys and let's
go," he told his daughter.

"Be right back, Daddy," she promised, flying out of
the room. He looked after her, mystified.

Definitely something off, he thought.

He was more convinced than ever when Ginny returned almost immediately, her backpack bulging with
her favorite toys.

It was almost, he speculated, as if she had them already packed and waiting.

Why would she do that?

The answer was she wouldn't. After all, she was only
four, he reminded himself, and that sort of thing would
have taken a little planning on her part. Four-year-olds—
even those who were almost five, like Ginny, didn't plan
anything.

Still, he commented, "That was fast," just to see what
she would say.

"I *am* fast, Daddy," Ginny informed him proudly,
puffing up her chest a little.

She was one of a kind, his Ginny, he couldn't help
thinking.

"And you know to be on your best behavior, right?"
he asked her even though Virginia had just said the same
thing to her less than five minutes ago.

"Right," she parroted back eagerly, then, for good measure, she crossed her heart and gave him her one-hundred-watt smile. "The bestest," she declared.

Stone nodded, trying to convince himself that he had nothing to worry about as he left the house. What was the worst thing that could happen? He supposed that his new client could quickly become his ex-new client. But he'd weathered things like that before—usually after his clients had made unreasonable demands on either a completion date, or a cost estimate.

This, Stone thought, would probably be the first time he would have a project terminated "on account of daughter."

Opening the rear passenger door to his wide-body truck, he stepped back to allow Ginny room to scramble up to her seat, then he lifted her onto the car seat he had secured there. Strapping her in, he checked to make sure the belts all held before shutting the door and then rounding the hood to get to the driver's side. He slid in behind the wheel, snapping in his own seat belt and then started up the truck.

"When can I ride shotgun in front with you, Daddy?" Ginny asked, raising her voice above the starting hum of the truck's engine.

"When your legs are long enough for your feet to touch the floor," he informed her automatically. This wasn't the first time she asked the question.

"Okay."

That sounded *much* too complacent for Ginny. Maybe, he thought as he glanced at his daughter in the rearview mirror, he should have checked his garage for a pod before he left.

But since he was already running late, "pod checking" was going to have to wait until later, when he got back, he told himself.

Until then, all he could do was pray that Ginny's good behavior somehow continued.

Chapter Five

When she was taping her cable cooking program, or meeting with the handful of business clients—she liked keeping her hand in the catering business just in case the cable program disappeared, as so many did—Danni made certain that she always dressed well. That meant wearing either attractive dresses or flattering skirts and matching tops. Either way, she always completed the outfit with killer high heels.

She usually picked the heels before she picked the outfit.

On her few days off, Danni did a complete about-face and dressed as casually and comfortably as possible. That translated to wearing either jeans or shorts when it was hot, accompanied by a colorful cotton T-shirt, the bottom of which usually conducted a flirtatious relationship with her midriff. And although she'd slip on a pair of mules if she was going to the mailbox or into the garage, for the most part, Danni would walk around her house and patio barefoot.

So, when Stone rang the front doorbell—after issuing one last warning to his daughter to remember to be on her very best behavior—and the door opened, he didn't recognize the barefoot female standing in the doorway at first.

The young woman looked far more like a carefree first-year college student than she did the central figure in a currently up-and-rising cable cooking program.

So much so that at first glance, Stone thought he was looking at the woman's younger cousin or maybe her kid sister. Since there didn't seem to be anyone else coming up behind the young woman, he asked, "Is Ms. Everett around? I'm Stone Scarborough and I'm supposed to start working on her house today." For emphasis, he nodded at the oversize toolbox he was holding. He took it with him to every job, a last Christmas present from his late wife.

Before the young woman in the thin sky-blue T-shirt—a T-shirt that seemed to be adhering to her torso closer than a second skin—could respond, Ginny, not to be left out, introduced herself.

"And I'm Virginia Scarborough," Ginny announced proudly to the pretty lady in the doorway. "Everybody calls me Ginny so they don't get confused between me and my aunt Virginia. You can call me Ginny, too," she told her, grinning from ear to ear. "Daddy told me you were a godmother. Does that mean you're God's mother?" Ginny asked, curious. "'Cause Aunt Virginia told me God already has a mother. Her first name's Mary, is that your first name?"

"Ginny, what did I tell you about talking too much?" Stone asked, trying to curtail his mini inquisitor, as well as his own impatience.

Ginny instantly looked down on the ground, as if that would summon a subdued nature. "Not to," she replied, mumbling the answer into her small chest.

"No," he answered patiently, "I said to remember to *breathe* in between sentences. You have to breathe, Ginny," he told her firmly. It was the only chance a person had to get a word in edgewise when his daughter started with her nonstop rhetoric.

That said, Stone raised his eyes to look at the petite, barefoot young woman. She appeared to be extremely amused by the whole scenario being acted out right in front of her.

"Sorry about that," he apologized. "Ginny tends to get carried away sometimes when she meets new people."

"Nothing to be sorry about," Danni assured him. She smiled warmly at the little girl. "I understand completely."

Ginny's eyes were all but shining.

"You do?" she asked, clearly thrilled and stunned at the same time.

"Absolutely. Sometimes I get so excited about something new, I don't know what to say first, so all the words seem to come tumbling out all at once, and they even get tangled up sometimes," Danni told her as solemnly as she could manage.

Ginny was literally beaming, Stone noted, as the little girl turned to momentarily look back at him. "She's nice, Daddy."

Danni suppressed a delighted laugh. "Glad I passed inspection." And then she looked at Stone. "And I do know who you are, Mr. Scarborough," she assured him. "We met when you came by to see my house and to work up an estimate after I told you what I wanted done. You told me I might want to consider buying another house. I didn't want to."

Amused by what she assumed was the reason for his repeated introduction, Danni said, "In case you're wondering, my memory is just fine. And the cookies that I bake just have the ingredients you can easily buy over the counter in any supermarket—nothing more," she informed him, ending her statement with a wink.

For some reason, the wink seemed to go straight to his gut.

For one of the very few times in his life—possibly the very first—Stone felt flustered. Because she looked so different from their first meeting, he didn't fully recognize the woman who would be signing his checks for a while. Maybe it was too early in the morning. Looking more closely now, he realized his mistake.

"I didn't mean to imply, that is—I didn't completely recognize you at first," Stone finally managed to say. "You look like your own kid sister," Stone added, at a loss as to how to rectify the situation and backtrack gracefully.

Was he actually telling her that she looked like a kid? The smile curving her mouth was somewhat bemused.

"I don't know if that's a good thing or a bad thing," Danni commented.

He didn't want her to think he was trying to get too personal—or flirt with her. "It's not supposed to be either, just an observation," he explained honestly.

Danni put her own interpretation to his response. "I didn't mean to make it sound as if I was fishing for a compliment," she told him. "It's just that nobody's ever said anything like that to me before, that I look too young," she added in case he wasn't following her line of thinking.

Stone thought of protesting that she didn't look too young, but that really wasn't the truth, because she did. So instead, he fell back on logic. "Do you have mirrors in the house?"

Danni blinked. "Yes, of course I do." There was one right over there, on the far wall, and she nodded toward it.

"Do you ever look in any of those mirrors when you're dressed like that?" he asked pointedly.

Aside from the shorts and clingy T-shirt, she was wearing her hair in two separate ponytails, jauntily perched high on her head. They swished back and forth as she moved. She didn't even look as if she was twenty, much less any older.

Danni looked down at her clothes, then back up again at him. She didn't need a mirror, she could just imagine that someone coming in, expecting to see the star of a new cable cooking program might think she was just some young relative hanging around.

She was also blessed with her mother's skin, which

seemed to defy age and didn't turn to leather despite her love of the outdoors—although lately, that love wasn't something she was able to indulge in very often.

She supposed, if it was a choice between looking older than she was or younger than she was, she'd choose the latter.

"Point taken," Danni told her contractor. Looking up, her wide smile was back in place. "Now, can I offer you something to eat or drink before you get started?"

He didn't believe in taking a break before getting started. Besides, he liked doing what he did and was eager to get started.

"If it's all the same to you, I'd like to begin working. Not really sure just how much time I can devote to anything today," he said, casting an apprehensive side glance toward his daughter.

The way he looked at his daughter was not wasted on Danni.

"Don't worry about Ginny," she told him, easily taking the little girl's hand in hers. "I have a project that needs some very valuable little-girl input," she said, addressing her words to Stone as well as to his daughter.

"What's input?" Ginny asked.

"Words," Danni said simply. "I want to find out what you think of some of these new desserts I'm going to be making for my viewers."

"Cool," Ginny declared, her eyes wide enough to pass for the proverbial saucers.

"But first, I'm going to have to make the desserts. For that, I'm going to need an assistant to help me. She needs to be about this tall." Danni held her hand up to indicate approximately Ginny's height. "Would you have any idea where I can find someone like that?"

"Me!" Ginny declared, raising her hand in the air as if she were in school, trying to get the teacher's attention. "Me, I can help and be your 'sistant," she told Danni with enthusiasm.

"You?" She glanced at Ginny, pretending that she was just seeing the little girl for the first time and was seriously considering the possibility of taking her up on her offer to help. "Are you sure that you have the time to help me?" Danni asked, keeping a perfectly straight face.

"Yes! Daddy said he was going to be here at least an hour, maybe two," she told her new best friend. "Or more," she added with a whisper. "So I can be your 'sistent!"

Danni peered over the little girl's head toward the man she had hired to bring new life to her house.

"An hour or two?" she questioned. She'd expected him to be here for most of the day. Just how fast did this man work?

Stone subtly indicated his daughter with his eyes, then looked back at her. "I thought that two hours might be all you could handle."

Danni smiled then, the same smile he'd seen the other day, the one that looked as if it had enough wattage to light up a good part of the first floor in the dead of night.

"I think you might be underestimating me, Mr. Scarborough," she told him.

"Apparently," he agreed, thinking of what he had just witnessed. In a few easy words, she'd seemed to have made a friend for life out of his daughter. Danni had certainly won the little girl's heart and made her feel useful at the same time. "And it's Stone," he told her. Addressing him formally just seemed out of place in this situation. "My name," he clarified.

"Yes, I know," she replied with the same warm smile that for some reason made him feel unseasonably hot.

Stone forced himself to look away. If he didn't, there was a very real danger of his just standing there, staring at Danni, being completely mesmerized by the woman, by her smile, and by the utter unassuming power she was able to wield over his firecracker of a daughter.

"I'll just go get started," he murmured, pointing toward the door and the driveway beyond where his truck was parked.

"You do that," Danni agreed. "And my assistant and I will do the same." She looked down at the little girl. "Right, Ginny?"

"Right!" the little girl declared happily.

Even though Stone allowed himself a slight, private smile, he still couldn't help wondering if this woman knew just what she was letting herself in for. Ginny could tire out a legion of saints once she got going.

He knew that whenever either he or his sister gave Ginny a time-out, it wasn't done so that she could sit in her room, reflecting on what she'd done wrong; it was so that he and Virginia could get a little break, a breather, before they began trying to regroup and prepare for the next onslaught of Ginny, The Tireless Warrior Princess.

From what he'd observed, although Danni seemed to be energetic and she was certainly imaginative, he wasn't all that certain that the newest cable personality would be equal to not just putting up with, but surviving his daughter.

He decided to work as quickly as possible and get as much done as he could before the call for help—following Danni's complete surrender—rang out through the house.

Stone glanced at his watch.

Immersing himself in his work—which required that he completely gut the first room he'd chosen to work on, the downstairs rear bedroom—he realized that he'd apparently lost track of time. Before he knew it, more than two hours had gone by. Two hours where the only sound he'd heard were the sounds he'd created himself when he turned his power tools on and used them.

Stone stood now in the middle of the barren room, looking at what was left after he'd ripped away the plasterboard and what had once been some rather awful-looking rust-colored shag rugs. He shook his head as he regarded the pile of off-colored orangey-rust. It was incredible what bad taste an entire generation had adopted, he'd thought when he began separating the pieces of rug from the floor.

But he wasn't thinking about bad taste at the moment, or even envisioning what he would eventually turn this room into. He was concerned that he hadn't heard any sounds coming from the kitchen where his daughter and Danni were supposed to be working.

Granted the machines he was operating tended to drown most things out, but they hadn't been on nonstop.

Taking off the safety glasses he was wearing and

turning off the sander he'd been using on a particularly
stubborn section of plasterboard, he left the room and
went in search of his daughter. He sincerely hoped nothing was wrong and that he hadn't lost one client before
he really had her, but he couldn't help having his doubts.

He needed to check on his daughter and what she'd
done to Danni.

The moment he walked out of the back bedroom, he
realized he could smell it. Smell a tantalizing aroma that
suggested something exceptionally pleasing to the palette was going on in the oven.

As he approached the kitchen, Stone looked around
and saw no one. He did detect a slight ticking sound,
once he acclimated himself to what he first presumed
was the silence. He quickly realized that what he was
listening to was a timer. A timer that had exactly ten
seconds left before it suddenly announced the end of
its journey.

Rather than ring, the timer, jauntily mounted on the
refrigerator, began to buzz. Buzz loudly and continu-
ously, pulsing demandingly until someone paid attention to it, shut it off and took out whatever it was timing.

"Ginny?" he called. "Ginny, where did you go off
to?" *And what have you done with Danni?*

"I'm right here, Daddy!" Ginny announced, all but
bouncing into the kitchen from the direction of the living room.

Danni strode in right behind her.

Stone hadn't noticed until just now that for what was
a rather petite woman, the cable channel's new cooking
darling had a really long pair of legs.

A very attractive, really long pair of legs.

He caught himself staring at them as he watched Danni hurrying into the room, and for just a moment, he forgot that he'd been taught as a child that it wasn't very polite to stare.

The word *polite* really wasn't entering into the equation at all at the moment. But other words, other sensations and feelings, were.

And not exclusively for Stone.

Because even as she hurried over to the stove, Danni saw her contractor staring. And it wasn't at the stove.

A warm shiver danced down her spine.

Chapter Six

"Where were you?" Stone asked, tearing his eyes away from Danni and making a conscious effort to focus only on his daughter.

"We were in the living room," Ginny answered before Danni had a chance to explain anything to her father. "Danni's got this really awesome gaming system."

And it was crystal clear to Stone, by the look on his daughter's face, that she was absolutely enamored with the video gaming system.

And just possibly, with the owner of the gaming system as well.

"You have kids?" he asked Danni. She'd only mentioned having a goddaughter when he'd called to cancel on her because he didn't have a sitter for Ginny. Who bought a gaming system for a goddaughter who was dropped off occasionally?

Danni shook her head. "No."

His eyebrows drew together into one perplexed, wavy line. The woman certainly didn't look like a computer geek or gaming nerd. But those were the only two options that might explain why someone over the age of eighteen would have a sophisticated gaming system— or any gaming system for that matter.

"Then why do you have a gaming system in your living room?" Stone asked her.

Danni went with the very obvious: She had money and she liked pleasing a child in her life.

"Because, even though I don't have a child, I *do* have a goddaughter and she likes to play competitively. I found some age-appropriate games for her—which meant I needed a system to play them on. It also meant I had to learn how to play and hold up my end if I ever hoped to have a chance of winning." She glanced over at Ginny. "She's very sharp, your daughter."

Danni would get no argument out of him on that count. "Like I said, four going on forty."

"I'm gonna be five very soon," Ginny volunteered to Danni proudly.

"Too soon," Stone commented. He could vividly remember bringing her home from the hospital, thinking, as he held her, that she was liable to break at any second. The fear stayed with him for a while.

Ginny sniffed as she put her hands on her very small, barely noticeable little hips and told her father in the oldest voice she could muster, "I can't stay a little girl forever, you know."

Danni laughed. "Sounds like she's already on her way to growing up."

Stone sighed as he shook his head. "Don't I know it. Well, I'll take her off your hands now."

Danni looked at him in surprise. "You're finished for the day?" By her reckoning, he'd only been at it for just a little under two hours.

"I gutted one room." But that wasn't why he was getting ready to pack up and leave for the day. "I thought my daughter would have tired you out by now."

Danni laughed softly. "We Georgia girls are a lot heartier than we look," she informed him with a touch of pride.

"I like your accent," he realized. That slight lilt in her voice he heard every now and then, the comfortable way she had of talking, it had a pleasing effect on him.

Danni had tried very hard to lose her accent, paying very close attention to the cadence of those who did not drawl, twang or have a nasal intonation.

She wanted to sound like a Midwesterner.

What she definitely didn't want was for someone to think that her Georgia accent was actually a gimmick she was falling back on to distinguish her from some of the other cable channel chefs.

She had never believed in gimmicks. She wanted to appeal to everyone across the board.

"I don't have an accent," Danni protested with alacrity.

There was just the barest hint of a smile curving the corners of Stone's mouth. How could a proverbial "Georgia Peach" think she didn't have a Southern accent?

"Yes, you do," Stone countered.

Ginny looked from one adult to the other and seemed very quickly to pick a side. She backed up her new best friend loyally and even moved a little bit closer to her, taking a couple of steps in her direction.

"No, she doesn't, Daddy," Ginny pronounced solemnly. "She sounds just like you and me. Well, me anyway, 'cause you don't really do much talking, Daddy," his daughter informed him.

Danni pressed her lips together to keep back her laugh, not wanting to hurt the little girl's feelings—or offend Ginny's father.

"Looks like I have a defender," she said with a warm smile. Danni ran her hand affectionately over the little girl's curly hair. If things had gone another way, she might have had a child of her own by now, rather than just her own cooking program.

Hey, things don't always work out the way we plan, a voice in her head reminded her. *Focus on what you do have, not what you don't.*

It was an adage her father had been fond of repeating often and she had to admit that it had helped to see her through some pretty rough times in the last couple of years.

Since the woman was apparently sensitive on the subject of accents, Stone let the matter drop—except for one consequence that had raised its head during the discussion. Ginny had been really quick to come to Danni's defense. He had to admit he'd never seen his daughter take to anyone as fast as she had to this woman. Not

that Ginny was exactly shy, but this had to be a new record, even for her.

"She really seems to have taken a shine to you," he
commented to Danni.

"The feeling is more than mutual," Danni assured
both father and daughter, winking at the latter as if they
had some sort of secret between them.

Ginny was apparently eager to show her father what
they'd been up to while he'd been working. The girl
looked toward the oven that was currently housing not
just the fruit of their effects, but the really delicious
aroma that came along it.

"You wanna try the pie we made?" Ginny asked her
father, looking ready to simply leap out of her skin with
enthusiasm.

He wasn't sure whether to say yes or no, neither was
he certain if the offering *was* his daughter's to make.

"I think that Danni has other ideas for the pie." He
assumed it was going with the woman to the cable studio, to be part of her program; the "after" photograph
used to encourage people who ordinarily burned water
not to give up.

"No, I don't," Danni corrected him cheerfully. "I
thought it might be a good experience for Ginny to help
me prepare and bake a pecan pie and then find out firsthand just how good it can turn out." She looked at the
little girl, who already needed no encouragement—or
any elaborate traveling directions—to make a beeline
for the stove.

Taking a pair of embroidered pot holders from a
drawer, Danni opened the oven door and then very care-

fully removed the chocolate pecan pie. She placed it on top of the stove to cool.

Noting the eager expression on the little girl's face, Danni cautioned, "It has to cool off first, honey. If you try to sample any of it now, you'll wind up burning your tongue."

Putting her hands behind her back, Ginny rocked back on her heels and said innocently, "Wasn't gonna try to eat it now. Not even one tiny piece," she declared, holding her small thumb and forefinger up and just a sliver apart to show just how small a piece she had no intentions of having.

Thoroughly amused, Danni continued the dialogue between herself and her Muppet-size assistant. "I see that you've thought this all out very carefully, haven't you?" Danni said to her, addressing Ginny the way she would another adult.

Her method completely won over Ginny's heart. "Yes, ma'am," she agreed.

Danni finally raised her eyes to look at Ginny's father and saw the very strange expression on his face. She made no effort to try to fathom what was behind it. That would only be a waste of time.

"Is there something wrong?" she asked.

Stone shook his head, still watching his daughter. "Not a thing. I was just thinking that I'd never seen Ginny respond to anyone the way she does to you." He made no effort to hide his unabashed wonder.

That was probably because—she would have placed a silent bet on the fact that—there wasn't overly much female traffic going back and forth from Stone's house.

He appeared too serious, too wrapped up in his work, to have time for "recreational activities" she believed one of those TV fix-all pseudo doctors had called it.

"Would you like to sample a piece once it cools off?" Danni offered.

He saw no reason to demur. The aroma was causing his stomach to almost contract in anticipation. "Sure, why not?" he agreed off-handedly, then added, "But you're sure we're not in your way?"

"What 'way'?" she asked. "I'm not doing anything except talking to you—and baking with a really good assistant," she added, flashing a wide smile at Ginny. "And for the record, if you feel like maybe doing a little more—gutting, is it?" Danni asked, referring to what he'd just told her he'd just finished doing to her back bedroom.

Stone nodded, confirming the term she'd just used.

"If you feel like doing a little more gutting today, there is another dish I thought that my willing assistant and I could try our hands at—but only if you have some work to do," she stipulated.

He had, technically, the whole house to work on. He just had to pick a spot. "You could make one hell of a negotiator, you know?" he said to her, then let her know that he had plenty of rooms to choose from for his next gutting.

"Sure," he told her agreeably. "If you really have more to do and my daughter's 'assisting' you hasn't pushed you over the edge yet—"

"It hasn't," she quickly interjected, not wanting to give Ginny anything remotely scary to think about late at night. "And it won't," she added with certainty, earning the little assistant's undying love right then and there.

"Then yeah, okay, I can do some more gutting," he agreed. "I thought that I'd do the bathroom off the back bedroom next, unless you'd rather I did another area instead."

That happened to be the only bathroom on the first floor. She decided that perhaps a question regarding timing might be in order right about here.

"How long between when you gut them and put them back into working order?" she asked.

Stone thought about it for a moment. He had no intentions of being vague or promising something he wouldn't be able to deliver on.

"Well, that really all depends on the size of the room that we're talking about," Stone qualified.

"The bathroom," Danni reminded him, nodding in the general direction of the room he'd told her he would do next.

That bathroom was considered a three-quarter model since there was no tub, only a shower. "I'd say about three, four days tops."

That sounded reasonable to her. She could certainly put up with that time frame. Going up and down the stairs more frequently was good for her, Danni told herself. It forced her to exercise her legs, never a bad thing.

Danni nodded her approval then said, "Go for it," out loud.

Stone didn't have to be told twice.

As he left the kitchen, in the background, he heard his daughter ask, "What are we gonna make next?"

"How do you feel about chicken potpie?" Danni asked her.

"I don't know," Ginny confessed honestly. "What is it?"

He didn't see the woman's smile, but he heard it in her voice. Though his back was to Danni just as he went into the hall, the smile in her voice had brought out one in kind to his lips.

"Absolutely delicious," Danni told her.

That was more than good enough for Ginny. "I like delicious," Ginny told her. "Let's make it!" she cried with enthusiasm and anticipation.

Stone picked up his sledge hammer and went back to work, marveling about what he'd just witnessed.

No matter how good a pastry chef the petite, sexy blonde was, she was really wasting her time at it. From the little bit he'd witnessed today, he could swear that Danielle Everett could be a really great child whisperer.

In the limited amount of time the woman had been with Ginny, she all but had the little girl wrapped around her little finger, ready to do anything she suggested.

He'd never seen anything like it before.

The tempting aroma of the cooling pie seemed to follow him all the way to the rear of the house. He could almost feel his mouth watering.

As he closed the door to minimize the noise of what he was about to do, he also deliberately sealed himself away from the tempting aroma that was wafting from the kitchen.

Even so, with the door closed and the aroma presumably barred from entering, he found that his mouth wouldn't stop watering.

He worked faster.

He had no other choice.

When Stone was finished and made his way back into the kitchen some ninety minutes later, he was rather spent and convinced that he now smelled far too gamey for mixed company. His new plan was to collect his daughter and go home, certain that by now Ginny had probably worn through all of the woman's steady nerves and that Danni in turn would be more than happy to see his truck pulling out of her driveway with Ginny strapped into the rear passenger seat, in a car seat.

"Daddy!" Ginny cried eagerly when she saw him coming into the room. "Are you finished for real this time?"

"I'm finished for real this time," he echoed instead of immediately telling his daughter that they were going home.

He saw the eager expression on his daughter's face. Was that due to what she'd been doing these last ninety minutes? Most likely it was, which made the woman with her nothing short of a real miracle worker.

Ginny ran up to him, no doubt very excited about what she'd been doing these last few hours. She moved in to hug him, then abruptly stopped and wrinkled her nose.

She gazed up at him with horror. "You smell funny, Daddy."

"That's just the scent of honest toil," Danni called out to Ginny from the far side of the kitchen. She was rummaging through the refrigerator. "Right?" she asked, making eye contact with Stone.

"Right," he agreed.

At least she wasn't wrinkling her nose at him, he thought. Whenever Elizabeth was around him right after he finished up a job, she'd flatly tell him that he needed to clean up first before he did anything else. Especially if he intended to do it around her.

"I'll just take Ginny and we'll get going," he told Danni.

"But, Daddy, you have to try what we've been making first. Danni said it was a late lunch. Your reward for all that hard work you did."

It was obvious that Ginny was quoting the woman, her new idol.

"I don't think that Danni wants to be around someone who smells like a barn," Stone said, trying to usher his daughter toward the front door.

"'Danni' knows how to make herself heard if she wants to," Danni informed him with an amused smile, as she walked toward him and his daughter. "However, if you feel uncomfortable about being a wee bit, um, sweaty," she said tactfully, "you're more than welcome to take a shower in one of the bathrooms upstairs. Ginny and I will wait until you come down again before eating," she promised. "Won't we, Ginny?"

"You bet!" Ginny cried.

"You're serious?" he asked Danni.

"Of course I'm serious. I can stop smiling and say it again with a frown if that would be more convincing,"

Danni offered, doing her best to suppress the grin trying to steal over her lips.

A shower would help, but that wasn't the total answer.
"Even if I take a shower, my clothes aren't exactly fresh."

"There're some clothes in a box in one of the upstairs bedrooms. You can't miss it. The box is in the
middle of the room. You might find something there
that'll fit you."

That sounded a bit odd to him.

"You just happen to have some spare men's clothing
that *might* fit me?" he asked incredulously.

The clothes had been some of the last ones she'd
bought her father. Up until now, she hadn't been able to
force herself to give them away to some charity where
they would do some good.

But she'd finally crossed that sentimental hurdle and
was ready to move on—to some extent. However, she
didn't really want to go into any of that in detail, at least
not yet.

"I just happen to be packing them up to give to charity. They're all still in good condition. I think they're
pretty much your size." Her father had been a big man.
He'd always made her feel safe, that nothing bad could
happen to her while she was with him.

She only wished that it had worked in reverse.

"Feel free to take anything you find there," she added.

He still hesitated, not wanting to take anything away
from someone else if they were in greater need than he
was.

But then Ginny delivered the winning argument. "Go,
take a shower, Daddy. So you can come back down and

taste the yummy stuff Danni taught me to make. Hurry, Daddy, before it gets all cold."

Danni smiled at him. "I believe you have your orders, *Daddy*."

He nodded and hurried away, absently wondering why hearing Danni call him that somehow felt really right.

He was probably just tired, Stone told himself.

Chapter Seven

Stone was back downstairs less than fifteen minutes later, his hair still damp and rakishly unkempt.

Returning to the kitchen, he found that the small, circular table in the nook had been set. His daughter was currently seated at one of the place settings and, miracle of miracles, she remained still.

Well, still for Ginny, he mentally amended.

"Daddy!" Her small face lit up when she saw him. "Now can we start?" she asked not him, the way he would have expected, but the woman setting out three small, perfect, golden-crusted potpies. No doubt prepared from scratch, they still had heat, not to mention tempting aroma, wafting from them.

"Well, that was a first," Stone murmured, sitting down on one side of his daughter.

"You don't take showers?" Danni asked.

"I don't take showers in other people's homes," he specified. "Especially not other people's homes that I'm working on."

After she finished putting out what she and Ginny had made for this rather late lunch, Danni sat down on the other side of Ginny—which also happened to be right next to Stone.

She liked his slightly messy and curly hair like that. It made him look more boyish and not quite so serious.

"You know, you could have taken longer," Danni told him. "Ginny and I would have still waited for you."

Stone realized that she was looking at his hair as she spoke. Probably thought he should have dried it before coming down, he guessed. There was a hair dryer plugged in just next to the sink, but he didn't feel quite right about using it. It was bad enough he'd had to use her towel to dry himself off. He couldn't get over feeling as if he was imposing.

"The shower was long enough," he told her matter-of-factly. And then he transformed into her contractor instead of a guest at her table. "I did hear some clanging coming from the pipes when I ran the hot water," he mentioned.

By the expression on Danni's face, he guessed he wasn't telling her anything new.

"I forgot to mention that the other day. It does that every time I take a shower or use the hot water in my bathroom. If I run cold water—" she waved her hand in the air "—nothing."

He nodded. What she'd just described wasn't that rare a problem. "I'll look into it when I'm remodeling the master bath," he promised. "Most likely, the pipe just needs to be bracketed down better."

As he talked, Stone sank his fork into the potpie on his plate and took his first tentative bite, his mind still on the noisy pipe.

The moment his taste buds kicked in and stood at attention, his mind did an instant about-face. Surprised, Stone looked down at the meal before him. The potpie was still rather hot, but that wasn't what had captured his attention. He was far from a discerning food critic with a delicate palette, but he wasn't one of those people who just ate to live, either. And even if he had been, the first bite he'd taken registered with quiet fanfare.

"This is good," he told her, making no effort to hide his surprise.

A smile played on her lips in response. "You were expecting to be poisoned?" Danni asked him, amused.

Stone raised his eyes and they held hers for a moment as he weighed his answer.

"Honestly?" he asked her.

Okay, this can't be good, not if he says it that way. Danni braced herself for what she thought *had* to be a strange answer. "Yes."

"I was actually expecting not to have any feelings about the food one way or another," he told her. Stone could see by her expression that Danni just couldn't relate to that sort of indifference when it came to food. "For the most part, food's pretty much just fuel to me. The decent kind of food I'll finish without noticing. The bad kind I'll notice and stop eating." He nodded at the potpie as he took another hefty forkful. "But this is *really* good."

Danni smiled broadly, more than a little relieved that she had managed to make something he enjoyed eating. "Thank you."

"No, *really* good," he emphasized with gusto, as surprised as she was that he was making this admission. "Which is unusual, seeing as how it's meant to be a soupy kind of thing and I don't really like soup."

"It's not soupy," Danni protested with a laugh. "This is what potpie is *supposed* to be like." She thought for a second, then felt she'd found the perfect analogy for this he-man type. "Just think of it as stew with a crust," she suggested.

Stone considered the description. "Not bad," he told her, nodding.

Danni cocked her head. "The description, or the pie?" she asked.

When she tilted her head like that, it made him want to sink his hands into her hair, frame her face and then discover what her lips tasted like.

"Both," he answered without pausing to think about it.

"Good, because I made a couple for you to take home with you—for you, Virginia and my young assistant here," Danni added, looking over toward Ginny and drawing the little girl into her inner circle.

For her part, Stone noticed, his daughter was far too busy eating to interrupt or insert her two cents into the conversation. Whatever secret ingredient the woman had put into the pie, it appeared to have a subduing effect on his daughter.

He could really get used to that.

"Just what's in this thing?" He nodded toward the almost-consumed potpie before him.

She thought of what she'd put in. "Diced chicken breasts, peas, carrots, corn, green beans, some broth mixed with flour, pepper, salt and a little parmesan cheese—why?"

That sounded almost painfully ordinary. There had to be something more. "What else?"

She didn't quite understand what he was trying to get her to say. She could only work with what she knew: the truth as it existed in this case.

"Nothing. It's all poured into a pie crust and covered with another crust, then baked."

He still found it hard to believe—not that the ingredients she'd just quoted had turned into an exceptionally tasty meal. The woman seemed to have a tight lock on the ability to make almost anything taste mouthwatering. What he found almost impossible to believe was that there wasn't something "extra" done to it before she put the potpies into the oven.

"What else did you think was in there?" she asked, curious to hear his answer.

"Oh, I don't know," he said and followed it up with pure speculation. "Extract of valerian root, a dose of tryptophan, something like that."

She looked at him, a little confused. Did he think she was trying to knock his daughter out, send her to slumber land until he was finished working? Just what sort of a person did he think she was?

"Why would I use something like that? This is supposed to be a potpie, not a sleeping aid."

"I wasn't thinking of sleeping, I was thinking more along the lines of tranquilizing," he corrected, subtly indicating his daughter with his eyes. "The last time I saw Ginny that still, she had a hundred and three fever and an upper-respiratory infection. Come to think of it, Virginia fed her chicken soup then."

"Chicken soup's supposed to have some medicinal properties," she told him. "But otherwise—the similarities in behavior are purely coincidental—maybe she just responds to good food." She smiled fondly at Ginny, watching her eat her potpie as if there would be nothing in the refrigerator for her to eat tomorrow. "She likes the epicurean experience."

"What's epi—epi—that word you just used," Ginny finally said in subdued frustration. "What's it mean?" she asked.

"It means that while you're eating, you focus on just that experience and nothing else," Danni explained to the little girl. "It also means that you know good food when you sample it," she concluded affectionately, giving the wiggling little girl a quick hug before releasing her again.

Ginny's eyes sparkled. "Yeah!" she responded with feeling. "And that was *real* good."

Danni noticed with pleasure that both father and daughter had done more than justice to their meals. All that remained were empty, miniature-size pie tins.

"Who's ready for dessert?" Danni asked, pretending to look around for takers.

"I am!" Ginny declared, raising her hand and waving it above her head just in case Danni hadn't noticed it.

"Well, by golly, it certainly does look like you are," Danni commented to the little girl, then stole a glance in Stone's direction. The man hadn't left behind so much as a crumb.

At least none that could be seen.

It gave her a warm glow inside. Seeing someone enjoy one of the meals she'd prepared always did that, and this time, even more so.

"But you're not," Stone pointed out, looking at the pie tin on her plate. "You didn't finish your meal. Something we should know about?"

The second he asked, he realized that it sounded as if he was teasing her. Something he hadn't engaged in since Eva had left his life.

Maybe there *was* something in the pie, he thought, something that took down his guard, or if not took down then definitely soften.

"Only that I'm a habitually slow eater, especially when I have guests," Danni said by way of a confession. "I get too caught up in watching their reaction to the meal I made to remember to eat it myself."

Danni rose from the small, circular table, taking both of their dishes, and putting them neatly down into the kitchen sink. She then took her plate and left it on the counter. She still had more than half the potpie left to eat.

"I'll have this for dinner later," she told him.

That done, she took the chocolate pecan pie from the

back of the stove where it was cooling and brought it to the table. She placed it in the middle, then got three dessert plates, which she distributed, placing one at each place setting, before she went to get a knife.

"I believe this is the first pecan pie your daughter's ever made," she told Stone, then asked for verification of her facts, not from him but from Ginny. "Am I right, Ginny?"

The little girl bobbed her head up and down vigorously, her curls flying to and fro about her face. "Uh-huh. The first. I never baked-ed a pie before today," she said with pride.

"Well, you did such a good job, I would have never guessed," Danni told her. "It just looks delicious. Don't you think so?" she asked, turning to Stone for back-up.

Danni knew firsthand how much a father's praise meant to a daughter. She still missed hearing her own father's enthusiastic encouragement.

Her father had been supportive of her right from the start, giving her heartfelt compliments even in the beginning, when her efforts were a great deal less than stellar. Sam Everett always made a point of telling her how much he enjoyed what she made, even when she had trouble choking it down herself.

It definitely made her want to do better next time. Made her want to be worthy of the praise her father gave her.

Even though she finally found her niche and hit a high plateau, she still strove very hard to do better "next time."

"Delicious," Stone echoed, nodding his head and looking right at Ginny.

Ginny looked as if she were bursting with pride. "I'll cut you a piece, Daddy, so you can taste it," Ginny volunteered. She started to reach for the knife Danni had set down.

Rather than chide her or pull the knife away before she could get it, Danni went with what she felt was an ego-saving approach.

"Oh, you've worked hard enough today," she told Ginny, deftly putting her hand over the knife before Ginny could wrap her fingers around it. "Why don't you let me serve *you* a piece?" she offered.

With that, Danni cut a healthy-sized sliver of pie and placed it on Ginny's plate, then cut a slightly wider piece and served it to Ginny's father.

A third sliver, more the size of what she'd just given Ginny, found its way to her plate.

Since both father and daughter were waiting on her, Danni proclaimed, "Okay, people, dig in." And three forks almost simultaneously sank into their own individual mound of pecans, brown sugar, two kinds of corn syrup and a few things Danni liked to refer to as her "secret" ingredients.

From beneath hooded eyes, Danni watched her guests' reaction to her latest version of crushed chocolate pecan pie.

While she was fairly confident that they would enjoy what they were eating, that wasn't why she was watching them. She just never tired of the look of pleasure that passed over people's faces when they first sampled something that she had made. It was like receiving a merit reward for a job well done and she was the first to admit—without shame—that she thrived on that sort of feedback. For her, it wasn't rooted in insecurity. The reason she liked it was because she had a desire for affirmation and reinforcement.

"Didn't Ginny do an absolutely outstanding job?" Danni asked the girl's father.

He didn't answer immediately. Instead, he looked at her for a long moment, then slanted a glance toward his daughter. Ginny was beaming from ear to ear, obviously pleased with herself and pleased with what she was eating. Moreover, from the look of it, his daughter was also half in love with this woman she had just met. This woman had a gift not just for cooking and baking, but for calming down overenergized little girls.

Hell of an asset to have, he couldn't help thinking, looking at Danni again.

"Yes," he said, "she did a *very* excellent job," he said, pausing briefly to glance over the woman whose house he was contracted to remodel before turning back toward his daughter.

In his estimation, Ginny looked as if she were ready to walk on air at any given moment. Thanks to Danni. The woman was extremely good with children.

"Maybe I can cook other things," Ginny said hopefully, looking at Danni as she nibbled on her lower lip, the way she always did when she was holding her breath over something.

"Maybe you can," Danni readily agreed. "The next time I'm off and your dad brings you along when he comes to work on the house, you and I can put our heads together and come up with another lunch."

Ginny watched her very thoughtfully. "Does it hurt?" she asked.

"Does what hurt?" Danni asked.

"Putting our heads together. Does it hurt? And do we have to keep them that way when we're cooking?" she asked with concern.

She could have eaten her up, Danni thought. "No, sweetie, it's just an expression. We don't really have to put our heads together. As a matter of fact, we'll probably get more done if we don't."

Ginny instantly clapped her hands together, ready to sign on. "Tomorrow?" she asked hopefully, her expressive big blue eyes dancing about.

"I'm afraid I'll be busy tomorrow—I have a job," she explained to the little girl. "But we can make arrangements for a next time," she promised. She saw Ginny's face fall a few degrees, as if she felt "next time" would never happen.

She didn't want the little girl to feel that way. She would have all the time in the world to experience disappointment. It shouldn't have to be at the age of four, she reasoned.

"Sometimes I get off early," she told Ginny, lowering her voice as if she was sharing some sort of state secret. "When I do, I'll call you and if you come over with your dad, you and I could make dinner."

Ginny turned her laser-beam eyes on her father. "Can we, Daddy? Can we?" Ginny begged.

"We'll see," he told her.

"We'll see *yes*, Daddy. We'll see *yes*," Ginny pleaded because she knew that when her father said the phrase, "we'll see," it usually meant no in the long run.

He looked at Danni then, not sure if he felt overwhelmed or just in awe of her methods.

"You were right," he told her.

Danni wasn't sure just what he was referring to. They'd found themselves on opposite sides of a few issues. "About what?"

"When you told me to bring Ginny with me because you were good with kids," he told her. "If anything, you didn't do yourself justice."

Danni laughed, more pleased than she thought she would have been to hear his praise.

"It's not a matter of being good with kids really. It's just a matter of being good with short people. That's what kids really are, you know. Just short people on their way to becoming tall people." She looked at Ginny with a warm smile. "What do you say to helping me pack up a few potpies and the rest of this chocolate pecan pie so that your dad can take it home and you two can have the rest of this later on tonight?"

Ginny needed no further convincing. Danni had had her with the phrase: "What do you say to—"

Ginny's response was a resounding "Sure!"

Stone had a feeling that if this woman with the hundred-watt smile and killer legs had asked his daughter to come slay dragons with her, she would have gotten the same response.

He wasn't doing remodeling for a celebrity chef,

Stone thought, he was remodeling the living quarters of a sorceress.

A damn *sexy* sorceress.

Which meant, among other things, that he was going to have to watch his step.

Chapter Eight

"**I** like her, Daddy. Do you like her?" Ginny asked some time later as they were driving home from Danni's house.

They had lingered awhile longer, after their hostess had packed up the extra potpies, along with what was left of the chocolate pecan pie, to take home with them. They had stayed predominantly to help with clean-up after the impromptu meal.

Stone had to admit that he was pretty stunned when it was Ginny, not Danni, who had come up with the suggestion to clean up.

And he was even *more* stunned when his daughter dove into said cleanup eagerly, especially since this was the child who couldn't be coaxed into cleaning her room and required excessive bribery to pick up her toys off the family room floor.

Eagerly, but slowly, he noted her pace. When he commented on her abbreviated speed, she'd looked at him with her doelike eyes and said, "If I'm too fast, then I'm not doing it well."

She had parroted back a sentiment that he had once expressed to her.

His daughter was clearly up to something.

The suspicion rose again now, with the question she'd just put to him. The one he hadn't answered yet.

"Well, do you, Daddy?" Ginny pressed.

Most of the time, when his pint-size woman-in-training asked a question, it was just sufficient for him to grunt or make some sort of noise that passed for a reply and she, in typical female fashion, just continued with her monologue. Rarely, if ever, did Ginny require an actual verbal response.

This was different.

After having asked her question, she obviously wanted some kind of input from him. Most likely, if he was any kind of judge of voice tones, Ginny was looking for him to agree with her and say that he liked the woman.

So, to bring an end to this, Stone told him daughter, "Yes, she's nice."

He hadn't expected Ginny to seize the word and all but run with it.

"Very, very nice," she declared with feeling. "I think Danni's the nicest lady I ever met."

This seemed to be getting a little out of hand, Stone thought. "Nicer than Aunt Virginia?" he asked Ginny, curious now to hear how his daughter would respond.

Ginny started to say "Yes," then stopped. He could almost hear her thinking.

"Not nicer," she finally said. "But she's just as nice as Aunt Virginia."

Well, at least Ginny's loyalty was still intact, he thought, somewhat amused. He quickly reviewed the day's events as he knew them. Granted he'd been working a good deal of the time that she had spent with Danni. Maybe something had happened when he wasn't around that had created this feeling about the woman. If so, he wanted to know just what had happened.

"Why are you so impressed with her?" Stone asked his daughter.

"'Cause," Ginny responded. No other words followed in the single word's wake. That alone was highly unusual.

The light up ahead at the major intersection was red. Stone eased to a stop behind a blue van with a dented bumper and took the opportunity to glance into the rear-view mirror.

Securely strapped into her car seat, Ginny was waving her feet back and forth like a metronome set on triple time, a sure sign that she was agitated or exceedingly excited about something.

He was right. Something was definitely up with his daughter, but he hadn't a clue what it was. Whatever it was, it had something to do with Danni Everett.

Was Ginny acting like this because, in a vague sort of way, Danni bore a slight resemblance to her mother, to Eva? Did some part of Ginny remember her mother and was responding to this new woman on that level?

No, Stone decided in the next moment, he was reading far too much into this. She'd been just a baby when Eva died.

The Smartcar behind him beeped. The high-pitched sound registered just as he saw that the light had turned green and the dented van that had been in front of him was now halfway down the next street. He took his foot off the brake and pressed down on the accelerator again.

There was probably a far simpler explanation for what was going on. Ginny was probably just responding to Danni because the woman had displayed an interest in her and had had Ginny "help" her make both the main dish and the dessert.

That was something a mother might do—and something he knew that Virginia had never done with Ginny. Virginia, God bless her, was good at a lot of things, but anything that involved preparing a meal was completely out of his sister's realm of expertise. Virginia's talent for cooking began and ended with dialing the phone for takeout.

So helping in the kitchen was an entirely new experience for Ginny, one that, from the bits and pieces of dialogue he had picked up at the table, made his daughter feel quite proud of herself. There was no underestimating the value of something like that, he thought.

Consequently, Ginny was associating that feeling of well-being and pride with Danni, which was why she was so high on the woman.

So, rather than try to explore any different reasons behind Ginny's sudden and strong attachment to Danni

Everett, he opted to go along with his daughter's enthusiastic pronouncement—and hope that was the end of it.

"She *is* pretty nice, isn't she?"

He didn't think he'd ever seen Ginny beam as hard as she did this time around.

"Yes!" she agreed with even more zest. He was definitely *not* prepared for what came out of her mouth next. "Can we go back there again tomorrow? To Danni's house?"

"Well, I have to," he told her, "because I'm working on her house. But you're going to be staying home with Aunt Virginia."

He trusted that his sister's "sudden emergency" meeting with her potential new client was a one-time occurrence and that she would once again be available to stay with Ginny while he worked. All they had to get through was the summer. Once they were past that, Ginny would be in first grade and things would get a little easier.

At least he could hope.

"But what if Aunt Virginia's busy again?" Ginny asked.

Was that a hopeful note he heard in Ginny's voice? "She won't be."

"But what if she *is?*" Ginny pressed, obviously determined to get an answer out of him.

Stone sighed. Ginny wasn't about to let this go. "Then you can come with me again," he told her. Darting a quick glance into the rearview mirror again before looking back at the road, he saw Ginny elaborately crossing her fingers as she squeezed her eyes shut.

His daughter was making a wish.

This woman had *really* cast a spell over the little girl. He had never seen her behaving like this. "But if that happens, it'll be just the two of us at the house."

Another quick glance showed him that Ginny's face had fallen. "Why?"

"Because Danni will be at work. She tapes that cooking program on some cable channel," he reminded Ginny. "I don't remember the name of the show."

"Danni's Desserts to Die For," Ginny rattled off. "Then can we go there?" Ginny asked. "To watch her make things?"

Her mind was like a steel trap. Even so, he was surprised she remembered the name of the program when he didn't. This woman *had* snared his daughter's heart. Maybe he should have paid a little closer attention to her, he told himself.

In the next moment, he reminded himself that he was currently "seeing" someone, which meant he should *be* paying closer attention to another woman, not Danni.

"Number one," he told Ginny, "Danni would have to invite us to come on the set, we can't just show up. And number two, if we *did* go there, then I wouldn't be working on her house, which is what she's paying me to do, remember?"

"Oh." It was a very small, sad little sound. His daughter knew how to play him, Stone couldn't help thinking. "Then I guess you'd better work on her house, huh?"

Stone struggled to suppress a laugh. "Yes, I guess I'd better," he agreed.

"But you will see her again, right, Daddy? If you

work on her house, she'll want to see what you're doing, right?"

Stone thought that was rather an odd question to be coming from a four-year-old, even if that four-year-old *was* going on forty. For now, he set her mind at ease. "I have to," he told Ginny.

She didn't leave it at that—not that he thought she would. His assurance just opened the door for yet another question. "Will you be seeing her a lot?"

Glancing to his right, he changed lanes, preparing to turn down the next corner. "Well, she's the one who has to make the final decisions about each of the rooms I'm remodeling for her, so yes, I'll probably be touching base with Danni pretty often." He waited until he turned at the end of the next block before asking, "What's this all about, Ginny? Why are you so interested in whether or not I'll be seeing Danni?"

Ginny raised and lowered her shoulders in an exaggerated shrug. A movement Stone caught the tail end of as he looked up into the rearview mirror for a split second.

"I dunno," she told him, suddenly looking every bit the four-year-old. "I think Danni's fun," she finally said.

So she'd already said. But this time it began making sense and falling into place for him. This woman had paid real attention to his daughter and she'd played with her. As opposed to Elizabeth, who was polite to Ginny, but for the most part, she didn't really seem to be able to relate to his daughter at all.

"And you don't think that Elizabeth's fun, do you?"

he asked, even though he was pretty sure he knew the answer to that.

"Elizabeth's not fun," Ginny answered flatly. The simple statement confirmed his suspicions.

"Well, we'll see if we can change that," Stone promised. He was going to talk to Elizabeth about their including Ginny the next time the two of them went out together.

When had life gotten to be so complicated and tricky? It used to be something he'd just glide through without any effort, and now, he was constantly facing choices, with forks in the road that necessitated decisions every step he took. He missed the simple times.

He missed Eva.

Elizabeth Wells was the first woman he'd gone out with since Eva had died. One of his friends, Jeremy Banks—they started out in the general contractor business together—had introduced him to Elizabeth. She was the cousin of Jeremy's wife and, at the time he'd introduced them, Elizabeth had just stopped seeing some politician. Jeremy thought the two of them might hit it off. He and his wife had invited them both to their house for dinner.

Elizabeth, who was a press secretary for the mayor's office, was certainly attractive enough and interesting enough to warrant his asking her out. Stone knew that he felt like half a person ever since Eva had left his life and, while the work he did as well as raising Ginny certainly kept him busy, there was this empty spot inside of him that nothing seemed to fill.

So he had agreed to give dating a try.

Dating, he thought with a shake of his head. Who would have ever thought that after having what he'd considered a perfect fairytale life with a woman he adored and a baby they were both crazy about, that he would suddenly find himself back trying to navigate the dating pool?

"Okay, Daddy," Ginny said gamely, agreeing to something he'd said earlier. Stone spent thirty seconds wracking his brain, trying to remember just what it was he'd said. "I'll try to like Elizabeth."

Well, that sounded hopeful, he thought, taking her words at face value. "That's my girl."

He noticed that this time, she didn't smile the way she usually did when he called her that.

He *definitely* needed to have a talk with Elizabeth about opening up more to his daughter.

Virginia was home by the time he and Ginny arrived. Parking the car, he undid his daughter's car-seat straps and placed her on the driveway, then went to take out the leftovers his newest client had all but forced on him.

Ginny was already at the door, standing on tiptoes and ringing the doorbell. "It's us, Aunt Virginia," she declared at the top of her lungs.

The door swung open less than half a minute later. "How did it go?" she asked her brother as he crossed the threshold after Ginny. "And what is that wonderful aroma?" she asked.

"Not badly and leftovers," Stone said, heading straight for the kitchen.

It took Virginia a moment to unscramble his answers

and assign them to the right questions. By then, Stone had put the leftovers down on the table. "How did it go for you?" he asked.

"For me?" Virginia asked, momentarily bewildered at his question.

"Yes, you told me that you had an interview. With a new client. That's why you said you couldn't watch Ginny, remember?" For the first time it occurred to him that perhaps Virginia *hadn't* had an interview to see to. But if she didn't, why had she said that she had? Things just weren't adding up.

"Of course I remember," she said almost indignantly. "And it went just the way I expected it to," she told him, mentally crossing her fingers and hoping, if this all went the way it should, that her brother would find it in his heart to forgive her for bending the truth this way.

What "bending?" You're lying and you know it. But it was for a good cause, she told herself.

"You landed the client?" he asked her, taking down three dessert plates out of the cupboard.

"Like he was a salmon and I got between him and upstream," Virginia said with a pleased laugh. She was rather proud of herself for the image she'd just verbally drawn.

"So you can watch Ginny for me tonight?" he asked Virginia.

"Sure." Following her brother's lead, she took out forks and placed them next to the plates. "Are you going out?" she asked hopefully.

"Going out," he confirmed.

There was no need for either Virginia or Ginny to

know that he was going to call Elizabeth first and see if perhaps he could either coax her to come over so that they, meaning she, could spend more time with Ginny. Or to at least broach the idea to her and perhaps make arrangements to bring Ginny along with them this weekend. Maybe they could take in a movie or go to an amusement park.

"That was fast work," Virginia couldn't help commenting.

Stone looked at her, confused. "I worked at my usual pace," he told her.

Trust Stone to be too literal. "Wait," Virginia said, putting her hand up. Something didn't feel right. "You're going out with—"

"Elizabeth," he answered, wondering why she had to ask. "Who else?"

"Who else indeed," Virginia said under her breath as she watched her brother go up the stairs to change into fresh clothing.

So far, this wasn't exactly going according to plan, she couldn't help thinking.

But then, as the cliché went, tomorrow was another day.

And she prayed it would go better tomorrow.

"You're joking, aren't you?" Elizabeth asked with a touch of impatience a few minutes later as they spoke on the phone.

He was getting a bad feeling about this. No part of his conversation so far had suggested that this was going to be the comedy portion of their verbal exchange. "No, I'm being serious."

"You want to include your four-year-old on our next date," Elizabeth repeated incredulously. And then, after a rather audible sigh, she seemed to regroup. "Stone, honey, if you feel you're not seeing enough of your daughter, I understand. Really," she emphasized, making him doubt that she understood anything at all. "Spend some time with her. Take her to one of those God-awful animated movies you just mentioned. We can go out some other night," Elizabeth told him.

He couldn't help feeling that the leash about his neck was being temporarily loosened. All he could focus on, though, was that there *was* a leash.

When had *that* happened?

One of his most cherished memories was the last time he, Eva and Ginny had gone out as a family. Ginny was two and a half at the time. They had gone to a matinee at the neighborhood movie theater to see a rerelease of a famous cartoon classic. He could have sworn that Eva enjoyed it just as much as Ginny had.

It was Ginny's first experience going to the movies and her eyes had been as big as saucers for the entire movie. She'd also insisted on standing up rather than sitting down, afraid that if she was sitting, she'd somehow miss something that was on the screen. She'd been incredibly excited about what they were watching.

They'd each sat on one side of Ginny, he and Eva, and he remembered thinking that this was the way life was supposed to be, enjoying these tiny, sparkling pockets of time that were absolutely perfect.

Less than two weeks later, Eva was gone. Just like that. And he'd felt as if someone had gutted him using a jagged spoon.

He'd started seeing Elizabeth in hopes of getting rid of that feeling. But maybe, he now thought, this wasn't the way to go.

"I take it you don't like animated movies," he said to Elizabeth, exhibiting a great deal of restraint as far as he was concerned. The fact that she didn't somehow insulted the memory of Eva for him.

Stone could almost envision Elizabeth's expression, half amazement that he should even ask such a question and half pity that he had entertained the thought that she might *like* watching cartoon characters cavorting across a movie screen.

"Should I?" she asked with a touch of disdain. "They're made for children."

Stone thought of letting that pass uncontested, but then he heard himself saying, "To appeal to the child in all of us."

Elizabeth laughed in response. "Now you sound like a production marketing executive. I like movies that are intended for adults, Stone. The 'child' in me grew up a long time ago. But, like I said, if you feel you need to connect with your daughter, then by all means, do it so that you can stop feeling so guilty. We'll just go out some other time."

It was on the tip of his tongue to inform her that this had nothing to do with guilt and that part of him actually resented the off-handed assessment. He'd spent the better part of the day, in one form or another, with

Ginny, so it wasn't a matter of needing to connect. *He* wasn't the one who needed to connect with his daughter.

Better luck next time, Stone thought philosophically.

"I'll be over by eight," he told her.

"I take it that eight *is* past her bedtime?"

"Yes." He told himself he shouldn't be feeling this sudden resentment toward the woman. She'd never had children of her own and this was a learning process for her.

But Danni didn't have any kids, either, a voice in his head said. *And she related to Ginny just fine.*

He shut the voice out.

"Wonderful," Elizabeth was saying with a note of triumph—as if she'd just thrown the dice and come up a winner. "I'll be here, waiting."

For some reason, Stone felt as if he'd just been put on notice.

Chapter Nine

"I have no kitchen," Danni cried as she walked into what had been, up until just now, the center of her home. She'd arrived from the studio early and had walked through the house, looking for Stone and curious as to his progress. The noise of groaning plasterboard under attack had led her to the back of the house.

Once on the scene, it took Danni a couple of moments to recover.

They were three weeks into renovating the forty-plus-year-old house and so far, she had dealt with looking at stripped walls and exposed, ugly pipes in all three of her bathrooms and had put up with a family room that looked as if a bomb had gone off in the middle of it.

But seeing her kitchen devoid of everything that made it a kitchen in the first place—the stove, the refrigerator, *both* sinks, everything, included the overhead light panels and the walls—well, it made her feel as if her very identity had been diced, sautéed and then thrown down the garbage disposal to be ripped into tiny bits.

Danni had deliberately come home early—having moved up her program's taping schedule for the day—so that she could touch base with her general contractor and discuss mundane things like where to shop for rugs and stone flooring. These areas, she was clueless about. Her life had always been filled with far too many details for her to take note of the best places that catered to home rejuvenation.

She hadn't expected to be jarred by the sight of a war-zone kitchen.

Surprised—she hadn't said anything about arriving home while he was still here, working—Stone dropped the crowbar he'd been using to pry away the discolored, cracked tile from the counter beside the gaping hole that had once been the double sink.

Recovering, Stone laughed at her exclamation. "For my sister, that would be a reason to rejoice and an excuse to go nuts, ordering takeout," he told her. For the first time, he took in Danni's shell-shocked expression. "But I guess not for you," he speculated.

What she was looking at took her breath away—and not in a good way. Even the floor—he'd removed the dark brown vinyl with its embossed, cracked octagon design—felt uneven beneath her feet. Splotches of dried glue yet to be pried off added to the unevenness.

Doing anything in this shell of a room before Stone got around to remodeling it would be immensely challenging, Danni thought, already trying to deal with the challenge. She couldn't conceive of not having some sort of a kitchen to work in.

"I guess I could put up a card table and have a hot plate on it." And then a thought hit her and she looked around at what was left of the walls—or where the walls had been this morning when she'd left for the studio. "I do still have sockets so I can plug in a hot plate and a coffeemaker, right?"

"One," he told her, pointing to the opposite wall. He hadn't gotten around to removing it yet so that he could check the wiring, making certain that it was sound.

Danni smiled as she nodded. "One's all I need to plug in the coffee in the morning and a hot plate to cook on at night."

The woman had to be one of the most exceedingly flexible people he'd ever met. He liked the way she was able to adjust to any circumstances. He'd certainly dealt with enough home owners to be impressed with Danni's low-key attitude. She hadn't gone off the deep end when she saw that her creative center had been demolished. That spoke well of her resilience.

"Like your morning coffee, eh?" he asked, amused. That gave them something in common. He couldn't fully function without his.

"My eyes don't officially open until the second cup," Danni willingly admitted.

Stone laughed, nodding his head. "Me, too," he told her. "I'm dead asleep until I've consumed my second cup of what I'm told passes as a giant cup of double espresso. My sister threatens to run a coffee IV through my arm so I sound human first thing in the morning instead of like—her word," he quoted, "Bigfoot."

As Danni listened to him, she looked around again, thinking she might have acclimated to what she saw. But the view was as abysmal the second time around as it had been the first. Maybe even a touch more, since there were gaping holes, which she now noticed.

She didn't want him to think she was trying to rush him in any way, but she needed something to hold on to and schedule around.

"Just how long does it have to stay like this?" she asked, doing her best to sound as if she were just curious and fighting off a full-blown panic attack. She didn't want him to think she was a flake, but she *did* need her kitchen.

Squatting down, he tucked the crowbar away into the larger of the two tool bags he'd brought into the house today.

That done, he rose again, looking into her eyes and thinking how incredibly blue they were before saying, "That depends."

Had she made a mistake in going with this man? She'd trusted Maizie's recommendation, but maybe Maizie hadn't actually been able to have him checked out, maybe *she* was going by someone else's recommendation. Someone who had something to gain from this man getting work. Now that he'd denuded her kitchen, was he going to hold it for ransom, stretch out the project as long as possible? She wasn't paying him per diem, but maybe he would begin hinting at "incentives" for finishing faster. Incentives in this case always translated into money.

"On?" she asked, holding her breath and waiting for him to lower the boom.

"On how long it takes you to pick up the kind of stone you want for your floors, whether you want tile or granite for your kitchen counter—both, by the way, come in an array of styles, colors and shapes so there's a lot to choose from. And then there are the appliances—you get to pick out the brands, the types, the colors, well, you get the picture. The upshot is it can take anywhere from three weeks to six—not to mention that there's also the delivery to factor in."

"The delivery to factor in?" she repeated, feeling utterly lost.

Stone nodded, then explained it as simply as he could. She looked a little stunned and he felt rather sorry for her—though for the life of him, he didn't know why. He'd been in this business for a number of years now, working pretty steadily, thank God, and he'd never really identified with the home owner before. He had no idea why he did this time, but something about the woman got to him and he couldn't even begin to guess why or how this had come about.

He supposed that Ginny was to blame if anyone was. If she hadn't asked him that first day if he liked Danni, hadn't pressed him for an answer while proclaiming that *she* liked the woman, maybe this thought about being attracted to her wouldn't be rattling around in his head.

"Some things are shipped from back East," he told her. "Others might have to come from somewhere in

Europe, depending on what you finally pick out." Stone saw the rather dazed expression on her face intensifying, as if she didn't know where to begin. There was no denying that she looked rather appealing like that, like a girl—not a woman—who had suddenly realized that she'd lost her way and was in way over her head.

"Overwhelmed?" he asked, managing to successfully hide his amusement.

You have no idea, Danni thought in response.

But there was no way she was going to admit that. At least, not to the extent that she felt it. Danni had made it a point never to let anyone know if she felt outnumbered, outflanked or unequal to a task.

For the last three years, since her father had died, although she made friends as easily as some people breathed, at bottom she felt alone, without anyone to turn to or depend on but herself.

Oh, there'd been a brief period when she'd thought she was in love, around the time of her father's passing, but she'd discovered that Bill had seen a great deal of potential in her and had gone out of his way to hitch his wagon to her star.

His intention, she'd discovered, was to get a free ride. Exchanging compliments for cash.

When she'd found out that his bottom line involved money, not love, she'd quickly sent him packing. So now she was her own person, no matter how lonely that turned out to be at times.

"Stone," she confessed, "I don't have the first clue where to go to find any of this stuff or how to go about finding out."

He *knew* she was going to say that, he could feel it in his bones. Lucky for her, he had the solution to her dilemma.

"No problem. I can give you addresses to different stores—there're a whole cluster of stores that deal with floor, wall and counter coverings on Katella Ave, in Anaheim. They've got tile, stone, carpets, tubs, showers, more fixtures than you'd think possible—"

She held her hand up, already overwhelmed by what he was telling her and the images his words were creating in her head.

"That's what I'm afraid of. I'm going to be like Alice in Wonderland, trying to find her way home while some saleswoman besotted with the latest color in rugs yells, 'Off with her head!' in the background."

"You don't *like* shopping?" he asked incredulously. He thought all women were born loving to shop. Even Ginny enjoyed going to the mall at her tender age.

"I like 'browsing,'" Danni emphasized. "This isn't browsing, this is 'make up your mind quick or your kitchen stays naked' shopping. I don't like shopping under pressure," she admitted. "And there's the other problem, I don't have all that much time to devote to it, which means I'm probably going to wind up settling." And that didn't even take into account the problem of possibly being taken advantage of.

Stone thought for a moment, weighing the pros and cons of what he was about to suggest. The pro would be that he'd be helping a client, not to mention that there was the added bonus of spending time with an attractive woman who got more attractive each time he saw her.

He had a feeling she wouldn't even mind if he brought Ginny along. Each evening when he came home, he was subjected to his daughter's youthful version of the Spanish Inquisition, asking him if he'd seen Danni that day. When he said no, she was disappointed. If he said yes, the questions became more involved. Three weeks into this renovation project and Ginny still hadn't lost her any of her enthusiasm for the woman. Not to mention that he'd be offering his expertise and guidance to someone who seemed to be badly in need of it. This was an area where he was pretty much of an expert. That was rather heady stuff on its own.

The con was...well, he'd be giving up his Saturday, not much of a con in the scheme of things, he supposed. Except that he had a feeling Elizabeth wouldn't be happy about his working on a Saturday. It *did* cut into their time together and she really wouldn't appreciate the fact that the person he was helping was neither a senior citizen nor someone whose face could make a clock stop— except, perhaps to stare in abject admiration.

But then, things between Elizabeth and him had been rather tense these last few weeks, ever since he'd suggested bringing Ginny along on one of their dates. Each time he tried to broach the idea to her, Elizabeth would blatantly change the subject.

While they still continued to see one another, he was beginning to feel that their relationship was facing an expiration date and that date was approaching a wee bit faster than Elizabeth was happy about.

Maybe things would work themselves out and if they

didn't, well, maybe they weren't meant to. But he felt he shouldn't waste time reflecting over it.

He made up his mind and proceeded full speed ahead. "Would you like some help with selecting some of the things you need for the renovations?"

At this point, she was opened to *any* suggestions. "You mean like a crib sheet or a book to help navigate me through the wonderful world of renovations?"

Maybe she didn't want him butting in, he thought. Some people thought of this as a very private process, wanting the house to reflect their taste and no one else's.

"Well, I don't have a crib sheet or a book like that," he told her, "but I'm pretty good at making recommendations if I see the material firsthand."

She wasn't sure where he was going with this. For the most part, after their initial meeting, he'd been working on his own here, which was why she'd decided to touch base with him. But so far, he'd only been tearing things down, not building them up.

"Are you offering to buy the materials for me?" Danni asked.

Maybe he needed to spell this out for her. "I'm offering to take you to the stores and give you the benefit of my experience."

A rush of pure relief washed over her. Suppressing a squeal of joy, Danni threw her arms around his neck and cried, "Offer accepted!" with such enthusiasm, Stone started to laugh.

The sound, since she'd thrown her arms around him to express her relief and thanks via an impromptu, warm hug, seemed to rumble right through her. Rumble through her in such a way that it felt almost seductive and exceedingly sensual.

It was then that she realized just how close her face was to his.

How close her mouth was to his.

And then, as an unknown, unforeseeable force suddenly seemed to grip her, her mouth wasn't close to his anymore. It was now occupying the same exact space, the same exact coordinates as his.

One second, there was laughter, the next, that laughter had given way to silence.

And passion.

Unexpected passion.

An entire moment packed so solidly with passion that there wasn't room for anything else.

Certainly not any common sense.

But the next moment, common sense returned, moving back in and making a valiant attempt to regain control of the situation, as well as of the two participants in that situation.

As with everything else that transpired in her life, Danni took full blame for what happened. It never occurred to her to do otherwise, to blame someone else for causing this lapse in control. She was at fault.

"I'm sorry," she all but whispered, not knowing exactly where to look, yet unable to tear her eyes away from his. "I didn't mean to do that."

"Understood," he replied, trying to regain his own composure.

In his case, it involved discovering that his insides were utterly scrambled. He might have not been the person to initiate the kiss between them but he had certainly been a willing participant the second he realized what was happening.

Moreover, he hadn't been plagued by pesky rules of decorum, or even remotely entertained the thought that this shouldn't be happening, or that he was being disloyal to Elizabeth, or even—laughingly—that his client was forcing herself on him because she'd misinterpreted his signals.

For the life of him, Stone had no idea what sort of signals he gave off. But he did know one thing for certain—Danni Everett had a sweet, sweet mouth and she was one hell of a kisser.

So much so that he was more than willing to go through the whole process again.

And again.

Danni dragged in a shaky breath, not bothering to pretend that she was unaffected by what had just taken place here. "I guess you won't be accompanying me to any of the stores this Saturday."

He looked at her for a long moment. "Was it that bad?" he finally asked, then, in case she wasn't following his thought process, he elaborated, "The kiss, was it that bad?"

Her mouth dropped open as she stared at him. How had he come to that conclusion?

"No. No," she sputtered loudly. "It was wonderful." The word echoed back to her and she could feel her cheeks beginning to burn. "I mean—I just thought that you wouldn't want to go with me after I just…well, because I just…"

The woman seemed to be drowning right before his eyes. Taking pity on Danni, Stone decided to come to her rescue. "Expressed your relief and gratitude with a friendly kiss?" he suggested.

Again she could only stare at him. "You consider that a *friendly* kiss?" she asked incredulously. If that was just friendly, then what did this man consider to be a torrid kiss?

"Well, it certainly wasn't a hostile one," he told her with a wide, amused grin.

When he grinned like that, his face transformed, changing from that of a man who looked as if he were carrying the weight of the world on his shoulders and who appeared to be the very embodiment of solemnity, to one who looked more like a free-spirited boy than a man. A very handsome, sexy, appealing, free-spirited boy. "We can pretend it never happened if that makes you feel more comfortable," he said.

"It would," she admitted, wishing that it could actually be that easy. But then, if it had never happened, she wouldn't have felt—and still be feeling—that small, amazing thrill vibrating all through her.

"All right, it never happened," Stone told her with a nod of his head. He put his hand out to her, as if to seal the deal.

Danni put her hand in his and they shook on it. But deep down, that didn't change a thing.

The kiss *had* happened and she would remember it happening for a long, long while, there was no getting around that. Because that kiss, begun in innocence and sheer exuberance, had shaken the foundations of a world that she believed to be secure. Humdrum, but definitely secure.

Just went to show her that she couldn't count on anything being true these days. Not even, she thought with a deep pang, herself. And that had been her last bastion of hope, being able to count on herself, being able to know what to expect from herself.

Being able to rise to the occasion, no matter what it was.

Now she no longer knew.

"So," Stone said to her, "if you're sure you'll be available, I can swing by around ten Saturday morning, pick you up and we can hit a few of those stores, get started on the selection process."

Danni nodded numbly, belatedly realizing that she was still holding his hand. Feeling awkward, she instantly released it and dropped her hand to her side.

"Oh, would you mind if I brought Ginny along?" he asked her.

Mind? She *welcomed* it. "No sitter?" she guessed.

"Something like that." Well, now he was stuck with the story, he thought, even though he knew that Virginia would be around. "I could call around to see if I could find someone at the last minute—"

"To come with us?" she asked, not really following him.

"No, to watch Ginny." He didn't like lying and he knew he wasn't very good at it *because* he disliked it and being lied to.

"No need for that," Danni told him. "I'd love to have

Ginny along." *She'll make the perfect chaperone*, Danni thought in relief. "I've missed her enthusiasm."

"She certainly has that," Stone agreed.

And she'll have even more of that when I tell her she'd be coming along with us Saturday.

The only element interfering with this scenario was telling Elizabeth that he wouldn't be able to see her Saturday afternoon because he was going to be busy, working.

Well, technically, he was, Stone silently insisted.

He knew that wasn't going to sit well with the woman and he began to brace himself for the torrent of displeasure coming his way.

Even so, he caught himself really looking forward to Saturday.

Chapter Ten

"You're breaking *another* date with me?"

Elizabeth Wells's voice went down an octave as she came to the end of her sentence.

Rather than put off the ordeal, Stone had decided to get it over with as soon as he came home. He called Elizabeth on her cell a few minutes after he'd walked in and greeted his daughter and sister.

He could gauge Elizabeth's displeasure by whether her voice rose or fell from its normal range. If it went up an octave or so, she was annoyed, but could be persuaded to come around and make the best of it. If her voice went down, the way it did now, then she was really angry, immovable and her forgiveness wouldn't be forthcoming any time soon.

She made it sound as if he canceled dates on a regular basis. He could only recall twice, and both had been for legitimate reasons.

"It doesn't happen that often," he pointed out.

"Often enough," Elizabeth informed him coolly. "I don't like coming in third, Stone. I can handle second once in a while, but not third."

He could almost hear the icicles forming in her voice. "Third?" he questioned. He had no idea what she was talking about.

"Yes, *third,*" Elizabeth emphasized. "After your work and your daughter. My job is just as demanding as yours, Stone. Probably more," she told him haughtily. "I haven't canceled on us even once."

For a moment, he lost his temper. What had started out as an exceedingly pleasant relationship with a great deal of promise had progressively become less so. The list of red flags he needed to ignore grew rather long.

He knew for a fact that Elizabeth looked down at anyone who worked with their hands, feeling intellectually superior to them. He suspected that the only reason she was still willing to see him was because he had a degree in engineering and had worked in aerospace until the industry had all but disappeared from Southern California.

His ties to the area had him reinventing himself and using his fall-back skill from when he was working his way through college: carpentry. That eventually led to his getting a general contracting license and graduating from making cabinets to building and remodeling almost anything.

Since Elizabeth worked for the mayor's office and had a degree in political science, she saw herself a cut above the people he associated with. Her attitude was getting to be a bit much to overlook.

"Did your boss ever ask you to?" he asked Elizabeth pointedly.

"What?" She snapped out the word impatiently. Elizabeth didn't like being on the receiving end of questions that challenged her statements.

"Did your boss ever ask you to cancel your plans for the evening and work on something he needed done ASAP?" Stone asked, deliberately enunciating each word so that there was no mistaking his meaning.

"That's not the point," Elizabeth informed him frostily.

"I think it is." This had all the earmarks of escalating into a full-fledged argument and he didn't want that. Taking a breath, Stone focused his efforts on calming down. After a half a beat, he tried again. "I'll make it up to you, Elizabeth."

"Don't bother," she snapped just before she slammed down the phone.

Stone stared at the phone receiver in his hand for a long moment, debating whether or not to call Elizabeth back and find some way to smooth the woman's ruffled feathers.

But then he wondered if he really *wanted* to make amends.

In the beginning, in addition to being quite attractive in a polished sort of way, Elizabeth had been bright and funny and he'd enjoyed listening to her biting wit. But, if he were being honest with himself, he never felt a hundred percent comfortable in Elizabeth's company.

A part of him sensed the woman was constantly scrutinizing him, evaluating him. It was a little like being a student in a prep school, knowing he didn't dare allow himself to slouch.

He'd never put on any airs to try to impress anyone. If anything, he *was* guilty of the sins of omission, of not saying what he knew might lead to a less than amicable conversation. He let her talk and at times let her believe that he agreed with her on some trivial matters close to her heart when he really *didn't* agree at all.

And, most important of all, even slightly more important than never feeling that he could really just be entirely himself, was the fact that Elizabeth didn't fill that emptiness within him.

That had been the whole original point for his giving in to Jeremy and going out with the woman to begin with, to try to fill that hole that Eva's passing had opened up in his gut.

"If you'd like to place a call…" the metallic, female voice was saying into his ear, accompanied by the annoying throbbing noise of a phone left too long off the hook.

Stone sighed. "No, I wouldn't," he muttered under his breath just before he returned the landline receiver back to its cradle.

As if guarding a major secret, Ginny stepped into the family room. She grinned from ear to ear and hugged herself gleefully.

Virginia looked up from her book.

"What's up, munchkin?" she asked, curious as to why

her niece seemed to be embracing herself while that wide grin of hers all but split her face in two. "Daddy and Elizabeth just had a fight," she announced happily.

The book about someone else's romance instantly ceased to be of interest to her, not when real life was unfolding something far more interesting before her. Virginia tossed the paperback on the coffee table.

"How do you know?" she asked.

"I heard him on the phone," Ginny told her, then, bobbing her head, she added, "I heard her, too."

"He had it on speaker phone?" Virginia asked, wondering why Stone would do that. Her brother was very big on privacy.

But how else could Ginny have overheard what Elizabeth was saying?

Ginny shook her head. "She was using a big voice. I could hear it coming out of Daddy's other ear."

Virginia paused, taking in a breath. Doing her best not to laugh. She supposed that was probably the most colorful, succinct explanation of why Ginny could hear what that snob was saying to her brother.

Virginia knew that she shouldn't be encouraging Ginny to eavesdrop, that she should tell her it's wrong. But they could have that heart-to-heart talk some other time. Right now, her curiosity was getting the better of her and she needed answers.

"So you know what they were arguing about?"

Ginny bobbed her head up and down like a dashboard bobble-head on a road trip. "Daddy told Elizabeth he couldn't see her on Saturday because he had to do something for his work. He said he'd make it up to her, but she yelled, 'Don't bother.'" Ginny cocked her head, her small eyebrows knitting together in confusion. "What's 'making it up to her' mean?" she asked.

"Doing something nice later on because you can't do something you promised right now" was the best way Virginia knew how to explain the phrase to her niece.

It seemed to do the trick because the little girl's eyes began to sparkle as her grin bloomed again. "You know what I think, Aunt Virginia? I think Elizabeth's going to go away." Ginny was practically beside herself with excitement.

Virginia nodded her head. Certainly sounded like that to her. "Looks promising," she agreed.

"What looks promising?" Stone asked as he entered the family room. After his less than cheerful phone conversation with Elizabeth, he needed a dose of sunshine and that meant being with his daughter.

"The weather on Saturday," Virginia said quickly before Ginny had a chance to blurt out the truth. Ginny was sharp enough, even at four, to play along.

"The weather here's always promising," he said, wondering why his sister would even think to say that. "You have plans?" he asked.

"Nothing special," Virginia answered with a vague shrug. She remembered that she was supposed to be watching Ginny because Stone had told her he was seeing Elizabeth on Saturday so she used that scenario to build on. "Just taking Ginny to the park for a while maybe. I haven't really decided yet."

"Well, you don't have to make any decisions," he told her. "You're getting the day off." He saw the quizzical look on Virginia's face and explained, "Ginny and I are going to pick out tile." Realizing that this was coming as a surprise to Ginny, Stone looked at his daughter. "I know it's boring, kiddo, but—"

He got no further as Ginny clapped her hands together as if she'd just been told she was going to live in Sleeping Beauty's castle.

"I love tile, Daddy!" she declared with gusto, fairly jumping up and down.

Stone could only stare at her. He knew she liked Danni, but he hadn't even told her that part yet. Had she just assumed they were shopping with Danni? Otherwise, this made no sense. "Since when?"

"Since I was a little girl, Daddy. A long time ago," she answered with a toss of her head.

Stone pressed his lips together, doing his damnedest not to laugh. "My mistake. I forgot," he solemnly "apologized." "By the way, Danni's coming with us. It's her tile we're going to be picking out."

Virginia rose from the sofa, more pleased than she could possibly put into words. "Looks like things are going well for you and Danni."

"The renovations are coming along, yeah," Stone agreed, deliberately avoiding assigning any other meaning to his sister's words. There was no *and* between Danni and him. They weren't a couple, a unit. They weren't *anything*.

You sure about that? She'd been on your mind a lot for someone who wasn't "anything," a small, annoying voice in his head insisted on pointing out.

Because she knew that no one could talk Stone into

anything or force him to do anything, Virginia let his answer ride for the time being. There was time enough to work on it—and him—later. Right now, all that mattered was that he was seeing Danni on Saturday and he *wasn't* seeing Elizabeth on that day.

"I'd better go see about dinner," she told him, then paused in the doorway, waiting for instructions. "Chinese or Italian?" she posed.

"Italian," he responded without thinking.

"Pizza it is," Virginia said as she went to place the order to the near-by restaurant that was on their speed dial.

Stone could have sworn he heard his sister singing, "Ding-dong, the witch is dead," under her breath and wondered what had come over her.

He also knew that there would be no finding out, no questions properly answered. Virginia could be very elusive when she wanted to be.

The older he got, he decided, the more mysterious women—all women—became. He resigned himself to the fact that trying to understand them was a losing battle and always would be.

"But, Barry," Danni lamented, "it's Saturday."

"I know it's Saturday, babe. I've got this handy-dandy thing on my desk called a calendar so I can tell people like you I know what day of the week it is." And then her producer's voice grew serious. "You think I'm happy about this? Saturday's the only day of the week I get to sleep in. Sally drags my butt to early mass every single Sunday. Like seeing me there, nodding off in the pew is going to change any plan He's got in store for me," he commented. "But the powers that be need this one segment of the show retaped," he stressed. "You gotta come in."

Barry reverted to his standard coaxing tone, the one he used dealing with studio heads and actors alike.

"Look, sweetheart, it'll only take an hour. Ninety minutes, tops. Then you can go do whatever it is you were going to do. At least you're only putting a little of your day on hold. I can't just go home and pretend nothing happened so I can get back to sleeping in once we're done," the man complained. He assumed that he'd convinced her and asked, "How soon can you get here?"

Danni heard her doorbell ringing.

They were here.

What was she going to tell them? she wondered, disappointment washing over her. She was looking forward to this on so many levels, not the least of which was finally picking out some of the things to keep the renovations moving along.

"Soon," she promised.

"Okay. Oh and don't forget to wear what you were wearing yesterday so there's continuity. Your viewers won't understand why you did a sudden costume change in the middle of making those cake pops."

"Fine. Same clothes," she parroted. "See you then," Danni said, quickly terminating the call just as she opened the door to Stone and his daughter.

The second she did, Ginny erupted like a happy firecracker.

"Hi!" she exclaimed with exuberance as she bounced

into the house. "Daddy said you need help picking out tile."

"Hi, yourself," Danni said, greeting the little girl. The grin on Ginny's face was infectious. Danni could feel it spreading to her lips even as she turned toward Stone to make her apologies and explanations.

But then she got an idea.

"There's been a slight change in plans," she started to explain, nodding at the phone in her hand. "My producer just called."

"You have to go in," Stone guessed.

She nodded her head, but before she could say anything, he was absolving her of any guilt she might be feeling. What he was feeling, oddly enough, was a sense of disappointment. He tried to pinpoint exactly why that was, even as he deliberately nixed that it could be because of Danni.

"Hey, I understand," he told her. "We can do this some other time."

"No," Ginny cried.

Danni took one look at the disappointed expression on Ginny's face and did a quick recalculation, going with the idea that had just popped into her head.

"No," she said, echoing Ginny's protest and accompanying it with a firm nod of her head.

Now he was really confused. "No?" Stone asked, looking for enlightenment.

"No, we don't have to do this some other time," she told him. "We really need to get started today." She was really tired of looking at naked, stripped-down walls when she came home at night.

He wasn't the one who had just said she had to go into the studio this morning. *She* had. "But you just said—"

Danni stopped him right there. They were wasting precious time. Every moment they stood here, talking was another moment that freeway traffic to the studio wound up doubling. They had to get going now if they wanted to have a prayer of getting to the studio at a relatively decent time.

She stopped to find her purse. "I know what I said and I do have to go to the studio, but how would you like to come with me?" She was addressing her words to Ginny. "You can sit in the studio audience—you can *be* my studio audience," she told her. "And once we get this one scene redone, we can go look at tile. Unless you'd rather not go to the studio," she said as that possibility occurred to her. Driving to Burbank and back might just be too much trouble to put Stone through.

Stone never got a chance to answer. Ginny beat him to it.

"I want to go to the studio," Ginny assured her. "Please, Daddy, can we? Can we?" she asked twice, just in case he'd missed hearing her beg the first time. Ginny grabbed his hand, all but jumping up and down, pulling on it, as if that would help persuade her father to agree.

There were very few times Stone said no when it came to his daughter. This was not one of them. Instead, he turned toward Danni.

"You don't mind?" he asked.

"Mind?" she repeated, mystified. "Why should I mind? In case you missed it, I'm the one who just suggested it. I've got people in the studio audience watching what I do every day. It might as well be people I like," she told him, then glanced down at Ginny. "The studio audience gets to sample what I make when I finish."

There, that should seal the deal for Ginny, she thought, just in case the little girl was thinking of changing her mind.

Changing her mind was the furthest thing from Ginny's mind right now. If anything, Ginny's eyes were shining. "Really?"

Danni's grin almost matched the little girl's. "Really."

Ginny swung around to make her final appeal to her father.

"Say yes, Daddy, say yes," she pleaded.

Stone responded with a deep, rumbling laugh. "As if I've ever said no to you."

"But you did say no to me, Daddy," Ginny reminded him very seriously. "I asked for a pony for Christmas and you said no. Don't you remember?"

He remembered very well. Remembered, too, feeling badly about denying the little girl *anything*. Even something as outlandish as her very own pony. There were times when he felt, if he looked up the term *pushover* in the dictionary, there would be a picture of his face in the reference area.

"That was different. I was thinking of the pony," he teased now. "And your aunt Virginia who'd be stuck cleaning up after the pony."

Ginny's small face scrunched up as if she were untangling what her father had just said.

But the bottom line was that she was really interested in one thing. "Then we can go with Danni?"

Stone nodded. "We can go."

He wasn't sure just which felt better, being on the receiving end of Ginny's hug or Danni's smile. He decided that it was a tie.

Chapter Eleven

Ginny, her hand wrapped tightly around Danni's as they walked onto the sound stage, appeared to be trying to take everything in at once.

"If your head spins any faster, it's going to fall off," Stone warned his daughter, amused as he watched her looking around.

"Is this where you work, Danni?" Ginny asked, no doubt overcome by the hugeness of it all.

"This is where I work." Danni had led the father and daughter duo in via the rear stage entrance, which brought them right to the actual set.

The set, with its gleaming new appliances, was the epitome of a state-of-the-art kitchen. It was, in a nutshell, her dream kitchen. Sometimes, after the show was done for the day, Danni would stay late to make something to take home with her or to give to one of the crew members as a gift if they happened to be celebrating some special occasion.

The crew all loved her.

Rather than behave like a diva, something that some celebrities did when they became caught up in their own press releases and started believing them, Danni never put on airs. She made it a point to know the entire staff and crew by their first names.

She also made it a point to find out about their families. Her accessibility as well as her likeability made the atmosphere on the set a great deal warmer and more laid-back than most sets.

The sound of her voice as she spoke to Ginny drew out both the producer who'd initially called her this morning and the director.

The latter looked more than anxious to get this re-taping over with and get back to his far-too-often-interrupted life.

"You came," Barry said needlessly as he came out onto the set to join her. That was when he saw Stone and Ginny for the first time. "And I see you brought reinforcements with you," he commented, looking the newcomers over rather intently.

Like most of the people on the set, he was protective of Danni.

"This is Stone Scarborough and his daughter, Ginny," Danni said, introducing them. "This is my producer, Barry McIntyre, and my director, Ryan Talbert." Each man nodded in turn. Barry gave her a questioning look and she knew that if she didn't want to walk onto a set full of speculation on Monday morning, she needed to set the record straight right now. "Stone and his daughter had just arrived at the house to take me tile hunting when you called this morning. Since you said it was only going to take up an hour—"

"Or so," Barry pointed out. "I said an hour or so."

"Actually, you said, 'Ninety minutes, tops,'" Danni quoted. "I'm planning on holding you to that because I don't think it's right to restrict Ginny for any longer than that."

Barry appeared a bit daunted as he glanced uncertainly over to his director.

Ryan sighed and nodded. All he could do was give it his best shot. "Let's get going then. We're reshooting the cake pops segment. For some reason, the tape on that didn't come out right."

She heard one of the cameramen chuckling. When she turned to look in the direction of the amused sound, she cocked her head as if to silently ask him why he was laughing.

The man wasn't shy about sharing. "My guess is that Wally probably ate that part of the tape—he's hoping you'll have to bake another batch of cake pops. I think the guy must have eaten about twenty of them. What he didn't eat, he took with him." The cameraman grinned. "Said it was for his kid but I've got a hunch his kid is never going to see them."

The gaffer they were talking about was the newest addition to their staff. He'd been there for a couple of months and was exceedingly friendly and talkative, but there was no denying that he really liked to eat. The man weighed about three hundred pounds and was already being referred to as a human vacuum cleaner—not always behind his back.

The term didn't appear to offend the man. At least, he just seemed to be able to laugh it off.

"Hey, where is the human vacuum cleaner?" another cameraman asked, looking around.

"Grady, don't call him that," Danni said.

"Ah, he doesn't care, Danni," Grady protested, waving away her protest.

"The man has feelings. Trust me, he cares," she stressed. Danni absolutely hated seeing any living thing picked on and teased, whether the act was blatant or covert.

Standing back, Stone was wordlessly taking in the exchange. He liked the fact that Danni was defending someone, thinking of the person's feelings when he wasn't even around. It gave Stone a little insight into the woman's character and her nature. He liked what he'd glimpsed in both cases.

"Okay, everyone, assume your positions," the director instructed, raising his voice.

"Where do you want us to sit?" Stone asked, addressing the question to the only person on the set who mattered to him besides his daughter.

"You can be the audience," Ryan told them, cutting in to answer before Danni had a chance to say a word. He pointed toward the small audience section. "Gemma, Roy, take seats in the second row. Let— Stone is it?" he asked, looking at the general contractor. Stone nodded. "Let Stone and the little princess here sit in the first row," he instructed.

Ginny giggled. "I'm not a princess," she protested—but not too strenuously.

"I don't want to bump anyone," Stone told the director.

"Don't worry about that. We couldn't get an audience back for the shoot on such short notice so we just gathered up friends and family members to serve as an audience. Audience at home is watching Danni, not memorizing who's in our studio audience and who went home. Since Danni brought you two with her, I figure she wants you to be up close and personal with the action—right, Danni?" Ryan asked, turning a weary, thousand-watt smile on his star for ten seconds.

"Whatever you say, Ryan," Danni responded, not wanting Stone to think she was making a big deal out of any of this—even though, now that she thought of it, she rather liked the idea of having the man and his daughter here, taking in what she did for a living.

By no means did she think of herself as a celebrity, but there were people who were impressed with *anyone* whose face wound up on the TV screen. She had a feeling Ginny might fall into that category—for the time being.

Danni pretended to be busy and not watch where Stone and his daughter finally wound up taking their seats, but she was acutely aware of where they sat down.

As far as she was concerned, they *were* her audience. She directed most of her words to that section of the seats—which turned out to be front and center.

"Okay, Danni, do what you do best. Action," Ryan declared.

Danni began talking to her audience in her laid-back, easy cadence. Traces of her Georgia accent wove their way through her sentences as she instructed the audience, both in the studio and at home, how to go about making one of the newest dessert fads to capture the public's fancy: elaborately decorated cake pops.

Just as she began, a heavyset man maneuvered his rather large frame into the seat next to Stone. "Made it," he sighed contentedly, more to himself than to anyone around him.

Then, as if he suddenly realized that he wasn't in the audience alone, he turned toward Stone and murmured, "I got stuck in traffic. Was afraid I was going to miss this."

This had to be that Wally character the others had talked about, Stone thought. The man's sentence was obviously begging for a reply. After a beat, Stone gave in and asked, "You enjoy watching her bake?"

"Mouth starts to water just thinking about it," Wally confessed. "The stuff she burns tastes better than what some people spend hours preparing—not that she ever burns anything," he added hastily, looking suddenly nervous, as if he realized he'd said too much. "You're not a blogger or anything, are you?" he asked.

"I'm her general contractor," Stone said to put the man at ease.

Wally immediately relaxed. "Yeah, she said something about having her house worked on. She's a real nice lady," he told Stone in a pseudo whisper. "Don't come any nicer. Knows the names and ages of my kids. And not just mine. Can't see why someone like that doesn't have a family of her own," he said with a shake of his head.

"Not always that easy," Stone commented.

Wally nodded his head in firm agreement. "No, I guess not. But she should." He took in a deep breath. The first batch of cake pops had gone into the oven and were already creating a tempting aroma. "Smell that?" he asked Stone. "That's pure talent. If I was married to a woman like that, I'd be fat," he speculated. Then as if he had a sudden reality check, Wally laughed and patted his large girth. "Or fatter," he amended with a wide grin.

The taping abruptly halted as Ryan cried, "Cut."

"Are we done already?" Danni asked hopefully. She glanced over toward the producer who was standing in the wings. The man had actually underestimated the time on this, she thought happily, glad she'd suggested having Stone bring his daughter and be part of her audience.

"No, and we won't be done unless the running commentary coming from the audience stops." Ryan glared at the late arrival.

"Sorry," Wally apologized. "Guess I got carried away with a surge of enthusiasm," he said, then raised his voice to promise, "Won't happen again."

"It does and today's desserts are going to go home with everyone *but* you," the director warned, obviously knowing that was the most effective threat he could issue to the gaffer.

Ryan's back was to Danni, so consequently he didn't see her looking at the wide staff member and he didn't see the wink she sent the man. A wink that silently assured him of his fair share of the loot as long as he played by the rules.

Taping resumed as Wally made a conscientious effort to maintain his silence.

Stone continued observing the woman. He had to admit that he really liked what he saw—she was bright, entertaining and funny—and the tempting scent of cake pops, decorated or simply rolled in powdered sugar, just seemed to enhance everything.

Especially, he noted, for his daughter.

"Well, I was almost right," Barry said the moment that the taping finally wrapped up for the day. "It was around ninety minutes."

"Not all that close," Danni contradicted, her eyes not on her producer but on the two people she'd dragged to the studio. It was time to get going. "I'll see you Monday," she told Barry, thereby effectively ending any further conversation he might have felt compelled to engage in.

Danni stripped off her coverall apron and placed it on the counter rather than going off set to put it away herself. She was constantly being told some people were paid to keep track of her aprons. Just this once, she decided to utilize said people—she hurried off the set and down into the audience seats.

"I'm so sorry," she apologized before she even reached them.

Stone was already on his feet, waiting for her. Ginny had bounced up to hers, energy about to be unharnessed.

"For what?" Stone asked. "The taping wasn't that much longer than ninety minutes," he told her.

Maybe it *was* but he didn't want her feeling badly about it. He—and more important, Ginny—had enjoyed themselves. Ginny had already consumed two cake pops—a lion and a giraffe—and she was holding two more in her hands.

His daughter, Stone thought, looked as if she were absolutely in heaven. Wisps of yellow and black frosting dotted her wide, smiling mouth. And her eyes could double as Fourth of July sparklers.

Danni flashed Stone a grateful smile. "Thanks for being so understanding. I really didn't want to miss out on getting your help selecting the tile and granite," she confessed. Turning toward Ginny, she asked, "So, what do you think? Do you like cake pops?" The answer was more than obvious, but she wanted the little girl to feel as if her opinion counted.

"I *love* cake pops," the little girl declared.

Stone laughed, thinking of the two cake pops she'd already made such short work of. "Just what she needs, a sugar high."

"I don't use sugar, I use apple sauce, remember?" Danni reminded him. "*Natural* apple sauce," she emphasized. "That's supposed to be even better than sugar in the recipe. Most people can't tell the difference."

Natural sugar or artificial sugar, the results were still going to be pretty much the same, Stone judged.

"Still going to have to scrape her off the ceiling," Stone predicted.

"But it won't be a cathedral ceiling," Danni pointed

out, as if that made all the difference in the world. "Just a normal-size one."

"You do try to find the silver lining in things, don't you?" Stone observed, amused and maybe just a little charmed by this exuberant woman as well.

"That's the only way I know how to survive," Danni admitted. The nature of her behavior was deeply rooted in her past. "Otherwise," she admitted in a rare moment of sharing, "I think I would have been pretty much plowed under by now."

"Oh? By what?" he asked. Then, the next moment he realized how that must have sounded to her, as if he was digging into her life. "Sorry, none of my business," he told her, raising his hands in symbolic surrender. "Didn't mean to pry."

She ignored his words of apology and the fact that he was backing away from the subject altogether. Granted she didn't owe him any explanations, but even so, maybe she owed herself a small twist of the release valve. She'd been carrying things around, bottled up inside her, for too long.

Danni made a conscious decision to share, telling herself that sometimes it was good to give voice to the things that weighed so heavily on her soul.

"My dad died just as I graduated college. He was a dear, sweet man who through no fault of his own left me with a mountain of bills to pay in addition to having to pay off my college loan. For about a month, I felt so swamped I could hardly breathe."

"Technically, you could have walked away from the medical bills," he told her. People did it all the time, either just picking up and moving away, or declaring bankruptcy.

Danni shook her head. Not that she hadn't considered it for all of a few minutes, but she'd come to the same conclusion she still espoused now.

"Not my style. My father would have been very disappointed in me if he knew," she confided. "Although, I do have to admit that I did lean in that direction for a little while, feeling that if I had to pay the bill, the least they could have done was save my father." She laughed shortly. "But there was no 'satisfaction guaranteed' stamped on the hospital bill. Just the words, Payment Due Now. And," she added with a shrug, "they *had* tried to save my dad, but the cancer was too far along, discovered too late…"

He filled in the blank. And what it told him was that the woman he was looking at had far more integrity than anyone he'd ever dealt with.

The lights all around them on the set suddenly dimmed. The set was being shut down, she realized. "I think they're hinting we should leave," Danni told her guests.

"Don't have to tell me twice," Stone said with a short laugh. Taking his daughter's small hand in his, he placed his other one against the small of Danni's back and said, "Let's go."

She could feel the slight pressure of his hand, could feel a wave of warmth pass all along her body. Danni had no idea why, but that in turn created a feeling of wellbeing, of being taken care of. It wafted through her as she allowed herself to be guided off the sound stage and out into the parking lot.

Just for a second, she pretended that for once there was someone looking after her, someone for her to lean on. It was an exceedingly good feeling.

Chapter Twelve

"I had no idea there were so many different stores that just sold tile," Danni sighed as she sank into the passenger seat of Stone's truck.

For the last two hours, ever since they'd left the studio in Burbank, she, Stone and Ginny had undertaken what amounted to a pilgrimage, going from one store after another, looking at miles and miles of tiles. So far, all the stores were located along the same stretch of road in Anaheim—many of them boasting that *their* collection of tile was *the* collection.

One store had tile only imported from Italy, another had their tile shipped in from different regions in South America. Still another only carried tile that came from France. A couple of stores got their tile from places she'd never even heard of. Each store had a slightly different twist to their collection, be it color, texture, locale of origin or something as simple as sporting a slightly different glaze.

And that, Danni discovered, didn't even begin to cover the army of cleaning products designed to keep those select pieces of tile looking brand new, or, in a couple of cases, older than time. Had it not been for the company she was keeping—both Ginny *and* Stone— Danni knew she would have been more than ready to throw in the towel after the third store.

Stone, standing outside the truck and directly next to the passenger seat, sympathized with how she had to be feeling right about now.

"Unless you know exactly what you're looking for, it can be pretty overwhelming," he agreed.

Now there was an understatement, she thought. "It makes me seriously consider living in a hotel."

Having secured Ginny's straps in her car seat, Stone came around to the driver's side and got in behind the steering wheel. He put the key into the ignition, but left it there for the moment.

"You don't strike me as the transient type," he told her.

"No, living in a hotel *permanently*," Danni underscored.

Stone paused for a moment to study her a bit more closely. And then he shook his head. "Still don't see you living out of a suitcase. You like owning things," he said, surprising her with his insight. "Don't worry, this gets better."

She'd believe it when it happened. "Are you talking

as a general contractor or as someone who's been on the other side of this process?" she asked.

"Both," he answered. There wasn't even a hint of a smile on his lips. "And I do know what you're going through," he assured her. "It feels as if you'll never make the right choice—and you're afraid of settling, but even more afraid that this process will go on forever—am I close?" he asked. This time he allowed the corners of his mouth to curve.

Danni shook her head. "No, you're not 'close,' you're dead on," she told him. Either he really *had* been through this process on his own, or someone had bared their soul to him in an attempt to get him to relate. Either way, she was glad that he understood how all this made her feel.

"If it makes you feel any better, most people don't go with the first selection they see," he said. "It usually takes more than a few trips to different stores before they find something that *really* moves them and then they go with that."

She laughed at his description of the process. "If I didn't know any better, I would have said you were describing the kind of search a person undertakes looking for a soul mate," she told him.

He didn't even need to reflect on what he'd said. Because he agreed with her. "Well, it is in a way. You make a commitment to what you pick out and wind up living with that commitment for a long time. Sometimes longer than some couples remain married. So, take your time," he advised. "You want to really like what you pick out. There's no advantage in going with the first thing you see."

She couldn't help thinking he was advising her about more than just the tile or the other household decorations they would be looking at in the near future.

Rousing herself, Danni focused on the business at hand. "Except that I'd be getting my house back," she pointed out.

"But you're having the remodeling done so that you'll *like* that house, right?" he reminded her. "Otherwise, there's no point in having it remodeled in the first place." He waited for his words to sink in. And enjoyed watching the bit of color rise up on her cheeks.

Danni was force to nod—and concede. "Makes sense."

"Now then, are you up for any more stores, or would you just rather call it a day and we can do this again some other time?" he asked.

If it were just up to her, she'd definitely opt to keep going. She liked spending this time with him. Liked his company, his wit, his masculinity that was so grounded. But there wasn't just her to consider here.

"That depends," she answered. Before he could ask her on what, Danni twisted around in her seat and looked at the little girl strapped in directly behind her. "Do you feel like going to any more stores, honey, or are you tired?"

"I'm not tired," Ginny proclaimed loudly. She kicked her feet a little as if to emphasize how *not* tired she was.

"I forgot to warn you. Ginny's a self-winding kid," Stone told her. "Just when you think she's going to be winding down, she surprises you by getting all wound up again."

Despite Ginny's overenergized state, Stone appreciated Danni's concern for his daughter and putting her comfort ahead of anything that she might have personally wanted.

"Well, then it's settled," Danni told him. "If you don't mind continuing to be my guide on this safari, let's just keep going."

"You heard the lady, Daddy, let's keep going!" Ginny called out excitedly, sounding as energetic as if she'd just taken a nap instead of run up and down the aisles of six different stores.

Stone laughed. "Well, I guess then I have my marching orders," he said as he started up the truck and pulled out of the parking lot.

"You're not marching, Daddy, you're driving," Ginny pointed out, giggling at his error.

"My mistake," Stone said "humbly."

Ginny giggled louder.

After another two hours of traipsing through stores that dealt predominantly with bathroom and kitchen tiles, as well as a couple of shops that specialized in tiles made out of marble, Danni decided that the excursion needed to come to an end for now.

"No more, please," she begged as they walked out of their umpteenth store, nauseatingly called, *Rocks to Riches*. "All the tile is beginning to look alike," she protested.

"That's because a lot of them *are* alike," he explained. "Some stores tend to carry the same thing, as well as a little bit extra, hoping that 'extra' will draw you in. Anyway, I think we've sufficiently gotten your feet wet."

"Her feet aren't wet, Daddy," Ginny corrected him, looking down at Danni's shoes. "It's not raining."

Ginny had been in rare form all day, he noted, and apparently on her best behavior as well. She wasn't a child given to tantrums, but she could get a bit cranky at times when she was tired, which by all rights, after walking around for four hours through stores that didn't have a single stuffed animal between them, she should have been. It seemed to Stone as if his small keg of dynamite was trying extra hard today.

It wasn't difficult to see why.

Ginny had taken a huge shine to Danni, so much more so than she ever had to Elizabeth. Now that he thought about it, Ginny hadn't really taken to any woman except for his sister, and now Danni, since her mother died. That said a great deal about the woman he'd been driving around for the last four hours, he mused.

"Nope, you're right," he agreed. "No rain." He looked now at Danni as they reached his truck. "What do you say to grabbing some dinner and then calling it a day?"

"Why don't we just go to my house and I'll whip up something for us?" Danni suggested, addressing her words to both Stone and his daughter.

"I think you're forgetting something," Stone pointed out.

She thought for a moment and nothing came to her. "What?"

"You have no kitchen." He hadn't thought he'd have to remind her of that.

"I have a plug and a hot plate," she countered, then grinned. "Never underestimate the ingenuity of a woman with a hot plate."

Stone laughed. "I have no intention of underestimating you," he told her sincerely. He already knew how capable and determined she was. He didn't need a refresher course. "But I thought it might be a nice change of pace for you to consume something you didn't have to slave over a hot plate to make," he told her, doing his best to look serious at the end.

His thoughtfulness left her momentarily speechless. Recovering, Danni said the first thing that came to her mind. "You forget, I *like* to cook."

He could just hear his sister's voice in her head, wholeheartedly endorsing this woman.

Stick with her, Stone. This woman's a keeper.

Most likely, his sister was also anticipating being invited over for meals a lot, he guessed. That was, if she ever did get around to moving out again.

"No, I didn't forget," he told her.

When it came to this woman, he'd found that he didn't forget anything he'd learned about her. Not the way she smiled, or the way she tilted her head when she was listening to him, or the way that she pressed her lips together when she was trying to make up her mind about something.

But that wasn't the point right now—or maybe he was just trying to bury the point because he wasn't ready to face it just yet. Because admitting, even just to himself, that he was drawn to this woman on any other level than just plain old basic physical attraction, would be leaving himself opened to the possibility of pain, raw, soul-shredding pain. He'd already been through that once and barely survived. He might not survive a second time around.

"There must be some part of you that likes to be waited on," he said.

"There is," she allowed, "but you just gave up your whole Saturday for me, so I want to do something in return."

"You did," he told her. When she looked at him quizzically, he explained, "You gave Ginny a bunch of cake pops."

"I gave Ginny cake pops because she was such a good audience," Danni said, twisting around to look at the little girl and give her a wink. Ginny beamed at her in response.

"Well, fortunately, I'm driving so that means you two have to go where I take you," Stone informed her with finality. "So I suggest you settle back and enjoy the ride, Ms. Everett."

"Guess I have no choice," Danni replied, amusement playing along her lips as she turned to face front again and settled into her seat. "But I intend to make a feast for you and Ginny once I get my kitchen back."

"It's a deal," Stone told her and, God help him, he realized that he was looking forward to the informal "date" he'd just made.

His reaction to Danni both intrigued Stone and worried him. He hadn't had feelings—real, *intense* feelings—for anyone since Eva had died. For the longest time, he actually didn't believe that he *could* feel anything again. What he'd had with Elizabeth was pleasant enough and he did like her. But he had resigned himself to his low-key attraction to the mayor's chief press secretary being as good as it got for him.

After all, he'd had passion already and while it had been wonderful, it had also led him into a land of desolation once Eva was no longer part of his life. It had taken him a very long time to heal, to feel something other than despair and dread.

Had he not had Ginny to care for, Stone didn't even want to think about the path he would have wound up taking.

Feelings were exhilarating, but they came with a price and he really didn't want to pay that price a second time.

But no matter how much he reasoned with himself, it felt as if he had no choice in the matter. Deliberately sabotaging his intent to do his job and leave before Danni came home, he caught himself lingering at her house longer and longer each evening, adding finishing touches on areas already finished, just so that their paths might briefly cross.

Just so he could see her before he went home to his daughter and his life. And even perhaps, just to touch her in passing, although the last time had resulted in not just an impersonal touch but a caress. A slow, languid caress along her jawline as he looked into her eyes. It had been on a pretext of removing a stray hair from her cheek. But there'd been no hair.

Only sizzle.

Sizzle that in turn lingered as well. Lingered because

he kissed her—although he wouldn't have been able to reconstruct the logistics if his life depended on it. One second, they were talking and he was saying, "Good night," the next, for a brief, shining, wondrous moment, their lips all but fused into one another, creating, among other things, their own personal bonfire.

But the next moment, they'd separated, each diving for cover behind inane words and cardboard sentiments they both knew didn't have a lick of truth to them.

He was later getting home than he'd ever been.

The funny thing was neither Ginny nor Virginia complained about his lateness. They hadn't even said a word when he began coming home later and later.

Ginny had always complained when he left her to see Elizabeth, but this, somehow, was different for her. Most likely it had to do with the fanciful desserts Danni began sending home with him right after they'd observed her taping that Saturday.

It got to the point where his concern wouldn't stay under wraps. He felt the need to share it with Ernie Walsh, the retired construction worker, now part-time handyman he utilized on occasion to speed up a job.

This job, he decided in a moment of raw honesty, needed speeding up. If only to get done faster because the sooner they were out of each others' lives the sooner things would go back to normal for him. Dull, but normal. Every treaty had an unpleasant part, he thought philosophically.

"Ginny acts like a kid in a candy store, waiting for me to come home," he told Ernie as they painted the renovated downstairs bathroom a shade of icy blue. "The minute I walk in through the door, she runs over to me and checks both my hands to see if I brought her anything."

Ernie dipped his roller into the tray, removing the excess paint before beginning to apply what was left on the roller onto the wall.

"And?"

"Usually, I have," Stone said with a somewhat helpless shrug.

Ernie paused, as if trying to get his facts straight. "So the woman whose house we're working on bakes for your daughter?" Ernie asked, momentarily taking a break—something he did with a fair amount of frequency.

Stone could hear the laugh in Ernie's voice. The handyman probably thought the woman slaved for hours making these edible "gifts" she was sending home with him. The way to a father's heart is through his kid, right?

"It's not like it's a hardship for her. The woman's a chef—"

"Wait, back up. You said her name was Danielle Everett?" he asked incredulously.

"Yes."

"You talking about *Danni* Everett?" Ernie asked, saying her name as it if was revered in his household. Or at least revered by him.

"Yes," Stone replied.

"As in *Danni's Desserts to Die For?*" he asked in disbelief. His voice quavered a little. "We're talking about the woman on the cable channel?" Ernie's voice rose a little higher with each sentence.

"Yes." Ernie was looking at him as if he were utterly starstruck. "I take it you've seen her show."

"Seen it?" Ernie repeated with a harsh laugh. "I never miss it. That woman cooks on all four burners and I'm not just talking about the stove." His laugh turned almost lusty. "*That's* who you're working for? Oh man, you lucky devil," Ernie crowed gleefully. "Anyone who looks like that has *got* to be able to really cook outside the kitchen, if you know what I mean." The man winked at Stone in an exaggerated fashion.

"My wife thinks I've developed an interest in her programs," he continued, chuckling. "I let her think whatever makes her happy." He scrubbed his hand over his face as he obviously envisioned the encounters between his one-time protégé and the woman who in his mind deserved a golden spatula. "So what's she like in person?" Ernie asked eagerly.

"She's nice." Stone thought that was a good, safe description, certainly not an offensive one and not one that could be regarded as giving away how he really felt about the woman.

"Nice?" Ernie echoed, then jeered. "Nice? An apple is 'nice,' a spring breeze is 'nice.' This woman is nothing short of hot. And if she's sending desserts home with you for your kid, that means she likes you," Ernie pointed out. "I mean *really* likes you."

Maybe he shouldn't have shared this, after all. He liked Ernie, but the man, now that he thought of it, wasn't exactly the last word when it came to being discreet. "I think you're reading too much into this, Ernie."

"And I think you're not reading enough into it," the handyman scoffed.

"Ernie, Danni and I have a professional relationship, that's all. I'm renovating her house and she's paying me to do it. End of story," he said firmly.

But Ernie remained unconvinced. He rolled his applicator down the wall one time, then paused again. "Huh. Nobody ever sent desserts home with me for my kid."

And there was a very good reason for that. "You don't have any kids, Ernie," Stone reminded him.

But Ernie was not about to be diverted from the stance he'd taken. "You're missing the point here, boy," he said impatiently.

There was no convincing the man tonight, Stone thought. The sooner he got him out of there, the sooner things would go back to normal—at least for the evening.

"And you're missing a spot," Stone said, pointing out a small section of the wall that Ernie's roller had skipped over. "Now stop making prophesies and finish that wall so we can get started on the upstairs bathrooms before she decides to hire another contractor."

"Will you introduce me?" Ernie asked.

"Sure, why not? I'll introduce you." Stone played his ace. "But only after you finish painting the bathroom."

"On it!" Ernie gleefully declared, putting some muscle into it.

Shaking his head, Stone got back to what he was doing.

Chapter Thirteen

Danni saw the truck from a distance as she turned down her block.

At first, she thought maybe it was just wishful thinking on her part, or she was seeing a truck that was actually sitting in the driveway next to hers.

But as she drew closer, she realized that it *was* her driveway. Stone's truck was still there, despite the fact that it was past six o'clock.

A smile curved her mouth as she pulled her car up next to the truck. Taping this week kept hitting snags and running way over the usual time, with her afternoons bleeding into her evenings.

Danni's sense of responsibility trumped her desire to get home early so that she could exchange a few words with Stone before he left for the day. She wanted to talk to him about how work was going, about how his daughter was doing.

About anything at all actually.

Lately, she found that she looked forward to seeing him. And never more than today.

Ever since he'd kissed her, she found that her mind kept straying at the most inopportune times to thoughts of Stone, to the way his laugh set off a reaction in the pit of her stomach.

The familiarity of that set off more chain reactions inside her.

So far, she and Stone, as well as his daughter, had spent several Saturdays visiting every conceivable store that carried tile, floor coverings and/or bathroom fixtures and accessories, within a forty-mile radius. She'd finally made all her selections, thanks to Stone's advice and guidance. But, he'd warned her, just because she'd placed the orders didn't mean that it was smooth sailing from then on. Not everything was arriving in a timely fashion as originally promised. There'd been delays and mishaps, and consequently, seven weeks into the remodeling she was still making do with a hot plate, a microwave and a plug-in grill.

When Stone apologized, she told him she knew it wasn't his fault and that she was getting used to "roughing it." The smile he gave her in return was well worth what she had to put up with.

If she didn't know any better, she would have said she was falling for the muscular contractor. But of course she knew better. Love took time. Time to cultivate, to develop. Stone had only been in her life for seven weeks.

That might be long enough for a fruit fly to fall in love, but not a woman, right?

Despite her sensible reasoning, Danni caught herself hurrying up the walkway to see Stone. However, she told herself it was for an entirely different reason than the fact that he made her pulse race.

Danni stopped at the door, forcing herself to take a deep breath. She needed to collect herself.

You're acting like a teenager hoping to ambush the school hunk, she chided herself. But the truth of it was, she had to admit, she *did* feel like a teenager. The idea of seeing Stone caused her pulse to pick up speed and anticipation to corkscrew all through her.

It had been a *long* time since she'd felt like this, she thought, opening her front door and walking in.

Even though she didn't see him, she could feel his presence—and right now, that was a very good thing.

She didn't want to be alone.

"Hello?" she called out.

"In here," the deep male voice called back. It was coming out of the kitchen.

Danni told herself not to pick up speed as she went through the house, but she did anyway. She stopped just short of the kitchen. Crossing the threshold, she made her way over to Stone. There he was carefully placing small tiles one at a time on the back wall, creating what would eventually be the backsplash over the new cook-top she'd selected last week.

"You're still here," she observed, pleased.

"Looks that way," he quipped. Then he glanced over his shoulder at her. "I felt bad about the kitchen still not being finished so I thought I'd stay longer to do some more work. I figured it was okay because you weren't home yet." Finished for now, he brushed his hands off on the back of his jeans. "But you're here now and you probably want the house to yourself, so I'll go."

She didn't want him to go, not yet. Rattling around the house tonight would feel exceptionally lonely to her. "Don't rush off on my account. I can always have the house to myself later," she told him. She needed to have a plausible reason to ask him to stay, otherwise, she would just seem needy to him. Danni fell back on a tried and true method. "Have you eaten yet?"

Stone nodded, thinking she meant had he eaten that day. "Had some kind of sandwich Virginia threw together for me for lunch—don't ask me what. I tend not to pay attention to things like that when I'm working."

That sounded like a typical male, Danni thought. Her father had been like that, eating without paying attention to what he was consuming.

"I can make some dinner for you," Danni offered, going into the family room where her old refrigerator was currently housed.

Stone knew better than to point out that she still had no stove. He'd watched her work miracles on her hot plate. She cooked better on the hot plate than most women did with a state-of-the-art stove.

Still, he didn't like putting her out on his account. "That's okay. Virginia probably has some takeout waiting for me."

The more the merrier, Danni thought. Especially tonight.

"Tell her to come by with Ginny," she said, impulsively extending an invitation to the rest of his family. "It's important for a little girl to eat dinner with her daddy."

Something in her voice caught his attention. A sadness he hadn't heard before. Granted he hadn't known her for that long, but he'd noticed that usually Danni was incredibly upbeat. And while there was a smile on her face right now, it appeared to be taking some effort on her part to maintain.

"Something wrong?" he asked her.

"No," she said quickly. "I just think that fathers and daughters should spend time together if they can." *When they can,* she added silently as another pang skewered through her.

"You'll get no argument from me, but Ginny's not neglected, if that's what you're thinking." And then he paused. Those were tears shimmering in her eyes even though she'd turned her head away quickly, he could swear to it. "There *is* something wrong, isn't there." It wasn't a question anymore. "Maybe it's none of my business," he acknowledged. "But I'm a pretty good listener if you want to talk."

She wanted to talk, but she didn't know if the words would even sound coherent when they came out. People endured loss all the time and went about their lives. For the most part, she'd gone on with hers, but there were just times, like now, when the loneliness threatened to undo her.

"I'd rather not be alone just yet, if you don't mind," she told him quietly.

That much he'd already gathered. "I'm not going anywhere," he told her. Gesturing toward the open boxes of tile he had on the kitchen floor, he told her, "I've got enough tile there to work straight through the night." But right now, work—though he loved it—wasn't uppermost on his mind.

Stone crossed to her, studying Danni's face. "Something did happen today," he guessed.

"No, not today. At least, not this year today." She blew out a breath. It was just as she'd thought, her words were getting jumbled. The man probably thought he was working for a lunatic. Maybe it was better if she explained. "My dad died four years ago today," she said, her voice barely audible.

"I'm so sorry," he told her compassionately.

She sighed and a shaky breath escaped her lips. "Yeah, me, too."

"You were close, you and your dad?" Stone guessed.

She wanted to say yes, but that really wasn't true. At least, not for most of her childhood.

"Just at the end. He was a traveling salesman," she said with a half smile on her lips. "The kind they always tell stories about. He was on the road for most of my childhood. I grew up missing him. One of the last things he told me just before he died was how much he regretted not being there for me, not being there to share the simple things as well as the milestones. It wasn't until after he became ill that I found how smart he was and how funny. I felt cheated." She looked at him. "Don't let Ginny feel that way years from now."

He laughed softly and shook his head. "Not a

chance. She'd going to have the exact opposite to complain about—an old man who glares at her boyfriends when they come to the door. Who keeps wanting to hang out with her even though she wants to pretend he doesn't exist because he's embarrassing her in front of her friends." There was more truth than he was happy about in his prophesy.

Danni smiled at him. He was instinctively a good father, she could just tell. "She might complain about it, but deep down inside, she'll be grateful that you love her enough to care."

"We'll see," he responded.

"I was serious about the invitation," she told him. "About having Ginny and your sister over for dinner."

"Sounds good," he agreed. "But we can do it some other night. I think that Virginia would appreciate a little heads-up first. But I'll stay," he told her quickly in case she thought he was trying to leave as well.

"I'm sorry. I'm acting like a child. You've put in a long day, I shouldn't be making you stay longer."

"Well, I'm standing over here and you're standing a couple of feet away from me and as far as I can see, there's been no arm twisting going on so you're not *making* me do anything. Now, you can't issue an invitation to dinner and then rescind it in the next breath. Not after my salivary glands have started to drool in heated anticipation. You don't want to be labeled a culinary tease now, do you?" He asked the question so seriously, for a moment she didn't realize that he was kidding her.

"Heaven forbid." She laughed, appreciating his kindness.

"Good, then go whip up dinner. Impress me with your ability to create something delicious out of nothing," he told her.

"I'll do my best." It felt good to laugh. Good to feel useful as well. A surge of deep gratitude spiked through her. "You're a good man, Stone Scarborough."

He shrugged off the compliment, not comfortable with its weight. "I'm only as good as I have to be," he told her.

Why that sounded like a promise of things to come to her she didn't know, but it did. And a little thrill of anticipation raced through her.

He was being awfully nice, which made her feel both vulnerable and guilty. Vulnerable because she was responding to this display of sensitivity on his part and guilty because she'd almost forced him to stay to keep her company. The man had a life waiting for him. Not to mention a girlfriend, the one that Ginny told her she didn't like.

"I'm sorry, I didn't mean to guilt you into staying. I'll be okay, really," she underscored. "You should go home to your daughter."

"So then you really are reneging on dinner?" he asked.

His expression seemed so serious, she didn't know if he was kidding or not. She told him the truth. "No, that's my way of telling you that you don't have to stay here and hold my hand."

"I know I don't *have* to stay," he replied. "Did it ever occur to you that maybe I was waiting for an invitation to stay?"

Danni shook her head, her eyes never leaving his. "No."

"No?" he questioned.

"No, it never occurred to me," she told him. She took another breath. She liked him and right now, he was keeping the shadows at bay for her, but she didn't want to be the cause of any discord in his life, no matter how innocent it actually was. "Stone, I have no right to ask you to stay for any reason other than work. You have a girlfriend—"

"Had," he corrected. Was that the problem? Talk about being selfless, she had to be at the head of the class. "I *had* a girlfriend."

He didn't ask Danni how she knew that he'd been seeing someone; he just assumed that any description of Elizabeth had to be something Ginny had told her. Most likely his daughter had complained about Elizabeth since she had never really warmed up to the woman— not that, looking back, he could blame her.

"You broke up?" she asked, stunned. Danni did her best to ignore the strong desire to cheer. "I'm so sorry." Danni tried to sound sincere, but it was hard sounding sincere when she felt like grinning.

"Don't be," Stone told her. "She gave me a choice, so I chose." It had been more of an ultimatum, and he didn't like ultimatums. He and Elizabeth weren't in a place in their relationship where that sort of thing mattered. "She didn't like the fact that I had canceled on her twice and she informed me that I had to choose between her and a job I was currently doing, so I chose the job. I don't like having my back against a wall," he told her simply. And then he shrugged again. "We weren't right for each other, anyway."

"I'm sorry to hear that," Danni said. But she really wasn't.

They talked all the way through dinner and Danni found herself laughing over his recollections of his first job in construction—when he had been less than able, just very willing.

For his part, Stone found her incredibly easy to talk to, which in his eyes was a big deal since he didn't readily share bits and pieces of himself with anyone.

That was how he found himself talking to her about Eva. About the four perfect years they had spent together and about how grief-stricken he was when the police came to his door late one afternoon to tell him that she'd been struck by a hit and run driver while she was out on her afternoon run. Eva was a physical fitness advocate who was always trying to get him to join her. He'd tried going out and running a few times before Ginny was born, but found he had no patience for it. He preferred lifting weights, so Eva ran alone.

Had he been with her that afternoon, he might have been able to push her out of the way, or gotten struck in her place.

For a very long time, he carried a great deal of guilt around with him. Guilt for being alive while Eva was dead.

"You can't do that to yourself," Danni told him, picking up his plate as well as her own and bringing them to the bathroom where the sink was still operational.

He followed behind her with the glasses and utensils. "Easier said than done," he pointed out.

Setting down the two plates in the bathroom sink, she turned in the doorway, about to get the rest of the dirty dishes.

She wound up brushing up against Stone. Startled, as lightning coursed through her at all the points of contact, she lost her train of thought for a second, then murmured, "Sorry."

He contradicted her by saying, "My fault."

Both apologies blended together and faded off into the netherworld. She offered him a small smile. "I've talked your ears off, I didn't mean to."

To which he went through the motions of touching his ears as if to see that they were still attached.

"Nope," he assured her, "they're still there. You didn't talk them off." And then he looked at her and smiled into her eyes. "Cut yourself some slack, Danni," he told her. "You've had a really rough time of it from what I've gathered."

She could feel the heat building up within her. Heat that the weather outside had nothing to do with.

"I could say the same thing to you," she told him, acutely aware of their close proximity, and how very easy it would be just to lean a little forward. Lean into him and from there, lean into a whole world of possibilities. Danni could feel her heart beginning to pound even harder than before.

"Would you mind if I kissed you?" he asked her, his voice lower than a whisper.

"No," she responded in the same sort of low voice

that Stone had just used. Danni could feel herself trembling inside.

Get a grip, Danni. Nothing's going to happen. Just stay firm and you'll be all right.

"I wouldn't mind," she told him.

He was asking for trouble and he knew it.

But her vulnerability spoke to him and the sadness in her eyes reached out to him, silently asking him for the only sort of comfort he could give her, comfort that transcended mere words.

Her breath caught in her throat as she felt him framing her face with his hands, felt his breath drifting along her face. Felt the almost fierce longing that had suddenly sprang up, fully formed, within her. Longing that reached out to him.

His lips came down on hers and this time, they both knew, there was no turning back.

Chapter Fourteen

Volleys of excitement shot through Danni.

It was too late to run for cover, too late to pretend that she didn't want this. She wanted it as much as she wanted to wake up tomorrow morning.

More.

Since her father had died, Danni had devoted herself exclusively to forging a future for herself, to making her cooking her own small cottage industry.

Other people with an aptitude for cooking or home-making had done it, putting their own spin on it, their own particular brand, and she felt that if she focused only on that, only on applying herself 24/7 to turning this goal into a reality, she stood a good chance of making it happen. That, in turn, would allow her to pay off the mountain of bills that all but haunted her.

She'd never thought she would take off the way she

had—which necessitated more energy, more focus and so much less "me" time for her.

Danni had almost forgotten that there was a "me" inside of her that required something other than working twenty-four hours a day. That knew how to do more than communicate with her audience, much as she cared about not disappointing them.

What she was feeling now, with Stone, opened a door for her to a place she'd ignored for so long, a place she hadn't even ever fully explored before.

A burst of sunshine went off inside of her as Stone's lips skimmed along the side of her neck, along the hollow of her throat. She could feel her insides quivering as anticipation began to swiftly build.

Without being aware of it, she dug her fingertips into the hard surface of his arms as she tried to anchor herself to him, to this wondrous sensation echoing through every fiber of her being. Glorying in it and wanting more, yet at the same time, being afraid of where this was taking her.

She felt disarmed, naked, vulnerable—and more alive than she'd been in far too long a time.

And then suddenly, as abruptly as it had begun, it stopped.

Stone stopped kissing her.

She felt him drawing away. Was something wrong? Had she done something to make him stop? Crossed some line she shouldn't have?

Confusion overtook her and she struggled to focus not just her eyes but her mind as well.

"Danni, are you sure?"

She saw his lips move, heard his voice echo in her head. The haze around her made it difficult for her to understand him at first.

It took her several moments to process the words. Several more to process the intent.

Dear God, was he being gallant? she wondered. She didn't know men like Stone existed outside of wishful thinking and maybe a few romantic comedies.

"And if I said no?" she asked, needing to hear what he would say.

Could he walk away from her, from this moment, just like that? Danni was fairly certain that she really couldn't walk at all right now. Her knees were weak and she'd all but turned into a swirling cauldron of pulsating needs. That made taking the smallest of steps all but impossible.

"If I asked you to, would you just back off?" she asked.

"Yes," he told her, his eyes caressing her even though his hands were still.

"Oh."

That meant he wasn't moved, didn't feel what she did. That he could take this or leave this at will. She could feel her heart sinking all the way down to her toes.

"It would kill me," Stone told her, "but I would." He framed her face again, his eyes intent on hers. "I won't lie. I really want you, Danni, but if you have the slightest bit of doubt, I'll stop. I don't want to force myself on you."

A laugh bubbled up in her throat. The rays of sunshine were back, stronger and brighter than they'd been before.

"What would you say to my forcing myself on you?" Danni whispered in his ear as the cauldron inside of her overflowed.

His mouth curved just a little, but she could feel the effects of his smile go all the way deep down into her soul.

"I'd say 'bring it,'" he told her.

And then there were no more words.

Words were next to impossible when he kissed her. Maybe she should have played harder to get, but the key word in that was *played* and she didn't want to play at this, didn't want to play any games at all. Games were for people who didn't feel what she was feeling. This sensation was far too serious for her to pretend otherwise, even if it meant saving face in the end.

She had no doubts that there would be regrets and possibly even soon. But Danni was certain that she'd regret not seizing this moment and making the most of it even more.

Heat soared through her as, wrapped in ardor, Stone and she moved from the barren kitchen with its patchwork of tile along one wall into the overly crowded family room with its makeshift, temporary obstacle course.

Danni was suddenly aware of the refrigerator directly at her back as Stone worked nothing short of magic with his lips along her torso, his fingers deftly removing more and more of her clothing as his clever mouth heated her skin.

Danni did her best to mimic his movements, letting

him take the lead only so that she could follow behind him almost immediately. Do what Stone did, create havoc within him the way he created it within her.

Her cool fingertips swept along his ribcage, pulling away the material that clung to his body by design as well as by his sweat.

Small, lethal tongues of fire licked at him as he felt her hands make short work of his T-shirt and his jeans, removing them almost as quickly as he was divesting her of hers.

And then, a short eternity later, there was nothing but skin between them. Stone trailed his hands along her body, memorizing curves and swells, committing every fraction of delicate inch to memory, lingering over every nuance he discovered.

Glorying in every involuntary sound conveying pleasure that she made.

Each time he heard one, he felt a corresponding surge of desire shoot through him, raising his need for the final moment. And yet, he wanted to keep it at bay for as long as he possibly could, wanting to revel in her, in holding her, in having her, for as long as he was able. Because, all things considered, there might not be another time and he needed to store up everything he was feeling against that eventuality.

The sofa, miraculously, didn't have a mountain of things piled onto its cushions. Somehow, it had escaped becoming a repository while everything else had been requisitioned to serve double duty when the kitchen appliances had moved in.

Consequently, that was where they ended up in their

blind dance of passion. On the sofa. Their bodies firmly molded against one another without an inch of space, or of sofa, to spare.

She found herself beneath him, with his weight just barely pressed against hers as he gathered her to him, covering every free inch of space on her body with his lips, his teeth, his tongue, effectively branding her from this day forward.

Danni tried to remain still, she really did, but she couldn't help herself. Twisting and turning, first into his kiss, then away as she savored what it was doing to her, was done almost involuntarily.

Done automatically.

Her body throbbing both in response to his actions and from a yet unfulfilled desire, Danni arched her back, pressing herself against him urgently. At the same time, she stroked any part of Stone she came in contact with, succeeding better than she'd possibly hoped when she heard him suddenly suck in his breath and he caught her hand.

She saw the look in his eyes and her heart all but stopped, then sped up again to the point that it felt as if it was challenging the speed of light.

Before she could say a word, she felt Stone parting her legs with his knee.

The next moment, they were joined together and another, far more intense, wave of heat flashed through her.

And then the race to the top, to the climax of their experience, began.

He set the tempo and she matched it, moving faster each time he did until finally, with his hands joined to hers just above her head, she felt the lightning explode and light the very sky in her world.

Felt the power seize and hold her before, all too soon, it began to recede.

Danni held on to it as long as possible, aware of just how tightly Stone was holding her to him, as if, were he able to, he would have absorbed her completely into himself.

A sense of loss nibbled away at the edges of her being when she felt the slight sag of his body against hers as Stone began the descent back down again.

Maybe it was selfish of her, but Danni wasn't quite ready to release the euphoria dancing through her. In a move more instinctive than anything else, she wrapped her legs around his torso, keeping him exactly where he was.

He raised himself up on his elbows and for a moment, just looked at her as he brushed the hair out of her face. She couldn't begin to gauge what he was thinking.

Stone smiled when he spoke. "Is that your way of saying you want more?"

"No," she answered, even though she *did* want more. "That's my way of saying I want to hold on to the sensation just a little bit longer."

About to roll off her and take his place right beside Danni, Stone remained where he was a while longer.

There were far worse places to be in the world, he thought with suppressed amusement. "Anything else?" he asked her.

She laughed then, a soft, gentle laugh that made him smile all the more. Things were going on inside of him that he didn't feel up to exploring. For now it was enough that there were these skyrocketing sensations going on in his body as a direct result of their close contact.

"You can relax," she told him. When he didn't move a muscle but continued looming over her, she added, "That means you can lie down next to me instead of staying where you are."

The next moment, he was rolling off her and gathering her to him. "Certainly didn't see that coming," he murmured under his breath.

"What?" She wasn't sure what he was referring to. "That I'd let you lie down?"

"No." He gently stroked her cheek, succeeding in arousing himself with the simple action. "That you'd let me—well, you know."

"There was no 'letting' going on," she assured him. "Whatever went on was done by mutual consent," she told him.

"Regrets?" he couldn't help asking her.

"Yes," she admitted. When she saw the sadness that entered his eyes, she was quick to add, "But not about this. Perhaps no one explained to you what the word *mutual* means?" she suggested.

He laughed and pulled her closer, then kissed the top of her forehead. "I know what it means. I suppose you'll want a friends-and-family discount on the work," he teased.

Danni raised herself up on one elbow, a part of her still rather stunned that she'd done what she had. Celibacy had become a way of life with her. "And just how does that work?" she teased back.

Stone did his best to keep a somber expression on his face as he said, "The closer a friend or a family member you are, the better the discount."

"I see." He was still flat on his back and she was looming over him on the limited space they were sharing. The ends of her hair were lightly flirting with his upper chest, tickling it. "And just how friendly am I allowed to get?"

"As friendly as you want," he told her solemnly—but his eyes were flirting with her the entire time.

"What if I want to be very, *very* friendly?" she pressed. "Then what?"

He pretended to think the matter over. And then he wove his fingers through her hair and said, "Then I just might wind up having to pay you for working on your house."

"Sounds tempting," she said, her eyes dancing as she regarded him.

"No, *you're* tempting," he corrected. Cupping the back of her head, he brought her face down closer to his. "So tempting that you'd probably be banned in at least seven Southern states," he theorized.

"How about you?" she asked. "Are you thinking about banning me?"

He slowly moved his head from side to side, his eyes never leaving hers. "My mother didn't raise any stupid children," he told her.

"Prove it," she whispered, her words feathering along his lips.

He laughed then, delighting in her, in the way she

made him feel. It had been a very long time since a woman had made him glad just to be alive.

"I thought you'd never ask," he told her, bringing her closer to him again.

It amazed Stone that he could want her again so soon, that he would be ready to make love with her all over again so quickly on the heels of what they had just done together.

He thought he knew his limitations, thought he knew himself as well as any man could know himself. But being with Danni had created a whole new set of parameters for him, parameters that both surprised him and pleased him at the same time.

He had no idea, at this moment, where any of this was going. All he knew right now was that he wanted her and that, for the first time in a very long time, he didn't feel as if there was a part of him that was empty, a part that was conspicuously missing. Maybe he wasn't exactly complete, but he wasn't empty, either.

And more than that, he realized as he began the journey back to paradise, he was happy.

Chapter Fifteen

"Happy" was a dangerous state to be in, Stone thought the next afternoon as he attempted to finish what he'd scheduled to be done for today.

He was hurrying. He wanted to be gone by the time Danni came home. The less temptation, the better.

"Happy" made you blind to the inevitable and set a man up to take a fall. And if ever a man was getting set up for a fall, it was him.

He *knew* there was no future for the two of them; he'd been here before. Granted, Danni was a far warmer person than Elizabeth had been, but they were both professional women, both smart and attractive—and Danni was a budding celebrity to boot. And he, he was a former aerospace engineer with a general contractor license who didn't talk all that much.

He just wasn't on the same level, the same rung in

society as Danni. Eventually that would hit her and become important enough to move to center stage even if it didn't seem that way now. He had nothing to offer her and he knew it. She outearned him and while that wasn't a problem for him, down the line it just might turn into one for her.

Elizabeth, he knew, was acutely aware of the fact that she earned more money than he did. She'd even mentioned it a couple of times in passing. The most notable time was when she'd talked about sending Ginny off to a "proper" private school, to use her words. She'd quickly followed that up by saying she knew he probably didn't have the money for that, given his job, but she did and she was quite willing to "lend" him the money so that Ginny could receive a decent education.

Though he'd tried to deny it to himself at first, it became very apparent that this was less about Ginny and more about her and how it would reflect on her to have a stepdaughter who went to public school.

After that incident, he was forced to acknowledge two things. One, Elizabeth apparently wanted to send his daughter away once they were married—something she'd obviously taken for granted despite his "station in life." And two, she did consider herself and what she did superior to what he did and consequently, to him.

After that, even if Danni hadn't come along, their relationship was scheduled for termination.

After measuring, he hung the last two tiles on the wall. He'd made a mistake last night. A glorious one, but a mistake nonetheless. To make certain that he wasn't tempted again—because the very thought of Danni sent him headlong into the land of heated desire—Stone decided that it was best not to be around her any more than was absolutely necessary. He only had so much willpower and no more.

Done! he congratulated himself as he rose to his feet.

Brushing off his hands, Stone looked around the immediate area to see what he needed to take with him. A quick assessment told him that he was going to need everything there tomorrow so there was no point in packing up.

Besides, it saved time.

Grabbing only the basic toolbox he brought with him to every job—a gift from Eva on their last Christmas together—he headed for the door.

As he put his hand on the doorknob, he felt it suddenly turning. The next second, the door was opening and Danni, her arms laden with bags and one large, opened box, came hurrying in.

The collision was inevitable. And jarring.

In that split second, Stone became acutely aware of her body and his own instant response to it. As if he needed to have that reinforced.

This would be a great deal more difficult than he'd foreseen, he thought with a suppressed sigh.

Steadying her even as he took a step back, Stone said, "You're home early."

Was that disappointment she heard in his voice, or just her imagination? Was she being insecure because she was still having trouble believing that something so perfect was happening to her at long last?

Damn it, Danni, you're overthinking things again. You plowed into him. He's just reacting to that.

"And you're leaving early," she noted, seeing the tool-box he'd dropped on the floor.

Suddenly feeling awkward, he said, "I got done ahead of schedule." It was only a partial lie; he'd gotten done early because he'd engineered it that way, but there was no way she could know about that. "So I thought I'd go home and spend some quality time with—um—with Ginny."

Great, forgetting your kid's name. If Danni needed any proof that you're less than brilliant, you just handed it to her.

If she noticed that he'd stumbled, she didn't show it. Instead, shifting the box and bags so she had a better grip, she told him, "Well, it looks like you can still get your wish."

Good, she wasn't going to try to make him stay, he thought. Maybe he'd overreacted as to the situation between them. Maybe she didn't feel the same way about him that he felt about her.

That was supposed to make him feel better, not worse, he upbraided himself. Just what the hell was the matter with him? Stone silently and impatiently demanded. Either he wanted her to be into him, or he didn't. He had to choose.

It was while he was confronted with this little dilemma that he realized she was all but completely overloaded with several bags and a large carton opened at the top.

And the most sensational aroma was wafting from it

all. "I'll just help you carry that in and then go," he said as he relieved her of the large opened box.

She looked up at him innocently. "I thought you said you wanted to spend some time with Ginny."

Confused, Stone followed her into the kitchen. The room now had a finished floor, so it could once more accommodate the table and chairs that had been there originally.

"I did—I mean—I do," he corrected.

"Then you'd better stay here because that's where they're coming," she told him matter-of-factly. Putting the bags down on the table she turned around to face him as she told him the rest of it. "I invited your sister and Ginny over for dinner."

"You're going to cook dinner now?" he asked, surprised.

She still didn't have a functioning stove, although that was next on his list of installations. Her new stove was currently in a box in her garage. He was waiting on the granite to be delivered for the counter. He knew, of course, the miracles she could accomplish with her hot plate, but that took time and it would be late before she would be finished.

"No, I'm going to *heat* dinner now, or at least keep it on a warming tray," she amended. "I made this at work before I left." She nodded toward the box and bags. "I'm kind of partial to the ovens we have on the set," she confessed. Which was why when she began ordering appliances to replace the ones she'd had before the remodeling began, she'd ordered the same brand of range and cooktop that was featured on her set. "This way Ginny and

Virginia won't have to sit around, starving and waiting for me to make a three-course meal one piece at a time on my struggling hot plate."

"When are they coming?" Stone asked.

He'd talked to Virginia earlier today and she hadn't mentioned anything about coming over for dinner. Why would she deliberately neglect to tell him that? Unless, it suddenly hit him, this was a last-minute idea on Danni's part.

The doorbell rang just then, interrupting his thoughts.

"Now," Danni said brightly, answering his question before she left the room.

She started to go to admit Virginia and Ginny. They were her buffer, because she really wanted to see Stone again, but at the same time, she didn't want either one of them to be tempted to repeat last night.

Not that she hadn't absolutely loved and thrilled at what happened between them. But an event of that magnitude stole away her ability to think clearly, causing her to focus on one thing and one thing only. And this was ever so much more complicated than "just one thing."

She didn't want him to feel pressured in the slightest while she needed to keep her intense, unvarnished reaction to him safely under wraps.

"You don't have to do this," he said just as she crossed the threshold.

She stopped and slowly turned around. Was he telling her, or actually ordering her not to do this?

"I know," she replied, flashing him a smile. "But I want to. From what you've told me, good, balanced meals aren't exactly a priority at your house."

With that, she hurried off before he could protest anymore. She didn't want to keep her two guests waiting any longer.

The second she opened the door, Ginny was quick to give her an energetic hug.

Virginia, on the other hand, hung back a little, which, Danni later discovered, that was rather foreign to her normal mode of behavior.

"You didn't have to invite me, too," Virginia told her. It was obvious that Danni had decided to make a play for her brother. Maybe she felt that the way to Stone was through his family.

Virginia smiled to herself. In that case, this woman was a very pleasant change from his last girlfriend. Elizabeth had made a point of looking down her perfectly shaped nose at her and the fact that she was self-employed, pulling in far less money than the other woman did.

But all this was supposition on her part and Virginia didn't want to seem as if she was presuming too much.

Danni laughed. "Well, it's certainly easy to see who you're related to. I'll tell you what I told your brother. 'I know I don't have to but I want to.' Come into the dining room while I still have a dining room where I can seat people," she said.

Taking Ginny's hand in hers, she led the way to the small room.

The only element that saved the dining room from arousing very real feelings of claustrophobia was that both sides of the room were open, leading into either the kitchen on one end or the living room on the other.

However the dining room itself was completely filled up by the scarred mahogany table with its six chairs. Of necessity, the table was placed at an angle so that people could pull out their chairs without slamming into walls on three of the table's four sides.

"Make yourselves comfortable," Danni told them. "Dinner will be ready in a few minutes."

Because she knew that form dictated it, Virginia felt she had to volunteer her services even though she was less than domestic.

"You need any help with dinner?" she asked Danni gamely.

Danni shook her head. "None whatsoever," she assured Virginia. "I prepared dinner at the studio. I just have to get all the covers off and make sure everything's the right temperature to serve," she told Stone's sister. "Besides, I wouldn't invite you to dinner and then put you to work cooking it. That wouldn't be right."

Virginia didn't bother hiding her relief. Turning toward her brother, she said, "I really like this woman, Stone," she said with sincerity as well as a bright, broad smile. Turning her head, she winked at her niece, who had been, after all, the start of it all when she'd brought her case to that Realtor. She'd had her doubts at first, but it looked now as if that woman was the genuine article. A matchmaker of the first caliber.

And neither one of these two people knew it, she realized. Somehow, that made this match all the more special.

"Me, too!" Ginny piped up, needlessly putting in her two cents.

No more than I do, Ginny, no more than I do, Stone said silently. Out loud he said to his daughter, "We already know that, kiddo."

If he didn't know better, he would have said that the female members of his family were actually trying to sell him on Danni.

As if they had to.

The real problem here was keeping his feelings under wraps—especially since he was so very tempted not to.

Had he been someone else, someone with fewer principles and more of an inclination to have a good time, he might have been tempted to go another route, to enjoy himself with Danni and live only within the moment without giving any thought to the future.

But that wasn't him.

He'd always done things with an eye to the future, ever mindful of the possible consequences of any action.

Stone already felt as if he cared more than he should for Danni. And he knew he was going to wind up paying for that. Because when the time came, and it would whenever he was finished with her renovations, they would inevitably go their separate ways.

He would move on to his next project and she would move on with the rest of her life. The life of a woman who had a bestselling cookbook to her name and a cable channel program that was swiftly growing in popularity. He'd heard somewhere that her audience was growing larger with each broadcast.

The last time he, Danni and Ginny had gone to look for new carpeting for her living room and bedrooms, the sales clerk had recognized her. And just like that, the man's clip, efficient manner transformed and he became a fawning fan who'd asked her for her autograph.

How could he possibly hope to compete with that? Stone wondered.

The simple truth of it was that he couldn't. He was destined to get lost somewhere in the background.

He was still mulling over this dark situation and its inevitable resolution when Danni returned with the main course and several side dishes. One that he was partial to, he noticed, while there were two others that would appeal to his daughter and his sister.

The woman thought of everything.

"Let me help," he offered, rising in his chair.

"You can help by eating," Danni told him, waving him back down with a plate of shredded hash browns covered in crushed cornflakes and mild, melted cheddar cheese. She placed the plate close to Ginny.

The asparagus, ham and cheese crepes found a home near Virginia while almond-sprinkled string beans were destined to keep Stone company.

The main course took the center of the table.

"Oh my God, what *is* this?" Virginia asked three minutes later as she took a second bite of the main course and rolled her eyes.

"Veal parmesan," Danni told her, carefully watching Virginia's reaction. It was hard to tell if that look was stunned appreciation—or aversion. "Why, is there something wrong with it?"

Danni had never made it a habit to taste her own food while she was preparing it, the way some other chefs did, so Virginia's question, voiced so quickly after she, Stone and Ginny had sat down to eat, made her a tad uneasy.

Still watching Virginia closely, Danni waited for more input.

"Wrong?" Virginia echoed incredulously. "Only in the sense that dying and going to heaven is wrong," she said with unabashed enthusiasm. "I've had veal parmesan once before, years ago, but I definitely would have remembered if it had tasted even a tiny bit as good as this does." She brought the next forkful to her mouth and it disappeared behind her lips. A contented sigh followed. "Definitely an out-of-this-world experience," she told Danni. "And you *made* this?" she asked, still unable to comprehend how a person could manage to make something so utterly spectacular.

"Yes," Danni replied with just the smallest touch of satisfaction and pride.

"Virginia," her brother said, a warning note suspended in the air.

"It's all right, Stone," Danni told him. "I really don't mind receiving positive comments. It's the negative ones that get to me."

"You get negative comments?" Virginia asked in utter disbelief.

"Sometimes," Danni answered.

Although, truthfully, she didn't remember the last time she had. Still, she wasn't one to take anything for granted and there had been a time when even though she'd always liked cooking, she hadn't been quite as good at it as she was now.

Stone listened in silence to the exchange between his

sister and the woman who made his body temperature rise just by smiling in his direction. The two, along with his daughter, seemed to be getting along rather well. From where he sat, the conversation seemed laid-back and completely unself-conscious, proceeding as if they had all known one other for years.

It filled him with a strange sort of melancholy, knowing that this was just temporary. That all too soon, this sort of contented air would all be in his past, a memory to be pulled out on occasion. When he finished the renovations to Danni's house, there'd be no more reason for them to see one another.

The renovations were what kept them together. It was the excuse he hid behind in order to see her.

Though it went against everything he believed in and practiced, Stone began to seriously entertain the idea of working just a little bit slower. Of getting less done each day, not more the way he'd initially planned.

It was the only way of hanging on to paradise a little longer. He knew he was just postponing the inevitable, but he didn't care. He was living within the moment and the moment contained Danni in it, which was all that really mattered to him.

Chapter Sixteen

It wasn't like him, but Stone found himself intentionally dragging his feet for as long as humanly possible.

He forced himself to work even slower after Ernie had called him. Prefacing his conversation by saying that he needed to pick up a little more extra work, Ernie asked him if he had anything available to throw his way. No job, Ernie told him, was too small. Then he'd asked him if work on "that cooking lady's house" was completed.

Ernie left him no choice.

It wasn't in Stone to lie, especially not to someone he knew and liked. So he'd said that he was still working on Danni Everett's house and that were a few things he could use a little help with completing.

Ernie was there the next morning, arriving before he did.

With Ernie working alongside of him, Stone did what

he could to stretch out the renovations on his end. He assuaged his conscience with the fact that Danni wasn't paying him by the hour, just by the project, so at least this wasn't costing her anything extra. And it was buying him some precious time.

But there was only so much he could do to stretch the process out without raising Ernie's suspicions and calling attention to the fact that he was moving like a man swimming in molasses.

The renovations, extensive as they were, were progressing smoothly with two pairs of hands working and completion was within sight.

Meanwhile, Stone's other campaign, the one whose theme was: look but don't touch, the one he'd come up with in hopes of keeping Danni at arm's length at all times, kept self-destructing at the starting line.

Most likely because his heart just wasn't in it.

Whenever they were alone together at the end of the day—after Ernie had left and Virginia and Ginny *weren't* coming over for dinner, all of Stone's attempts to strictly focus on his work just went flying out one of the newly installed double-paned windows.

Stone admittedly had gotten used to this, used to being with Danni, used to making love with her, to hearing the sound of her voice or catching a whiff of her perfume. In what amounted to an incredibly short amount of time, she had become part of his life.

Part of *him*.

Getting over Danielle Everett would be as hard as getting over an addiction.

Harder, because he couldn't hold an addiction in his arms the way he could hold her.

As if by mutual agreement, Stone noticed, they had both put off talking about it. Put off talking about life after the renovations were finally finished.

That's because there isn't going to be a life after the renovations are over, idiot, Stone upbraided himself. Danni was an intelligent woman. Which meant that she knew there was no future for them even better than he did. She was just too inherently polite to say as much out loud.

Maybe she even saw him as a guilty pleasure, he speculated. He certainly thought of her that way. Because she was. For him she was a very guilty pleasure and so much more.

No matter what he was doing, or what he was initially contemplating, thoughts of Danni would suddenly invade everything he did, everything he thought about.

With a flash of self-awareness, he came face-to-face with a truth that had somehow, without any warning, sneaked up on him.

He was in love with her.

Really in love with her.

"In love with a celebrity chef," he muttered under his breath, mocking himself as he laid there in her bed, watching her sleep.

They'd made love again at the end of the day, despite his very real determination—again—not to and afterward, she'd dozed off for a few moments.

"Hmm? Did you say something?" Danni asked, opening her eyes and looking at him.

Danni stretched languidly and he almost swallowed his tongue, becoming aroused all over again.

"What? No. I guess you must have dreamed it," he told her, the lie chaffing his conscience.

An embarrassed smile curved her mouth. "I must have dozed off," she realized aloud.

They'd made love, wonderful, exquisite love, and she'd been so very comfortable with him, she'd drifted off to sleep. It made her realize that he had become part of her life, a very integral part. How was she going to keep him that way?

"Can I make you something to eat before you go?" she asked, swinging her legs out of bed and then reaching down for her robe. The robe was usually at the foot of her bed, but it had managed to slide onto the floor, a casualty of their last lovemaking session.

"No," he murmured as he did his best to memorize her every movement. The way she stretched before she slipped the robe on, the way the silky material clung to her every curve. The way she breathed.

Everything.

Because it would have to last him a very long time.

Pulling her hair out from the back of her robe and letting it fall free, Danni turned around to look at the man who had so easily, so effortlessly infiltrated every corner of her life. "Are you all right? You sound a little strange." There was something different in his voice. She wondered if she should be worried.

The thought came out of nowhere.

Getting out of bed, in her estimation Stone pulled his clothes on like a man in a hurry.

"I'm finished," he told her, his voice still strained, distant.

"Finished dressing? Finished for the day? Or—finished with me?" she asked. There was something unsettling about his declaration and maybe she was being paranoid, but she needed him to clear it up.

To set her mind at ease.

He drew in a breath, as if to fortify himself, then said, "Finished with the renovations."

She pulled the robe tighter around her, suddenly feeling very cold despite the warm weather outside her bedroom window.

Was she being put on notice?

"There's nothing left to do?" she asked, feeling very nervous inside, like someone waiting for the bottom to drop out from beneath her feet.

He shrugged, trying to look casual about it even though there was nothing casual about the situation. "Just to collect payment on the final bill."

Was that it? Was that all what they had boiled down to? A final payment?

Money?

"And then what?" she heard someone with her voice ask.

Stone watched her for a sign, some indication that she wanted him to stay, to be something more than just this intense fling in her life.

He saw nothing.

Stone shrugged, feeling an emptiness already beginning to form in the pit of his stomach. "And then I guess I'll go on to another project."

"I see."

Not a word, not a single word from him about *them* as a couple. Nothing to indicate that any of this meant anything other than a hot time.

Suddenly unable to support her weight, Danni abruptly sat down on the edge of the bed.

There it went, she thought, the bottom. Dropping out from beneath her feet, sending her plummeting into an endless abyss.

"How much do I still owe you?" she asked, her voice echoing hollowly to her own ear.

The rest of your life. You owe me the rest of your life. Didn't you feel anything at all? How can you just sit there, sounding so controlled?

"I'll send you a bill," Stone said out loud.

"You do that," she told him. He was dressed and standing at her bedroom's threshold. *This is it, he's going. He's really leaving.* "Would you mind letting yourself out? I'm feeling a little tired."

Why wasn't she saying something? his mind shouted. *Because she's relieved, that's why,* a voice in his head mocked.

"No problem."

Yes, problem, Danni thought. *A huge problem. You just ripped out my heart and tap-danced all over it. Was this just another gig for you? Was that what I was to you, a 'project'? Nothing more than a pastime? While you were renovating my house, were you also renovating me just to satisfy your ego?*

She heard the front door closing downstairs. Hot tears stung her eyelashes.

The sound of the closing door was like a knife scraping across her heart, drawing blood. Danni shuddered as she began to cry in earnest.

Ginny came bouncing into the small bedroom Stone had converted into his office.

"Can I come with you when you go to work at Danni's house, Daddy? It's been a week and you haven't taken me." The little girl pouted as she looked at him.

He'd done his best to avoid talking about Danni and, up until now, Ginny hadn't asked anything. But he'd known it was just a matter of time before she did.

Time to clear this up and get it out of the way, he thought, resigned. "That's because I finished working on her house."

Ginny scrunched up her face. As if his words didn't compute. "You *finished* it? What does that mean?"

Ginny was far too gifted a child to not know what that meant, Stone thought, but he told her anyway. "That means that everything she asked me to do to the house is done and I won't be going over there anymore."

Ginny's smile drooped and she looked crushed. "But I thought you *liked* her."

This was just what he'd been afraid of. "That had nothing to do with it one way or another. Of course I liked her, Ginny. She was a nice lady."

"And that's all?" Ginny pressed, as if his words still weren't making any sense.

"What else is there?" her father asked, looking at her suspiciously.

Ginny seemed on the verge of blurting out something but instead shrugged and murmured, "Nothing, I guess."

Leaving the room, the disappointed little girl went out into her backyard. Planting herself on the swing her father had built for her, she began to think.

"Daddy!" Ginny called out, running to him as he let himself in the front door. It was the next day and she seemed impatient for him to come home. "Danni called and said you had to come right over."

Why wouldn't the woman call him on his cell, he wondered. "Why?" he asked suspiciously.

"She said her new shower was leaking all over the place and the water was raining in the kitchen."

He stared at his daughter for a moment, convinced she must have gotten the message garbled. "Water was 'raining' in the kitchen?" he repeated in confusion.

Ginny nodded her head vigorously. "From the shower," she said."

Stone thought a moment, trying to visualize what Ginny was telling him. "It's leaking through the floor?" he asked incredulously.

Ginny bobbed her head up and down again, no doubt grateful her father had filled in the blanks.

"Uh-huh. She said for you to come right away."

"Why didn't she call me on my cell?" he wondered again, this time asking the question out loud.

The small shoulders rose and fell in an exaggerated shrug. "I dunno. But she said to hurry."

"I'm going to call her—" he began, taking out his cell phone.

"She won't answer," Virginia said, coming into the room and to Ginny's rescue. The little girl had shared her impromptu idea with her. Virginia, impressed with the rather clever, if shaky, plan, decided there was nothing to lose by implementing it. "She said she was going to be too busy bailing. She said that you should just come right over."

"So you talked to her?" he asked, trying to get the story straight.

"After Ginny answered the phone, yes," Virginia confirmed. "Poor woman sounds frantic. Go rescue her," she ordered.

Stone sighed, shaking his head. He never took shortcuts with his work or with the materials he used. Something like this had never happened before, but he supposed there was always a first time.

"I'm on my way," Stone called out, hurrying out the front door.

Only after the door closed did Virginia and Ginny grin at one another as they high-fived.

That's odd.

Mystified, Danni placed the phone back in its cradle. Ginny had just hung up after telling her that her father had instructed her to call and say he was coming to check out the upstairs-bathroom plumbing.

Ginny hadn't been very clear, saying it was something about a leak, but that she wasn't very sure because her father was hurrying out the door when he asked her to call for him.

Danni supposed it was all part of the contract and

his standing behind his work. If only he was that conscientious about standing behind his silent promises...

Stop it. He left you. His choice, not yours. You're not to look needy around him, understand?

Danni told herself to remain aloof when he came over. But in her heart she knew it was going to be damn hard not to just throw herself at him.

Maybe this was just an excuse on his part to come see her. Maybe—

If it was an excuse, then he'd act on it and she'd know. No point in getting ahead of things and letting her imagination run away with her.

God, but she had missed him, Danni couldn't help thinking as she checked her makeup in the mirror—a mirror he'd picked out for her. One week and it felt like one eternity.

"That's it, Danni, play hard to get," she upbraided herself, annoyed at her lack of resistance to the very idea of Stone. "He walked away from you, you didn't push him out the door, remember?"

The pep talk wasn't working.

She almost jumped out of her skin when the doorbell rang a few minutes later. It took everything she had not to just fly to the front door to answer it. But she did hurry, stopping just at the door.

Taking a deep breath, she opened it. When she did, when she admitted him and looked up at Stone, her heart hurt.

"Hello," she said formally. Stiffly.

Oh God, maybe he should have sent Ernie in his place. The handyman was equal to anything and he would have paid Ernie well to stand in for him. To take this bullet to the chest for him.

Stone walked in and she closed the door behind him. "Well, I'm here."

Danni stepped away from the door and in front of him again. Was he playing some game? Why? Did he want to see how unhappy his walking out had left her? "I can see that."

He couldn't continue addressing his words to the air. Bracing himself, Stone turned around to face her. "So, where's the emergency?"

She looked at him, confused. "Excuse me?"

"The leak," he emphasized. "Where is it?"

Why was he almost shouting at her? "I don't know, you tell me. You're the one who wants to check it out."

Was this some kind of game? Why was she playing dumb like this, as if she didn't know why he was here? "Because you called about it."

Now Stone was just plain making things up. "No, I didn't."

Her indignation seemed sincere. Stone regarded her closely. "Ginny told me you called and said the upstairs shower was leaking."

What was he talking about? "Ginny called to tell me you were coming to check out the pipes," she countered.

Something didn't smell right to him. He needed to get to the bottom of all this. "That doesn't make any sense, why would I want to check out your pipes—"

"Maybe you *like* them," she shouted at him, her nerves utterly frayed.

Stone could only stare at her. "What?"

Danni threw up her hands. "Never mind, I'm babbling." And then, abruptly, it hit her. "We've been set up. Think about it," she stressed, waiting for the light to dawn on him.

It did—even though it seemed impossible. "By a four-year-old?" he asked in disbelief.

"A very intelligent four-year-old. 'Four going on forty.' Those were your words, remember?" Danni pointed out.

"Yeah, I do." He looked at her for a long moment. It seemed almost inconceivable to him to have missed someone as much as he had missed Danni—but he had. With every fiber of his being. "Maybe she saw something we didn't."

Danni's eyes met his. "Or saw something we did, but refused to acknowledge."

Stone was about to tell her that she wasn't making any sense—except that she was. What hadn't made any sense, he realized, was his accepting defeat before a single shot had been fired. That wasn't like him. Because Eva's death had devastated him the way it had, it made him afraid of reaching out for what was right in front of him. That was no way to live. That wasn't life, that was as good as being dead and he wasn't going to accept it anymore. "Yeah, maybe that's it." He took a breath. "Danni, will you marry me?"

Her mouth dropped open. They had just gone from *A* to *Z* without stopping at any of the other letters. "What?"

"Will you marry me?" he repeated more forcefully. "I don't care that you earn more money than I do, I don't care that you're famous and I'm not—and I'm betting that you don't care, either. I did you a huge disservice before, thinking those things mattered to you, that because I was a contractor, you'd think I had nothing to offer you, but I do. I have my heart to offer you, freely and unconditionally and nobody's going to make you a better offer than that or ever love you more than I do." He had all but run out of breath, getting all that out before Danni could interrupt him. "So, again, will you marry me?"

Stunned, Danni could only stare at him in silence.

The silence stretched out between them, growing longer. And more silent. Until it became unbearable for Stone to endure a moment longer.

He'd finally said it, finally put himself on the line. He'd given her the gist of why he'd left and told her how he felt about her. Told her that he wanted her to marry him.

But she wasn't saying anything.

Why wasn't she saying anything?

Had he presumed too much after all? Stone wondered nervously.

Wasn't she *ever* going to say anything?

"Danni, I'm standing here, naked, out on a limb," he told her impatiently. "Aren't you going to say *anything* to me?"

"Wait," Danni ordered, putting up a hand for him to hold his tongue. "I'm savoring the image of you standing there, naked." Unable to maintain a straight face any longer, she burst out laughing. She felt like hugging the immediate world. "What do you want me to say?"

He was through beating around the bush. "'Yes' would be nice."

She smiled again, a softer killer of a smile. "Yes would be very nice," she agreed. Threading her arms around Stone's neck, she looked up into his eyes and said, "So yes. I say yes. Yes, I will marry you. Yes!" Her voice grew louder in volume each time she said the all important word.

Laughing, he pulled her closer to him. "And now you can stop saying it." And just to insure that she understood, he sealed his lips to hers.

Danni stopped saying yes verbally, but she continued saying it in other ways—just so that there would be no misunderstanding.

* * * * *

"Don't break any rules on my account."

"Not to worry. But there is something I plan to do on your account."

"Don't do me any favors."

"Actually it's myself I'm concerned about." He picked up his ice cream again and started eating. "It seems the people here in town are all very protective of you. To win their hearts and minds I need to prove myself to you, earn your friendship. And that's exactly what I intend to do."

"Good luck with that." She struggled for a flip attitude, but was pretty sure it didn't work, what with her heart pounding so hard. "I've built up an immunity to nice, charming men."

"Then it's a good thing I'm not nice or charming."

THE DOCTOR
AND THE
SINGLE MUM

BY
TERESA SOUTHWICK

First published in Great Britain 2013
by Mills & Boon, an imprint of Harlequin (UK) Limited,
Eton House, 18-24 Paradise Road, Richmond, Surrey TW9 1SR

© Teresa Southwick 2012

ISBN: 978 0 263 90126 9
ebook ISBN: 978 1 472 00506 9

23-0713

Harlequin (UK) policy is to use papers that are natural, renewable and recyclable products and made from wood grown in sustainable forests. The logging and manufacturing processes conform to the legal environmental regulations of the country of origin.

Printed and bound in Spain
by Blackprint CPI, Barcelona

Teresa Southwick lives with her husband in Las Vegas, the city that reinvents itself every day. An avid fan of romance novels, she is delighted to be living out her dream of writing for Mills & Boon.

To my husband, Tom.
I love you—first, last, always.

Chapter One

"I really like what I see."

Adam Stone wasn't just talking about the apartment for rent. The same applied to the pretty lady renting it. Jill Beck was hot, and not just because of all that curly red hair. The thought of asking her out crossed his mind, but that wasn't why he was here. A truck with his stuff was on the way from Dallas to Montana and he needed to find a place to live here in Blackwater Lake before it arrived.

"Isn't this a little too small for you, Dr. Stone?" When Jill settled her brown-eyed gaze on him, he momentarily lost the power of speech.

The two of them were standing in a spacious living room. One window looked out at a dense forest of evergreen trees, and the other had a view of the wide expanse of sparkling blue water known as Blackwater Lake. Only the woman in front of him was a better view than either.

"Call me Adam."

He glanced at the body of water that gave the town one hundred miles north of Billings, Montana, its name. Then he looked around the apartment again. It seemed like just what the doctor ordered. The unit had an eat-in kitchen plus two bedrooms and baths. The walls were painted a light olive-green and trimmed with wide white baseboards that butted up against the pinewood floor. Crown molding highlighted the nine-foot ceilings.

The stairs up to this apartment were located to the side of her front door. He'd seen her place and it was identical to this one, although her walls were painted a particularly sunny shade of yellow that was appealing. He'd thought it suited her, until he turned serious about becoming her tenant. Wariness now replaced her cheery expression.

He folded his arms over his chest and looked down at her. "I'm a single guy. How much room do you think I need?"

"I have a feeling it's more than you can find in my upstairs." The clouds swirling in her beautiful eyes definitely wouldn't drop precipitation in the light-to-moderate range.

Adam could tell he was in for a hard time. A family practice doctor learned to listen, note verbal cues and read between the lines. He was a really good family practice doctor and knew her jeans were in a knot about something. Maybe when they'd climbed the stairs she'd caught him checking out her butt.

It was in his top five, hovering around one or two in the shapeliest category. He was a guy and guys were hardwired to notice girls, especially pretty ones. As far as looks, Jill Beck wasn't in the top ten, but there was something about her. And not just her chest. Yeah, he'd noticed that, too, but had been very careful to look at her face during this conversation.

The positive part of that was appreciating the cute splash of freckles on her upturned nose. But admiring her butt and the freckles on her face wasn't a hanging offense, so he was at a loss about what was bugging her.

Talking was the best way for him to find out. "If I was a family man instead of a family practice doctor, your upstairs would present some space challenges. But that's not the case. I was told it's the best place to rent and I can see why."

"Someone at Mercy Medical Clinic told you about me?"

"Yes." The retiring doctor he was replacing had given him the scoop. Along with two thumbs-up from the receptionist and the nurse.

"Have you looked anywhere else?" she asked.

"I have," he admitted. "But there's not a lot available."

"There are a couple of houses," she said helpfully. "And the Blackwater Lake Lodge probably has a room until you find just what you're looking for."

"Yeah. But the houses aren't as convenient to town and the clinic. The lodge—" He shrugged. "I want to settle somewhere. By process of elimination, that puts this property in the lead."

"Lucky me." Her tone struggled for upbeat but fell way short.

Adam could feel his stubbornness kicking in, and that wasn't necessarily a good thing. "I'd like to rent your apartment, Miss Beck."

If she noticed he didn't call her Jill, she didn't say anything. She shrugged. "The lease is on my desk. I suggest you read it before making a final decision."

There was a warning in the words, but he followed her downstairs to the computer desk tucked into a corner of her living room. This furnished twin of the upstairs apartment gave him an idea how homey it could be.

A chocolate-brown sofa sat in front of the fireplace with a flat-screen TV on the wall over it. The couch partitioned the room into work and relaxation spaces and with warm touches in both. Brass lamps with scalloped shades on tables. In framed pictures covering the walls he recognized the lake outside and the surrounding mountains. Photographs were everywhere. On the desk beside the computer was one of Jill with a little boy whose curly red hair gave a clue who his mother was. As far as he could tell, there were no photos of the boy's father.

She handed him the paperwork. "Look it over carefully."

Adam didn't need a microscope or a magnifying glass to see that the terms of the agreement favored the landlady. Big-time.

"I wasn't aware that this was the down payment on purchasing the property."

"A landlord needs some safeguards," she explained.

If she was a single mom, that would account for the financial safeguards stipulated in the agreement. "That's quite a hefty security deposit."

"But necessary."

"And this penalty for early lease termination seems excessive in addition to spelling out that a tenant is on the hook to pay the agreed-upon rent for the duration of the contract or until an alternative renter is secured."

"Also necessary," she said. "The costs of cleaning and painting between renters adds up. Then I have the costs of advertising to fill the vacancy on top of the lost revenue."

"But I'm not going to skip out on the rent."

"That's what they all say." Even if the tone hadn't given her away, skepticism was there in the expression on her face. "This covers the winter months. In spring and summer there's a better chance of getting a tenant who sticks."

"What makes you so sure I won't?"

"The last doctor took off after the first snow."

"I'm not the last doctor."

"Right," she said. "The clinic will replace you when you go."

"That's not what I meant and I'm pretty sure you know it."

"Doesn't make it any less true."

He leaned a hip against her desk. "Are you trying to talk me out of renting from you?"

"Is it working?" she asked, neither confirming nor denying the accusation.

"Correct me if I'm wrong, but real estate is business. It feels like you're making this personal."

"It's both. I already spelled out the business part in the contract." Her gaze rested on the photo he'd noticed moments ago. "I'm a single woman with a child. That gives me a personal interest in who lives upstairs. It's why I do a pretty thorough background screening before even showing the place to a prospective tenant. The town sheriff is a good friend of mine."

He guessed that she'd hoped to turn up something that would give her a reason to tell him no. As a businesswoman she needed to show the empty apartment to everyone who didn't have a black mark on their record. But he asked anyway. "Did I pass the test?"

Her smile seemed reluctant, but that didn't detract from its beauty. "I usually take families' testimonials with a grain of salt, but yours are different."

"I'm aware of that, but why do *you* think so?"

"When your dad is a Nobel Prize–winning economist and your mother a nationally known biomedical engineer, not to mention your brother is one of the country's top cardiac surgeons, that tends to carry some weight."

"You have no idea." The burden of being related to the gifted and geekish had finally worked in his favor.

"And you're a family practice doctor." There was a thoughtful expression on her face as she tucked a strand of curly red hair behind her ear. "Did your folks bring the wrong baby home from the hospital?"

"I get that a lot." Long ago he'd learned not to take it personally. His line of work was exactly what he wanted. "I'd probably have done a DNA test except I look like my dad and I have a twin sister."

"Is she a doctor, too?"

"Yeah. Rocket science. She works for NASA."

"Wow. Your family has some very impressive credentials," she commented.

"So you know my background. That doesn't explain your hard-line rental policy."

"If you think about it, it kind of does."

Adam looked at her. "How?"

"I have to wonder why you're here at all."

"I'm not sure I understand what you're asking." Actually he understood exactly what was on her mind.

He'd fielded lots of endless questions about his career and life choice, especially from the overachievers in his family. The perception was that he wasn't as good if this was the best medical specialty he could do. His ex-wife had no problem dumping him when he'd made the decision. It wasn't flashy enough for her and Adam was still bitter enough to make Jill say straight out what he knew she was thinking.

"Blackwater Lake is a small town."

"But growing," he pointed out.

"Yes." There was a sexy little dent in her chin that was more pronounced when her full lips were pulled tight. "But right now it's not very big. Summer is winding down and winter comes early in northern Montana. You could have your pick of warm places to practice medicine."

Someone, probably his mother, had shared information about offers he'd fielded from Los Angeles, San Francisco, Miami and Dallas, where he'd been working until recently.

Taking any one of them in a major metropolitan area would have gone a long way toward reassuring his family about what they considered his lack of ambition.

He'd accepted a long time ago that they would never understand why he wanted to treat the whole person, whole families, rather than be a world-renowned expert in a single body part. If the people who knew him best didn't get it, there was no way to explain it to a woman with a chip on her shoulder.

Adam decided to try anyway. "I found out early in medical school that factors beyond disease and diagnosis affect an individual's health. Treating the whole patient and not simply specializing in a certain organ of the body was important to me. Knowing the people in their world factors into the medical protocols. I like people."

"That's very noble of you." She sounded sincere and hopefully impressed. "But why here?"

"I came to a camp in Blackwater Lake. My parents were busy and gone a lot, so keeping us kids busy and out of trouble was important. I fell in love with this place and never forgot it. Being part of a community is important to me. So, when an opening came up in the clinic, I applied."

"I'm guessing you spent more than one summer here at camp?"

"Every one for nine years." He nodded emphatically. "Dallas is great, but big. Seeing the contrast between there and here convinced me that small-town life was just my cup of tea. I want to live and work here in Blackwater Lake."

"That's easy for you to say when the weather is beautiful, like it is today. But what about when you have to fight your way to the clinic through a blizzard?" She held up a hand when he opened his mouth to protest. "I can tell you what happens. You change your mind about small-town life. You run, not walk, to the closest airport and it's not all that close.

You get on a flight to the nearest big city and guess who's left holding the bag—or the lease. I have a family to support."

That sounded like confirmation that there was no ex helping her out with raising her son. Someone had obviously done her wrong, so he had to sign a legal contract to give her peace of mind.

Adam didn't react well to negative vibes, and Jill Beck had *N-O* with a capital *N* coming off her in waves. That made him want to challenge her and he could feel his stubborn streak going radioactive. It didn't always lead to the best personal decisions, and he had the only divorce in the family to prove the point. But the obstinate side always made his life interesting.

"I still want to rent your apartment, Miss Beck."

Her gaze narrowed on him. "You do realize what kind of money is involved?"

"In spite of my less challenging career choice, I did make it through medical school. I can do the math." He looked around at the living room with fresh flowers and more than one oval-framed needlepoint sampler. "This is charming. And the cost is not a problem."

"All right, Doctor—"

"If my personal check isn't satisfactory, I'd be happy to stop at the bank for cash or a cashier's check." He took a pen from her desk and signed the agreement. After handing it back he said, "You're going to be my landlady. It's time you started calling me Adam."

Adam.

Stone.

The name suited him, Jill thought. He was immovable like a rock. A tall, good-looking rock.

The man was her worst nightmare and he was settling in upstairs. The moving truck had brought his stuff and then rumbled away a while ago. On paper he was the perfect tenant. A doctor. Gainfully employed at Mercy Medical Clinic. He came from a prominent family. And the hefty check he'd given her had cleared the bank. Probably soared more than cleared. There was that prominent, wealthy family. But the doctor gig no doubt paid pretty well without help from the folks. That was the business part of her talking.

From Jill's personal perspective, he couldn't have been worse. Young. Too handsome for her own good. He reminded her of the actor who had played the most recent Captain James T. Kirk in *Star Trek*. She had a crush on that actor, and now his clone was living upstairs. Even worse, she liked him. He was funny and charming. Damn him.

None of that was even a problem—until he left. And he would. Like she'd told him, they all left. She should be used to men walking away from her by now, but apparently one never quite got the hang of having one's hopes crushed into dust. It still smarted. But she was a big girl and understood what was going on. Her son was just a little boy and she wouldn't stand by and allow a good-looking tenant to trample on C.J.'s feelings again.

Speaking of her son…

Jill pushed away from her desk and rubbed her eyes after looking at a computer screen for so long. This economics assignment for her online class had taken more time than anticipated. "C.J.?"

There was no answer and the house was too hushed and silent. He was a six-year-old boy, not a cat burglar, and quiet wasn't hardwired into him.

"C.J., are you hiding?" She stood, then listened for the giggling, a clue there was an unannounced game under way.

The only sounds came from overhead—faint footsteps and a thump. Doctor Dazzling was putting things away. Should she offer to help? Not if she was smart.

She walked down the hall to her son's room, which was where she'd last seen him, playing with action figures now abandoned on the beige area rug. His bed was made, the lumps and bumps in the superhero spread evidence of the small hands doing the big job. The boy attached to those hands was nowhere in sight.

"C.J.?" Jill opened the closet to make sure her mischievous little man wasn't playing with her.

The interior looked as if a clothing and toy store had thrown up. When he was ordered to put his stuff away, this was where C.J. stashed everything. But if he were hiding in here, there would be giggling and wiggling. His skill level for holding still was on a par with keeping quiet.

Now she was starting to get concerned. He couldn't maintain the cone of silence for very long, but sneaking out of the house without being heard was something he was pretty good at. If he'd left the premises, she knew where to find him.

She walked over to her desk, picked up the phone and hit speed dial. It rang several times before the man who worked her marina business on the lake answered. "Blackwater Lake Marina and Bait Shop."

"Brewster? It's Jill."

"Hey, boss. What's up?"

"Tell C.J. it's time for him to come home. And he's in big trouble." She half sat on the edge of her desk.

"I'd be happy to except he's not here."

Her stomach knotted with worry. "Are you sure? Maybe he sneaked in quietly. You know how he loves to jump out and scare you."

"That's a fact. But I've been out front all afternoon straightening up. No way he could get by me."

"Okay. Thanks."

"You want me to look for him?"

"No. I'm sure he's in the house somewhere. Bye, Brew."

No need to panic. This was probably a new unannounced game, something he did frequently. But from the moment he was born she'd used all her senses to keep tabs on her little guy, and sight was the one that brought her the most comfort. Seeing him safe and sound always made her breathe a sigh of relief. She badly wanted that sigh now.

Overhead she heard more footsteps followed by another thump. Her eyes narrowed as a thought formed. "He wouldn't dare—"

Jill walked out her front door and turned right, then went up the stairs and knocked on her new tenant's door. Moments later he opened it and smiled. Her stomach boomeranged down to her toes and back up. It had happened the first time she saw him, but she'd been sure the reaction was a one-time deal and was now under control. Apparently it needed some more work.

"Hi," he said. "What's up? Do you need more money?"

"Not until next month." In spite of the niggling guilt she smiled. Might as well be friendly. No way she could avoid dealing with him. "Are you settling in okay?"

"Yeah. Thanks for asking." His gaze sharpened a fraction as he studied her. "Is something wrong?"

Jill figured either he was superobservant, or she should never try to improve her financial situation by playing poker.

"Actually," she said, "I was wondering if you'd seen my son."

"Is he about this high?" Adam put his hand about C.J.'s height. "Curly red hair? Wearing jeans, sneakers and a Spider-Man T-shirt? Looks a lot like you."

"A perfect description. That means you've spotted him recently." The knot of anxiety in her stomach loosened.

"Yeah. He's been helping me put things away."

"You should have sent him home." The anxiety snapped

back, but for a different reason. "He knows better than to pester our renter."

Adam folded his arms over his chest. There was something so blatantly masculine in the movement that her mouth went dry. Until that moment, Jill hadn't considered how long it had been since her last date. Apparently too long. Might be time to do something about that.

"By 'knows better,' do you mean he had specific instructions not to come upstairs?"

She nodded. "The exact words were that there would be dire consequences if he bothered you."

"Then he's off the hook."

"How do you figure?" she asked.

"Because he's not bothering me."

Adam Stone was covering for C.J., she realized. It was protective and sweet. Unfortunately, she couldn't afford to give in to that "aww" feeling. It would open the door for the "oh, damn" feeling when he left. She was the only one C.J. could count on. It was *her* job to protect him.

The sound of small sneakers running sounded just before the little guy appeared beside the big guy. "Hi, Mom. I didn't sneak out and help Brew at the dock because I had to help Adam."

There were so many things wrong with that statement she didn't know where to start, but he was gone before she could say anything. And that was classic C.J. They needed to have a conversation, but before that she needed to set boundaries with Adam. When she did, it would be best if her son was out of earshot.

"He didn't tell me where he was going," she started.

"You were worried."

"Of course." It was probably an educated guess, because her background check confirmed he was a bachelor without children. He had no frame of reference to empathize with a parent.

"I should have asked if he had permission." There was annoyance in his expression that looked to be self-directed. "It won't happen again. You have my word."

"That's very much appreciated," she said sincerely. "But here's the thing. Probably it's better for C.J. if you don't encourage him to hang out with you at all."

Adam leaned a broad shoulder against the doorjamb. "Are you telling me to stay away from him?"

"No. Not exactly." Unable to meet his gaze, she looked down at the wood floor on the landing outside his door. "Kind of."

"I expect you've got a good reason." The deep tone dripping with sarcasm said he didn't believe there was such a thing.

"I'm a single parent—"

"So you said."

"And C.J. is an active, outgoing little boy."

That made him smile. "He's a really great kid."

"I know." She smiled, too. Then grew serious. "He's a great kid who badly wants a man in his life to hang out with."

"Just my opinion as a family practice doctor, but that's perfectly normal."

"It's probably not a good idea for him to get attached to you." She met his gaze. "That's just my opinion as his mother."

"Because you think I won't stick."

"Exactly. I just don't want him to get his little heart broken again—" A lump of emotion lodged in her throat and it was mortifying in front of this man.

"The last doctor," he guessed.

His parents and siblings weren't the only smart ones in

the Stone family. She was trying to be vague, but apparently he had a gift for connecting the dots. "Yeah."

"I wouldn't hurt him, Jill." The tone was extraordinarily gentle.

"Not deliberately," she said. "I know that. But it concerns me."

"I admire your impulse to protect him and will do my best to help you out."

Jill hadn't realized she was spoiling for a fight until he didn't give her one. She appreciated the compliment about her maternal instincts, and the admiration went both ways. He seemed like a good guy, but another seemingly good guy had once stood right where he was now. That guy broke his promise and her son's heart. Jill's had been nicked, too.

"Thanks for understanding." What else could she say?

"I'm still not going anywhere." Before that could be challenged, he called out, "C.J.? Your mom says it's time to go home."

"Do I have to?" The question was followed by the *tap, tap* of running sneakers. The boy stopped beside Adam. "My tummy isn't tellin' me it's time for dinner yet, Mom."

"It's still time to go home," she said firmly, noting the way Adam's mouth twitched as he struggled not to laugh.

"Why?" the boy asked.

"Because you've bothered Adam enough for one day."

"I didn't bother him. Did I?" C.J. looked up, the beginnings of hero worship on his freckled face.

Adam glanced at her, caught between a rock and a hard place. Then he answered without actually answering. "Your mom has her reasons. If I were you, I'd do what she says."

"Okay." Then a thought chased away his disappointment. "Can Adam have dinner with us?"

"It's Dr. Stone," she corrected the little boy.

"He said to call him Adam," C.J. protested.

"I did," he confirmed. "You could take lessons."

"Right." Jill smiled. "How about a compromise, kiddo? What do you think of Dr. Adam?"

"I think he's cool," C.J. answered.

"I meant that's what you should call him. Remember, respect for your elders."

"Moving day is always tough," Adam said, "but I didn't feel quite so old until just now."

"Can Dr. Adam have dinner with us?" the relentless child persisted.

"I don't think so, kiddo." She looked at Dr. Adam, and there must have been pleading in her eyes.

"Not tonight, buddy." Adam's expression was half amused, half regretful. "I still have a lot of boxes to unpack."

Jill appreciated his cooperation and knew what was coming from her son. "No, you can't help, C.J."

"Aw, Mom—" Hope filled his brown eyes. "What about when he's done unpacking? He might get lonesome."

"You're pushing it, mister. Downstairs. On the double." She glanced over her shoulder and thought Dr. Adam might have been looking at her butt.

It was a nice thought, but a waste of his time and energy. A crush on the movie star type notwithstanding, she would never let Adam Stone be her type.

Jill walked C.J. down the stairs and when they got to the bottom she saw Brewster Smith walking up the path. He stopped in front of her, on the covered porch.

"Just came by to see if you found C.J." The man was in his fifties and had a full head of gray hair and a beard to match. Very mountain-man-looking. He was an employee, but more important, her friend. "I see you did."

"Yes, he was—"

"Hey, Brew," C.J. said. "I was helpin' Dr. Adam unpack

his stuff and he's got a lot! Mostly books. Really big, fat ones. He said they're too heavy for me."

Jill put a hand on her son's small shoulder. "I'm sorry if I worried you, Brew. He neglected to tell me where he was going."

"Figured that." The man's pale blue eyes narrowed. "If he had, you'd have put a stop to it."

This man knew her better than anyone, knew how hard it had been when she'd been left behind by the doctor. He was the one who'd held her when she cried.

The door at the top of the stairs opened and heavy footsteps sounded on the wood tread behind them. There was only one person it could be.

"C.J.? You forgot these." Adam handed over Batman and Captain America action figures. He nodded at Brew. "Hi."

The older man's eyes narrowed on the new guy in town. "You're the renter."

"Yeah." He held out his hand. "Adam Stone."

"Brewster Smith," he answered, taking the offered hand. "Nice to meet you."

"Hope you still think that when I say what's on my mind."

"Okay. Shoot."

"This woman is like a daughter to me." Brewster's face was all warning, no warmth. "Treat her right or I won't be a happy man."

"You're already not happy," Adam pointed out cheerfully, apparently not intimidated at all.

"If you do anything to hurt her, I'll be a whole lot not happier. And that goes for a lot of folks in town, too." The older man's gaze never wavered, before he abruptly turned and walked down the front porch steps. At the bottom he headed in the direction of the marina.

"Nice guy," Adam said. "Straightforward."

"He's a good friend."

Jill was grateful for his friendship and something else, too. The town was circling the wagons around her. It wasn't the first time this had happened, but it still made her very happy. In the case of Dr. Adam Stone it made her incredibly grateful. He'd done nothing to anesthetize her attraction and she'd need all the protection those circled wagons could give her.

Chapter Two

Adam had just seen his last patient on his first day at the clinic. He wouldn't say this was the worst day he'd ever had as a doctor, but moving from Texas and unpacking boxes had been a piece of cake compared to cutting through the glacial attitude of the people he'd seen today. Of course none of those people had been C. J. Beck, who couldn't have been cuter or friendlier, unlike his mom. Except for the cute part. Jill was more than cute. And that was nothing more than a guy's appreciative take on a very pretty, very sexy woman.

The surroundings were different from any office he'd ever worked in. Mercy Medical Clinic was set up in a large Victorian house that had been donated to the town years ago. The kitchen had been turned into an outpatient lab and the spacious living room now had sofas, chairs and tables for a waiting area. Bedrooms had been converted to exam rooms, and closets held medical and office supplies. That morning he'd had the two-cent tour from nurse Virginia Irvin, who was no warmer than the patients he'd seen. She was like a glacier in scrubs.

He grabbed a cup of coffee from the break area in the small alcove near the back door that was once a mudroom, then went back down the long hallway, past the exam rooms and to his office. It was time to catch up on paperwork.

So as not to keep patients waiting too long, there hadn't been time to do more than look at the updated medical information form he'd asked each patient to fill out and skim the chart for drug allergies. Now he wanted to look at all the information on each person he'd seen, including notes from the physicians who'd come before him. Including "the last doctor."

Those words worked on his nerves like something in his eye that wouldn't come out. Everyone he'd seen today had said it and in exactly the tone Jill used, the one that put him in the same slimy subspecies as the physician who'd run out on her and the rest of the town.

"There you are, Doctor."

He looked up from the stack of charts on his desk. Mercy Medical Clinic's nurse stood in the doorway. "Hi, Ginny."

"It's Virginia."

Apparently only to him, because everyone who wasn't gum on the bottom of her shoe called her Ginny. Somewhere in her late fifties or early sixties, she had silver hair cut in a pixie, blue eyes that missed nothing and no filter between her brain and her mouth. At least one knew where one stood with her. In his case, he was pretty sure she wished he was standing in Alaska. She was short on stature and long on attitude.

"Can I ask you something, Virginia?"

"Thought doctors knew everything. Like God." She folded her arms over her chest, and the body language felt like a *yes* to his question, so he continued.

"We just pretend to know everything. It makes the patients feel better." Maybe self-deprecation would thaw her out.

"Uh-huh."

Maybe not so much. "As a boy I spent a lot of summers here in Blackwater Lake and folks seemed a lot friendlier."

She looked down at him. "We're not in the habit of being mean to kids, especially ones who are visiting."

"So the friendly pill wears off when that kid grows up and moves here?"

"Something like that."

He was the new guy and she knew this clinic and everyone who used it inside and out, by all accounts an excellent nurse who would be difficult to replace. So he hid his frustration when he asked, "Can you be more specific?"

The gaze she leveled at him could laser a person's heart out. "It would help if you looked less like the good-looking actor in that space movie and more like Quasimodo."

Huh? There was a compliment in there somewhere, but he'd need a scalpel to remove it. "I'm not sure what you mean by that."

"Then I'll explain." She moved farther into the room. "If you were ugly as a mud fence and didn't rent a place from Jill Beck, folks here in town would give you the benefit of the doubt. But that's not the case. The last doctor—"

"Didn't stick," he interrupted. "Jill mentioned that."

"She's one of ours," the nurse continued. "Her mother was my best friend since third grade. The last thing I said to Dottie before she died was that I'd watch out for her little girl and her grandson."

Adam remembered what Brewster had said and figured Virginia and the patients he'd seen today were some of the folks who'd be a whole lot not happy if Jill got hurt.

"What happened to her mom?" he asked.

"Breast cancer." The woman's mouth pulled tight as if her lips would tremble without the control.

"I'm sorry."

"Me, too."

"The thing is, you don't need to protect Jill from me," Adam assured her.

"Uh-huh."

The sarcastic tone said there was nothing he could say to convince her, so he wasn't going to waste his breath trying. "Did you want something?" At her blank look, he added, "You were looking for me?"

"Right." The puzzled expression disappeared. "You've got one more patient. Little boy with a fever and sore throat. His daddy sweet-talked Liz into letting him come by."

Liz Carpenter was the clinic receptionist, a pretty young woman who apparently didn't need protecting from the big, bad outsider.

"Is he here?" Adam asked.

"Exam room one," the nurse answered.

"I'll be right there."

"He's ready for you." She turned and left his office.

It had been a warm, September day in Blackwater Lake, Montana, but Adam felt like digging out his winter parka before seeing the patient. He left his office and walked back down the hall. Exam one was the farthest away and the others were empty, so it wasn't hard to do the math. New doctor hazing, with a generous dose of warning tossed in.

He pulled the chart from the plastic holder on the wall beside the door and read the patient's name. Tyler Dixon. The last name was familiar.

Before going in he read the medical information. Tyler was six, about the same age as C. J. Beck. Not allergic to anything. An otherwise healthy boy with a sore throat and fever. His father was Cabot Dixon, and Adam grinned as he walked inside.

The dark-haired, dark-eyed little guy sitting on the exam table looked exactly like the boy his father had been when Adam had met him years ago. The Dixons owned the ranch where he'd gone to camp every summer and the two had become friends.

He held out his hand. "Cab, it's good to see you again."

"Adam." The other man's smile was sincere and friendly, a first for the day. "Heard you moved here, but didn't think I'd have to see you in a professional way so soon."

"Your boy's not feeling well?"

"This is Tyler."

"I didn't wanna miss school, but my froat hurts," the child informed him. "And I don't like shots."

"Me either." Adam smiled as he studied the boy's feverish eyes and flushed cheeks. "Would it be okay if I just take a peek in your throat?"

"Just look?" The boy didn't trust him, but that had nothing to do with Jill Beck and everything to do with being six years old.

"I want to feel your neck, too, but it won't hurt."

"Promise?"

Adam crossed his heart and held up his palm. "Word of honor."

"Okay."

Beside the exam table on a metal tray, nurse Virginia had put out some things. He picked up the wooden tongue blade and the handheld light and told Tyler to say "ah." Then he ran his fingers over the boy's neck and asked the father, "Has he had a cough or runny nose?"

"No."

Adam took the stethoscope from around his neck and listened to the small chest and back. "Strong heartbeat. Good bilateral breath sounds. No wheezing from upper or lower lobes of the lungs," he said.

"What is it, Adam?"

"My guess is strep throat. It usually shows up late fall to spring, so this is early, but symptoms are classic, including yellow patches on the back of his throat. I'll swab it and we can do a rapid strep test to confirm."

After Cabot nodded approval, Adam promised the little guy a "good boy" toy, then rubbed a cotton swab in the back of his throat. When Virginia came into the room he asked her to do the test on the sample and Tyler went with her to pick out his reward. That gave Adam a chance to talk to the man who'd befriended him when they were boys.

"Don't worry, Cab. It's not serious. Strep usually goes away without treatment and only rarely turns into something more serious. I'll give you prescription for an antibiotic, but it's just a precaution."

"That's a relief." The rugged man clearly had a soft spot where his son was concerned, and that was as it should be. "Anything else I should do?"

"Make sure Ty gets over-the-counter meds for the fever and lots of fluids—soda in moderation, popsicles, juice and water." But Adam wondered about Cabot's wife. It was most often the mother who came in with a sick child. "So, when did you get married?"

"Six years, eight months ago." There was no mistaking the anger that slid, hot and intense, into those dark eyes. "And I got divorced right after Ty was born because she walked out. Left me with an infant and no idea how to take care of him. Still, he's the best thing she gave me and I have to thank her for him. Just an FYI, don't bring a city girl to Blackwater Lake. If you want to be happy for the rest of your life, make a local girl your wife."

"Had a wife once," Adam said. "Don't want another one, thanks."

"Want to talk about it?"

"No. You?"

"No." His friend smiled. "So, how's Blackwater Lake treating you?"

"Like a leper," he admitted.

"I heard you rented Jill Beck's apartment."

"Guilty. And apparently that's a hanging offense as far as people in this town are concerned, because I haven't even screwed up yet."

Cabot shrugged. "You're paying the price for the doctor who rented her place and then charmed and harmed her. Folks don't like it when an outsider dumps on one of their own."

"She's safe from me," Adam protested. "I just want to be part of the community. End of story. Honest."

"I believe you." The other man's expression was amused and sympathetic. "But you'll never belong until you prove you're not going to 'do Jill wrong.'"

"Tell me how to convince folks and I'll do it." Adam figured he'd take all the help he could get, especially from someone who knew the locals.

"You're on your own with that."

Before he could say more, Tyler came back into the room to show off his toy car and Adam was no closer to solving his problem. He liked Jill. He was attracted to her, but starting something was problematic. A single mom in Blackwater Lake would want promises and vows, and that was something he'd never do again.

To start anything he had no intention of following through on would make him no better than the last doctor, which would only drive the wedge deeper between him and the community. He didn't get through medical school being stupid, so somehow he'd find a way to live under her roof and not complicate the situation by getting personal.

The best approach was to take the advice he so often gave his patients. Give it time. Unfortunately, he *wasn't* patient.

Potter's Ice Cream Parlor wasn't busy on a weeknight now that the kids had returned to school from summer vacation. Jill was filling in for her friend Maggie and it was kind of a relief to be here as opposed to her own house where she couldn't stop thinking about Adam Stone and the fact that only a ceiling separated them. Glancing at the display case, she made sure none of the ice cream flavors needed a refill. Beside it, all the sundae toppings, including nuts, crushed candy and fruit, were all full.

In front of the counter, all the cute little chairs with heart-shaped backs were tucked neatly under circular tables. The walls were filled with brightly colored prints of candy sprinkles, nuts and cherries. Right behind the cash register was a photo of Maggie Potter and her husband, Dan, in his Army National Guard uniform, hugging and happy on the day they'd opened this place a couple of years ago. Now her husband was dead and Maggie was dealing with everything by herself. Jill was going to help as best she could.

There wasn't much to do, so she grabbed a damp rag and started to wipe down the stainless-steel counters. With her back to the front door she relied on the old-fashioned bell above it to alert her to a customer. When it rang she turned to see who was there.

"Hey, you two." She smiled at Norm and Diane Schurr, friends of her mom. He was about six feet five and thin, with white hair. His blonde wife was about a foot shorter and always watching her weight. "What'll you have?"

"Three scoops of vanilla in a cup with caramel and nuts," Norm said.

Like the retired school teacher she was, Diane gave him a stern look. "You're supposed to be watching your cholesterol."

"Okay, then," her husband said good-naturedly, "make it two scoops."

"Oh, for goodness' sake." His wife laughed and shook her head. "I'll have the nonfat cookies 'n' cream yogurt— a small."

"Coming right up." While Jill worked on filling their order she asked, "What's new?"

"Not much with us, but Brewster Smith says you filled your vacancy. Mercy Medical Clinic's new doctor." Diane's gaze was full of warning.

"It's true." Gosh darn it.

"The doctor is very good-looking," the woman added.

"You've met him?" Jill handed over Norm's sundae above the high glass of the display case.

"Had an appointment today for my checkup," he answered.

"We both did," his wife said. "The thing is, sweetheart, you shouldn't let a pretty face tempt you into letting your guard down again."

"Don't worry." She turned to the yogurt dispenser and depressed the handle to let the creamy stuff make a volcano-shaped mound in the cup. "Even if I weakened, I know I can count on good friends like you to pull me back from the edge."

"Darn right," Norm said.

"That'll be seven dollars and three cents," she said.

Norm put down his cup and reached for his wallet. "It's too bad."

"I know, but Maggie wouldn't make any money if the order was free," Jill teased.

"Not that," he said, waving away her words with a twenty-dollar bill in his hand. "It's a shame you can't go after the doc. He seems like a real nice young man."

So did the last doctor, until he left. *Fool me once, shame on you. Fool me twice, shame on me,* Jill thought.

After handing over change, she said, "So, how did your appointment go? You guys doing okay?"

"Pretty good," the man answered. "I'm not gettin' any younger, but I got a strong body. Doc said it's like a muscle car. If you put junk in the tank, you're gonna get a junk performance."

"So you have three scoops of ice cream," his wife said wryly.

"Only two, dear." His blue eyes twinkled with mischief. "Dr. Stone told us we have the time to take care of ourselves because we're retired. We want to enjoy it."

"Of course you do." Who wouldn't? Jill thought. She just couldn't imagine leisure time for herself. Ever.

There were bills to pay and a son to raise, plus a little bit to put away for the college fund he would need someday. She barely scraped by now and only had herself to depend on. The idea of not working was a luxury she couldn't even think about. "But you guys are okay?"

Diane nodded. "The doctor says we're both healthy, but to watch our cholesterol and blood pressure."

"So Dr. Stone didn't tell you anything you didn't already know?" Jill asked.

"No. But he spent a lot of time doing it, not like the one who always rushed us in and out. Dr. Stone said our hearts are strong. Walking is a good exercise and he couldn't think of a more beautiful place than Blackwater Lake to do it in. Clean air. Majestic mountains. Trees. Said a person could exercise body and soul at the same time."

The bell over the door jangled and in walked the doctor/poet himself. Jill wondered if her own heart was strong enough to survive the pounding it took every time she saw him, and now was no exception. The Schurrs looked like twin deer caught in headlights. Or kids with their hands in the cookie jar.

"Dr. Stone," Diane said. "Speaking of the devil. We didn't expect to see you here."

"Besides being the devil," he said with a straight face and a gleam of amusement in his eyes, "I'm also the food police."

"This is yogurt." The older woman's voice was only a little bit defensive. "Ask Jill."

Apparently Adam hadn't noticed her behind the tall glass case, because he looked surprised. "So you're the witness for the defense?"

"Mrs. Schurr is telling the whole truth and nothing but." She couldn't stop a smile. "And as chief of the food police, you should deputize her. She cut Mr. Schurr back from three scoops to two."

The doctor nodded. "Have you thought about coming out of retirement and taking on a new career in diplomatic negotiations? You'd be good at it."

"I should be after all those years in the classroom. Girls and boys need a firm hand and the voice of reason." She finished the last of her yogurt and looked at Jill. "Norm and I have to be going. It's good to see you, sweetheart. Take good care."

"Will do," Jill answered, reading the real meaning between the lines. "Night, Mrs. Schurr. Mr. Schurr."

The two waved, and then the bell above the door jangled before they walked out and she was alone with Adam. He was wearing worn jeans and a black T-shirt that snugly covered his broad chest like a second skin. The sleeves stretched over his biceps and drew her attention to the contour of muscle there. The devil impressed her female hormones, she thought.

And it was okay to be impressed as long as that didn't blind her to reality.

"So, you didn't really come in here to be the food police, did you? That could put a big dent in Maggie's income. She does a lot of business with the town's retired demographic."

"No, I'm not checking up." He laughed. "I have a confession to make, though."

Being married, having a girlfriend and leaving tomorrow were the top three declarations of guilt that popped into Jill's mind. But all she said was, "Oh? What?"

"I can't say no to ice cream."

"Neither can my son, which I guess makes me the food police."

"Good luck with that. C.J. is resourceful and could join Mrs. Schurr in diplomatic negotiations."

"Or undiplomatic," she added. "What can I get you?"

"I'll have what Mr. Schurr had." Adam folded his arms over his chest and studied her as if she were a new and exotic flavor in the display case.

She scooped the ice cream into a cup, then took the ladle to drizzle caramel over the two vanilla mounds. She was grateful to have something to do with her hands and very aware that his gaze never left her. "Is something wrong?"

"You tell me." He took the cup she handed him. "Where's C.J.? And what are you doing here?"

"My son is with Brewster and his wife, Hildie." Not that it was any of his business. "And I'm here because Maggie Potter is pregnant and having contractions. Her brother drove her to the hospital."

"The closest one is over seventy miles away. And she's only seven months along."

"How do you know that?"

A wry expression chased away the concern for a moment. "This isn't my first time here in the parlor."

"Right. Ice cream obsession." She nodded.

He moved to the lower counter where the cash register was located and braced a hip against it as he ate. "Why did her brother take her? Where's her husband?"

"He was in the army. Killed in Afghanistan. She found out not long ago." And obviously hadn't shared the information with a stranger, even if he was a doctor and a regular customer.

"Damn it. I don't even know what to say. That…" Adam jammed his plastic spoon into the ice cream and set it down. He shook his head and the sympathy in his eyes was wrapped in an anger that looked sincere. "It just sucks."

"I know."

"The shock could have brought on early labor," he said. "I hope not. Baby's still small."

"She's pretty upset," Jill confirmed.

"So you're filling in."

"It's the least I can do," she said. "Maggie and Dan built this business from scratch. I've known them both since we were all in kindergarten together. They were high school sweethearts. He was the love of her life and my good friend. No one can bring him back, but if there's anything I can do to save his child, I'll do it. And keeping this place alive is as much for him as for Maggie."

"It's a wonderful gesture."

There was a hint of surprise in his voice that Jill resented. Or maybe she just took exception to him, however unfair that was. Or it could be her reaction was more about looking for a reason to keep up a robust level of mad to squash or squeeze out the stubborn attraction to him that she couldn't seem to shake.

Whatever her motivation, there was an edge to her voice when she said, "Friends are *there* for each other."

"I couldn't agree more." His voice had an edge, too, and

the words clearly indicated he hadn't missed the underlying meaning in her words. There was a spark of anger in his blue eyes that had nothing to do with loss from a war halfway around the world and everything to do with conflict between the two of them. "And I'll look forward to someone being there for me when I have more than one friend in town."

"You actually have one now?" she asked, leaning a hip on the other side of the counter.

"As a matter of fact, I do. Cabot Dixon and I go way back to my summer camp days. His father's ranch is where my parents sent me, and we hit it off."

"C.J. and Tyler are good buddies," she said.

"I wondered. Cab brought the boy in and I noticed that he's the same age."

"Hope it was nothing serious."

"No." Adam shook his head. "But because of patient privacy laws I can't say more than that."

"Don't break any rules on my account."

"Not to worry. But there is something I plan to do on your account."

"Don't do me any favors."

"Actually it's me I'm concerned about." He picked up his ice cream again and started eating. "It seems the people here in town are all very protective of you. To win their hearts and minds I need to prove myself to you, earn your friendship. And that's exactly what I intend to do."

"Good luck with that." She struggled for a flip attitude but was pretty sure it didn't work, what with her heart pounding so hard. "I've built up an immunity to nice, charming men."

"Then it's a good thing I'm not nice or charming." He finished the last of his sundae and dropped the cup and spoon in the trash.

Suddenly Jill realized he hadn't paid for it. "I forgot to

ring up that ice cream. Some friend I am. That's no way to mind Maggie's store."

He reached into his jeans pocket and slid out some folded bills. After pulling one from the wad, he put it on the counter and said, "Keep the change." Then he met her gaze and said, "Jill?"

She couldn't look away even if she wanted to. "What?"

"I'm really not the devil."

She'd have to take his word on that because right now she was pretty sure he was. He tempted her just by walking in and breathing the same air. Technically he lived right above her and probably they were trading oxygen and carbon monoxide all night long. That could do a number on her if she thought about it too long.

So she wouldn't think about it, and no way was friendship a possibility. Men and women couldn't be friends. More often than not, it went bad. She didn't need any more bad in her life than she'd already had.

Chapter Three

It was Saturday and Adam didn't know what to do with his first real weekend off since moving to Blackwater Lake. He wandered around the apartment that grew on him more every day. The boxes were gone, stuff was put away and pictures were hung. They weren't as soul-stunning as Jill's, but he planned to take his own photos and get some shots that were wall-worthy.

His computer was hooked up and on the desk in the second bedroom he was using as a home office. Medical books and a few fiction paperbacks were stacked on the floor, and he could use some bookcases. A trip to the antiques and furniture stores in town could fill some time today.

Then he looked out the living room window with a view of the lake. There was a small wooden building nearby with a sign that read Blackwater Lake Marina and Bait Shop. It was about time he explored his new hometown, starting with what was right in his own backyard.

He grabbed his keys, locked the front door, then jogged down the stairs to the covered porch. Beside Jill's door sat a pair of C.J.-sized muddy sneakers and a small baseball mitt. Just a guess but both probably belonged to the little guy who lived downstairs. Thoughts of the redheaded rascal made him smile and he wondered what the kid was up to on a day off from school. Hopefully hanging out with Tyler Dixon on the ranch where a kid could be a kid. Adam wouldn't trade his time there for anything. And what C.J. did was none of his business since his redheaded, red-hot mom had warned him off.

He walked down the path and turned right, heading for the marina store. A few minutes later he stepped onto the wooden walkway outside. A few yards from the door, the dock jutted into the lake, a small number of boats tied up on either side.

He entered the store and waited for his eyes to adjust from the bright sunshine outside. Bending over a box, Jill had her back to the door and was restocking the tall, refrigerated case with bottled water. Before she straightened he had time to look his fill and conclude that she did have one terrific tush.

And that kind of thinking was to his goal what the iceberg was to the *Titanic*. To win over the people of Blackwater Lake, he had to be her friend, nothing more.

"Mom?" That was C.J.'s voice.

Adam moved a step farther inside and saw the kid. Racks of souvenir T-shirts had hidden him, sitting cross-legged on the floor beside the cold case. His elbows were resting on his knees, and his small, freckled face was cradled in both hands. If he was a photo, Adam would title it *Boredom*.

"Mom," he said again, louder this time.

"What, kiddo?"

"Why can't I go outside?"

"Because you're not allowed to play by the lake when there's no one to watch you. That's the rule."

"It's a stupid rule. I know how to swim."

"True. But better safe than sorry," she said.

"I'm already sorry because I can't go outside."

Adam smothered a laugh. This kid was priceless.

"I wanna go to Ty's house," he said, taking a new direction.

"We've been through this already. I have to mind the store, so I can't drive you."

"I could call Ty. I bet Mr. Dixon could come and get me, Mom."

"He's busy running his ranch. You shouldn't bother him," she said.

"When's Brew coming back?"

"A couple of hours."

The kid let out a big sigh. "I don't got nothin' to do for a couple hours."

"I don't have anything to do," she corrected.

"Then you can drive me to Ty's."

Adam cleared his throat to cover a laugh and let them know he was standing there. "Hi."

"Dr. Adam!" C.J. jumped up and ran over.

"Hi, champ." He made a fist and the kid did the same and bumped it. Looking at Jill, he said, "Good morning."

"How are you?" She brushed the curly red hair off her forehead.

"Good. Enjoying a day off."

"Must be nice," she said wistfully.

"It is."

He saw the dark circles under her eyes and asked, "Is there any place in town you don't work?"

She laughed, which was a nice surprise. "Potter's Parlor was for Maggie, but this store is mine."

"Interesting place," he said, glancing around.

Fishing poles were standing along one wooden wall, and

above them was a divided case with lures, sinkers and bait. Another wall had cubbyholes holding hats, and beside it were stacks of ice chests. In the center space were racks of outdoor clothing—quilted vests, flannel shirts, windbreakers and light jackets.

"Brewster works for me, so I take over when he's off."

"Who takes over when you're off?"

"It's not an issue."

The subtext was that she never had time off. But there wasn't any trace of self-pity in her tone or expression. All he saw was strength and pride. The combination made her stunning, the kind of woman he wanted to get to know better.

He started to say something but was interrupted by the sound of heavy footsteps on the wooden walkway outside just before three men came into the store. They were all about the same age, in their late fifties or early sixties.

Jill smiled. "Welcome to Blackwater Lake."

Adam listened to the conversation and figured out that these guys were strangers to her, new to the area and looking for fishing gear. Jill led them to the wall with rods and reels, then began answering their questions regarding the pros and cons of each type and its relation to their skill level.

While she was preoccupied with customers and a potentially lucrative sale, her son slipped outside, unnoticed by anyone but Adam. He stood in the store's doorway and saw C.J. race down to the lake's edge, then bend to grab a rock and throw it into the water. So much for mom's rule. And Jill was right to worry about safety around the water.

Adam walked down the path and stopped beside the boy. He picked up a smooth stone, then flicked his wrist and watched it skip three times before disappearing.

"Cool," C.J. said. "How did you learn to do that?"

"Tyler's dad showed me when I was just about your age."

The boy looked up, squinting into the sun. "Did you live here then?"

"I only visited during the summer."

"Are you and Mr. Dixon friends?"

"Yes." So far the only one he had in Blackwater Lake. As far as Jill was concerned, C.J. didn't count.

"Can you teach me how to skip rocks?" he asked eagerly.

"I can show you. Then it's just practice to get the hang of it."

"Forget it, then. I'll never get good." C.J. kicked at the rocky shore with the toe of a sneaker. "I'm not s'posed to be here alone. But Mom never has time to watch me."

"She has a lot of responsibility." He could relate. Jill was a single mom, but Adam had two parents, and their demanding careers had left little time to spend with a boy who wanted to play. He'd been turned over to others to be supervised, then spent summers here. As an adult he understood, but thank goodness for those summers. "But I'm here now."

"You can watch me?"

"Yeah." He picked up another stone and demonstrated the proper way to hold it, between thumb and forefinger. "It's all in the wrist."

C.J. watched as he threw it and said, "Let me try."

They worked on the skill for five minutes, which is about all the attention span a six-year-old has. After that the boy used the rocks like a depth charge, aiming for the fish darting around just below the surface.

"I'm a mighty hunter," he said, moving so close the water almost lapped over his shoe.

Adam was ready to grab him if there was a chance he'd fall in. "Do you have a fishing pole?"

"Not yet. Mom says when I'm seven."

"When's that?"

"When it gets cold."

He remembered Jill telling him that the doctor had left as soon as it turned cold. Had he been there for the kid's birthday or skipped out before? She'd said she wouldn't allow her son's heart to be broken *again,* which meant he'd already been hurt once. That sucked.

"Does it hurt the fish when you hook 'em?"

Probably, Adam thought. But he didn't want to tell the boy that. The crunch of footsteps behind them saved him from having to answer, but the look on Jill's face told him he wasn't saved from anything else.

"Uh-oh," C.J. said. "It's my mom."

Uh-oh, indeed.

"I'm very disappointed in you, C.J."

Adam knew from personal experience that the disappointment card was the biggest gun in the parental arsenal. But a safety rule had been broken.

"Are you mad, Mom?"

"Do I look mad?" Her voice was deadly quiet and calm. Shouting would have been easier to take.

C.J. studied her expression. "No?" he asked hopefully.

She shook her head. "You disobeyed a direct order right after we talked about it."

Adam looked from her to C.J., knowing she'd just taken the "I forgot" defense out of play.

"There has to be consequences, kiddo."

"Am I grounded?"

"I have to think about this," she said.

"While you're thinkin'," he said, rubbing a finger along the side of his nose, "remember Ty's birthday party is in a week."

"Thank you for reminding me," she said.

It was that quiet voice that finally got to Adam. He couldn't just stand there and say nothing. "Look, Jill, it's Saturday and the sun is out. Awfully tough for a guy to be cooped up indoors. I was here—"

"About that," she said, her tone edging up. She looked at her son. "Run up to the store and get a drink of water, C.J. I need to talk to Adam."

For just a second he teetered on the verge of argument, then just nodded. Without a word he trudged back up the path and disappeared through the door to the marina store.

"Jill, don't take it out on him. I'm the one you're really mad at."

Her brown eyes darkened with anger. "I made it clear that letting him get attached to you isn't an option. Water safety isn't the only issue here. It's my job to look out for him emotionally, too."

"And I made it clear that I wouldn't hurt him."

"Talk is cheap." The breeze blew a strand of hair across her eyes and she angrily brushed it away.

"I was just keeping him company—in the spirit of helping someone out," he said.

"I don't need that kind of help. When he gets attached to you and is left behind—"

"I'm going to be a part of this community where people look out for one another." He hadn't planned to defend himself, but hearing about the last doctor was getting old. "Blackwater Lake is a place where neighbors pitch in. It's what you did for Maggie. That's all I was doing with C.J."

"*I* look out for him," she said.

"So you can be there for a friend, but I can't? Smacks of a double standard to me."

"That's because you're not a single mom." She nodded for emphasis, then turned away and walked back up the path after her son.

Adam watched her stiff back and not for the first time he thought she had a little too much spine. Bending a little would do her good, and he was just the guy who could out-stubborn her.

That's when it hit him that instead of diminishing his fascination for her, the arm's length she was trying to put between them just intrigued him more. It was all kinds of bad because relationships were not his specialty. So far he'd been less than successful in staying uninvolved, and one wrong move could cost him the community approval he needed to make this career move and the life he wanted a success.

Now that he had a diagnosis, it was time to come up with the treatment. So far, he had nothing.

Potter's Ice Cream Parlor was hosting a fundraiser for Blackwater Lake High School's football team, and Jill had just finished her two-hour volunteer shift. She was grateful for the break because her hands ached from nonstop scooping. It was standing-room only except for Maggie Potter. Her early labor pains were under control, but she was under obstetrician's orders to stay off her feet and was sitting at a table for two in the center of the room. Her job was to collect cash donations from folks who were watching their calories but still wanted to help out.

Jill sat in the empty chair across from her friend. "You should be at home with your feet up."

"At least I'm off them." Maggie was a pretty brunette, petite and fragile-looking. Her beautiful brown eyes were sad and hadn't lost their haunted look since she'd gotten the news that her husband had died in Afghanistan. "It's been a week since I saw the doctor, and doing nothing is driving me crazy."

"You have to put crazy on a back burner and take care of that baby."

"I'm doing my best. Now that Dan is gone, there's nothing more important than this baby. I have to make sure a part of his father goes on." She settled her palms on the baby bump. "You can put your own maternal instinct on a back burner because I called the doctor for permission. He said it's okay to be out of the house as long as I'm taking it easy. If I get wild and end up behind the counter, Brady has orders to pick me up bodily and take me home to solitary confinement."

Jill laughed. "So it's your big brother's day to watch you."

"Every day is his day, poor guy." The sadness in her eyes deepened. "He's running the parlor right now, until the baby is born and I'm back on my feet."

"He's a really good guy."

Jill had often wondered why she hadn't fallen for Brady O'Keefe in high school instead of Buddy Henderson. The only good thing that jerk had left her was C.J. Other than that, it was a lot of bad memories and no desire to fall in love again. Ever. The one time she'd even thought about it, the doctor took off and she wasn't in the mood to test the theory about third time's the charm.

"It doesn't hurt that Brady owns a successful business of his own. He can structure his time to give me a hand, but he's really stretched thin." Maggie was looking at the door. "Speaking of good-looking men…"

Jill knew by the expression on her friend's face that she was looking at Blackwater Lake's newest doctor. She hadn't seen him since the incident by the lake a few days ago. Thinking about it afterward, she'd been unable to decide if he was a good, softhearted guy or an interfering jerk who wasn't going to be around and had no emotional investment in whether or not C.J. became a responsible adult.

When her friend started to wave him over, Jill protested, "No."

Maggie's eyebrow rose questioningly. "Oh, really?"

"What 'oh, really'?"

"Don't play dumb with me. I've known you too long. What's up with you and your newest tenant?"

"Who says anything is? Can't I just not want to talk to him?"

"Not unless you have your eyesight checked and your head examined," Maggie said, her gaze tracking him as he moved farther into the crowded room. "He's gorgeous and seems really nice. I know everyone in town hates his guts because of what the last doctor did to you, but I believe in giving people the benefit of the doubt."

"Only because he's got an ice-cream obsession and is a good customer," Jill retorted.

"That doesn't hurt. But, for goodness' sake, he's a bachelor without children and is here to support the football team. That gets a check mark in the 'pro' column." The sadness in her eyes deepened. "Danny loved playing football for Blackwater Lake High. It was his idea to do this annual fundraiser, and I'll defend anyone who is here to support it." Unexpectedly a small smile turned up the corners of her beautiful mouth. "And by the looks of it he's not just buying for himself."

Jill turned and followed her friend's gaze, noting that there were four kids with Adam in line. Reading the body language, she could see that he was relaying questions and answers from volunteers behind the counter and the boys giving their orders. When each sundae was ready, he handed it over to the child.

"Wow," Maggie said.

"What?" Jill turned back to her.

"He's buying the Mag-nificent Mocha and the Dan-dee Delight, the two most expensive things I have."

Jill knew her husband had created and named them after the two of them. She also knew Adam was trying to win over the community and wondered if this was a bribe or he was being extra nice to Maggie. She hated being that cynical. It would be shallow, self-centered and just plain wrong to compare what she'd experienced to Maggie's incomprehensible loss, but something had died inside Jill, and a couple of men were responsible. Now she looked at everything involving men through a magnifying glass made of skepticism.

"I hope the kids don't get sick," Maggie said, watching the boys juggle their treats over to a table while the doctor paid the bill. "Now Adam is looking around for a place to sit."

"Are you going to do a running commentary on his movements all night?"

Maggie folded her arms and rested them on her ballooning belly. "Someone took a crabby pill. Maybe you need something to sweeten your disposition."

"If you're suggesting ice cream, I've already had mine."

"Finishing C.J.'s doesn't count."

Jill automatically looked for her son and saw him in a far corner with Tyler Dixon and his dad. There was a part of her that always breathed a sigh of relief when she could see him happy and healthy.

"I may have finished his, but that means we both took one for the team." The comment made her friend smile, and that was enough to sweeten her disposition.

"Hello, ladies."

"Adam." Maggie's voice was dripping with friendly and topped with welcome. "Why don't you pull up a chair?"

Even if Maggie hadn't announced him, Jill would know that voice anywhere. It was deep and rugged and seemed to have a direct line to her heart, kicking up the beat until surely everyone in the noisy, crowded room could hear.

Jill saw the mischievous gleam in the other woman's eyes. It momentarily blocked out the sad, and for that she was grateful. When he moved into her view she said, "Hi, Adam. Join us."

He glanced from one to the other. "You two looked serious about something. I don't want to interrupt any soul-baring confessions."

Jill was doing her level best to keep this guy from searing her soul and wanted to tell him he was absolutely interrupting them, but had a bad feeling Maggie wanted him to sit down. There was probably no way to avoid it, so she sweetened her disposition and aimed all that sugar in his direction.

"We were just chatting," she said to him. "Nothing important. Sit with us."

"Okay." A faint look of surprise flitted across his face just before he grabbed a recently vacated chair from a nearby table. He pulled it over and sat. "How's the mother-to-be?"

"Doing nothing, as ordered, and teetering on the edge of insanity," Maggie answered.

He laughed. "Apparently the edge agrees with you. Glowing is an understatement."

Definitely he was being extra nice to her, Jill thought. "Is that your official medical opinion, Doctor?"

"It is." Then he studied her. "And you look like a woman who could use a day off."

When he turned his baby blues on her, she felt the effects just short of her soul. Then the meaning of his words sank in. Tired? Bags under her eyes? She looked like something the cat yakked up?

Glancing at her best friend's amused expression, Jill knew Maggie knew what she was thinking. Before she could decide how to sugarcoat her response, Mayor Loretta Goodson stopped beside the table.

"Hi, Jill." Her Honor was a tall, slender, attractive woman who made the mid-forties look like the new thirty. Her shiny, shoulder-length brown hair was stylishly cut in layers and her jeans, white blouse and navy blazer struck just the right balance between friendly elected official and professional businesswoman. As far as anyone knew, she'd never been married and when she looked at the pregnant lady, there was a mirror image of sadness in her gray eyes. "You look good, Maggie."

"I feel good."

The mayor nodded, then extended her hand to Adam. "We haven't met, Doctor. Mayor Loretta Goodson."

"It's a pleasure," he said.

"How are you settling in?"

He hesitated just a second before responding, "Making a change is always a challenge."

Loretta nodded. "Folks in Blackwater Lake pride themselves on loyalty."

"And they're good at it," he said wryly.

Jill knew it was a veiled reference to everyone in town freezing him out to protect her.

"Their attitude will change. Doing physicals at no charge for the football team helps," the mayor said. "And it's important for everyone to accept you. I was elected to grow the tax base here in town, and to do that we need to attract business. People work in businesses and they'll need services, like health care."

Now Jill felt really guilty and personally responsible for hindering town expansion. On her account Adam was being treated as if he'd already screwed up just for being a doctor who rented her apartment.

The mayor smiled at him. "It occurs to me that you might want to do a booth at the Harvest Festival next month."

"I don't make quilts or pickle cucumbers," he joked.

"Health screenings were more what I had in mind."

"Taking blood pressure, cholesterol and diabetes checks. Eye exams," he said, thinking out loud.

"We could set you up between the pumpkin pies and corn dogs," she teased.

"That'll make folks love me," he said ruefully. "A terrible warning."

Loretta laughed. "Just a healthy reminder. It would be great exposure and a good way for people to get to know you."

"Sounds like an idea, Madam Mayor. Who should I talk to about setting it all up?"

"Calvin Johnson." She pointed out a man across the room who had his arm draped across one of the teenage football players. "I'll take you over there right now and make introductions."

"I'd like that. I actually came over here to give you a donation for the team," he said to Maggie. "Give me a couple minutes and I'll be back with a check." Then he looked down at Jill. "See you later."

Speechless, Jill smiled and nodded, then watched him walk away. The information about contributing his medical expertise to the kids was new, unexpected and something the last doctor hadn't done. She understood that the money he'd spent tonight was about buying town approval and it was for a good cause. But free physicals was time-consuming, not to mention above and beyond the call of duty. That made it awfully difficult not to respect the gesture. And like him for it.

It was a disconcerting realization. How could she hold out against the new doctor who went out of his way for the high school football team and was extra nice to a pregnant war widow? What could a girl do to put up a defense against a man like that?

Somewhere between talking to the mayor and sweetening her disposition, Jill had misplaced the hostility that was her best weapon.

Chapter Four

Adam drove home from the clinic along Lakeview Road, and it hadn't been called that for no reason. The street curved around the lake and the view was pretty spectacular. Hence the name. The thing was, no matter how difficult his day, looking at the sparkling expanse of water and the tree-covered mountains of Montana seemed to suck out the bad mood and pump up his spirits. At least that part of his career move had gone according to plan. As for the rest, time would tell.

He stopped at the two side-by-side Quonset hut-shaped boxes on the road leading to the house and retrieved his mail, then pulled into the driveway and parked beside Jill's small, older, gas-efficient car. Somehow it suited her, he thought, copper-colored and compact. But her curves were the kind that kept him up nights because his imagination tried to fill in the blanks of what it would feel like to explore her.

After turning off the SUV, he headed for the house.

Rounding the corner, he spotted C.J. sitting on the front step with a baseball glove beside him. His bony elbows dug into his knees, and his face rested in his hands.

Adam stopped in front of him. "Hey, champ."

"Hi, Dr. Adam."

"What's going on?"

"Nothin'."

"You didn't get sick from all that ice cream you ate last night, did you?"

The boy shook his head.

"Are you okay?"

He nodded.

This wasn't the never-still, never-silent child Adam had come to know. Something was up with him. "Why are you sitting here by yourself?"

"My mom is doing homework. She told me to go outside and play."

Homework? A question for another time. "So, how come you're not playing?"

C.J. shrugged. "There's nobody to play with."

And there was the downside of living on Lakeview Road near Blackwater Lake. The land wasn't developed and there weren't any kids right next door to hang out with like a tract home neighborhood. The closest house was almost a mile down the road. Even if a kid C.J.'s age lived there, a vigilant mom like Jill wouldn't be comfortable letting him walk there on his own. Besides being cautious, she was a busy working mom, not a chauffeur, and badly needed a day off.

C.J. looked at him. "Will you play catch with me?"

Adam recognized the pleading in those sad brown eyes so like his mother's. Memories of all the times his father had come home and he'd asked the very same question came back to him now. But his father, the Nobel Prize–winning economist, was always too busy or tired to play.

"Sure, champ. I'd love to throw the ball around."

C.J. sat up straighter. "Really?"

He nodded. "Playing catch is one of my favorite things to do."

The boy jumped up, then froze. "Do you have a mitt?"

"No." Adam held back a grin. "But if you go easy throwing the ball, I think I can handle it."

"Okay."

They stood several feet apart on the grass to the side of the walkway. The sun was just going behind the mountain; it wouldn't be light for long.

Adam braced his feet shoulder-length apart, bent his knees and held out his hands. "Ready."

The kid threw the ball wide. "Sorry, Dr. Adam. I don't throw so good."

"No problem. Just takes practice." Moving to the side, he bent to pick up the ball and realized it was hard rubber, not a hardball. He gave it a soft underhanded toss back that was right on the money but fell between C.J.'s hands.

"I'm really bad at catchin', too."

"You'll get the hang of it. Just keep your eye on the ball, champ."

"Okay." There was still a discouraged, defeated tone in his voice.

"How was school today?" Adam lunged a foot to his right and managed a bare-handed catch of the ball.

"Not good."

He tossed it back through the kid's hands again. "What happened?"

"I didn't get picked for the baseball team." There was a world of hurt in his voice. "The yard duty lady told 'em they had to let me play, but I didn't want to then."

Adam was angry even though he knew this kind of crap was all part of growing up. This was the part that built character, but it didn't come without pain. What ticked him off most was that there wasn't any injectable medication or pill, or words, to make that pain better. Then C.J. threw the ball over his head and he jogged over to pick it up.

"That sucks." He met the boy's gaze and said, "Did you say anything to your mom about it?"

"No. When I do it makes her sad."

"It's pretty cool that you're taking care of her." The little hero already had enough character to be the man in his mother's life and protect her. She'd done a great job with him on her own. "Was your friend Tyler there when they were picking teams?"

"Nope. He was playin' soccer."

"So you like baseball better?"

"Yeah, but I'm not very good at it."

Adam held his hands out in front of him to give the kid a target for his throw. This time the ball came right to him. "Says who?"

He shrugged. "I didn't get picked 'cuz they said I can't catch or throw or hit very good."

"Keep your eye on the ball," Adam said, then gently lobbed it practically into the mitt.

C.J. closed the glove and put his hand over it to hold on to the ball. He jumped up and down. "I did it!"

"Nice job. Way to go, champ. See? It just takes some practice."

"This is fun!"

It was, Adam realized. Watching a child blossom with a little attention was the most fun he'd had in a long time. For the next ten minutes they tossed the ball back and forth with more drops than catches, but success couldn't necessarily be measured by runs scored. The kid had his enthusiasm back and some self-esteem, too. If that wasn't a victory, he didn't know what was.

Finally Adam realized they'd lost the light and it was time to call it a day. "I think it's getting too dark, C.J. Better go inside."

"I can turn on the porch light," C.J. offered eagerly.

"It won't be enough."

"O-okay." He dragged his feet and moved closer, then looked up. "Dr. Adam?"

"Yeah?"

"Do you need help unpackin' any more boxes? You got any stuff to put away?"

Adam grinned at the transparent attempt to prolong the hanging out. "Actually, I think I'm all settled. But if I find something I missed and need help with it, I'll let you know."

"Got anything to do now?"

"Not really. I just have to go find something for dinner," he said.

"We're havin' my favorite," C.J. said.

"What's that?"

"Hot dogs with mashed potatoes on 'em."

"Sounds good." To his credit Adam didn't shudder, although it was probably too dark to see even if he did.

"If you don't have any food, you can come to my house and eat."

Adam figured that would go over like mouse droppings in the pantry. Jill had made it pretty clear that he should avoid C.J. and her. "I don't think your mom would be happy about that."

"She won't mind."

Adam glanced at the front window and the light inside. The view on his drive home, spectacular though it was, couldn't fill the simmering sense of loneliness his landlady's window generated in him as he passed by it every night. He knew she and her son were inside laughing, talking and being together. She'd smiled at him last night at the ice-cream parlor and seemed friendlier, but it could have been for the benefit of the mayor and her friend Maggie. It wasn't necessarily a reaction he could afford to trust or test too far.

"I don't know, champ. It's probably not a good idea for me to come over without asking her. There might not be enough food. Maybe another time."

"Nah. She always tells me I can have friends over anytime I want to. And we always have enough hot dogs."

The light from the window outlined the eagerness in C.J.'s expression. This child had been rejected once today, and there was no way to prevent that, but a yes from him now would avoid two rejections in a row. Adam didn't have the heart to disappoint him.

If she had a problem with him showing up, it would be her responsibility to explain to her son why. Would that put her on the spot? Heck yes. But maybe it was time to shake things up. Jill needed to get used to the fact that he wasn't going anywhere.

C.J. tugged on his hand. "Please say yes, Dr. Adam."

"Okay. You talked me into it. What time?"

"We eat at six."

"I'll be there."

And that would give him just enough time to run an errand first.

Jill pulled the hot dogs topped with mashed potatoes out of the oven and set the cookie sheet holding them on top of the stove. Her mother had come up with this simple dinner after Jill's father had left. Money was tight and it was especially sinful to throw food away.

Dottie had called the meals clean-out-the-refrigerator-for-two and sometimes they involved creative ways to use vegetables, potatoes and whatever leftover meat hadn't entered an altered state that resembled a science experiment gone terribly wrong. Dinners weren't always a culinary triumph, but hot dogs with mashed potatoes was one of Jill's favorites and fortunately her son liked it, too.

There was a knock on the front door followed quickly by the galumphing sound of C.J.'s sneakers coming down the hallway from his bedroom. "I'll get it," he hollered.

"No!" She rushed out of the kitchen to beat him to the front door. It was unusual to get visitors out here by the lake, especially this time of the evening. "We don't know who's out there. I'm not expecting anyone."

"I am."

In front of the door she stared down at her little guy, an uneasy feeling knotting her insides. "Just who are you expecting?"

"Dr. Adam."

Before she could quiz him further, there was another, more forceful knock. Jill peeked through the shutter and, sure enough, Adam was standing there on the porch.

"Open the door, Mom. Don't make him stand out there all night." C.J.'s tone sounded suspiciously like hers. "You're being kind of rude."

And so the child becomes the parent. Unfortunately he was right, and not just about this moment. At the very least, she'd been borderline rude since Adam expressed interest in renting her upstairs apartment. That's not how she was raised.

"You're right, C.J." She opened the door and started to say hello, but the flowers and bottle of wine Adam was holding kept her speechless. The front porch was dark and unwelcoming, kind of like her, and when she peeked out, she hadn't seen what he was holding.

"Hi." Adam smiled down at C.J. "Hey, buddy."

Jill finally found her voice. "This is a surprise."

"I came for dinner."

"I 'vited him," her son added.

She looked down at him. "You should have asked me first. So I could be prepared. I'd have made more food." And better food.

"If this isn't a good time, I'll take a rain check." Adam held out the flowers, daisies mixed with baby's breath, and the bottle of wine. Numbly she took them from him.

"It's okay, Mom. Dr. Adam can have my hot dog. I'll make myself a peanut butter and jelly." Her son must have seen the protest forming because he added, "You always tell me we hafta help people who don't have anything, and Dr. Adam doesn't have any dinner. He told me he had to go find something."

Jill had often said that herself, but C.J. was taking the statement literally. This wasn't the time to explain, especially because she was actually pretty proud of him. All her preaching and lecturing had produced fruit, although it was probably the most inopportune time for the most inconvenient man.

"You're welcome to stay." She met Adam's amused gaze. "It's not fancy. An old family recipe."

"C.J. told me what's on the menu."

She closed the door with her hip because her hands were full. "And you're here in spite of full disclosure."

"I keep telling you I don't cut-and-run. Or scare easily."

That made one of them because the smile he dropped on her was equal parts charm and sex appeal, which scared her a lot. It was unnerving how easily, how fast, the combination stole her breath away, but she was stuck now.

"I'll set another place at the table and put a couple more hot dogs in the oven."

"Come and see my room, Dr. Adam." C.J. tugged on his hand.

"Lead the way, champ."

Jill half expected him to brush off her son the way the

last doctor had done. It still made her spitting mad that the jerk had broken C.J.'s heart even though he'd never gone out of his way to spend time with her son. The fallout could be worse if her boy formed a relationship with Adam. But she was borrowing trouble and it was becoming a habit.

In the kitchen, Jill put the already-cooked hot dogs in foil and set them on a warming tray. She made more of her specialty, then set out another plate and eating utensils on the round oak table. The flowers went into the crystal vase that had been her mother's and she set them in the center of the place settings. Part of her was hoping to hide behind the arrangement.

Looking at the label on the wine, she wondered if cabernet sauvignon paired well with hot dogs. Smiling, she opened the bottle and poured the deep red liquid into the two glasses she'd bought for a dollar apiece at the thrift store on Main Street.

After fixing a salad, she was just about to call out that dinner was ready when C.J. tugged the affable doctor into the room and announced, "Me and Dr. Adam are hungry, Mom."

"Then it's a good thing dinner is ready." She looked at Adam. "Don't say I didn't warn you."

"You're gonna like it, Dr. Adam. This is my favorite food."

"I thought ice cream was number one." Jill watched her son plop his tush on a chair where the place setting had a glass of wine.

"Ice cream is my favorite dessert. And I'm sittin' here tonight."

"Okay." Jill switched the wine with his tumbler of milk. "But that doesn't mean you get a pass on drinking this."

"But, Mom—"

"No buts, Christopher John. It has calcium and that's good for your bones and teeth."

"Then how come my teeth still fall out?" he grumbled.

"Not all of them." Jill glanced at Adam, who was biting his lip to keep from laughing. That made it harder for her to keep her serious mom-face in place. "Your baby teeth came out to make room for the permanent ones. All the more reason to take care of them because that's all you're going to get. So, drink up or no dessert."

"Yes, ma'am." He took a token sip that left a white mustache.

Jill watched Adam's face as he cut off a bite of hot dog and potato. She'd added slices of cheese to spruce things up a little, but it was still a hot dog.

After swallowing he said, "Not bad."

"Told you," C.J. said, stuffing a too-big piece in his own mouth.

"Chew that carefully," Jill warned. "You're going to choke." When he mumbled something unintelligible she added, "Don't talk with your mouth full."

She took a sip of wine and nodded at their guest who had brought it. "This is really good."

"I'm glad you like it." He pushed the vase of flowers aside to the empty place at the table. "I was surprised to find it at the store in town. It's a label my parents like."

"They have good taste."

"Of course. They're practically perfect. It's not easy being the flawed offspring of such gifted and talented people."

"They must be pretty busy with their demanding careers."

"Mom is starting to cut back some."

"What about your dad?"

"When he isn't winning Nobel Prizes for economics, he teaches college classes on the subject."

"Wow." Feeling like a particularly dim country bumpkin, she took another sip of wine. "How do they feel about you moving to Blackwater Lake?"

He'd already polished off one of his hot dogs and a good portion of salad. "How can I put this delicately?"

"Careful." She glanced at her son, who was soaking up every word. "There's a minor present."

"Understood. I'll say it this way. My mother isn't subtle. She never misses an opportunity to ask if I'm bored yet with my Daniel Boone imitation and ready to move back to Dallas."

"You're leaving?" C.J.'s voice rose an octave, a big clue that he wouldn't be happy about that.

"No, champ. I'm staying put. I like it here."

He was looking at Jill when he said it, and there was mischief in his eyes. A wicked expression that made her want to get into trouble with him. Even if he invited her, she didn't have to say yes. For tonight she could just enjoy conversation with an adult male and not be in danger of making a mistake. No matter how often he swore that sticking around was the plan, she knew better than to picture him in her tomorrow, let alone forever. One night didn't have to cost her.

"C.J. tells me you were doing homework." There was a question in Adam's voice.

"When did he say that?"

C.J. put his milk glass back on the table. "Dr. Adam played catch with me."

"I hope he didn't bother you," she said quickly.

"It was fun." Adam smiled at the boy. "He's got a lot of potential."

"Yes, he does."

The wickedness faded from Adam's eyes and she had a feeling that her son had confided in him earlier. Now wasn't the time to ask what was said.

"I was doing an assignment. I'm taking online classes for a bachelor's degree in business. Better late than never." She shrugged. "I was in junior college intending to transfer, but then C.J. was born. My mom got sick. And I had to put school on hold for a while."

Adam put his knife and fork on the empty plate. "I can't think of a better way to show your son how much value you put on education and a work ethic."

"I never thought about it like that." His words started a glow inside her. "Honestly, I just got thrown into the deep end of the pool and continued to run the marina like my mother did. The classes are to make sure I'm doing it right."

"Doing what right, Mom?" C.J. couldn't hold back a big yawn.

"Making sure you get enough sleep, big guy. Time for your shower."

"But Dr. Adam's here. And I didn't have my dessert yet. I ate all my dinner, too. See?" He held up the empty plate for inspection. "And I'm havin' so much fun. It's almost as good as goin' out to dinner." He looked at Adam. "We never get to except for special stuff 'cuz it's awful expensive."

Jill figured that after six years she should be used to her son sharing embarrassing aspects of their life, but she wasn't. She didn't want to be pitied, especially by Adam Stone.

She ignored the statement. "You can have some ice cream after you get ready for bed, C.J."

"I'll be here when you're finished," Adam promised.

C.J. looked at her, gauging his response. "Is this one of those times that no means no 'cuz you're the mom?"

"Yes."

"Okay. But—" He pointed at Adam. "Don't go. I'll hurry."

"Be sure to wash your feet," she called after him.

When they were alone, she looked at Adam and saw that his shoulders were shaking. She burst out laughing, too.

"He's something else." Adam chuckled. "Really a bright kid."

"Tell me about it. Makes mothering a challenge." She stood and started stacking plates.

"I'll give you a hand." He carried his own plate to the sink.

Jill followed and stood beside him, looking up. "Did he tell you about not getting picked for a team at recess?"

"He said you didn't know about that."

"His teacher called to clue me in, just in case he was upset."

"He was," Adam confirmed.

"And so am I. I'd like to throttle the little stinkers, but it's not in anyone's best interest."

"I have to agree with you there."

"Part of being a mother is stepping aside to let your child fight his own battles. Or fall on his face. To handle it in his own way." She met his gaze. "I'm a little concerned that he's more upset than he let on because of talking to you about what happened."

"It was a guy thing." Adam rested a hip against the counter and studied her. "That was him trying to protect you. He said it makes you sad."

"Of course it does. No one wants to see their child left out—" Emotion choked off her words, and tears burned her eyes.

"Jill—"

He touched her shoulder and something that felt a lot like an electric current arced between them. The sadness vanished, replaced by a hot, spicy sizzle. She didn't know which one of them moved first, but all of a sudden his arms were around her and their lips were a whisper apart.

Chapter Five

Before Jill could even whisper "no," Adam's mouth was on hers. His lips were soft and he smelled so good—manly and spicy and sexy. In a heartbeat the contact grew more intense and he wrapped his arms around her waist and pressed her body to his, her breasts flat against his hard chest. Her breathing was shallow, fast and mingled with his as the harsh sound of it filled her small kitchen.

Her pulse was throbbing and the blood pounded in her ears as he kissed the living daylights out of her. Liquid heat poured through her and settled in places that proved her feminine parts still worked.

When he traced her top lip with his tongue, she opened eagerly, letting him explore and take what he wanted. Happily, willingly she went along for the ride. She slid her palms up and over his chest, soaking up that exquisitely muscular masculine contour. He kissed her over and over, then let his mouth wander to the corner of hers before sliding to her cheek and that take-me-now spot just by her ear. If there was a God, this moment would go on forever.

Adam Stone was rocking her world.

Until he wasn't.

She didn't know which of them had moved first and started it, but there was no doubt who was responsible for ending it. He went still, as if some sound, some thought, breached the sensual haze, bringing the equivalent of a glass of cold water to the face with it.

He took her hands, squeezed tight, then lowered them from his chest. "I'm sorry."

A nanosecond ago she wasn't sorry, but that was beginning to change. From the moment they'd met, her defenses had been in place, with a firm negative repeating over and over in her head. Who knew hot dogs, mashed potatoes and wine were such a powerful aphrodisiac that one touch of his mouth made her his for the taking? It was kind of humiliating.

Jill shook her head, as much to clear it as a disapproving reaction to his words. "You have nothing to be sorry for."

"I shouldn't have done that. It's all my fault." He stood with his back to her sink and dragged his fingers through his hair.

Part of her wanted him to define *it,* but she didn't ask, probably because she didn't want to hear the answer. Taking two steps away from him, she said, "Wow. Words every girl is just dying to hear…being someone's fault."

All hint of charm disappeared from his face, leaving behind an intense expression that looked a lot like self-recrimination. "This isn't a good idea. You. Me." He moved his hand, indicating both of them. "I'm not good at relationships."

"Neither am I." She knew what was coming and couldn't believe he was gallant enough to say what she was thinking.

"I want to be the best family practice doctor possible," he

explained. "To do that I can't be an outsider. This community needs to accept me as one of its own. So far that's not going as well as it could."

"On account of me," she said.

"Not your fault I'm paying the price for another guy's mistake. I can get past that as long as I don't screw up, too."

"Right." Jill forced a sunny smile that threatened to crack her face. *Please let this conversation be over.* "I see what you mean."

He didn't look convinced. "I think we can be good friends, but anything else has the potential to go badly based on my history. That could get awkward, complicated and counterproductive to what I'm trying to accomplish."

"You're absolutely right." Her tone had more enthusiasm than sincerity. "You may be bad at relationships, but I'll go you one better. I've already lived this one. I can give you a blow-by-blow of how this will play out. Spoiler alert—it's not pretty."

For some reason her agreement intensified his frown. "So we're on the same page. Best to sidestep this land mine."

"Absolutely." She caught her bottom lip between her teeth. "But I have a favor to ask."

"Anything."

"Mayor Goodson says good health care is important for area growth. I can do friends with you." She blew out a long breath. "But don't pretend it just to fit in."

"I'd never do that." Frustration and anger wrapped around the words.

"That's what the last doctor said." She held up her hand to stop him when he started to protest. "There's one more thing."

"That's two favors."

"It's important."

He nodded. "Okay. What?"

"Don't start anything with C.J. Don't pretend to be his friend. Don't play catch and pay attention to him if you're going to drop him like a hot rock. He's vulnerable. And you may have noticed that he's hungry for male companionship—"

"I'd never hurt him. I'm not leaving." A muscle worked in his jaw as his fingers curled into his palms. "*You* may have noticed that I'm doing everything possible to build a life here."

She stared at him for several moments and realized he wasn't faking the same frustration she was feeling at calling off that kiss. That made her feel much better and slightly more willing to believe him.

Then she heard the sound of bare feet running through the living room before C.J. hollered, "Mommy, I'm all clean."

Call her naive, but she didn't believe Adam had planned to put moves on her tonight. If so, he'd have waited until C.J. was in bed. There was some comfort in that, but not nearly enough.

With wet hair and wearing superhero pajamas, the little boy appeared in the doorway and came to a sudden halt. "Dr. Adam, you're still here."

The doctor's eyes never left hers when he said, "I told you I'd stay."

"Cool." C.J. stared first at her, then Adam. "How come you guys look weird?"

"Maybe you still have water in your eyes?" she said, trying to deflect with humor.

"Nope. I dried real good. And I washed my feet. See?" He held up a foot and would have toppled sideways if she hadn't caught him.

"Nice job, kiddo."

Better than her. She was a complete failure at the objectives for which she'd been preparing. She wasn't supposed to crumple like a used tissue the first time Dr. Adam Stone showed the slightest interest. Ironically they were in complete agreement about how unwise it was to pursue anything personal, but the disappointment flooding through her took her completely by surprise. Still, what she resented the most was that he'd been the strong one and actually had the will-power to pull away before things got out of control.

"Mom? I want dessert now."

Yeah, Jill thought darkly, there was a lot of that going around.

Adam had thought a strenuous hike in the mountains around Blackwater Lake would relieve the tension coiled like a rattler in his gut. Three hours later he walked out of the woods sweaty, tired and more tense than when he'd left. Jill's car was gone, which was both a blessing and curse. He couldn't look forward to seeing her, because she wasn't there, but then the wondering where she'd gone and what she was doing kicked in.

This was nothing new since he'd moved in upstairs. It had just become more intense since he'd kissed her the other night. He needed a tension-relieving activity, and he needed it bad. Specifically something to take his mind off Jill. More specifically her mouth. And to put a finer point on it, the necessity of finding something to keep him from thinking about kissing those full, tempting lips was getting more urgent every day.

If he hadn't slipped up and gone there, it wouldn't be an acute problem now because he wouldn't have any idea about the sweet secrets her mouth had promised. But he did screw up, and doing it again would be an even bigger mistake. So he had to find something to fill his free time.

Adam walked around the front of the house, toward the stairway leading to his apartment. Glancing down at the dock on the lake, he noticed a sign in front of the marina store. Sale—All Fishing Gear Twenty-Five Percent Off. He hadn't cast a line in the water since his time at camp. Maybe it was time he did.

Fishing could distract him. Die-hard fishermen swore the sport was relaxing and put all your troubles on hold. If nothing else, the smell of lake trout wasn't the least bit like the sweet scent of Jill's soft skin.

It was a plan and he went to the little store to take action. There was a display of fishing poles on the wooden walkway beside the door, but they all looked the same as far as he was concerned. Different-sized sutures or medical equipment, he was your guy, but this was Greek to him.

He walked inside and looked around. Not much had changed since the day he'd hung out with C.J. by the lake. The biggest difference was that signs were everywhere advertising markdowns. His guess was the summer merchandise had to be sold before winter set in. Anything not moved out would have to be stored.

Adam didn't see anyone minding the shop and noticed there was another door on the opposite side that looked out onto the marina. He stepped outside and saw Brewster Smith hosing down fishing poles, rubber boots, tackle boxes and an ice chest beneath a sign that said Equipment Rental. "Hi." Adam raised his hand in greeting.

The other man nodded, but didn't say anything, then turned his attention back to what he was doing.

"Journey of a thousand miles..." Adam muttered, then walked over. The sun was shining in a clear blue sky and pine trees covering the mountains looked even greener. "Beautiful day."

Brewster looked up. "Yeah. Winter will be here before too long."

Mr. Glass-Half-Empty, Adam thought. "How's business?"

"Same as always this time of year."

The older man was wearing a blue work shirt with the sleeves rolled to the elbows and faded-to-almost-white jeans. His scuffed boots were well-worn and wet, along with the one knee resting on the ground. His thick gray hair could use a trim, as could the beard, and the skin showing was leathery, the sign of a man who'd labored outside for most of his life.

Adam wanted to recommend a sunblock with SPF fifty for face, neck, hands and even the skin under the shirt. He didn't say anything, figuring they needed to bond a little more first.

"Looks like there's a big sale going on," he said, setting the bonding process in motion.

"Noticed that, did you?" There was irony in the pale blue gaze the older man turned on him. "It's a comfort to know you can read."

Adam took the high road and ignored the sarcasm. "Might be a good time to buy a fishing pole."

"Rod." Brewster used a bristle brush on one of the rubber boots.

"Excuse me?"

"Fishing *rod,*" he said. "Only greenhorns or city slickers call it a pole."

"Good to know." Adam silently counted to ten, determined to maintain a cheerful and unruffled appearance. "I'm thinking of taking up fishing. I hear it's relaxing."

"Where'd you hear that?"

What the hell difference did it make? "I'm not sure. Around."

"Hmm," was the only response.

"Maybe you could recommend equipment for a beginner?"

"Best advice?" Brewster looked up and there wasn't a hint of friendliness in his expression. "Just rent or go cheap."

"Because it's less complex and easier to use?"

"Nope. Just practical."

"Why?"

"Best not to put a lot of money into something you'll leave behind after pulling up stakes." Brewster went to work cleaning the other rubber boot.

Adam refused to rise to the bait, no pun intended, but an appropriate metaphor in a fishing store. "I'm here for the long haul and money's not an issue. What do you think I should start with?"

"Depends."

I'll bite, Adam thought. Again with the fishing figure of speech. "On what?"

"On what your intentions are."

This guy was already looking to cut his heart out with a spoon. No way would Adam try to bond over the fact that he'd kissed Jill and was now looking for a way to forget about her. Brewster would never understand that Adam's intentions were to fix the mistake, that it was best for both of them. And C.J.

He remembered Jill saying that she could give him a blow-by-blow of what would happen if they tried a relationship. But, damn it, he wasn't the last doctor and it bugged him that he was painted with the jerk brush. There was no point in challenging her because he wasn't willing to start something just to prove her wrong. He wasn't going to take the risk.

"Define *intentions*," he finally said.

"You planning to hang around and look busy or actually catch something?" Brewster rested his forearm on his thigh. "If you're figuring on volume, there's trolling gear."

Adam had a fairly high I.Q. He'd made it through medical school at the top of his class, after all. But Jill Beck's self-appointed protector was making this clear as mud. On purpose. "I'm not following."

"There's simple cane rods—some call 'em bank rods."

"Why?"

Again irony in the older man's expression. "Because you stand on the bank of the water to use it."

"Ah." Adam had actually guessed that. "What else?"

"Some rods and trolling equipment are meant to be used on a boat, either anchored or moving."

"I see." Adam nodded. "I hadn't thought about a boat. Is the fishing better in deep lake water?"

"Maybe. Maybe not."

"How does one go about buying a boat?"

Brewster rubbed a leathery hand across his neck. "Got some docked here at the marina that folks are trying to sell. But they're mostly bigger, for longer trips."

The implication was that anything for sale here would be too much for Adam to handle, and that was probably true. "Is there something smaller that you know about?"

The older man reached over and turned off the hose at the spigot. "Rowboat."

"Can I see it?"

"Over there." He cocked his thumb, indicating the big, open area of the dock behind the store.

Adam walked over and saw a tarp tented over something. Since there was nothing else around, he lifted the canvas to have a look. Underneath was a stack of wood and the skeleton of what appeared to be a rowboat-under-construction. Obviously the older man was messing with him. Another frustrating moment in an increasingly frustrating conversation.

Moving back to where the man was coiling the hose, Adam struggled with his patience. "Looks like it will be a boat when it grows up."

"Been like that for a while," Brewster confirmed. "Started it on commission for that doctor who skipped town. He left Jill blowing in the wind for the money she put out on materials. At least she kept the deposit."

"Good for her." Adam nodded thoughtfully. "Might be

nice to have something like that in the spring. Can you finish it for me? I'll pay up front."

"You're still here in the spring we can talk about it. No point in wasting energy, or storing something that won't get used."

Adam's turn-the-other-cheek attitude was just about played out. He had one nerve left, and Brewster Smith was standing on it. "I'll be here in the spring."

"Heard that before."

"That's it." Adam's temper snapped. The cheerful well dried up and he was too pissed off to care about bonding or diplomacy. He took a step closer to the other man. "I'm sick and tired of everyone in Blackwater Lake assuming I'm just like the guy who hurt Jill."

Brewster didn't back down. His steely-eyed gaze never wavered as he planted his hands on his hips. "And I'm sick of seeing that girl cry over men who aren't worth spit. It's not happening again. Not on my watch."

Adam decided not to waste his breath repeating the fact that he wasn't going anywhere. He said something else that was just as true. "I'm not going to make her cry."

"I'll believe that when I see it. And make no mistake. I'm watching you," he added before walking away.

Adam knew the older man would also be passing along anything he saw to Jill. He blew out a long breath as he stood outside in the sun. It was hard enough to prove yourself in a new job, but he had the added pressure of proving to the whole town that he wasn't the other guy. The entire population of Blackwater Lake was watching him, waiting for him to screw up.

If he gave in to temptation and kissed Jill again, there was little doubt in his mind that he'd take her to bed. That would be a slippery slope into the relationship pool. After that it was

a hop, skip and jump into her wanting more—commitment
and vows. That wasn't something he could do again.

The disappointment had the potential to make her cry, and
he'd just sworn not to do that. But if he didn't stop thinking
about her, all his promises could go up in smoke, right along
with his dream of a life in Blackwater Lake.

If he took her to bed, there was very little doubt that everyone in town would know.

And he would pay.

Chapter Six

Jill walked into Mercy Medical Clinic with C.J. even though it was the last place she wanted to be, for so many reasons. C.J. was holding a towel to his injured chin, which had bled on his shirt and sneakers. His freckled face was dirty from playing outside after school, and tears had made tracks through the grime.

They walked over to the flat desk in what was once the living room of the converted Victorian house. The receptionist, Liz Carpenter, was a pretty brunette in her twenties.

She smiled sympathetically. "Got a boo-boo, big guy?"

C.J. nodded solemnly and his mouth quivered. "Mommy says it might need stitches."

Jill looked down and saw tears pooling in his eyes again. Her heart squeezed painfully as it always did when her child was hurting and scared. She wasn't sure which hurts were the worst—physical or emotional—but hated both with a fierce passion fueled by maternal instinct.

"Thanks for getting us in, Liz. I know it's past time for you to go home." Clinic hours were from eight to five and Jill's watch had said six-thirty when she'd pulled the car into a parking space outside.

The receptionist waved her hand in a don't-worry-about-it gesture. "We ran way behind schedule today. You're not the first emergency. I'm used to it. Happens all the time."

"Well, I appreciate it. And hopefully it's not a problem."

"Nope. I checked with Dr. Stone and mentioned C.J. is the patient. He seemed really concerned. Does C.J. need to lie down?"

"No." The panicky tone said he'd rather put off going into an exam room for as long as possible.

"Okay, then." She indicated the chairs in the waiting area. "Just have a seat. The doctor is with his last patient now. It won't be long."

Jill smiled automatically even though crying was what she badly wanted to do, but she had to stay strong for C.J. If she fell apart, this whole thing would be even scarier for him. Putting a hand on his small shoulder, she guided him to an empty row of chairs with a view of the hallway. "Hang in there, kiddo. Before you know it we'll be home and I'll make your favorite dinner."

"Hot dogs and mashed potatoes?"

"Of course." Would she ever make that again without thinking about Adam and what had happened after dinner? That kiss was epic, at least in her experience. Not epic enough, though, if he could back off so easily.

For so many reasons Jill hoped she was wrong about the gash on her son's chin needing stitches. First and foremost she didn't want him to go through any more trauma. And she'd give almost anything to avoid seeing Adam, anything except take C.J. to the hospital that was so far away, which was her only other choice.

Then there was the fact that she hadn't seen Adam since the night he'd kissed her *and* taken it back, which was a personal worst for her. Other men had kissed her, but not one had asked to be friends after doing it.

She wasn't sure if friendship could be pulled off, but it was best to try. Maintaining the appropriate level of hostility to neutralize his charm was an energy suck and she didn't have much to spare.

"Do you want to look at a magazine?" she asked, glancing at the stack on the end table beside her.

C.J. sat stiffly, still holding the cloth to his chin. "No."

She knew his arm had to be getting tired and this was probably as good a time as any to get a good look at the injury. It had been hardly more than a glance at the house. Her first instinct was to stop the bleeding and she'd grabbed the kitchen towel from a drawer. C.J. was crying, scared and wouldn't lower the cloth to let her examine his chin.

"Can I look at your boo-boo?"

"No! Don't touch it." His voice was just this side of a meltdown, which didn't bode well for letting the doctor have a peek, which was the whole reason they were here.

"Okay."

Just then she heard a door open down the hall. There were footsteps on the wooden floor and a murmured conversation that grew louder. Adam appeared in the doorway with Brewster Smith's wife.

Jill shouldn't be surprised, but she was. "Hildie."

"Hey, what are you two doing here?" The older, gray-haired woman smiled and sat in a chair next to C.J. A quick look and she figured out the reason for the visit. "What happened, honey?"

"I fell and hit my chin. Don't touch it," he warned.

"Don't even want to see it," Hildie said with a shudder. She looked at Jill. "Are you holding up okay?"

What other choice did she have? "Yes."

"That's my girl." Hildie reached over and patted her hand. "Do you need me to stay?"

"No. It's getting late."

"Tell me about it. Brew's dinner is not going to be on time tonight." She glanced at Adam as if he were personally responsible.

He smiled, but it looked tired around the edges. "Don't forget to have that prescription filled, Mrs. Smith."

"Are you sick?" Jill asked the older woman.

"No." There was a defensiveness in her voice. "Just out of sorts. I swear there's a pill these days for everything from putting you to sleep to helping a man perform."

Adam laughed. "Some of them actually improve your quality of life. I promise the one I prescribed will do that for you."

"Uh-huh." Clearly Hildie wasn't convinced.

"And I'd like to see you for a follow-up." Obviously he wasn't easily intimidated.

"I'll make an appointment if you're still here," she said skeptically.

Jill didn't miss the way Adam's mouth pulled tight, and it was the first time she'd seen any sign that even subtle comparisons with the last doctor irritated him.

Still his voice was nothing but pleasant when he said, "Then go ahead and make the appointment now. Save yourself a phone call."

Hildie sniffed, and then her face softened when she looked at C.J. "Be a brave boy. Next time you stay with Brew and me I'll bake your favorite cookies."

"The white ones?" As opposed to chocolate chip, which were brown, or the oatmeal raisin variety that he called bumpy.

"Of course."

"Can I help?"

"You always do," Hildie said.

"But this time I want to roll out the dough. And put on a whole bunch of sprinkles."

"It's a deal." The older woman leaned down and gently kissed his forehead, then said to Jill, "Call me when you get home. Let me know how everything goes."

"I will."

Adam cleared his throat. "Follow me, champ."

"Can't you just look at it right here?" C.J. glanced apprehensively at the doorway that led to the exam rooms. "Maybe I don't need stitches. Then Mommy can just put on the anny bactria cream and a superhero Band-Aid."

"He doesn't like going into the room," Adam said, meeting her gaze.

Jill nodded. "The clinic is not his favorite place."

"I can understand that." Adam squatted down and talked directly to C.J. "I could take a look at it here, but the other room has a big light and everything else I need to take good care of you."

"Do I hafta go?" he asked Jill.

"'Fraid so, buddy." She met Adam's gaze and her heart tripped up for reasons that had nothing to do with her son and everything to do with memories of their mouths devouring each other. What kind of mother was she, thinking stuff like that at a time like this?

"How about if I give you a lift?" Adam offered, holding out his arms.

C.J. hesitated for several moments, then said, "I guess."

The doctor picked him up as if he weighed nothing, but Jill knew that wasn't the case. It made her sad that this child she'd easily carried around as an infant was getting too heavy for her to lift at all.

Jill followed them down the hall, the tall, broad-shouldered man in the white lab coat carrying the small boy who had one arm around the strong neck. They went into the first room on the right, where Adam set him down on the paper-covered table. She stood beside her son while Adam washed his hands and then pulled disposable gloves from the box on the counter by the sink.

"Okay, champ, let's have a look."

Those were the magic words that set off her child's classic, clichéd redheaded stubbornness. This time it was fueled by fear. "No. No. Don't touch it."

"I won't." Adam folded his arms over his chest. "Not until you're ready."

"It's gonna hurt. I wanna go home," he wailed.

Jill squeezed his shoulder. "Soon, C.J. Just hold still."

"I can't. I don't wanna hold still."

A look slid into Adam's face as he studied the tantrum-throwing, terror-stricken child. "C.J., have you ever had stitches before?"

Jill was about to answer, but something about the way the doctor was talking directly to her son stopped her. She'd step in if necessary, but maybe the little boy needed to feel as if he was in control.

"C.J.?" Adam prompted.

He nodded. "My knee. I fell on a sprinkler. The other doctor said it wouldn't hurt. But it did. Then Mommy had to change the bandage and she poured watery stuff on it. I looked and it was gross. I told her I was gonna throw up."

"He did warn me," she confirmed. "And he was telling the truth."

"Apparently your son is more honest than the other doctor." His mouth pulled tight and his eyes flashed with anger, but none of that was obvious in his calm voice. "Okay, C.J. Here's the deal."

"I don't want any needles."

"I can't promise anything until you let me look."

"Just look?" the little guy asked skeptically.

"Yes, then we'll talk."

Without a word he slowly lowered the towel from his chin. Jill was standing to the side and could only see the dried blood. Adam moved close enough to inspect the injury.

"What happened?" he asked, looking it over carefully, his arms still folded over his chest. The posture was completely nonthreatening.

"I was runnin' on the front porch and fell. I hit my chin."

"On that old rocking chair?" Adam asked.

"Yeah. The one Mommy got at the garage sale to fix up."

"That rocker isn't all that needs fixing. Your mom is right," Adam said seriously. "You need a couple stitches to close this up."

"No." C.J.'s injured chin took on a stubborn tilt.

"I could put a bandage on it," Adam said slowly. "But it's deep and that means healing will take a long time. And that means no baseball for a while."

"Okay." His tone said he could live with that.

"And there will be a pretty bad scar." Adam stepped back, deliberately giving the child space. "Don't get me wrong. Scars aren't a bad thing. A lot of manly men have them on their chins."

"You don't," C.J. pointed out. "Are you manly?"

There was amusement in Adam's gaze when he looked at her, but Jill felt her cheeks burn. She could vouch for his manliness. She had firsthand experience with it, or rather her mouth did.

Adam laughed. "I guess I'm just not one of the lucky guys."

C.J. squirmed on the exam table. "It hurts to get stitches."

"I have to give you some medicine with a little tiny needle, so it doesn't hurt while I'm putting them in. That will be like a pinch but it'll go away pretty fast. Then we'll wait till it works and you need to hold really still while I fix it up. Afterward it will ache, but not too bad."

"I don't know if I can hold still."

"I'll make a deal," Adam said. "If you hold as still as you can, I'll take you out to dinner. Anywhere you want to go."

"Really?"

"I promise." Adam held up his hand, palm out.

C.J. didn't look at her for an okay. Adam had put him in control and this was a man-to-man deal. Finally he nodded and said, "Okay. I'll be so still I won't even breathe."

"Breathing is okay." Adam laughed. "If it hurts more than I said, I'll even buy you ice cream after dinner."

"Cool."

Then Adam did exactly what he said and C.J. was calm and quiet because he hadn't been lied to. There were no surprises and he'd been well prepared for what was going to happen. He held still, didn't cry and actually gave the doctor a hug when it was all over. Jill was grateful to Adam, but that was the easy part. Everything else was incredibly complicated.

Not only was Dr. Stone easy on the eyes, he was good with kids. Also good with mothers, Jill thought. The man was a double threat. She needed that like she needed a sharp stick in the eye.

It got too late last night for dinner out after Adam stitched up C.J.'s chin. For all his talk about the cool factor of scars, he'd worked hard and taken his time putting in the tiniest stitches possible to minimize any mark the repair would leave. How was a mom supposed to resist a guy like that? It was the reason she kept her inner skeptic on high alert, although Jill conceded, if only to herself, that it was handy to have a doctor in the house. Technically not *in,* but just upstairs was close enough.

This morning before heading to the clinic, Doctor Dashing had stopped by to inspect the injury for infection and ask about pain. Both were a negative. Then he'd mentioned his promise and asked if it was okay to take C.J. to dinner that night. How could she object to a man who kept a promise?

Adam had come home from the clinic about fifteen minutes ago. She knew that because C.J. had been waiting and looking out the window. When he spotted the doctor's car in the driveway, her son had made the announcement at the top of his lungs and in a pitch only dogs could hear. Now he was getting ready to go out.

She was happy her little wounded soldier wasn't disappointed this time, but disillusionment was coming. Maybe not tonight or tomorrow, but sooner or later her little guy was going to get his heart stomped on and crushed when Adam decided his wilderness experiment wasn't the rollicking good time he'd expected and left Blackwater Lake. There was no way to prepare C.J. for that.

"How do I look, Mom?"

Jill glanced away from the computer screen she hadn't really been looking at anyway. C.J. stood beside her desk in his navy blue Sunday pants and long-sleeved yellow checked shirt. He was wearing sneakers because that was his only pair of shoes. Church and Sunday school were once a week, but his feet grew every day. Shoes got too small too fast and were too expensive for a dress-up pair. She figured God didn't mind a boy wearing sneakers instead of dress shoes as long as they walked into His house.

Her son's wavy red hair was slicked down with what looked like a *very* generous amount of gel. And water. Drops of it glistened on his forehead. Waiting for her approval, he was almost as still as he'd been last night while Adam had gently and skillfully closed the gash on his chin. The only evidence of yesterday's trauma was a small white bandage.

"Earth to Mom—"

She should get used to hearing her own words tossed back at her. This was another of many signs that he was growing up far too fast, and unshed tears burned her eyes. She was able to hold them back and chalked one up for Mom.

"You look more handsome than usual tonight," she said. "It must be the manly scar on your chin. Does it hurt?"

"Nah. Dr. Adam was wrong about that. It doesn't ache at all."

Just then there was a knock on the door. Speaking of the devil...

C.J. ran to answer it. "Hi, Dr. Adam."

"Hi, champ." He smiled when she moved behind her son. "Hello, mother of champ."

Jill wasn't sure how he managed to look better every time she saw him, but it was a fact. In his battered brown leather jacket and jeans that were worn almost white in the most interesting places, he had the rugged appearance every woman expected of a Montana man. Maybe that was why she felt a constant need to remind him he wasn't from there.

"Hi, Adam." Her voice had a breathless quality that she couldn't seem to control. "C.J. was just saying that you were wrong."

"Really?" He looked down. "About what?"

"My chin didn't hurt at all after you got done fixin' it. And it doesn't ache now."

"That's a very good thing to be wrong about."

Jill couldn't agree more. "He's doing great, Adam. You were so good with him. And now taking him to dinner— I can't thank you enough."

"Don't mention it." He looked at the little guy and whistled. "You look spiffy."

"Is that good?"

"Yes." Adam's expression was wry when he met her gaze. "I feel officially old now."

Jill laughed. "Then you won't be keeping him out too late. An old guy like you should be able to get him home in time for bed."

"Not a problem."

His blue eyes sparkled with something that made Jill's pulse stutter. Somehow she knew the deceptively simple word *bed* was making him think about that complicated kiss. God knew memories of it were never far from her mind, but she had high hopes of them fading very soon.

"Take good care of him—" Jill pressed her lips together. "Sorry. I'm sure you will. That's just automatic."

"I understand. It's a mom thing." He snapped his fingers as if an idea just occurred to him. "You should come with us."

"Oh, no. I couldn't." She looked down at her own jeans, worn all day at the marina, and seized on that as an excuse. "I'm not dressed for it."

"You can change. We'll wait, right, C.J.?"

Her son rubbed a finger beneath his nose. "Do we hafta?"

"No." Adam folded his arms over his chest. "But waiting for women is something we men do. It's probably time for you to start learning. I promise the wait is worth it."

"Now, there's something you're wrong about." Jill prayed that would discourage him. There was a very real possibility that her resolve to resist him was no match for that roguish sparkle in his eyes. "You and C.J. go on. There's a microwave dinner with my name on it in the freezer."

"That's just too sad." Adam met her gaze, and his own was potent with challenge. "Are you afraid to go?"

C.J. studied her. "It's the Grizzly Bear Diner, Mom. And the ones they got there are just stuffed."

"Like you are after eating there." She started to ruffle his hair, then remembered his effort to tame his curls. "Thanks for the support, sweetie."

"Does that mean you're comin' with us?" he asked impatiently.

"Yeah," Adam said. "Are you?"

Jill wasn't sure whether it was the sparkle in his eyes or the charming grin, but her resistance to the invitation was a miserable failure. "It will just take me a couple of minutes to change."

In her room Jill slipped into a pair of dark slacks and pulled a black-and-white sweater over her head. She twisted her hair into a knot and secured it with a clip, lifting some curls for height at her crown. Then she brushed some blush on her cheeks and smoothed tinted gloss over her lips.

Adam whistled when he saw her. "That wasn't much of a wait, but definitely worth it."

"Can we go now?" C.J. looked up at them. "I'm really starvin'."

"Me, too." A huskiness crept into the doctor's voice that hinted at exactly what he was hungry for and it had nothing to do with food.

Heart pounding, Jill got her son into his jacket and the three of them out the door in record time. Fifteen minutes later they were sitting in a booth at the grizzly bear–themed diner with C.J. next to Adam and the two of them across the table from her. She wasn't sure if a full-on view of the doctor was less dangerous than being on the same side and brushing arms, but that was the way it worked out. The Grizzly had a pretty decent crowd for a weeknight and she knew practically everyone here. They all stared at Adam as if the enemy had waltzed into their territory and taken it without a shot being fired.

Before they had their jackets off, Harriet Marlow, the owner of the diner, walked over with three glasses of water and set them down on the table. The blonde, who was somewhere in her forties and what people diplomatically called "fluffy," had twenty extra pounds, which were her own best advertisement for the food she served in her establishment.

"Hey, Jill, haven't seen you in here for a while."

"Hi, Harriet." She silently pleaded that her son wouldn't share the reason why it had been so long was financial. "I've been busy."

Harriet studied the man across from her. "You must be the new doctor here in town."

"Adam Stone." He smiled as if the mistrust in her eyes wasn't there.

"He put stitches in my chin 'cuz I fell and hurt it. Wanna see?" C.J. offered.

"Maybe later."

"He said if I held really still while he did it, I could have dinner out wherever I wanted. I didn't move even once."

"Good for you, big guy."

"And I wanted to come here. I really like the bear paw burger and fries."

"As I recall, you get that with cheese," Harriet said, pulling a pencil and pad from her apron pocket.

"Yes, ma'am." C.J. grinned. "And I'd like a Coke."

"Sorry, kiddo," Jill cut in. "I know you were promised whatever you wanted, but I have to rule out anything with caffeine."

"O-okay," he said grudgingly. "Then lemonade."

"Coming right up." The plump woman smiled for the first time and almost included Adam. "Do you two need a minute?"

"I do." Jill always savored the luxury of a dinner she didn't have to prepare by looking at all the choices on the menu. But meals out were so rare, her usual burger would be the selection just because she knew she liked it and wouldn't be let down.

"Since this is my first time, I'll need to check it all out," Adam said.

"I'll give you a few minutes. Nice to see you, Jill."

"You, too, Harriet." She reached for two menus stacked behind the napkin holder and condiment containers, then handed one across to Adam.

As they were flipping through, Mayor Goodson stopped by the table. She smiled at C.J. "I heard about your adventure at the clinic yesterday."

"I bleeded a lot," he confirmed eagerly. Now that the pain and suffering were over, the story would take on a legend of its own. "Wanna see my stitches?"

"No, I'm sure Dr. Stone did a fine job."

"Took him forever," C.J. groaned. "I thought he'd never be done, but I didn't move. Not even my eyes. I just closed 'em."

"It's true," Adam agreed. "He was very manly."

"And I'm gonna have a big scar."

"He was very brave," Jill added. "And Adam was kind enough to reward him with dinner here because he was so good."

"That's the spirit, Doc." The mayor nodded her approval. "I hear we're going to see you at the Harvest Festival."

"I'm all signed up."

"Good." Loretta lifted a hand to wave goodbye. "Gotta run. See you there."

"She's stopping at every table," Adam commented.

Jill glanced over her shoulder and noticed that the people talking to the mayor were looking in this direction and the hostility level had gone down several notches. "I think Mayor Goodson is spreading the news of your good deed."

"I didn't put her up to it," Adam said quickly.

"That actually never crossed my mind. Because you didn't

know this place would be C.J.'s choice or that the mayor would be here."

"Wow." There was a teasing expression in his voice. "Good to know you trust me without any evidence to back it up."

"I trust you, too, Dr. Adam." C.J. was kneeling on the plastic booth bench, his elbows on the table. "Does it hurt to get stitches out? Can I keep 'em in forever?"

"They can't stay in more than a week." Adam thought for a moment. "It doesn't hurt, but you'll feel a little pulling. I'll do it really fast."

"Okay." There was no sign of apprehension as he blew on the straw in his water glass. He had complete faith in this man.

As it turned out, a full-on view of Adam wasn't the most dangerous thing that night. It was the hero worship in her son's eyes. It was seeing him so happy to be hanging around with another guy, the three of them having fun. This outing was a glimpse of what being a family was like. She'd experienced it a long time ago, before her father walked out, but C.J. never had. The yearning to give it to him welled up inside her.

Why did Adam have to be the one she pictured a family with? That was just crazy, especially when he'd flat out told her he wasn't interested. If she knew how to get the thought out of her head, Jill would do it in a heartbeat. Holding out hope for something like that with Adam Stone was just asking for trouble. If life had taught her anything, it was that she didn't have to ask for trouble.

It had a way of finding her on its own.

Chapter Seven

When Adam had made the decision to move to Montana, it never crossed his mind that he'd be the man voted most likely to be hate-stared out of town. In his medical station at the annual Harvest Festival he felt the vibe in a more public way than ever before. Folks walked by and looked at him as if an alien would burst out of his chest.

So far he had a boyhood friend and a six-year-old boy in the friends column. Mayor Goodson was civil to him mostly because she was a civil servant and it was literally in her job description. So here he sat by himself trying to rally some character and not let the isolation bother him, but that was hard for a guy who'd been popular in high school and college. Even in med school and afterward, people had accepted him easily. Shoot, he was an easygoing and likable guy— everywhere but Blackwater Lake.

Cars had been detoured off Main Street to close it off for the festival, and the booths were set up in the road. All the retail stores were open and hoping to take advantage of foot traffic.

Adam was situated between the Chamber of Commerce and Tourism booths. Behind him there was a big sign in blue letters advertising Mercy Medical Clinic health screenings. He'd been there since 10:00 a.m. and it was now past one. A handful of people who probably weren't Jill's friends had stopped by for blood pressure screenings, flu shots and cholesterol checks. The stack of brochures regarding healthy lifestyles and warning signals for stroke had hardly gone down at all.

Mostly he was doing nothing except fielding hostile looks from the residents of Blackwater Lake and really starting to resent taking the heat for "the last doctor" who had done Jill wrong. He was beginning to wonder if folks would ever give him a chance. At this point convincing them he was different looked doubtful.

Cabot Dixon separated from the people meandering down the street and walked over. He was carrying Tyler, who had his head on his father's shoulder. "How's it going?"

"Quiet. Not much has changed since the last time I saw you at the clinic."

That wasn't completely true. He'd kissed Jill, but it seemed that would stay between the two of them. If she'd mentioned anything, a lynch mob would have come after him with a whole lot to say before hanging him from the highest tree. Since he was still getting the silent treatment, the obvious conclusion was that no one else knew. Looking at it that way, he was doing all right.

"Give it time," his friend said.

"I'm a doctor. That's my line."

Cabot shrugged. "Apparently it's universal advice."

"Maybe, but at this rate I'll be retired before there's a

crack in the attitude." He folded his arms over his chest. "Hey, Tyler."

"Hi." He didn't lift his head, which was uncharacteristic of a six-year-old boy.

"You feeling okay?" Adam asked.

"He went on the roller coaster and Ferris wheel back-to-back. That was a couple of twists, rolls and turns too many after a hot dog and cotton candy. My fault." There was a dark look in Cab's eyes, something that said he blamed himself for a lot. "I'm taking him home."

"Wish I could go with you," Adam said.

"How long are you here at the festival?" Cabot asked.

"The booth is open till four. Although I'm on call for the clinic, too."

"Something tells me you're hoping to hear from the answering service."

Adam shrugged. "It would break up the monotony."

"Hang in there," the other man advised.

"Daddy, my tummy hurts," Tyler groaned. "Can we go home now?"

"Yeah, buddy. I'll get you there soon." He looked at Adam. "Any advice for a stomachache, Doc?"

"Time."

Cabot smiled ruefully. "See you later."

"Yeah. Feel better, Tyler."

Adam watched father and son move quickly away in the direction of the temporary lot at the edge of town set up for public parking. He looked at his watch and noted the friendly interlude had lasted the better part of five minutes. It was a nice break.

He could use more of them. And that's when he saw a familiar redhead in the flow of people walking by. Jill. A feeling of profound lust poured through him. He wanted her so bad he could taste it. Just from one look. It was a damn good thing he didn't see her every day. When his vision cleared and the blood started circulating back to his brain, he noticed that C.J. was beside her.

The kid glanced around and spotted Adam, then ran toward him, grinning. "Hi, Dr. Adam."

"Hey, champ. It's good to see you." A smiling face in this town was priceless. "Are you having fun?"

"Sort of."

Jill followed her son. She wasn't smiling, but she didn't look like she wanted him lynched either. "Hi."

"What are you up to?"

"Not much," she answered.

"That would explain the 'sort of' response to having fun." At the sight of her, Adam's spirits rose in a very different way from talking with Cabot.

"No, the explanation for that is his friend Tyler got a tummy ache and had to go home."

"Tyler and me were s'posed to ride *all* the rides and then go to the baseball booth. The one where you knock the bottles down and win somethin'. I been practicin'. I coulda won a really good prize."

"You can still go," his mother pointed out.

"It's no fun by myself."

"What am I, chopped liver?" she protested.

He plopped his tush down on the folding chair set up for patients. "You're a girl."

Not new information, Adam thought. The slender legs and curvy curves were a giveaway. And, after more clinical evaluation in the weeks since he'd been there, his assessment of her excellent derriere hadn't changed. It was still in the top five, although he was leaning toward a number one ranking now.

"Sorry, kiddo." Jill sighed. "I'm sure Tyler doesn't like not feeling well even more than you miss him being here."

"What's this thing?" He picked up the cuff with the attached bulb to inflate it.

Adam squatted down in front of him. "That's a blood pressure cuff."

"What's it for?"

"Taking people's blood pressure." Adam knew what was coming. "It goes on your arm and measures the force of blood pushing against the walls of your arteries. If the needle on the gauge reads too high, that means the blood is moving at a pressure not within normal range. That could be dangerous."

"Can you take mine?" Pleading brown eyes blinked at him.

"This one's too big for you. It's for grown-ups."

"Oh, man." C.J.'s posture was pure dejection. "I can't do anything. I wish you could go with me to the baseball booth."

Adam wasn't quite sure how the two thoughts connected, but the meaning of both was clear. "Me, too. But I can't leave here for a while."

"Why not?" The boy looked around. "There's no one here."

"Someone might come by," he explained. Although the odds weren't good on that. "High blood pressure screening is really important because there are no warnings if you have it."

"No tummy ache?" he asked.

"Nope. So, just in case, I need to be here."

"Dr. Adam is checking other things, too," Jill explained. "And giving flu shots for anyone who needs one."

"I don't," the boy said. "I don't like needles."

"I remember." Adam smiled as he inspected the red line under the small chin. He'd taken the stitches out a few weeks ago. There'd been no drama or tears, which could mean the kid trusted him more after dinner out. He'd really enjoyed spending time with the two of them. "That's a good-looking scar."

"It's hardly noticeable," Jill said. "You did an amazing job."

He smiled at her. "Happy to help."

"Can't someone take your place here?" C.J. persisted.

"Sorry, champ. I gave my word."

"What does that mean?"

"I promised and have to follow through. It's a responsibility."

Jill looked at her watch. "Have you had lunch?"

"No."

"You must be starving." There was concern in her voice.

"I'm okay."

"C.J. and I can get you something," she offered.

It surprised and pleased him that she'd go out of her way. Just talking about eating had his stomach rumbling, especially with all the food smells in the air. "Is someone selling pizza?"

"By the slice," she confirmed.

C.J. pointed. "Just down there."

"Tell me what you want."

"Let me go, Mommy." C.J. slid off the chair. "You can watch me. I wanna do it for Dr. Adam. He might get cranky if his sugar gets low."

Her smile was sheepish. "Can you tell we've talked about that?"

"Figured."

There was uncertainty in Jill's eyes. "I don't know, sweetie. Why don't we go together?"

"She never lets me do anything by myself," he grumbled to Adam. "Even though I'm gettin' bigger every day."

The "she" in question chewed on her bottom lip, clearly

conflicted. "You're right, C.J. You are a big boy. And I can see you from right here."

He looked up at Adam. "What kind do you want?"

"Pepperoni." Adam reached into his pocket and pulled out a twenty-dollar bill, then handed it over. "And a bottle of water. Can you carry all that?"

"'Course I can."

"Get something for yourself, too."

"Nah. I don't wanna get sick like Ty." He took the money and raced to the booth where the pizza was.

Adam watched him. "That hair makes him easy to spot."

The color was identical to Jill's. He studied her, never looking away from her son. She was definitely not hard on the eyes and he felt the wanting well up the way it always did when she was near. If she was just beautiful, the knot in his gut wouldn't be so bad. He'd met a lot of beautiful women who didn't get to him, but there was something about this woman that did. Unfortunately acting on the attraction complicated everything he was trying to accomplish.

"Hi, Jill." A tiny, gray-haired woman stopped.

"Mrs. Carberry. I haven't seen you in ages. How are you?"

"Pretty well." She glanced at Adam. "You're the new doctor?"

"Yes, ma'am."

"He's doing free blood pressure checks, among other things," Jill said. "You should do it."

"Really?"

"I promise it won't hurt," Adam said. "Unless you want a flu shot, but that's only a little stick. I recommend it. Risk factors are higher in your age demographic."

"Are you saying I'm old?" she demanded, although there was a twinkle in her blue eyes.

"No." He shook his head. "I just meant—"

The woman grinned and sat in the folding chair. "Just messing with you, Doc. If Jill thinks I should, then I will."

Adam did his thing and Mrs. Carberry decided to get the shot because she'd had a bad case of flu the year before. As he worked, he noticed a few more people chatting with Jill. She was pointing in his direction and it looked as though a small line was forming. Maybe the town sweetheart was starting to like him and would pass along the sentiment to her friends and neighbors.

That would help his cause, if he could only forget how good it had felt to kiss that hometown sweetheart. If only he could unkiss her, because the memory was powerful and just made him want her more. The temptation was damned inconvenient, especially with the thaw in her attitude. Because he didn't have the aptitude to do it right, pursuing a relationship with Jill Beck would be a big mistake.

Based on the Blackwater Lake cold shoulder he'd already experienced, if he screwed it up, acceptance in this town would be next to impossible.

Jill rubbed her eyes and then glanced at her watch, surprised at the time. It was Saturday, but unlike most people she wasn't off. She'd been at the computer for several hours, still making up for the half a day she'd squeezed out of her schedule for the Harvest Festival a week ago. First she'd completed an assignment for an online class, then her own budget. Adam Stone's rent check had cleared and it hit her that he'd been upstairs for two months now. Since renters paid ahead, he was going on number three.

When they'd first met, the weather had been sunny and warm, one of those perfect Montana days that made you forget the awful ones. And the awful ones were coming soon. Last night on the news the anchor had warned that a cold front was coming.

She stood and pressed her hands to her back, then raised her arms over her head and stretched from side to side. C.J. had been at the marina store with Brew all afternoon. It was almost time for dinner and she decided to walk down to get him. A phone call would do the job, but she needed some exercise after sitting for so long. Grabbing her quilted jacket from the hall tree, she opened the front door and gasped. The glare had her shielding her eyes.

"Snow."

Normally the first storm of the season was exciting, but not this one. A vague sensation of depression settled over her.

Footsteps sounded on the stairway to the upstairs apartment and moments later Adam appeared at the bottom. The last time they'd seen each other was when he'd given Mrs. Carberry a flu shot. Somehow, maybe by unspoken mutual agreement, they steered clear of meeting like this and she wasn't used to bumping into him. That was definitely for the best since she knew he was the reason for her lack of first snowfall joy. This was the kind of weather that would send a doctor from Dallas back to his warmer natural habitat.

"It's snowing." He was just shrugging into his jacket.

"The weather guy said it was a possibility, but I figured he was wrong. It's early." And just this once she'd so hoped winter would hold off. "You've been keeping long hours at the clinic."

"I've been pretty busy. Thanks to you." He slid his hands into the pockets of his sheepskin-lined jacket. "Haven't even had a chance to thank you for not only acknowledging me in public, but giving a recommendation, too."

"You're a good doctor, Adam. And definitely C.J.'s hero. Not only did you convince my son the wiggle worm to hold still, but the care you took closing up that nasty gash on his chin was amazing."

"I'd have turned C.J. over to someone in plastics if they were close by."

Jill had considered trekking to the hospital, but that was about her personal reasons for avoiding Adam. "I can't imagine a plastic surgeon doing a better job."

"A specialist knows the latest and best techniques in the field so patients get the most positive outcome possible." He blew out a breath, and a white cloud appeared in front of his face. "Family practice physicians see anyone with any problem and become experts in common problems. With C.J., I just used the smallest sutures available and put in as many as possible to minimize scarring."

"Clearly you've patched up little boys before." She rocked back on her heels.

"Accidents happen to everyone, all ages. I treated a grown woman who decided to go after an avocado pit with the business end of her paring knife. The pit shifted and the point of the blade went straight into her palm."

"Ouch." Jill winced.

"I'm told it wasn't painful in spite of the blood splatter. But her husband was kind of freaked out."

"That doesn't surprise me." She smiled at him and he smiled back. It was too nice and to break the spell she glanced away. "Boy, the snow is coming down even harder now. At this rate, the roads could be a problem."

"Yeah." His expression turned grim.

"What's wrong?"

"Mommy, look!" C.J. came running up the front walk. "It's snowing."

"I see that," she said.

"Hey, Dr. Adam, wanna have a snowball fight?"

The doctor smiled and ruffled the red hair. "Wish I could, champ, but—"

"Hey, Jill." Brewster was hurrying up the front path. The

walkway was now covered with snow and only someone familiar with the property would know where it was. Although her son's small footprints were still there, they were quickly being obscured. "It's comin' down hard."

"Yeah." What was it about the first snow that made everyone, including her, state the obvious?

Brewster stepped on the porch and stomped his feet. "If it's all the same to you, I'd like to head out before I get stuck here. You know how Hildie worries about her man."

"I do. Definitely go home," she said.

"Thanks." He looked at Adam. A friendly look that was new and different. "Hi, Doc."

"Mr. Smith."

Brew held out his hand. "Wanted to say thanks."

"For what?" Adam squeezed the other man's palm.

"I don't know what kind of medicine you gave my wife, but she's a new woman." He rubbed his chin. "It's more like she's back to her old self. Only better."

"I'm glad to hear it."

There was a twinkle in Brewster's blue eyes. "She's frisky again, if you know what I mean."

"I don't know," C.J. said. "What do you mean?"

"Just that," Jill interrupted, "Hildie has more energy. Right, Dr. Adam?"

"That's right." His grin was the epitome of male satisfaction. "More energy."

"And how." The older man grinned. "Doc, let me know if you decide you want that boat finished. It's the least I can do."

"I will, Mr. Smith—"

"Call me Brew." He turned and headed for the steps. With a wave, he said, "Talk to you tomorrow, Jill."

"Okay." Bewildered, she met Adam's gaze. "I think I just witnessed a miracle."

"What?" Adam said.

"Don't pretend you don't know. Brewster was nice to you."

"I got that. I'm pretty observant. I tend to notice when someone isn't trying to rip my head off."

"Brew tried to do that?" C.J. said, bewildered in his six-year-old way.

"Not recently," Adam clarified.

"What did you give Hildie?" Jill asked.

"I could tell you, but then I'd have to kill you. That's just a funny grown-up expression, champ," he explained to the boy. "Patient privacy laws are carved in stone—no pun intended." The cell phone in the case hooked to his belt vibrated and he plucked it out and answered, "Stone." He listened and his expression grew serious. "I'll meet you at the clinic. Be careful, Brady."

"Brady O'Keefe?" Jill took a wild guess and Adam's nod confirmed it.

"Maggie's in labor. He called me earlier and said he was taking her to the hospital. In case he couldn't get through because of the storm, he wanted to give me a heads-up."

"So, you're going to deliver her baby." It wasn't a question. He was the only doctor around.

"Yeah."

"Is her mom with her? Maureen is her birth coach."

"Brady didn't say. But don't worry. Delivering babies is another one of those common problems we family doctors face every day. And first babies, like all of them, are notoriously unpredictable. I have to run." He smiled at C.J. "We'll have that snowball fight another time."

"Okay."

"Bye." He waved, then jogged down the steps and turned left toward his car.

Jill watched the big, fat flakes falling out of the gray sky quickly start to obscure his footprints in the snow. Hildie wasn't the only one worried about her man out in the snow.

But Adam wasn't Jill's man. She didn't have the right to worry about him.

Did he know how to drive in snow? Did he have chains? Four-wheel drive? What if he had an accident? Would anyone notify her?

She didn't like this thought process one single bit but couldn't seem to turn it off. Fretting wasn't something you did for just anyone. It was something you did for someone you had feelings for. She didn't want to have feelings for Adam. Especially not now.

She looked up at the snow falling and sighed. An early winter just meant he'd skip out that much sooner. It was impossible to ignore how sad her heart was at the thought of him not in the apartment upstairs.

Chapter Eight

Jill woke early the next morning tired and crabby. She hadn't slept well, which was unusual for her during a snowstorm. The falling flakes always made everything especially hushed and still. It felt as if Mother Nature tucked the world in for a nap. Outside, everything was quiet and serene, but apparently not inside, at least for her. She couldn't stop herself from worrying about Adam driving in bad weather. And her friend Maggie was giving birth without the baby's father, the love of her life, by her side. Nothing was right and Jill felt helpless.

At least C.J. wasn't stirring yet. It was Sunday and he didn't have to get up for school. She hoped he would sleep in for a while.

She got up and dressed in warm clothes—jeans, sweater, boots—then went to the kitchen for coffee. Grounds and water were ready, but she was up before the automatic timer was set to go off. She hit the on button and soon heard the hiss and sizzle of the water followed by the warm, rich smell of her morning pick-me-up. Normally the familiar routine made her happy. There was comfort and stability in sameness, but nothing had been the same since Adam Stone had showed up in her life.

He hadn't returned before she went to bed last night and she'd stayed awake listening for the sound of his car. Sometime during the night she fell asleep and didn't know if he'd come home or not. Had he made it to the clinic? Were the roads passable? And if not, what happened to Maggie? She didn't like this at all. She didn't like that he was important enough for her to actively worry about. It wasn't the general concern of one human being for another. This was more, and scary.

She poured herself a cup of coffee, then went to the living room window to check out the driveway for his car. Her inspection never made it past the front walk where Adam was shoveling snow. Her snow, from her front walk.

The surge of joy coursing through her was a dangerous thing and she knew it, but there was no controlling something with a life of its own. If she were smart, she'd turn around, go to the computer and use this quiet time for her online econ class. It seemed she wasn't very bright because she poured coffee into a second mug, put on her jacket and gloves, then went outside and stood on the porch.

He was facing away and apparently hadn't heard her because the shoveling continued. He kept moving the snow from her walkway to the growing white pile beside it. The first rays of sun were just peeking over the top of the mountains and gave her more light to admire the broad expanse of his shoulders that made this tedious job far easier for him than it would be for her. His jacket hung over the porch railing and he was wearing jeans and a navy-and-brown plaid flannel shirt. The look was very geek-meets-lumberjack and worked for her in a very big, very unsettling way.

"Good morning," she said, her voice sounding louder in the early stillness. She started down the steps toward him.

He turned and spotted her with the coffee. It wasn't clear if one or both were responsible for the wide smile. "Hi."

She handed him the still-steaming mug. "I wasn't sure whether you like it black or not. There's milk and sugar inside."

"This is fine." He took a sip and his face registered sheer pleasure. "Better than fine."

"You're up early."

"Actually, I never went to bed. Just got home a little while ago."

Maybe the sound of his car had awakened her so early, possibly because on a subconscious level she'd been listening for him. Then she remembered why he'd been up all night. What with checking him out in detail, she'd forgotten about the reason he'd rushed off to the clinic—was it really yesterday?

"How's Maggie?" she asked.

"She's the proud mother of a beautiful, healthy baby girl—seven pounds, four ounces, twenty inches long."

"Danielle Maureen," Jill whispered, knowing the child would have been named after her father. "Maggie and Danny chose not to find out the sex of the baby, but he wanted a girl who looks just like her mother. That's the name they picked out."

Adam's brooding expression indicated that his thoughts turned a little sad. "It's hard to tell just yet who she looks like, but Danny got his little girl."

"I'm glad you were here to help her into the world."

"Me, too." He jammed the shovel into the snow, then went to sit on the top porch step, holding the mug between his palms. When she sat beside him, he said with a touch of awe and pride, "I just delivered my first Blackwater Lake baby."

First, as in he would be bringing more babies into this town, which meant he was planning to stay.

Happiness bubbled up inside her. "I think Maggie's baby should get some kind of award."

Adam looked sideways at her. "Do you, now?"

"Seems fair." She shrugged. "A blue ribbon—maybe pink, considering she's a girl."

"I can do better than a prize. I'm going to set up a college fund for her and make the first contribution."

Jill's heart melted like snow in the sun. "That's very thoughtful."

"It's only right. Her father gave his life for this country. The least I can do is make an investment in a good life for his daughter."

Jill couldn't think of a way to express how sweet this gesture was, and that was just as well. She had a lump in her throat the size of Montana and couldn't get words past it.

She swallowed hard. "I'm surprised Brady didn't call me about the baby," she said instead.

"He and Maureen talked about the list of people to notify, but there was a lot to do first what with getting mother and baby settled at home."

"She doesn't need to be in the hospital?" Jill asked.

"No. Everything about the birth was textbook normal and the baby's Apgar—the score for evaluating newborns," he explained, "was right on target. Virginia, my nurse, is going to check in on mother and baby. Of course I'm on call. After all that, they decided to wait for morning to make calls," he finished.

"That makes sense. Everyone is fine. That's most important." She looked at him and then the snow shovel. "And you're still here." She hadn't meant to lump that in the "most important" category, but somehow it came out that way. "Shoveling snow on my walkway."

"I am." He took a sip of coffee. "For the record, I wouldn't have been able to pull off a clandestine getaway since there's an apartment up there with a lot of stuff in it. But the point is that I'm not going anywhere. Talk is cheap. The best way to prove I'm not afraid of a little cold weather is to embrace it."

"Put your money where your mouth is? So to speak," she added.

"Exactly." He rubbed the back of his neck. "If I were a mean-spirited sort of person, I'd have you take a picture of me with the snow shovel and text it to my mother."

"Cell service is spotty here in the mountains, and why would you want to?"

"As a giant 'take that,'" he admitted. "I've been getting pressure from the home front."

She finished the last of the cold coffee in her mug, then asked, "About what?"

"Going home."

"To Dallas?"

"Yeah." He looked at her. "Mom called when she heard about the storm on the news. She wanted to know if I'm finished playing country doctor yet. Was I cold and ready to end this back-to-nature experiment? Did I miss the Dallas Metroplex where it's flat and the sun is shining on roads not covered with snow?"

"And?"

"No."

"No, what?" she nudged.

"I don't miss Texas. I like the mountains and the cold. Shoveling snow is good exercise and I'm staying put." He grinned. "The text picture would be me letting my actions speak louder than words my mother refuses to hear."

"I think your mother's reaction is understandable."

The surprise on his face said that wasn't what he'd expected from her. "*Understandable* isn't a word I normally hear coming out of your mouth."

"I deserve that. I've been skeptical about your longevity here in Blackwater Lake."

"You and everyone else," he added wryly.

Jill ignored that. "But this is your mother we're talking about. Of course she'd like her son to be close by. God knows if it were C.J., I'd want him under my roof forever."

"Trust me on this. No guy wants to live with his mother, and if he does, serious therapy should be considered, stat." He rested his forearms on his knees. "Don't get me wrong. I love my folks. And I plan to visit them. But the life they made for themselves isn't the one I want for me."

Jill smiled. "Then I'm sure your family is pleased that you have it. From the maternal perspective, I can say with absolute certainty that parents ultimately want their children to be happy. It's what I want for my son."

And just then the front door opened and the son in question raced outside. "It's all white out here!" he declared as if he were the only one who could see and the world needed a newsflash.

Jill couldn't help smiling at the fact that snow was one of the things that always rated an exclamation point from her little guy. "Want to shovel it?"

"I wanna have a snowball fight first." He ran down the porch steps and shoved his hands into the white stuff. After mounding the snow into a ball, he threw it at Adam and made a direct hit.

Brushing at the wetness on his face, the doctor pretended anger that fooled no one, least of all C.J. "I can't believe I practiced throwing a baseball with you. I taught you everything you know and this is the thanks I get?"

"I'm gettin' pretty good. Betcha can't hit me." C.J. stood there, making himself a target. He was goading Adam to play.

"I'll show you good." And just like that Adam took the bait. He set down his mug and in one athletic motion descended the stairs and reached down for a handful of snow. "It's every man for himself."

C.J. waved his hands. "Can't hit me!" Famous last words because the first shot hit him in the chest with a gentle splat. "Lucky shot. Betcha can't hit me again."

But he didn't stand still and Adam chased him. This went on for a while and Jill couldn't figure out where Adam got the energy after being up all night. Then things shifted. Apparently there was unspoken male communication and they both turned on her, dragging her into the fray. After that it was a free-for-all. There was running, laughing, ducking around the house and behind bushes. Adam grabbed up C.J. and tickled him, making him squeal with laughter. Snowballs were flying and the spirit of revenge filled the air.

Ten minutes later they were all wet, cold and laughing. Jill hadn't had such carefree fun for longer than she could remember, but all good things must come to an end. "It's time to go inside."

"Aw, Mom. I want to play with Dr. Adam some more."

"Adam needs some sleep. He was up all night delivering Aunt Maggie's baby girl."

C.J. looked unimpressed. "Tyler and me wanted a boy."

"Sorry. That doesn't change the fact that he needs to rest and you have to get out of those wet things before you get sick."

"Okay," the boy said, trudging reluctantly up the porch steps. "Bye, Dr. Adam."

"Bye." Adam pushed the wet hair off his forehead. "See you later, Jill."

"Yeah." After her son disappeared inside, she watched the doctor walk toward the stairs leading to the second floor-apartment. A thought flashed into her mind and out came the words. "Hey, Adam, want to have dinner with us tonight?"

He stopped and looked over his shoulder. "To what do I owe the invitation?"

"Let's call it a thank-you for shoveling snow."

"Okay, let's." But the intense look in his eyes called it something else entirely. "What time?"

"How about five-thirty?"

"I'll be there."

And she'd be waiting.

At five-twenty-five Adam stood on Jill's porch where light spilled from her front window. Inside, there was laughter, love and hugs—and somehow he felt as if he was on the outside looking in, all of that happiness just out of his reach. It was as if his nose was pressed up against the window and he was getting a glimpse of what he could never have. Being punished because he'd had his chance and blown it. Now he was a family practice doctor without a family.

The life I want for me.

He'd said that to Jill earlier but wasn't sure what that meant anymore. He hadn't thought past just wanting to move to Blackwater Lake, Montana. He loved the mountains, lake, outdoors. It was a place where he'd been happy. This probation period the town put him through was unexpected. They had their reasons, and all of them were about Jill.

She was unexpected, too.

All this soul-searching, deep thought and questioning wasn't like him. Maybe he was overtired. Being up all night to deliver a baby could do that. The high of bringing a new life into the world had worn off. Even after sleeping for a few hours today, he couldn't seem to get it back. He couldn't shake the feeling that accepting this dinner invitation had been a bad idea, that no good would come of it. Just like the last time.

But he had accepted and not showing up would undo all the positive steps he'd taken. It was dinner with Jill and C.J. He would leave right after eating. What could happen?

After knocking he'd expected to hear the sound of six-year-old running feet. He didn't and was surprised when Jill answered.

"Hi. You're right on time."

"That happens when you don't have to worry about traffic on the drive over." He walked inside. "Where's C.J.?"

"Finishing up his shower. He didn't want to miss anything this time."

Adam remembered in vivid detail what the kid had missed last time. Heat poured through him at the memories of his mouth on Jill's, her soft body pressed against his. The feel of her in his arms was too perfect, but that was chemistry and physiology. Neither of those two things made the kiss right. He promised himself that there wouldn't be anything to miss tonight. It was just dinner. C.J. would be there. They'd eat, and then he would plead fatigue and go home. He would spread goodwill by keeping his word. Mission accomplished. End of story.

"It's cold out here." Jill rubbed her arms. "Come on in."

"Thanks."

He walked past her and looked around. The inside wasn't exactly as he remembered; Halloween decorations were everywhere. Fake webs hung on lamp shades, and picture frames had black plastic spiders stuck in them. Orange pumpkins of various sizes sat on flat surfaces throughout the living room. On Jill's desk was a stand about a foot high with hanging wooden cutouts of orange and white triangular candy corn, a witch's hat, ghosts and black bats.

"This looks very cool," he said.

"C.J. did a lot of it. I think he likes Halloween almost better than Christmas."

Adam could relate. But he didn't remember his house looking like this. His mother was too busy working. Except that excuse didn't quite cut it any more than he believed C.J. had done most of this. Jill worked, took classes online and was a single mom who found the time to decorate for a holiday.

Then he heard the sound of bare running feet slapping against the wooden floor just before the redheaded chaperone burst through the hall doorway.

"Hi, Dr. Adam."

"Hey, champ." He squatted down and the boy unexpectedly ran into his arms. The smell of freshly washed little boy slipped into a soft spot inside him. "You look clean."

"I am."

"Come on, you two. Dinner is ready." Jill walked toward the kitchen and glanced over her shoulder as she talked. "It's nothing fancy. Just homemade soup, salad and bread."

Adam followed, unable to resist a chance to appreciate the Beck backside at its best in a snug pair of jeans. "You baked bread?"

"I have a bread maker and a mix. Not a big deal."

"But it's not store-bought?" he clarified.

"No," she confirmed. "Soup is chicken and rice. C.J. and I like that when the weather turns cold."

"Mommy makes the best," her loyal son piped up.

"Sure smells good." Felt good. Too good. He took the same seat as last time and realized this was the beginning of a habit.

Jill put a tureen and ladle on the table, then pulled a bowl filled with greens from the refrigerator. After that she assembled the sliced homemade bread and butter and proceeded to toss the salad. "I hope you like oil and red wine vinegar."

"My favorite."

"Not mine." C.J. wrinkled his nose. "I don't like salad."

"Which is why you need to eat all the carrots in your soup." She sat down and gave her son a "mom" look. "I expect you to put some vegetables in your bowl along with the chicken and rice."

"Okay." The guilty expression was a clue that they'd been through this before.

After the boy was finished ladling, Adam helped himself. "Looks good."

"It's not mashed potatoes and hot dogs." Jill's eyes sparkled with mischief. "But it's filling."

Adam ate a spoonful and nodded appreciatively. It was hot, tasty and just the thing for a snowy evening. They ate in silence for a few moments before he asked, "So, C.J., what are you going to be for Halloween?"

"Maybe a doctor." He chewed on a carrot.

Jill looked uneasy as she warned, "That's not a for-sure."

A life lesson from mother to son, Adam thought. Never count on anything. Everyone learned it sooner or later. He'd gone into marriage thinking it would be forever and found out just how wrong he could be.

"Where do you go trick or treating?" he asked. "It's pretty isolated out here. The next house is a long way down the road."

Jill buttered a piece of bread. "I take C.J. into town and hit a few streets before the party at the town hall. The kids get the door-to-door experience in a safe environment."

"I can't imagine anything about Blackwater Lake being unsafe."

"True," she said. "We're lucky that way, but I don't take anything for granted."

"What are you gonna be, Dr. Adam?"

"I hadn't thought about it," he admitted. "I'll have to find out if the staff at the clinic dresses up." He grinned. "I can picture Virginia in a witch's hat, a big wart on her nose."

"Gives you a hard time, does she?" Jill's eyes twinkled.

"In a word? Yes." He shrugged. "There's no way to sugarcoat it."

Jill took a bite of her salad. "I don't know what I'd have done without Ginny when my mom got sick."

"She told me. I'm glad someone was there for you." He truly meant that.

"Mom, I'm finished with my soup. See?" He tilted his empty bowl for inspection.

"Good job, kiddo. All that outdoor activity must have made you hungry."

"I still am. Can I have dessert?"

"Yes. But you have to wait patiently until Adam and I are finished."

"Okay." The agreement was automatic, but actual compliance was like trying to hold back a tsunami after a magnitude-nine earthquake. He wiggled and watched, but there was nothing patient about his waiting. After a minute or two he asked, "Aren't you guys done yet?"

Jill met his gaze across the table as she scooped up the last of her soup.

"I'm finished. Adam?"

"Me, too." He tilted his empty bowl for them to see.

"Would you like more soup?" Clearly she enjoyed just the tiniest bit of teasing.

"He's full," C.J. said quickly. "Right, Dr. Adam?"

"Not quite." Adam couldn't resist a little ribbing of his own. But only a little. "I have just enough room left for dessert."

"Is it time now, Mom?"

"Yes." She smiled at her son, then said, "It's just ice cream."

"My favorite."

"Mine, too," the little guy added.

"I picked up a couple of quarts from Maggie's place. There was a picture of her and the baby up behind the cash register." She stood and carried her dishes to the sink.

"I'll get those." Adam stood and picked up the remaining plates, bowls and spoons.

"I wanna help." C.J. slid off his chair and followed Adam.

Jill pulled the ice cream out of the freezer, then scooped it into bowls and set them on the table. "Dig in, guys."

"Can I watch the movie about the toys while I eat my dessert? Please, Mommy. I won't spill."

She thought for a moment, but the soft look on her face wasn't leading up to a negative response. "Okay. Just this once."

"Can we all watch the movie?" C.J.'s expression was eager.

"Why not?"

So all of them trooped into the living room and Adam held her bowl while she put the DVD in the player and turned on the TV. The studio logo filled the screen, and the three of them sat on the sofa in front of it with the little boy in the middle. This scenario was not in Adam's frame of reference. A quiet night watching television and not being alone felt really nice, which was why he knew it was past time to leave. And he would, as soon as a decent amount of time passed so it didn't seem rude.

When they'd all finished their dessert, Jill took the empty bowls. "I'm just going to put everything in the dishwasher."

"Do you need some help?"

"No. Enjoy the movie." She smiled, then turned toward the kitchen.

He watched her walk away, the unconsciously sexy sway of her hips. Her curly hair spilled over the collar of her green sweater, and all he could think about was how beautiful she'd look naked, how much he wanted to see her thick red hair spread over a pillow. It was definitely time for him to say good-night.

About ten minutes later she was back, looking down at her son. "Someone's out cold."

"Not me." Adam was too hot to be cold, and that was all her fault. But that's not what she meant and she wasn't talking about him.

C.J. had curled against him, his head resting on Adam's chest. The slow, even breathing was a clue that the boy had fallen asleep.

She bent and tenderly brushed the hair off her son's forehead. "I guess he's worn out from all the activity today."

"Yeah."

With the sweet scent of her skin filling his head and her mouth so close, activities came to Adam's mind that were all about tangled legs and twisted sheets.

"He needs to be in bed," she said softly. "He's gotten so heavy it's not easy for me to pick him up. I'll try not to rouse him too much while I walk him to his room."

"I'll carry him in."

"That would be great. Thanks." Her gaze met his. "I'll turn down the bed."

He nodded, then picked up C.J., who mumbled something before curling into his chest. He was solid, all boy, and tugged at Adam's heart. This was just one more reason why coming tonight had been a boneheaded idea. But as soon as the kid was settled, he'd be out of there.

He followed Jill to the second bedroom and as gently as possible put the little guy on the superhero sheets. When C.J. turned on his side without waking, his mom pulled the matching comforter over him. After kissing the freckled cheek, she quietly walked out with Adam behind her.

In the living room, the movie was still softly playing. They stood by the back of the couch and looked at each other. Her eyes were liquid and soft and he could easily drown in them.

"I should go." Because he so badly wanted to stay.

"Yeah. You must be tired after pulling an all-nighter."

Not that tired, he thought, but kept the words inside. "I'm hanging in there."

She walked him to the door. "Thanks for shoveling my snow."

"You're welcome. Thanks for dinner." He put his hand on the knob and opened the door. Frigid air blew in and mixed with the seductive warmth of her. It took every ounce of his willpower to say, "Good night, Jill."

Adam looked down at her, the way she rubbed her arms against the cold, and couldn't make himself walk out. He wanted to keep her warm. He wanted to hold her.

He simply wanted her more than he'd wanted a woman in his life. When something in her eyes made him lean toward her, he lowered his head and she went up on tiptoe until their lips met.

No way was he leaving now.

Chapter Nine

The gentleness Adam had shown her son was Jill's undoing. The strong man, so careful with C.J., had made her all gooey and warm inside. How could a woman resist the sight of a strong man carrying a child, *her* child, with such obvious caring? And he'd shoveled her snow, for goodness' sake. The best she could do was soup and salad, but he'd been happy with that. She'd been fighting this overwhelming attraction since the first moment they'd met, and she just couldn't do it anymore. All of the above pushed her over the edge.

Their mouths touched and the contact unleashed everything she'd been holding back. She frantically tugged at the shirt tucked into his jeans. He groaned and settled his hands at her waist, sliding them under her sweater to touch her bare skin. His palms were warm and he moved them up slowly until his thumbs brushed the undersides of her breasts. She couldn't hold back a moan. It had been so long since she'd had a man's hands on her like this, she nearly wept from the sheer joy in the sensation.

When she undid the top button of his shirt and ran her finger over the dusting of hair in the V, he sucked in a quick breath and took her hand in his. He kissed each fingertip before drawing the index finger into his mouth and sucking deeply. She felt the pull all the way to her belly, and between her thighs an aching need started pulsing.

"I want you." Adam's eyes burned with intensity. "But not here."

"C.J.," she whispered.

He nodded and took her hand, tugging her down the hall, past where her son was sleeping and into the master bedroom. He closed and locked the door. Again her insides turned into melted goo at the sweet and considerate act.

The garage-sale bedside lamp with the scalloped, off-white shade was turned on, but Adam's tall form blocked the light. He took her closer to the bed, then stopped and cupped her face in his hands and kissed her. He tasted like chicken soup and ice cream, so ordinary—yet not. As kisses went, it was probably the best of her life. Not too slow or too fast. Not too hard or soft. Just the right amount of pressure to prime the passion. But she didn't need priming, she needed him.

Jill reached up and slid her finger over his earlobe, then down his neck and stopped at his collarbone. His groan of need at the lightest of touches made her smile and then he kissed it away. Tension arced between them and they pulled at each other's clothes again. Shirt and sweater came off and were tossed away. They worked the snaps and zippers on jeans and yanked them off, taking shoes and socks, too. The sound of their harsh breathing filled the room, but it was fueled by passion, not exertion.

She stood still while Adam reached around and undid the

clasp of her bra. The straps slid down her arms and he helped it along, his eyes intense and approving as he stared at her.

"You are so beautiful," he breathed, cupping her in his palms.

The feel of his hands on her bare flesh was too exquisite for words and she pressed herself more firmly against him. When he brushed his thumbs over her nipples, the sensation rocked her world and kicked her breathing up higher.

"That's so good," she whispered. "Too good."

She pulled away and yanked the throw pillows off the bed and pitched them over the other side onto the floor. Then she turned down the comforter and crawled onto the mattress before dragging the top sheet over her. Finally she wiggled out of her panties and tossed them on the floor.

Lifting herself up onto her forearm, she studied him, standing there in his boxers. He looked pretty spectacular. Wide shoulders, broad chest with just the right amount of hair, a flat belly and muscular legs. She judged him a fifteen on a scale of one to ten. And her gaze slid to that part of him that made him so male, so ready. It had been a long time for her. She was out of practice, not that she'd ever been in practice, and groaned as a thought struck her.

"What's wrong?"

She met his concerned gaze. "I don't have protection. Oh, Adam… This is awful. We can't… I can't…"

"I have a condom." He shrugged at her look. "I always have one. Don't leave home without it. Guy thing. Just don't read anything into it."

"Not judging, just grateful."

She watched the play of muscle on his back as he reached for his jeans, pulled out the wallet, then put the square packet on the nightstand.

Jill held out her arms and he dropped his boxers, and came to her in the bed. He pulled her against him and lowered them both to the mattress. He kissed her lips, her neck, her breasts, until she could hardly draw air into her lungs. She kissed him back, sliding her hands over his shoulders, arms and chest. They were touching everywhere except where she most wanted.

"Oh, God, Adam…"

"I know."

He rolled away and reached for the condom, then ripped it open. After covering himself, he pulled her back into his arms and shifted his body over hers. Taking his weight on his elbows, he entered her slowly, letting her body accept him. Moments later, he reached his hand between them to brush his thumb over the bundle of nerve endings at the juncture of her thighs. The touch was like a jolt from a live electrical wire that sent vibrations rippling through her, pleasure pulsing everywhere. She clung to him as her body shattered into a million pieces.

Breathing harsh and shallow, Adam thrust once more before he groaned and went still, then shuddered as he buried his face in her neck.

Jill wasn't sure how long they stayed like that or where Adam found the energy to move, but he did and went into the bathroom. The light went on and she heard water running. A few minutes later he was back and the mattress dipped from his weight as he slid back in bed and reached for her.

"That was really…" She stopped and sighed, unable to come up with a good enough adjective.

"I know." He linked her fingers with his, then rested their joined hands on his belly.

"This is nice." She yawned and snuggled against him.

There was something about a warm man beside you on a cold night. She missed it and sighed again as her eyes drifted closed. She must have slept because sometime during the night she woke up cold. Sliding her hand over, she searched for Adam, but he wasn't there. And the house was quiet. There were no unusual sounds suggesting he might still be around.

The disappointment of being alone was bigger and harder than she'd expected. Damn the cuddling. Sex was sex and it had been pretty fabulous, but holding each other after was intimate, and personal and really lovely. She hated the weakness, hated that she knew better but had ignored her own warnings.

Adam had left her bedroom door open and she heard C.J. call out in his sleep, probably a nightmare, which happened from time to time. Still naked, she slid out of bed and put on flannel pajamas. Maybe it was the cold air hitting her body, but common sense came back in a rush. What if C.J. had tried to come in and the door was locked? It never was and he'd have known something was up.

Her son badly wanted a man in his life, and finding his hero here would give him ideas. When it didn't work out the way he hoped, the fall would be even harder. As disappointed as she was, maybe it was for the best that Adam had left.

But, oh, how she wished his arms were still around her. The intensity of that feeling was a very scary thing.

Just before six in the evening Adam heard a knock on his door and the fact that it was Halloween gave him a big clue who was on the other side. He opened it and, as he'd thought, C.J. was there.

"Trick or treat!" The kid was wearing a small white coat with his name embroidered on the pocket, black horn-rimmed glasses and a plastic stethoscope around his neck.

"Hey, champ. You look like a doctor."

"I don't give shots," he said. "Mommy bought me a doctor set from the toy store with the thing that goes around your arm and a shot-giver, but I left that home."

"Good to know." He looked past the boy and saw Jill on the landing. "Hi."

She lifted a hand in greeting, then slid her fingers into the pockets of her jeans. It was possible for her to look more uncomfortable, but he wasn't sure how. He hadn't seen her since that mind-blowing night a couple of days ago. The look he saw on her face now said she was having second thoughts about sex.

Adam looked down at C.J. "I don't have any candy. I wasn't expecting trick or treaters."

"Aw, that's okay. I just wanted to show you my costume anyways."

"How about if I make it up to you with ice cream from Potter's?"

"Cool!"

"C.J.?" Jill's voice was strained. "Why don't you run down to the marina and show Brew your costume before he goes home?"

"Okay." He lifted his hand in a wave. "Bye, Dr. Adam."

"Bye. Have fun tonight."

"Don't stay long, C.J. And meet me at the car."

"Okay." The boy was already at the bottom of the stairs.

Light from inside spilled over the tension in Jill's face. "Don't make promises to him, Adam. Don't make a date with him."

"Why not?"

"Because he believes. He'll count on it."

"There's no reason he shouldn't." Adam had a feeling they weren't talking about C.J. or ice cream now. "What's really on your mind?" Sex was on his. It shouldn't be, but no one was perfect.

"About the other night," she said, folding her arms over her chest. "It can't happen again."

"I see."

"No, you don't. There are reasons. A lot of them."

"It's not necessary to justify anything to me. If the spark isn't there…"

"This has nothing to do with sparks. It's a distraction and I can't afford that right now."

"Right now? What's changed?" Adam wasn't sure why he felt the urge to push back. She was right and he had his own reasons for putting on the brakes.

"The thing is…" She caught the corner of her lip between her teeth. "Before… With the other doctor… I let myself have feelings. It had been a long time since I put myself out there. Everything was fun and flirty, but all of a sudden there was a future to think about and it made me happy. Then, he said he was leaving. Small-town life wasn't for him."

"He was an idiot. Probably still is."

"I agree. But my little boy thought the sun rose and set on that idiot and he just walked away."

Adam had thought he was past having to reassure her that he wasn't leaving. "We've been through this."

"That was before we— You know." Now she was shy and awkward as opposed to uncomfortable.

"You're right. The 'you know' does change things." He knew exactly what she was saying. "And I agree that it can't happen again."

"You do?"

He nodded. "You're a single mother. I think I know you well enough to know that an intimate relationship needs to mean something. You just talked about a future. And there wouldn't be one with me."

She looked surprised, but said, "Okay."

She'd felt the need to explain and so did he. "I'm divorced. College sweetheart."

"Why didn't it work out?"

"I have a complicated relationship with my parents. That

sounds so stupid, but we're all a product of our environment." He sighed. "In any other family, my academic accomplishments would have been considered stellar, but not with my folks."

"I know how brilliant and accomplished your family is." She'd done the background check.

"I put a lot of energy into not caring about their approval. I told myself that the effort I was putting into being at the top of my class was only for me, that I didn't care what they thought about my life and my choices. But my parents loved Judith Bennett. Even my grandmother was a fan. So I proposed and we were happy right up until I didn't meet her expectations."

"So she turned to someone else? There was another man?"

"I think that would have been easier to take. I chose a medical specialty that she didn't consider special." He remembered the betrayal on Judy's face when he broke the news that he wanted to be a family practice doctor. "She thought she was marrying into a family of high achievers and that I would be famous like the rest of the Stones. Obviously we had a failure to communicate. Failure leaves a mark when you're a Stone, so now I make sure to put all my cards on the table. No assumptions, no misunderstandings."

"What are you saying?"

"Marriage isn't something I'm interested in doing again."

"Good to know." Her voice was steady, but there was a bruised look in her eyes and he hated himself for putting it there.

"It's for the best."

"I agree straightforward communication is the way to go. For me that's about C.J."

"What about him?"

"He's my first priority. His welfare and happiness."

"So you've said."

"But it's more important now." She blew out a long breath. "After you left the other night, I realized how easily C.J. could have found you there. He'd have asked questions."

"Kids aren't easily fooled."

"I dodged a bullet this time, but taking another chance isn't something I'm willing to do. If we continue seeing each other, he'll get ideas about you, me, a future. Believe me, he doesn't need encouragement for that, but there's no win in this situation, especially since you've been completely honest about your intentions. I don't want him hurt."

Adam understood and respected her for protecting her child. "He's a great kid. I like hanging out with him."

"For now. But what happens when you don't?"

He knew she was referring to the other doctor who'd hurt them both. "That's not going to happen. I moved here because of the small-town life."

"And you spent summers here, so you knew what you were getting into." She settled her purse more securely on her shoulder. "But no one knows better than me that there are lots of ways to leave even if you're still here."

"Mom?" The small voice carried up the stairway. "It's time to go trick or treatin'."

"Coming, sweetie." She smiled, but the look was brittle around the edges. "Thanks for understanding. Bye, Adam."

He watched her stiff back as she descended the stairs. Shouldn't he be more relieved after the straightforward talk? Now she knew he was a confirmed bachelor and he was completely on the same page with her about not setting C.J. up for a fall. Everybody was happy.

He should be, but not so much.

That warm and gooey feeling inside could turn on you in a heartbeat, Jill decided.

She should be pleased that Adam had been so understanding about ending any future physical relationship. Maybe she would be if he hadn't dropped his own bombshell.

Married? Really? And no one knew this? She'd done the background, but the marital status came up single, not divorced. And why did it really matter? At least she found out he wasn't on the market before her heart got sucked in and she got hurt. Maybe a little hurt. Nothing that spending time at this Halloween party couldn't fix, although if she'd known it would be necessary to hide her hurt feelings from people who knew her too well, she'd have planned to wear a full face mask.

Children and adults were gathered in the town hall, which was located one street over from Main, next to the courthouse. Hanging from the ceiling were orange-and-black streamers, cobwebs and tissue paper ghosts. One fourth of the big room was partitioned off into a haunted house, complete with zombie guide, squeaky door and eerie laughter sound effects.

On tables along the wall, potluck food was set up. On the other side of the room, games for the younger children were in progress. C.J. was with a group of boys in the corner who had dumped already-inspected candy from their trick-or-treat pumpkins. Tyler was there and it looked as though the two of them were in negotiations for a major trade.

Jill was checking out the choices on the food table, although her appetite had been missing since that informative chat with Adam. The mayor stopped beside her, paper plate in hand.

"Hey, Jill. How are you?"

"Good," she lied. "Yourself?"

"Can't complain. Technically, I could, but who would listen?"

"I would," Jill volunteered. She'd rather focus on someone else's problems than her own.

"I'm really fine." The sad gray eyes said something else.

It was said that eyes were a window to the soul, and with a flash of insight, Jill somehow knew that Loretta Goodson had loved deeply once and it hadn't ended well. She wondered if her own experience with Adam Stone had somehow made her more perceptive. It certainly made her empathize.

"What's going on with you? I haven't seen you since the football fundraiser at Potter's Ice Cream Parlor, before Maggie's baby was born. Have you seen her yet?" the mayor asked.

"Yes, but just for a couple of minutes. I remember how it feels when you're so tired you can't see straight and want to cry with the newborn, but you're the grown-up and can't."

Her Honor looked wistful. "I've heard it's really hard."

With the new insight Jill realized she'd touched a nerve with the mayor and a change of subject would be good. "The baby is beautiful and healthy. Or so Adam says and he's the expert."

"How is that hunky health care professional who's renting your upstairs apartment?"

"Still renting it." *For now,* Jill added to herself. When she'd left him earlier, he'd seemed far too relieved that she was ending it before anything really got started. And she didn't want to talk about Adam. Getting him out of her head would be better. *Good luck with that,* she thought bitterly. "What's new, Your Honor?"

"Still trying to get that golf course and club idea off the ground, but so far I can't get anyone to commit resources to the project."

"That would create some jobs, which would be a good thing." Jill felt the sluggish economy just as much as every business owner in town.

"More leisure activities would boost tourism, but it would also attract the retired demographic, which is good for construction. More folks moving here would pump money into the town's existing infrastructure." The mayor sighed. "It's giving me gray hair."

"Oh, please. Don't even complain about yours." Jill tugged on a lock of her red hair sticking out from under her hat. "Compared to mine, yours should be in a national ad campaign for product."

"Thank you." Loretta grinned. "And for this flattering shade of brown I'm incredibly grateful to Susie at A Wild Hair. On a man, gray hair is distinguished. A silver-haired woman isn't a fox, just old. It's my plan to keep everyone guessing about my age, but not out loud or to my face."

Jill laughed. "C.J. thinks anyone over twelve is ancient."

"Ah, the world according to a six-year-old. To be that innocent again."

Jill wasn't sure she'd ever been so innocent at that young an age. She remembered hearing her mother cry on those nights her father didn't come home and the fights on the nights he did. Finally he just left and her mother looked sad. As a single mom, she knew it was important that she not bring any pain or distress into her son's life. He might not get the male influence or the family he craved, but there was something to be said for a stable environment.

"So C.J. had the stitches removed from his chin all right?" The mayor took the tongs from a bucket of chicken and put a drumstick on her plate.

"He did," Jill confirmed. "And the jury's still out on who was more traumatized, him or me."

Loretta glanced at C.J., roughhousing in the corner with his friend. "It's purely an observation, but I'd say Dr. Stone worked magic on that boy since he's dressed for Halloween as a health care professional."

"I have to admit Adam was really good with him. And you can hardly see the scar on his chin."

"And what about your scars?" Those sharp gray eyes didn't miss much.

"I'm doing fine." If you didn't count sleeping with Adam, loving every minute of it and telling him not ever again.

"Has Adam worked his magic on you?"

Jill shook her head. "I didn't split open my chin."

"No, your wounds are on the inside where no one can see them."

There was no arguing with that, so she didn't try. "I'm fine."

"But are you happy?" Loretta's voice was kind. "Dr. Stone is an attractive man. I know there are people in this town who haven't welcomed him as warmly as they might have if you hadn't been hurt by that one who shall remain nameless. There's no reason to believe that this one will abruptly pick up and leave."

"Are you trying to talk me into going after him?" Jill stared at the older woman. "Since when does your job description include matchmaking?"

"It's a chick thing, not a mayor thing." Loretta grinned. "In my humble opinion you and Adam Stone would make a lovely couple."

"And if it didn't work out, what happens to C.J.?"

"You can't protect him from everything, Jill, and if you try it's not doing him any favors."

"Keeping my son from harm is in my job description."

"Absolutely—to a point. But you can't surround him with bubble wrap. Sure, you take a chance and he could get hurt and mope around. It might even leave a scar on the inside like the one on his chin. But it's experiences that give him the character to deal with what life will throw at him. He needs to learn that not every kid on a team with a losing record should get a trophy. That's not a realistic view of the world."

"Every child needs to know he has value."

"I couldn't agree more. But they need to find goals and work for them. You can't give C.J. his self-esteem, he's got to earn that on his own. Like you. Taking over your mother's business, raising your child and taking classes for your degree. I can't tell you how much I admire what you're doing. And what an amazing example you are to your son."

Jill knew the words made a lot of sense and she appreciated the approval. "Thank you, Your Honor."

"And while I'm on my soapbox, let me give you some words of advice. No one can guarantee that Dr. Stone will be any different from the doctor who disappointed your little guy. But he's here now and we might as well use him."

She was pretty sure Her Honor, the mayor, wasn't talking about sex, but the fact that Jill's thoughts went there wasn't comforting. How did she protect herself from that?

Chapter Ten

Adam was driving too fast and his tires squealed when he turned off Lakeview Road and into his driveway. Jill's car was there and he parked beside it. He was frustrated and pissed off. On top of that, it was late and he was tired. There was a gnawing in his gut that was mostly about feeling powerless and a little about being hungry.

He turned off the car then got out and slammed the door harder than necessary. Walking around the corner, he saw the lights on in Jill's place. That didn't help the gnawing in his gut.

Every night Adam walked up the steps to the porch that led straight to her front door and bypassed it for the stairs up to his place. The difference tonight was that it was harder than normal to head for the stairs and not stop to knock on that door.

Behind it Jill and C.J. ate dinner, laughed and talked. It should be the little guy's bedtime, but maybe he got to stay up a little later on Friday night since there was no school the next day. Now Adam knew what it was like to hang out with them.

He knew what it was like to make love to her.

Temptation pulsed through him, but he tamped it down and took the stairs two at a time. He unlocked his door and flipped the light switch on the wall just inside. There was a small table where he usually dropped his mail, but he couldn't do that because he had forgotten to stop and get it.

"Damn it."

Turning lights on, he went to the kitchen, opened the fridge and grabbed a beer. After twisting off the cap, he took a long pull of the cold brew. It did nothing to smooth out the edges of his aggravation or the emptiness in his belly.

He yanked open the freezer hoping a complete microwavable meal in a box would be there. Since he hadn't been to the market, it would take a loaves-and-fishes miracle to accomplish that. The best he could do was a couple slices of ham on stale wheat bread. He slapped a sandwich together and ate it standing up. Not nearly the gourmet quality of hot dogs and mashed potatoes, but it took care of the hunger if not the gnawing emptiness.

He needed to do email and, beer in hand, headed to his second bedroom that was used as an office. On the way he heard a knock on the door. A couple of thoughts flashed through his mind. If there was a medical emergency, someone would call.

It was too late for C.J. to be there and Jill wouldn't let him come upstairs, per their agreement about not giving him ideas. She wouldn't be there, also per their agreement. He opened the door and saw Jill standing there with a big box in her hands.

Adam had never been happier to be wrong. "Hi."

"This wouldn't fit in your mailbox, so the postman left it with me. Mail, too." She nodded at the envelopes on top.

"I'd have come down to get this." He took the box from her and set everything on the table beside the door.

"No problem. I thought something that heavy might be important."

"Books." He liked to read, but lately that was more about filling up the long evenings than pleasurable leisure time.

"Okay. Well, I heard you come home and just wanted you to have your mail. Landlady duty fulfilled."

"Right. Thanks. You should get back to C.J."

"Actually, Ty asked him to sleep over since tomorrow is Saturday."

"Ah." Adam nodded. "So Cabot has the boys."

"He took them to the high school football game," she explained. "The kids love that. They get to run around like wild Indians and fit right in with the Blackwater Lake High mascot, which conveniently happens to be an Indian. Cabot gets to watch the game and relive his glory days as star quarterback."

"Yeah." He hoped the boys had been running around and were not aware of what had happened on the field at the beginning of the game.

"What's wrong, Adam?"

"Just a bad day." He finished the last of his beer, then held on to the bottle and stared at the label.

Jill was half turned away from him, leaning toward the stairway, poised for a quick escape. Her body language all but screamed that she really didn't want to be here. There was reluctance in her voice when she asked, "Do you want to talk about it?"

"Wouldn't do any good."

"You're sure?" She took a step back.

"It's just frustration. Comes with the territory." But when

that territory could be different, it was damned hard to let go of the restlessness and discontent. "I'm okay."

"You don't look okay."

"Really?"

"Yeah, really," she said. "Your mouth is all pinchy and tight. There's a look in your eyes like you want to put your fist through a wall."

"Interesting diagnosis, Dr. Beck. I thought medical school taught me how to assume an indecipherable poker face."

"Not so much. Either you need a poker face refresher course or whatever happened that made your day really bad got to you more than it normally would."

"Probably all of the above." He blew out a long breath.

"Now you're scaring me." She studied him carefully. "Did you lose a patient?"

"No," he said quickly.

She was shaking and the cold air made white clouds of her breath. "Then why the bad day?"

"Something happened at the football game."

"Oh, no—" Shivering cut off her words.

"Come inside before you freeze." He curled his fingers around her upper arm and tugged her forward.

"O-okay."

He shut the door and said, "I'd offer you wine or hot tea, but they're only on my grocery list and not actually on premises yet. Beer?"

"No, thanks."

"Then the best I can do is a seat on the couch in front of a fireplace without a fire." If he'd known, he'd have made one.

"I'll take it." She moved farther into the room and looked around. This was the first time she'd been inside since showing him around. "Love what you've done with the place."

"Really? It's just furniture. I haven't had time to decorate—" He saw the teasing in her eyes. "Oh. That was sarcasm."

"Just a little." She sat at the far end of his brown leather sofa. "Tell me what happened at the game."

"I'm surprised you haven't heard. It's all over the local news." He sat down, too, but left as much space as possible between them. Feeling the warmth of her skin would likely bring on temptation that would jeopardize their fragile understanding. "One of the football players, Jimmy Kowalski, broke an ankle. Or I should say a linebacker on the opposing team did it for him."

"Oh, no." Her expressive face filled with sympathy. "Aren't there emergency medical technicians on hand at the games?"

"Yeah. They stabilized him on the field and then provided transport to the closest medical facility. I got the call and met them at the clinic."

"I don't mean to be insensitive, but physical contact is part of the game. And the single most important reason C.J. will never play it. But I don't understand why this got to you so much."

"The X-rays showed that both bones in the leg are broken and will require surgery to repair." Feeling helpless made him angry all over again. "He's a senior and hoping for a football scholarship because his father is out of work and without one he can't go to college. All I could do to help was ship him off to the hospital, which is close to a hundred miles away. So, on top of the trauma and pain, he gets plenty of time on that drive to worry about a surgery and its effect on his future."

"I can understand a little of what his parents feel." She slid over and narrowed the space between them on the sofa. "When C.J. cut his chin we would have had to make that drive if you hadn't been here."

"That was different."

"Why?"

"Because I could help C.J. A family practice doctor is sort of a jack-of-all-trades, but orthopedics isn't my specialty. All I could do was confirm that it was worse than a simple break, immobilize the leg and give him something for pain."

"I'd say you fixed the immediate problem. He can't thrash around, possibly doing more damage. And he won't be hurting on the way to the hospital."

"I hated shipping that kid off." He curled his fingers into a fist. "The situation really sucks. In a big city everything necessary would be under one roof."

"You could still be in the big city if you wanted. Or go back," she said.

"I just get angry when I feel helpless. That's not what I want." He saw traces of the wariness she'd worn like a cloak since the first time he'd seen her. Part of her was still protecting herself and probably always would. "The best-case scenario would be for that kid to be here in Blackwater Lake among family and friends."

"You really do know this community, don't you?" She smiled as if he were the star pupil.

"I'm getting there." He shook his head. "And what else I know is that this town is into skiing, snowboarding, boating and water sports—activities which aren't particularly user-friendly to bones. If Blackwater Lake is going to attract development, the scope of medical services has to expand. I know that small-town sensibilities and big-city services are in conflict with the growing pains. And that high school kid is caught in the middle. It makes me mad but there's no one to be mad at and that's even more frustrating."

"Ginny always says don't get mad, get even."

"Virginia is quite the philosopher," he said diplomatically. "What does that even mean?"

"I think in this case it's about channeling energy into finding a way to change circumstances that you don't like."

"I knew that." He shrugged. "On some level where I wasn't too angry to think straight. But in this case change will take time, but mostly money."

"So how do you get it?"

"Mercy Medical Center Corporation needs to approve a position for an orthopedic specialist for the clinic. And Blackwater Lake needs to step up and make the bureaucrats see that. It's an investment in the future. *I* need to get involved and make that happen."

"See?" She smiled and put her hand on his arm. "No more frowny face. You look better already."

"And you look beautiful as always." Did he really just say that out loud?

The way her eyes widened said he did. While they stared at each other, the warmth of her fingers penetrated the material of his long-sleeved shirt. It felt too good and he didn't just mean her touch. Having someone to talk to was a rare comfort, an extraordinary pleasure. He'd been lonely, but that was nothing new for him and wasn't really a factor in how he felt about her.

And he didn't want to lose the privilege of having her in his life. "It's getting late, Jill."

"Yeah." But she didn't move.

"If you don't go now, I'm going to kiss you. I made a promise not to do that and I need your help to keep it."

"Right." She blinked twice, then stood and hurried to the door. "Good night."

No, not good, he thought. Now the scent of her was in his house as well as his head. That was going to make it even harder to resist her than it already was.

Early Saturday morning Jill left C.J. at the marina with Brewster to visit Maggie Potter and her baby girl. And now she was sitting in the state-of-the-art glider chair with the infant in her arms.

"I love her name. Danielle Maureen. I bet your mom is excited."

"She's been so anxious to be a grandmother and Brady isn't cooperating."

"That's because he isn't married and not showing any signs that he wants to be." Jill snuggled the little pink bundle to her chest and breathed in the indescribably sweet scent of her skin. "I don't think there's anything more wonderful than holding a tiny, warm baby in your arms or that special smell babies have."

"Oh, she's made some extraordinarily special smells," Maggie said, grinning.

"You're already a high achiever, Dani Mo." The little girl continued to stare up at her while valiantly trying to suck on a tiny fist. "She is just more beautiful than I can even tell you."

"Really?" Her friend sat on the chocolate-brown sofa nearby.

Jill met her gaze. "We're friends, Maggie. I wouldn't lie about something like that."

A new mother's anxiety had replaced the sadness in her brown eyes. "Even if she was so homely she'd have to wear a bag over her head to go to preschool?"

"Oh, please." Jill stroked the baby, snugly swaddled in a pink receiving blanket. "She's already gorgeous. On a baby beauty scale of one to ten, she's easily a twenty-five. How could she miss with parents like you and Danny?"

And Jill could have smacked herself because the sadness was back in her friend's eyes.

"I wish he could have seen her," Maggie said.

"Oh, sweetie, I'm sorry. I didn't mean to remind you or make you sad about something so happy and wonderful."

"You don't have to remind me. The memories surround me

every day." She looked at the pine logs that formed the walls of her home. "When Danny built this place, he took extra care with the bedrooms for the two kids we were planning to have, making sure to double insulate so they wouldn't get cold."

Maggie's house was a log cabin a couple of miles from town, and Danny had done all the work himself. The floors were pine and had brightly colored oval braided rugs throughout. A crocheted afghan in multiple shades of green was thrown across the back of the sofa where Maggie sat. In the stone fireplace, flames crackled and popped, giving the room a cheerful warmth that didn't reach her eyes.

Jill effortlessly moved the glider chair forward and backward. She looked into the baby's big serene eyes that were so much like her mother's, at least for now. "I believe wherever he is, Danny can see his daughter. He's her guardian angel."

"I know, right?" Maggie scooted forward on the couch. "He sent Adam Stone here to work at the clinic because there would be a snowstorm and I couldn't get to the hospital."

Jill wasn't sure Danny had sent the doctor, but he was definitely here. And he had been there for her friend. "Everything went okay with the birth, he said."

"Normal in every way," Maggie confirmed. "But Adam was so calm, so steady, that he kept me calm and steady. I know it was a textbook delivery and probably Ginny could have handled it, but I'd never had a baby before. Having a doctor there gave me peace of mind. I'm so glad you were wrong about him leaving town at the first sign of winter."

"I was more wrong than you know." If he'd left, she wouldn't have slept with him and wouldn't now be so badly wanting more. "But I wasn't the only one who misjudged him. The whole town felt the same way."

"Not everyone," her friend reminded her. "I gave him the benefit of the doubt and not just because he's a good customer. You have to admit that Mayor Goodson never had a bad word to say about him."

"Is this an election year?" Jill asked wryly.

"Never alienate a potential voter. Political rule number one. But it's more than that."

"I know. But I don't trust him." Jill thought about Adam and what he'd done. In the spirit of fairness, she shared. "He shoveled snow off my walkway after being up all night delivering this little girl."

Maggie's gasp was teasing. "Clearly he has underhanded intentions."

"And that's not all."

"Tell me more."

"He prescribed some kind of medication for Hildie Smith that apparently gave her an attitude adjustment. Brew has a twinkle in his eyes and a spring in his step. He pretty much thinks Adam walks on water."

"Oh." Maggie covered her mouth with her hand, faking shock. "Skullduggery afoot."

"No kidding." Jill rolled her eyes. "Just last night I went upstairs to bring him his mail—"

"Do you go to his apartment often?" Maggie's eyes sparkled with innuendo.

"First time since I showed him around. Anyway, I could tell he was upset about something and finally got him to talk."

"Did it involve flashing him with a little skin?"

"It didn't." *Not that time anyway,* Jill thought. "He took it pretty hard that one of the high school football players was hurt in the game. Adam couldn't really help because orthopedics isn't his specialty and the kid had to go to the hospital so far away."

"Yeah, it's not exactly convenient when you're giving birth in a snowstorm either," Maggie said wryly.

"Turns out Adam is going to work on a plan to expand

the clinic and eventually build a hospital right here in Blackwater Lake."

"Sounds like a man ready to run out on us at the first opportunity," Maggie teased. "Watch out for that one."

"Okay, I'll admit my judgment about him is flawed." Jill thought for a second. "The thing is, he seems very sincere about his long-term plans here in Montana."

"You think?"

"I'm afraid to consider anything where Adam is concerned. I've been fooled before and I can't afford to slip up with him again—"

"Again? You're not talking about the last doctor." Maggie studied her friend. "You slept with Adam Stone, didn't you?"

"No."

"You're so lying."

"How do you do that?" Jill just shook her head in awe. She hadn't said anything incriminating, yet her friend had busted her big-time.

"I know you. Tone of voice. Guilty body language. Pensive frown that means a questionable decision, probably in regard to behavior." Maggie shrugged. "Was it when you played mail lady and the doctor upstairs?"

"No," Jill said. "It was when the doctor shoveled snow for his landlady."

"And how was it?"

"I'm sure it was a lot of work and his back was sore after he finished."

"No. I meant the sex and you know it."

"Oh. Sex. Actually it was pretty amazing." The earth moved, Jill remembered. And she saw fireworks. "But he and I agreed that it can't happen again."

"What?" Maggie's voice rose and brought a whimper from the baby, who was starting to show signs of discontent. "Sorry, Dani, but seriously. Auntie Jill needs to have her head examined."

"You know how I feel. C.J. and I are doing fine. Why let someone in and chance rocking the boat?"

"I don't say this lightly because I'm a mother now, too. I completely understand this maternal love that makes you want to surround your child with bumper guards and keep him safe." Maggie met her gaze. "But you can't protect him from everything and everyone forever."

"That's what Loretta Goodson said." Maggie raised the baby to her shoulder when she started to fuss. "She said when life throws him a curve, he won't have developed the skills to deal with it."

"Wow." Maggie's expression was filled with awe. "I wonder how she acquired so much kid wisdom without kids of her own."

"I'll ask her sometime."

"Take notes," her friend advised. "Now, back to the doctor. I think everyone realizes that he's not going anywhere. You don't need to hold back your feelings—or anything else."

"You're wrong, Mags. The reason he agreed we can't—get personal—again is that he's a confirmed bachelor. Carrying on with someone and settling for less than a committed relationship isn't the message I want my son to get."

"It's a valid concern. Again, motherhood does give you a different perspective." Maggie nodded thoughtfully. "But I just need to say a couple of things before I stop ragging on you."

"Okay, shoot." Jill steeled herself for the lecture.

"First, don't borrow trouble."

"If I do, does that mean I have to give it back?"

"Smart aleck." She shook her head. "It means you've already written an ending to the story. But you can't see the future any more than anyone else can. You have to take the journey, take a chance."

Jill wondered if Maggie would do it all again if she'd known what she knew now about how hard it was to lose the man you loved. But that wasn't a question she could bring up.

Instead she asked, "What's number two?"

The sadness returned to Maggie's eyes, clearly indicating that this part had to do with the love she'd lost. "This is one thing I know with my whole heart and soul. If you don't live in each and every moment, you're not really living at all. Don't miss an opportunity. Don't let yourself have regrets."

In spite of the fact that Maggie's wisdom had come from tragic personal experience, she wasn't recommending surrender.

When Dani started a full-on wail, Jill handed her over so her friend could breast-feed her baby. She missed having the warm body in her arms. She'd never been anyone's wife, but loved being a mother, and it made her sad that C.J. wouldn't have a brother or sister. She was sure of that because, in spite of her friend's sad insight, Jill had a different take on it.

She couldn't, just couldn't, throw caution to the wind and risk being hurt, no matter how much she might want Adam to hold her and kiss her again.

Chapter Eleven

Adam stepped off the last stair onto the porch just in time to see Jill coming around the corner of the house hefting an eight-foot ladder.

"Stop right there," he ordered, then hurried over. "Why didn't you ask for help with that?"

She brushed a strand of red hair off her forehead and huffed out a breath. "First of all, I do this all the time and don't need help. Second, I wouldn't bother a tenant with something like this. It's Saturday."

"What's your point? The ladder is still heavy and I'm stronger than you."

"My point is that I wouldn't disturb you on your day off. Maybe if there was a fire or the threat of a meteor strike. Possibly a NASA satellite hurtling toward the house. Otherwise, no."

He grinned at her. She was possibly the only woman on

the planet who could make him smile when she was telling him to mind his own business.

"First of all," he said, echoing her words, "I'm pretty sure that we're also friends in spite of the fact that I give you money every month and you let me live under your roof. Second, if you hurt yourself carrying something that's too heavy for you, I won't be off because I'll get called in to work. On you." He walked closer and put both hands on the ladder, stopping short of taking it away. "Where do you want this?"

"You're awfully bossy."

"It's one of my best qualities." The stubborn look in his eyes said he wasn't letting go.

"In the house." She stepped away and smiled. "Thanks, Adam. It is heavy."

"Don't mention it. I'll follow you."

Partly so he'd know exactly where to put it, but mostly to check her out from the back. The Blackwater Lake Marina sweatshirt she had on was pretty shapeless, but those jeans were perfect. If looking at her butt was an Olympic sport, he'd get all tens because practicing would be easy. He could watch all day. The only thing better would be cupping those soft curves in his hands, and his palms tingled now from wanting so badly to do it again.

"You okay?" she asked when he tripped on the top porch step.

"Fine." Distracted and disgusted with himself maybe, but all in one piece.

Watching where he was going was important and he didn't just mean right this moment. He had to keep focused. Eyes on the prize, which was building credibility along with a career in Blackwater Lake. No detour with his lovely, sexy landlady because it could cost him the fragile and hard-won respect of the people in this town.

Inside the house, she walked down the hall and stopped

beneath an access panel in the ceiling. "If you could set it down right here, that would be great."

The front door opened and slammed shut, followed by the sound of six-year-old feet running through the living room.

C.J. came to a screeching halt in the hall. "Dr. Adam!"

"Hey, champ. What's up?"

"I was at the marina with Brew while Mommy went to visit Maggie and baby Dani. Then I saw you carryin' the ladder for her. Whatcha doin'?"

"What are we doing?" he asked her.

"Furnace filters. They need attention twice a year, before summer and winter," she said. "I'm actually late this year. That snowstorm threw me off schedule, but fortunately it's all melted now and I'm good to go. Saturday is chores day and I've got a long list."

"Okay." Adam put one foot on the bottom rung of the ladder. "I'll get it down."

"Wait. I thought you were just carrying the ladder for me."

"Now I'm volunteering for chores duty."

"You don't have to do that," she protested.

"I know." He climbed until he could reach the metal closures for the vent. When he slid them sideways and it dropped, he saw the metal filter. "This isn't the disposable kind."

"In my humble opinion these are better quality. I hose them off. Just lift it out and hand it down."

"I wanna help," C.J. said.

"Hold on, champ." Adam did as Jill instructed, but handed the lightweight square filter to the boy and said, "Take that out back by the hose. There's another one in the living room, right?"

"How did you know?"

"I wish I could say I'm psychic, but upstairs is the same

floor plan. In fact, we might as well do those, too." He braced himself for another protest.

"You're sure you don't mind?"

There was nothing on his day-off agenda except possibly a movie all by himself. "I'm sure."

He moved the ladder and took out the filter behind the living room vent, then handed it to C.J., who was quivering with excitement while he waited. The boy took it outside and returned just in time to see Adam at the front with the folded ladder.

"Where ya goin'?"

"Don't bother Dr. Adam, kiddo." Jill put her hand on the boy's shoulder, a subtle cue to stay put.

"The filters in my apartment need cleaning, too," Adam explained.

"I can help, just like I helped now."

Adam knew the job would go faster if he did it by himself, but the eagerness and vulnerability in that small face tugged at him. With his chin tilted up, the scar was visible and Adam suspected there were more on the inside that didn't show. His mom, too. The kid was soaking up the attention, craving the male bonding just as Jill had said. The chore might go faster alone, but alone wasn't all it was cracked up to be.

"Okay, C.J.," he said, "Let's go upstairs."

"What can I do?" The boy followed him out the door.

"Same thing you did in your house. It saves a lot of time if you're there. I don't have to climb down the ladder. You're a really big help."

"That's 'cuz I'm six. Pretty soon I'll be seven. Mommy said in a couple of weeks."

"What do you want for your birthday?"

"A video-game player for the TV," he said without hesitation.

Adam knew it was pricey. "Have you told your mom?"

"Yup." The boy reached up and took the square filter.

"Just set that by the door. We'll get the other one and take them both down for hosing off. I'll leave the ladder here to put them back up after they dry."

"Okay."

"What did your mom say about the player?" he asked, folding the ladder to move it to his living room.

"Nothin'." C.J. shrugged, but he wasn't any better at hiding his feelings than his mom. "She asked what else I wanted, but that just means I won't get what I really want."

Adam could easily afford it and almost said so. He stopped just in time as an idea occurred to him. "Maybe you could do some extra chores for me and earn the money to buy it."

"Really?" The hope in those bright brown eyes could steal a heart if you weren't careful.

"Maybe."

"What do you want me to do?"

"Give me a chance to talk to your mom. If she's okay with it I'll come up with a list."

"Oh, boy!"

This time Adam followed C.J. downstairs and carried the filters. It was one thing to take a handoff, another to hang on and navigate stairs when you were six going on seven. They took them out back, where Jill was just putting the first two in the sun to dry.

"Hey, you," she said to her son.

"Mommy, Dr. Adam is going to give me stuff to do so I can make money."

"What?"

"For my game player," he clarified.

Adam liked it a lot better when she smiled. There wasn't a hint of a smile now and he felt the need to explain. "I can help and figured it would give him a sense of accomplishment."

"I see." The tone of her voice said she wasn't happy about

whatever it was she saw. "C.J., it's time for your favorite chore of the whole week."

"Aw, Mom. Do I hafta clean my room?"

"Yes. Now scoot."

Apparently he knew resistance was futile because he said, "O-okay." Then he looked at Adam. "I won't be long."

When they were alone, Jill's eyes filled with something, but it wasn't the anger he'd come to expect. If he had to name the emotion, he'd say dread. Apprehension.

"What's wrong?" He took a step closer.

"You know the game player he wants is expensive and that I can't afford it."

"From what he said, I connected the dots."

She lifted a hand to her forehead to shield her eyes from the sun that was dropping lower in the sky. "Don't think I don't appreciate the gesture, but taking care of what C.J. wants is my responsibility."

"I'm just trying to help," he defended.

"Not a good idea." She shook her head. "I'm the one he depends on."

The only one he can depend on. She didn't say that, but he read between the lines. "Jill, I—"

"Please don't." She held up a hand to stop the words. "This subject isn't up for debate. Thanks for helping with everything today. Now I better go supervise. To a six-year-old, cleaning his room means playing with the toys scattered around. Short attention span."

When she walked inside, Adam was less interested in her butt than her story. It was the first time that had happened. No matter how much reassurance and evidence to the contrary, she just wouldn't let go of the idea that he was leaving. He was no shrink, but it didn't take one to know that she'd been deeply hurt by someone who walked out on her, someone other than "the last doctor." He intended to find out just what had happened to her, mostly because he was curious and wanted to help if possible. But part of his motivation was just being selfish.

Adam badly wanted to sleep with her again, but he'd given his word that he wouldn't. If only words would make the temptation go away. He had a feeling Jill was fighting the attraction, too. An agreement made with all the good intentions in the world wouldn't hold up to a double dose of desire. When sex happened again, and it would happen, she was going to have to be the one to break the bargain.

Jill wasn't quite sure how they ended up at Blackwater Lake Hardware late in the afternoon. Chores were completed and before Adam put away the ladder he asked about changing batteries in the smoke detectors, pointing out that it should be done twice a year. Some people thought when the clocks were turned ahead and back was a good rule of thumb, but for her it could be filter cleaning. She agreed.

Since she didn't have the required 9-volt replacements, the doctor offered to drive her into town. If C.J. hadn't overheard, she could have gracefully declined, but... Oh, who was she kidding? Adam offered and she didn't want to decline, gracefully or any other way. So she was going to hell.

They walked past a winter preparedness display and Adam was carrying the two-handled blue basket. "What about flashlights and extra batteries? Snowstorms can snap tree limbs and bring down power lines."

"I know," she said. "And as far out as we are, you can be stuck for a few days. Sometimes it takes that long for the plows to get to us. If you don't already have snow tires now might be a good time to get some. Phone reception can be spotty, too, cell and landlines."

He picked up a flashlight. "So that's a yes?"

"The old one broke." When she nodded, he set it beside the package of square batteries in the basket.

"Can I have one, Mommy?" C.J. looked up at her with pleading in his eyes. "It's dark outside and I really need to see where I'm going so I don't fall and hit my chin and need stitches again."

"Wow, that argument was well thought out and emotionally motivated," Adam said, his voice full of admiration. "I see a career in law someday."

"When he's a lawyer, he can buy all the flashlights and batteries his little heart desires, but until then…" Jill sighed. "For now I have to say no. You can use mine, kiddo."

Looking into two pairs of eyes—one brown and disappointed, the other blue and wanting to offer help—Jill felt as if she was letting everyone down. Adam had just been trying to help earlier. The idea of giving C.J. chores to earn the money for something he wanted was a good one and showed great father instincts for a guy who had no intention of being a father.

Maybe that's why she'd gotten so defensive, that and her independent streak. Counting on anyone else was setting herself up for a big fall. She hated denying her son anything, but her budget was pretty tight and she still had to squeeze out enough for his birthday presents.

She added flashlight batteries to the basket. "I think that's all we need. Let's go pay."

Moving ahead, she got to the front of the store first. The kid behind the cash register was a stranger to her, but apparently he knew Adam.

"Hi, Doc."

"Hey, Landin. How's it going?"

"Could be better. Jimmy's out for the rest of the season."

"I know. Got a call from the orthopedic specialist at the

hospital." Adam didn't say more, probably because of patient privacy issues.

Obviously he was talking about the football player with broken bones. This kid was a tall, skinny, brown-haired teen with gray eyes and a cute smile who didn't look big enough for football.

"There goes our division championship. He's the best wide receiver we've got."

"Wait and see. Maybe John McLaughlin can step up. He's in good shape and pretty fast." How did Adam know all this? The question must have shown on her face because he said to her, "I did the team physicals before they started practicing. How could I not go to the games?"

That explained it. Apparently the teens embraced him in a way the adults loyal to her hadn't. When the kid gave her a total for the purchases, Jill swiped her debit card, then keyed in the PIN. Before she could take her bag with receipt, Adam grabbed it.

"Good luck next week," he said.

Landin nodded. "We'll need it."

A cold wind hit her when she walked out the front door toward Adam's SUV at the curb. Then C.J. hit her with something else. "Mommy, my tummy's so hungry."

"We're going straight home now and I'll make dinner," she promised.

"I can't wait. It's too far." In his uniquely dramatic way, her son dragged his feet and limped along as if about to drop from lack of nourishment.

Jill met Adam's amused gaze. "He goes from zero to starvation without any warning."

"Growing boys will do that." He snapped his fingers. "I've got an idea."

C.J. stood up straight. "Is it ice cream at Potter's?"

"Close. How about dinner at the Grizzly Bear Diner?" Adam met her gaze. "My treat. It's the least I can do."

"And why is that?" she asked wryly. "If anything I owe you for helping out with chores today."

"Give me a minute. I'll think of a reason."

"How about you just like takin' us to the diner?" C.J. suggested.

"That works for me." Adam grinned at the boy.

It worked for Jill, too. Way better than she wanted. For the second time that day she didn't have the will to decline. "Thank you, Adam. That's really nice of you. But, C.J., it's a block down Main Street. Do you really think you can walk that far being so hungry?"

"Yeah!" He took off at a run.

"Stop at the light," she called after him.

"'Kay, Mom!"

Side by side, she and Adam walked at a brisk pace mostly because it was cold. Jill wanted to snuggle into him for warmth and kept fighting the urge. It seemed so natural; he made everything seem so natural. She was getting awfully tired of fighting.

C.J. was already waiting for them up ahead at the red light on Pine Street. "Hurry up, you guys."

"Your son is pretty fast," Adam commented. "I wonder if he can catch a ball."

"He's not ever playing football. I'm pretty sure a parent has to sign a permission slip or something if a student is under eighteen."

"Good luck with telling him no." Adam's hand brushed hers and when he slid his fingers into the pocket of his jacket, it crossed her mind that he felt the temptation, too. "He struck out on the flashlight tonight, but give him time. He'll have a few years to perfect his pitch and I wouldn't want to be in your shoes if he decides to play."

They finally reached the corner and when the light turned green the three of them crossed the street to where Grizzly Bear Diner took up the corner. Inside it was warm and very crowded.

"Apparently this is the happening place," she said.

Even if one didn't know the diner's name, a theme would be obvious. There were bears everywhere. Wallpaper, menus and logo T-shirts on the employees.

Jill knew the hostess behind the podium displaying the sign Please Wait to be Seated. "Hi, Mrs. Taylor."

"Hey, Jill." The older woman gave the man behind her a wide smile. "Hi, Dr. Stone."

"Hi, Iris."

Iris?

"It's nice to see you." Iris Taylor was under five feet tall and in her late fifties.

"Same here." Adam met her gaze. "How are you?"

"Doing great. Now," she added. "That prescription you gave me really helped the pain from my arthritis."

"Good." He looked around the crowded waiting room. "Are there always this many people?"

"It's Saturday. I guess you're here for dinner." There was a curious expression in her eyes when she made the connection that Jill and C.J. were with him. "Three of you?"

"How long is the wait?"

"I'm really hungry, Mrs. Taylor," C.J. said.

"I bet you are. About thirty minutes." She looked at her list with some of the names highlighted in hot pink. "But for you, Doc, I think I can find a booth pretty quick."

"Thanks." He looked down at the boy, who was peeking into the glass case displaying grizzly bear T-shirts, sweatshirts and figurines. "Starvation can set in pretty quick when you're six."

"Give me a minute. Can you hang on?" she asked C.J.

"I could if I had one of those bears to play with," he said to his mother.

Jill rolled her eyes and knew by the sparkle in his that Adam was thinking, *Watch out when the kid wants to play football.*

Five minutes later Iris led them out of the waiting area and past the counter with swivel chairs. Carl Hayes, the plumber hired by her mother to do the upstairs work when Adam's apartment was being built, sat there.

"Hi, Mr. Hayes," she said.

"Howdy, Jill." The balding man smiled and lifted a hand in greeting. "Hey, Doc. Carl Hayes," he said.

"I remember," Adam said. "How are the leg cramps?"

The older man swiveled his counter stool around to look at them. "It was the darnedest thing. Vitamins, Gatorade and water sure did the trick just like you said. I've been sleeping like a baby ever since I saw you."

"Excellent news." Adam grinned. "Keep it up."

"Don't worry. I couldn't stop even if I wanted to. My wife keeps shoving water and vitamins at me."

"Good for her." Adam laughed and shook his hand.

They made it a little farther toward the back before a gray-haired man called out, "Hey, Dr. Stone."

Adam stopped at the end of a booth. "Mr. Gerard."

"Call me Alan. This is my wife, Winnie."

"Nice to meet you," he said. "How are you feeling, Alan?"

"Stomach pain is gone. More fiber is just what the doctor ordered." He laughed at his joke.

"That's good to hear. It's important. Nice to meet you, Winnie."

"Same here. I've got an appointment at the clinic next week," she said. "Nothing serious. Just my yearly checkup."

"I'll look forward to seeing you."

"Jill's a nice girl. And that little guy of hers is a hoot," the woman told him.

"I know." Adam waved a goodbye, then turned to her.

Jill felt the warmth in her cheeks. Could the matchmaking be any more obvious? She wished the earth would open and swallow her whole. Agreeing to come here was a mistake on many levels, but mostly she tried not to resent the fact that these people were *her* friends, supposedly loyal to her. But they were treating "the new doctor" like a rock star. She followed Iris to a booth in the back and slid into it. That's when she realized Adam and C.J. weren't behind her.

He'd been stopped yet again and was chatting with someone she didn't know. His hand was on C.J.'s shoulder in a friendly, familiar way that tugged at her heart. The little boy had lifted his chin, pointing to the place where Adam had stitched it up, and people were admiring a job well done.

Adam looked comfortable, as if he'd known everyone for years instead of just months. He fit right in and she hadn't done much to help except being seen with him here in the diner that one time. He had gained town confidence all on his own.

She was happy for him. Really. It was just that now her already complex feelings grew even more complicated. The last doctor she'd dated hadn't stayed past the first snow, which made him a wimp and an outsider as far as this town was concerned. When another single, good-looking doctor showed up, everyone circled the wagons around her and she felt safe, protected. Now Adam was no longer an outsider. Blackwater Lake embraced him as one of their own and he had their loyalty. Like her. It was a level playing field.

And she'd seen tonight that her friends and neighbors were putting them together as a couple, a family, which made the potential for pain shoot way up. When things with Adam didn't work out, and she refused to let herself believe that they could, she would let down the whole town.

Just like when C.J.'s father had walked out.

Chapter Twelve

All the way home from the diner C.J. kept up a nonstop monologue and Jill wasn't exactly sure when he took a breath, but the words kept on coming.

"When can we go to the hardware store again?"

"Next time we need hardware. Aren't you tired?" she asked.

"No."

"My ears are tired."

"You're funny, Mom. How can ears get tired? Are yours tired, too, Dr. Adam?"

"I think my ears are more used to it because I listen to patients all day." He was the soul of diplomacy.

"My ears aren't sleepy at all," C.J. said. "And next time we go to the hardware store, I hope we can go to the Grizzly Bear Diner, too. It was fun."

"And now it's late," Jill said. "I need to get those batteries in the smoke detectors."

"I'll do it." Adam turned the SUV into the drive, then came to a stop beside her car and turned off the ignition.

"Can I help?" C.J. piped up from the backseat.

"It's time for bed." Jill wanted desperately to be by herself, distance herself from Adam.

"But, Mom, it's too early to go to sleep."

"Don't forget about your shower." She released her seat belt and opened the front passenger door.

"But Dr. Adam needs me to help him put the new batteries in. Right, Dr. Adam?" C.J. opened the right rear door and jumped out.

"I'm Switzerland." The interior light illuminated Adam's wry expression as he met her gaze.

"Huh?" C.J. looked up for an explanation.

Jill couldn't help smiling. "That means he's not taking sides, kiddo."

"But, Mom, I hafta watch. How else am I gonna learn?"

Why couldn't she be Switzerland, too? Jill wondered. And why couldn't it be a country without guilt? A place where a mother could give her son a man in his life who wouldn't leave, a man he could count on. Right now she lived in the land of reality and a decision had to be made.

"Maybe just this once, since it's Saturday."

"Yay!" C.J. ran toward the front steps and called over his shoulder, "Hurry up, Dr. Adam. I don't have all night."

"Right behind you, champ." Adam laughed as he fell into step beside her. "If only I had that much energy."

"Yeah."

And if only Adam's arm didn't brush hers. The touch made her yearn for the right to snuggle closer to his lean strength. But that was part of a relationship, and all she had with Adam was sex, followed by a verbal agreement not to let it happen again.

While Adam took her son upstairs to replace his smoke

detector batteries and bring down the ladder, Jill unlocked her front door and went inside. She turned on lights and set her purse and the bag with the new flashlight on her desk. The quiet surrounded her and that wasn't about C.J. not being here. It was a sign that she was getting used to Adam being around. How did one go about growing *un*accustomed to a charming man who wasn't hard on the eyes and had a great sense of humor?

Ten minutes later the front door burst open and C.J. came in. "Mom? We're here and Dr. Adam brought the ladder."

And made it look incredibly easy because he *was* stronger than her. "I can see that."

"He let me climb up it."

"Not by himself," Adam assured her.

"Dr. Adam had to do the battery 'cuz I can't reach it yet. But I watched really good."

"It would have been a lot harder without his help. I needed the extra weight to steady the ladder so I could connect the battery."

C.J.'s freckled face beamed with pleasure. "Let's do the rest!"

Jill watched her son race out of the room, and his enthusiasm nearly broke her heart. It was all about having a man to do guy stuff with. In the kitchen, C.J. climbed the ladder and Adam was right there to make sure he didn't fall. Each time they went through the process, she marveled at his protectiveness and patience considering the chore took five times longer because a little boy wanted to help.

If there was a way to resist this doctor, she'd give almost anything to know the secret because falling in love wasn't something she ever wanted to do again.

"Okay, C.J., your reprieve is over. Now you really do have to get ready for bed."

"But, Mom—"

"No buts." She pointed in the direction of his room. "March. Or there won't be time for a story."

"Can Dr. Adam read it to me?"

"That's your call," the doctor in question said.

"You've already done too much."

"I was happy to help out."

She shook her head. "We've monopolized your day off."

"I didn't feel monopolized. It was fun hanging with you guys."

"And we appreciate everything you did, but you probably want some time to yourself."

"Solitary isn't all it's cracked up to be."

It sounded an awful lot like he was saying he'd really wanted to be there, but that was the very hardest thing for her to believe.

"C'mon, Mom. Just tell him it's okay."

She looked at her son and the heartbreaking hope so visible in his eyes. How could you say no to that? "Okay."

"Awesome." Without another word he turned and ran toward his bedroom. Several moments later she heard the sound of the shower.

"I'll put the ladder away," Adam offered.

"Thanks."

"Don't mention it."

C.J. was finished showering when Adam came back. With wet hair slicked down, teeth freshly brushed and wearing Superman pajamas, he looked up at the tall man. "I'm ready for my story now."

"Good, because I'm ready to read."

They all trooped down the hall with the redheaded child in the lead. Jill folded the bedspread down and pulled back the covers while he chose a book from his shelf.

"I want the baby animal book," he told Adam before climbing into bed.

"Looks like a good one." Adam waited until he was all tucked in before sitting beside him.

Jill stood nearby, listening to the sound of his deep voice as he read the child's story. She fell further under his spell with every word. When he read "The End," she wasn't ready for it to be over any more than C.J. was.

"Dr. Adam?"

"Yeah, champ?"

"Where do babies come from?" A question clearly designed to stall just a little longer and who could blame him? Certainly not Jill.

Adam looked at her. "Have you discussed this?"

"A little," she said.

"Mommy told me that the man has a seed and the woman has the egg and when they love each other a baby happens." C.J. yawned.

Adam looked relieved. "Your mom is exactly right. I have nothing to add."

C.J. yawned again before saying, "Dr. Adam, did you have a dog when you were six, almost seven?"

"Yes."

"I knew I was old enough for a puppy."

"I didn't say that." Adam pulled the covers more snugly over the small chest. "I had an older brother and a sister to help with the responsibility."

"Dr. Adam, is it—"

"Enough," Jill interrupted. "Lights out, kiddo."

"O-okay." He rolled onto his side.

"Good night, C.J." Adam gently brushed the hair off the child's forehead, then stood and backed away from the bed.

"I love you." Jill moved forward and kissed her son's cheek. "Sweet dreams. See you in the morning."

"Love you, Mommy." His eyes drifted closed and he said sleepily, "See you tomorrow, Dr. Adam."

Please don't count so much on tomorrow, she wanted to tell him. Just because Adam was doing all the right things to put down roots in Blackwater Lake didn't mean he would be part of their lives. She'd gone down that path and been fooled before.

She followed Adam out of the room and pulled the door nearly closed. Then she led the way into the living room to see Adam out.

"Free at last." She tried to make her voice light and breezy but didn't quite pull it off.

"What's wrong, Jill?"

"How do you know anything is?"

"Your mouth is tight. Your tone is tense. And your forehead has frown lines." He gently touched his fingertip to a spot just above her eyebrow.

If he hadn't done that, saying good-night would have been almost easy, but he had to go and lay a finger on her.

"You're way too observant. I thought I was hiding it pretty well." Resentment tinged her words as she met his gaze and the stubborn set of his jaw. "You're the toast of Blackwater Lake. At the Grizzly Bear tonight it was clear that you've bonded with the people of this town. You're everyone's new best friend."

"And you were hoping I wouldn't be?"

"It's not that. Not exactly."

"Then what?" He nudged her chin up when she tried to look away. "You haven't done a great job of hiding the fact that you're holding back, refusing to get attached. Tell me why. And before you start, I know it's not about the last doctor."

"You're right." She slid her fingertips into the pockets of her jeans and sighed. The words came with surprising ease. "My father left my mother and me when I was about C.J.'s age."

"So you were abandoned."

"I had my mom. And friends here. But, like so many other people, I have abandonment issues." It was a weak attempt at humor, but she couldn't manage a smile and didn't want his pity.

"Not having a father leaves a hole in a kid's life." He wasn't asking a question.

"Yeah." She nodded. "It hurt. And more than anything I wanted my child to have a traditional family. There was a time when I thought it would happen, too."

"But it didn't."

"Right in one." Her heart hurt for C.J. "I fell in love with Buddy Henderson when we were juniors in high school and thought we'd be together forever. Everyone in town expected us to get married the spring after graduation. Then the spring after that."

"Why didn't you?"

"He never proposed. But Blackwater Lake expected a wedding. Especially after I got pregnant."

"He still didn't ask you to marry him?" His blue eyes darkened with anger.

"It's hard to propose when you're not around."

"He left?" Surprise mixed with fury in his voice.

"When I needed him most," she confirmed.

"Son of a bitch—"

"My sentiments exactly." She met his gaze and willed him to understand. "C.J. never knew his father but I remember mine. I know what it's like to blame yourself when someone you love, someone you believe with all your heart cares about you, walks away. That's why I don't want *him* to get attached."

"I see." Adam rubbed a hand across the back of his neck, then nodded. "Thanks for telling me."

"Thanks for listening."

She would never have believed that explaining everything would lift a weight from her heart, but it actually did. Maybe confession was good for the soul.

"For the last time," he said, "I'm not leaving."

She smiled. "Okay."

He put his hand on the doorknob and the intensity in his eyes said loud and clear that he would stay if she asked. "If there's anything else you want to talk about—"

There was something she wanted, but it had nothing to do with talking. She remembered what Maggie had said about living in the moment so life wouldn't pass her by. Adam was simply too tempting to resist.

Jill moved close and put her hand on his chest, then stood on tiptoe and touched her mouth to his. Simmering desire exploded into flame and he wrapped his arms around her, then kissed her as if he'd been starving for this and could devour her. She felt the same way. Breathing hard, she broke off the kiss and took his hand in hers, leading him toward her bedroom.

Adam stopped and looked down at her, his eyes intense. "Are you sure about this? We talked about 'you know.'"

"I remember." She smiled because all the rational arguments in the world didn't seem to matter in this moment. "We both said it couldn't happen again."

"We both have our reasons." He reached out and tucked a strand of hair behind her ear. "Are they still a problem for you?"

"No." She was tired of fighting what she felt. Tomorrow regrets might come, but tonight she wanted him. And sometimes wasn't it okay to be selfish? "Is it a problem for you?"

"No."

She gave him a flirty look and said, "Then quit stalling, Doctor."

Without another word he tugged her into the bedroom

and locked the door behind them. In what had to be a world record they undressed each other and crawled into her bed, under the quilt. The sheets were cold against her back, but Adam was there to warm her.

He brushed his hand up and down the bare skin of her side, barely touching her breast. She moaned, a sound of need that couldn't be held back. It was like pouring gas on a fire, making the flames burn higher and hotter. His hands were everywhere and he never stopped kissing her. When he slid inside, she was ready, wanting and willing. She lifted her hips and wrapped her legs around his waist, drawing him in deeper.

They moved together in a frantic, sensual rhythm that pushed her to the edge, where she gladly stepped off. His breathing was a rough rasp in her ear and she gloried in the sound and feel of his hard chest pressed to her soft curves. In what felt like a heartbeat she came apart as pleasure exploded through her body. Seconds later Adam followed her over and they held on to each other through the aftershocks, too spent to move.

Finally he lifted his weight to his forearms and grinned down at her. "That was pretty good."

"Is that your expert diagnosis, Doctor?"

"You think I'm an expert?"

"Oh, yeah."

"Okay, then."

He went into the bathroom and she missed his warmth in the bed. Moments later he was back and pulled her against him. She settled her cheek on his chest, content and sleepy and happy.

The next morning Adam woke up with Jill curled against him. It was a little past six-thirty and the house was quiet. Obviously C.J. was still asleep, just like his mom, he thought. Her red hair was a mass of curls against the pink flowered pillowcase and he ached to run his fingers through it again because he wanted her again. But he kept his hands to himself and let her sleep. Anyone who worked as hard as she did needed the rest.

He needed to get out of here before her son woke up and started asking questions more complicated than where babies come from. Still, he couldn't resist just a few more seconds of watching while her guard was down. She looked so young and innocent, too young and too innocent to be the mother of an almost seven-year-old and carrying a whole lot of emotional baggage from getting dumped on and abandoned.

Adam had taken an oath to do no harm, but five minutes alone and no questions asked with the jerk who'd left her alone and pregnant was really tempting. How could any guy do that, especially to Jill? It wasn't just looking so vulnerable while she slept that made him want to protect her. He felt the same way when she was wide-awake and arguing with him until hell wouldn't have it.

He knew his decision to relocate to Blackwater Lake was a good one. He loved it here and wasn't pulling up stakes, but she'd pointed out that there were lots of ways to leave that had nothing to do with geography. He didn't know where things were going with Jill, didn't know if he had it in him to commit to someone again and risk another mistake. It seemed unfair to pursue anything and chance hurting her when his track record was less than stellar.

Glancing at the clock on her side of the bed nudged him into action since the digital display was inching toward seven o'clock.

"Gotta get out of here," he whispered to himself.

He eased out of bed and dressed quickly, leaving his shirt untucked. His cell phone was still clipped to his belt because he'd been in such a hurry to have her. With shoes in hand, he unlocked the bedroom door and tiptoed out. It bothered him to leave without saying goodbye, but a note? What would he say? Thanks for last night? See you later? Nothing seemed right.

He put his shoes by the front door and went to the kitchen. The least he could do was get the coffee ready to go for her. That was a statement, although what it said or why he was making it were less clear. Something to do with being happy and wanting to do a nice thing for her. How sappy was that?

After filling the water reservoir in the coffeemaker, he measured grounds into a filter and closed the lid.

"Good morning."

His heart stuttered at the sleepy, sexy female voice, but that was nothing compared to what he felt when he turned around. Her hair was tousled in that way a woman's hair should be the morning after making love the night before. Her eyes had the heavy-lidded, well-pleasured look of a satisfied female and made him want to satisfy her again.

"I was trying not to wake you," he said when finally able to form words.

"You didn't." She smiled and her expression was more contented than he'd ever seen. "I actually overslept. I'm usually up earlier than this."

"Good. I'm glad." That came out wrong. He was usually more articulate than this. "I mean that I'm glad I didn't disturb you."

She sure disturbed him—sound asleep or wide-awake. Right this minute he was disturbed because she was wearing a robe and he really wanted to know if she was naked underneath. The fuzzy, peach-colored, floor-length thing had a zipper up the front and it would be so easy to…

"Why don't you turn on the coffeemaker and stay for a cup?" she suggested.

He knew it wasn't the best idea, but was too grateful for the invitation to say no. "Don't mind if I do."

Almost instantly after he flipped the switch, the machine started to sizzle and drip. Jill moved beside him and opened the cupboard above to pull down two mugs. The scent of her filled his head just like last night when he'd held her and loved her. It wasn't just sex, but for the life of him he couldn't define what "it" was.

She set cream and sugar, spoons and napkins on the table. "Are you hungry?"

Loaded question, and he hoped the knot of need inside him didn't show on his face. "Maybe."

Color crept into her cheeks and the pulse in her neck fluttered, telling him she knew exactly what he was thinking. When the coffee was ready, she picked up the pot, her hand unsteady as she poured the rich, steaming liquid into the mugs. Then they sat down at the table and stared at each other without saying a word.

She picked up her mug and blew on the steaming coffee before taking a sip. "It's good."

"A skill acquired out of necessity during my medical training."

"When your wife left." It wasn't a question.

"Yeah. Right around then."

"Did you miss her?"

"I didn't have time to think about her." That wasn't really an answer but it was partly true.

He thought about it now, his wife walking out because the specialty he wanted so badly wasn't flashy, prestigious or high profile enough for her. He remembered coming home to an empty apartment and realized that he hadn't missed her or been especially hurt. Moving on with his life had been easy, which made him merely stupid for choosing her in the first place. The problem was that he hated feeling stupid.

"Mom?" C.J. stood in the kitchen doorway rubbing his eyes. When he stopped and looked, his face lit up and all traces of sleepiness disappeared. "Dr. Adam! Are you havin' coffee?"

"Yes." Adam was grateful that the question was simple and he merely had to confirm the obvious.

"Did you come over for breakfast?"

That one was harder to answer truthfully since he'd actually never left.

Fortunately Jill bailed him out, but her brown eyes sparkled with the mischief of their secret. "I'm going to make scrambled eggs, bacon, hash browns and toast for Dr. Adam."

"Awesome." That seemed to be the kid's new favorite word.

"I'll be right back." As she walked out of the room, Jill said over her shoulder, "Just talk amongst yourselves."

C.J. climbed up on the chair. "I'm glad you're here."

"How come, champ?"

"'Cuz I like eggs and Mommy doesn't make them very much."

"Why?" Adam figured it was a time issue.

"I don't know." The boy shrugged his small shoulders. "But I guess this is a special occasion."

Definitely special, Adam thought, and not just for the food. "I'm looking forward to it. Your mom's a good cook."

C.J. nodded slowly. "I got a really good idea."

"What?" Adam sipped his coffee.

"You should come to my birthday party. Mommy's makin' lasagna. Brew and Hildie are comin'. And Maggie." He wrinkled his freckled nose. "She's bringin' the baby, though."

Adam struggled not to smile at that. "Is the baby a problem?"

"Boy, is she!" The kid sighed dramatically. "Tyler said she cries all the time. And poops. It's pretty stinky."

Apparently Cabot and Maggie were friends if they'd gone

to visit the new mom and baby. "I can deal with noisy and smelly."

"Really?" C.J.'s eyes widened. "You mean you'll come to my party?"

"I wouldn't miss it for anything."

"Awesome!"

"Thanks for inviting me."

C.J. was giving him a rundown on what he wanted for his birthday when Jill walked back into the kitchen wearing jeans and a sweater. He missed the sensual mystery of what was or was not underneath the robe, but the way she filled out the denim was a pretty good trade-off.

She got to work cooking while he and C.J. set the table. The smell of frying bacon filled the kitchen, and his stomach growled, telling him he was hungry for food, too. And something else that was less basic and easy to identify. Something more elusive. He just knew that hanging out with Jill and her son filled him up in places he hadn't known were empty.

His phone rang and he hoped it wasn't a patient emergency, which was never good, but he was looking forward to a home-cooked breakfast that wasn't oatmeal or toast. He pulled the phone from the case and looked at the caller ID, but the number was blocked.

After pushing the talk button and putting the phone to his ear, he said, "Dr. Stone."

"Hello, Adam. This is your grandmother."

He hadn't heard from Eugenia Stone since his move. "Is everything okay?"

"No. But if that was an inquiry about my health you'll be relieved to know that I've never been better."

"I'm glad to hear that." Adam shrugged when Jill gave him a quizzical look. "So what's up?"

There was static on the other end of the line for several seconds, but he caught the last words. "…arriving around noon. Pick me up at the Blackwater Lake Lodge at one-thirty."

She was on her way?

He had questions, so many questions, and started to ask, but the line cut out again, then dropped the call. Soon enough he'd find out why she was coming, although he had a pretty good idea.

Jill turned a piece of bacon sizzling in the pan, then looked at him. "Is there a problem?"

"That's a very good question."

"Who was on the phone?"

"My grandmother." He ran his fingers through his hair. "She's on her way to Blackwater Lake."

Chapter Thirteen

Jill knew the sound of Adam's car. When she heard it pull into the drive, she waited for footsteps on the porch, then discreetly peeked out the front window. It was hard to see all the details she wanted while trying not to be seen herself, but she managed to form a general impression of Adam's grandmother. Eugenia Stone was a tall, trim woman, probably in her seventies, and wearing a navy crepe pantsuit and matching low-heeled pumps. They moved out of sight and up the stairs to Adam's place, so the woman must be in pretty good physical shape.

"Show's over," she said to herself. "Time to get back to work."

She sat down at the computer to finish the statistics assignment due the following day. Unfortunately focus for the tedious task was hard to come by. She'd spent the most wonderful night of her life in Adam's arms. That morning she'd awakened with the place beside her in bed still warm from his body and the spicy scent of his skin filling her head. He'd made her coffee, for goodness' sake, and seemed eager to stay for breakfast. God help her, she'd actually allowed the thought into her head that it was what being a family would feel like.

Then his grandmother showed up. He'd mentioned once that his family wasn't pleased he'd moved to Blackwater Lake. They'd probably sent an emissary to bring him home.

C.J. ran into the room and for once she was glad he'd interrupted her train of thought. "What's up, kiddo?"

"I'm bored. Can I go down to the marina and see Brew? Please, Mom?"

"Sorry. He's doing inventory and can't keep an eye on you today. How about watching TV or reading a book?"

"Do I hafta?" The expression on his face said he'd rather go to Mercy Medical Clinic for more stitches in his chin.

"No. But I have computer work to do, so you're going to have to entertain yourself for a while. Quietly."

"I can't be quiet." He flopped on the couch with a dramatic sigh.

"We've talked about this, C.J. I have to—" A knock on the door interrupted the lecture she hated having to deliver again. She stood and walked over to answer it, saying over her shoulder, "That's probably Brew. Maybe he's finished with inventory and can hang out."

"Awesome."

But when she opened the door Brewster Smith wasn't on the other side. "Adam—"

"Hi." He reached out and ruffled C.J.'s hair. "I want you to meet my grandmother. Eugenia Stone, this is my landlady Jill Beck—"

"And I'm C.J."

"Ms. Beck." The older woman had silver hair and blue

eyes the same shade as Adam's. She took Jill's measure, then looked down. "What do those initials stand for, young man?"

"What are nishuls?"

"His name is Christopher John, but everyone calls him C.J.," Jill explained. "It's a pleasure to meet you, Mrs. Stone."

"Thank you. May we come in?"

"Of course. I'm sorry. Please." She stepped back and opened the door wider. Adam walked in behind his grandmother and sent her a sympathetic glance.

The older woman looked around the room, and the sharp gaze no doubt missed nothing. "My grandson told me a lot about you."

"Did he? I'm sure it was all good." If you didn't count the very beginning. Jill noticed the corners of his mouth curve up. At least one of them was amused.

C.J.'s expression was filled with rampant curiosity. "I don't remember my grandma. I only saw pictures 'cuz I was a baby when she died."

"That's too bad, young man. Grandmother and grandson is a very special relationship."

Adam put his arm around the older woman's shoulders. "I'm her favorite grandchild. Right, Grandmother?"

"I love all my grandchildren equally." But her grave expression softened when she looked at Adam. "You were and always shall be a rascal."

"Are you movin' to Blackwater Lake?" C.J. asked her.

"Goodness no."

"Then why are you here?" the child wanted to know, not the least bit intimidated.

Jill couldn't say the same. She considered herself a strong woman who could deal with raising a child by herself, running a business alone and not backing down from anyone. But Eugenia Stone scared the living daylights out of her and that could only mean one thing. This woman's good opinion mattered, and that wouldn't be the case if Jill didn't have feelings for Adam.

"May I sit down?"

Jill gave herself a mental forehead slap. "Yes. Please. Can I get you anything? Coffee? Tea?"

The older woman sat on the couch. "Nothing, thank you."

One by one C.J. looked at the adults in the room. "Are you guys just gonna sit around and talk?"

"That's how people become acquainted, young man. I would like to get to know your mother."

"Then I have an idea," he said. "How about if Dr. Adam and I go outside and play ball? That way I won't interrupt when you're talkin'."

"Oh, sweetie—" Jill put her hand on his small shoulder. "Dr. Adam wants to visit with his grandmother because he doesn't get to see her as much as he'd like."

"On the contrary," she said. "We have time to catch up. I think that's a wonderful idea, Christopher. Why don't you take the child outside, Adam?"

"Really?" He gave her a skeptical look. "You don't mind?"

"Not at all." She looked at Jill. "We'll have a chance for girl talk."

"Yuk." C.J. raced out of the room and came back moments later with his mitt. He handed the ball to Adam. "Let's go."

"Have fun, you two," the older woman said.

"Be good, Gram," he said playfully on his way outside.

"I always am." Her voice oozed cool confidence.

The door closed and Jill wished with all her heart that she could go with them. "Are you sure I can't get you anything, Mrs. Stone?"

"Thank you, no. Please sit. I'd like to chat." She looked at the expanse of sofa beside her.

Jill sat and tried to think of something to say that wasn't about herself. Clearly the Stone family of Dallas had money and manners that would set too high a bar for a girl from Blackwater Lake, Montana, who had a child outside of marriage.

"Your son is very cute."

"Thank you."

"He reminds me of Adam when he was that age." There was a wistful expression on the woman's face. "Not in looks, but that mischievous personality."

"He's a handful," Jill said fondly. There were several moments of awkward silence before she thought of something to fill it. "How was your trip?"

"Grueling. This isn't an easy place to get to, is it?"

"I suppose not." Jill felt the judgment vibes big-time, and the need to defend her home became uncontrollable. "Some people find the peace and quiet of a small town appealing. We often get visitors who come here for a break from big-city stress."

"There's something to be said for a hospital and an airport nearby," the other woman pointed out.

"It's not perfect, but no place is."

"The Dallas Metroplex comes very close."

Jill could read between the lines and couldn't help pushing back. "Obviously you're very happy living there, but Adam wasn't."

"In my opinion, he simply needed to get the back-to-nature phase out of his system. He'll come to his senses."

"That's what I thought originally. In fact I told him the first hint of winter would have him throwing in the towel and heading for the hills, but I was wrong." Jill remembered that time in the beginning, using her hostility against his charm. Now her antagonism was gone, leaving her with nothing to power her anti-Adam shield. "Not only did he stay, but he delivered my best friend's baby in a blizzard, then came home and shoveled snow off my walkway."

"I know that dewy-eyed look, Ms. Beck. And I feel it's my duty to warn you it would be unwise to start picking out wedding invitations and china patterns."

Jill badly wanted to tell this woman what she could do with her warning. Fury vibrated through her until she was shaking with it, but no way would she show weakness. She linked her fingers to stop her hands from trembling, then settled them in her lap.

When under control, she met the other woman's gaze and refused to look away, keeping her tone cool when she asked, "What makes you think I want to marry Adam?"

"Because he's quite a catch. Handsome. Rich. A doctor."

"Apparently he wasn't enough for his ex-wife."

"So, he told you about that." His grandmother's mouth pulled tight, deepening the lines around her mouth. "Stupid girl."

Jill was surprised to find any common ground with this woman, but she totally agreed with that. "Her loss is Blackwater Lake's gain."

"Not for long. His family is not happy about this decision."

"That's unfortunate because Adam seems very happy with it."

"Maybe temporarily. It's my impression that he's—oh, what's the word? Infatuated with you, Ms. Beck. But that won't be enough to keep him here. He will come to his senses and return to Dallas. I assure you of that."

"You're wrong, Mrs. Stone. He's worked very hard to make himself a part of this community. People here don't trust easily, but when you finally earn it, it's yours forever. Adam has earned it. The man I know and—" Love? She couldn't go there. Not yet and maybe never, but she had to say what was in her heart. "He's content right where he is."

"You're wrong, Ms. Beck. And sleeping with him isn't

love." She stood and gracefully walked toward the door. "I truly hope you don't get hurt when he realizes his mistake."

The only reason Eugenia Stone got the last word was that Jill was stunned into silence because the other woman knew she and Adam had sex. When she was done being stunned, Jill's insecurity kicked in, fueled by the old woman's words. Letting herself think about a family with Adam was like writing a prescription for heartbreak. She should have known better.

Based on her experience, she should have known that when things were going well it was time to run in the other direction.

While driving his grandmother into town, Adam pointed out the scenic beauty of Blackwater Lake and the towering, snow-tinged mountains beyond. Her only comment was, "Hmm."

Maybe she was speechless with awe, but he didn't think so. This place filled up his soul, but the difference in people was what made being a family practice doctor interesting and challenging. It was possible that Eugenia Stone's soul was stirred by looking at the ocean. Or flowers. Or a closet full of designer shoes. Or maybe she didn't have a soul.

That wasn't fair. She'd been good to him; he was her favorite. And he loved her very much.

She was sitting at rigid attention when he glanced over to the passenger seat. It was on the tip of his tongue to ask why she was here, what the purpose of the visit was, but she'd only say that she didn't need a reason to come and see her grandson. After that she'd add something snarky about it being difficult to visit a destination in the middle of nowhere.

"So, how's the family?" he asked instead.

"Fine. Mostly."

This part of the road leading into town was winding and

he had to keep his eye on it, so looking at her expression to read between the lines wasn't an option. Questions were required.

"Mostly fine? Or mostly not fine?"

"Your mother is well. She's in the process of losing ten pounds for your brother's wedding."

"So Spencer has set a date?"

"It seems Avery has her heart set on being a June bride."

"I wish someone had let me know," he said.

"Consider yourself informed now."

When his brother and Avery O'Neill had visited Dallas, his grandmother had been traveling and didn't meet her with the rest of the family. Since Spencer was clearly head over heels in love, Adam assumed Eugenia had corrected the oversight. "What do you think of Avery?"

"Charming girl." There was real warmth in her tone. "Smart as a whip. Witty. Pretty. She's absolutely perfect for Spencer."

And how did she feel about Jill? Adam only wondered because there'd been tension between the two women. After he and C.J. came back inside, it had been impossible not to notice the coolness.

He wasn't going there. Why open that can of worms since he had no intention of declaring any intentions? "Okay, so Mom and Spencer are fine. That leaves Dad and my twin, Becky. Which one of them isn't fine?"

"Both."

"What? Really?" This time he did glance at her because the road was straight and just entering the town of Blackwater Lake. Her mouth was pulled tight, which he didn't much like.

"Your sister and her husband are going to marriage counseling. No one will tell me why they need it."

And Adam wouldn't either. His sister had confided in them about her husband's one-night stand, but she didn't want their grandmother to know. Becky was confident the marriage could be saved and Eugenia Stone held a grudge if anyone had the audacity to wrong a member of her family. And she took her grudges very seriously. She'd treated his ex-wife like her own daughter, but when the marriage ended, some very unladylike language had come out of his grandmother's mouth. No one could speak his ex's name in her presence.

Adam only said, "I think Becky and Dan will be able to work things out. They have demanding careers and twins of their own. Taking time for them as a couple isn't easy, but it's necessary to the relationship."

"Speaking of relationships… Can we talk about your landlady?"

"Look," he said. "There's the Blackwater Lake Lodge."

"Don't get me started on the things wrong with that place."

"Okay. Tell me about Dad." Maybe he'd successfully deflected the personal question.

She sighed loudly. "Other than the fact that he won't listen to me or your mother?"

"About?"

"He's working too hard and won't slow down. He's tired all the time and won't see his doctor for a physical. So far our nagging has been unsuccessful."

"It sounds like you and my mother need to nag harder."

"It won't work. I'm his mother. I know."

"Has Spencer talked to him?" If he tuned out his wife and mother, maybe he'd take the advice of one of the country's leading cardiothoracic surgeons.

"I think your mother is coordinating that endeavor."

"I'll talk to Dad, too. We're both doctors."

His grandmother waved her hand dismissively. "You and your brother may be physicians, but you're also his children and by virtue of your youth, you don't have the life experience to give him perspective."

He could see where this was headed and decided to change the subject again. Potter's Ice Cream Parlor was just coming up on the right and there was a convenient parking space out front. He pulled into the diagonal lines. "How about some ice cream?"

"I'd love some. If it's good," she added skeptically.

He'd inherited his love of the stuff from her and knew her high standards would be met. "Best I've ever tasted."

After exiting the driver's side, he walked around and opened the door for his grandmother. A cold wind was blowing from the north and he knew real winter was bearing down on them. Quickly he hustled her inside where it was warm, and crowded. He was surprised he'd been able to park out front.

Carl Hayes was sitting with his wife at a table for two just inside the door. "Hey, Doc, how are you?"

"You stole my line." Adam grinned. "I'm doing great. Got family in town. This is my grandmother."

"That explains the resemblance. Except I can't believe this young lady is old enough to be your grandmother." He held out his hand. "Welcome to Blackwater Lake."

She smiled warmly at the compliment. "Thank you."

"We're very lucky to have Adam here in town. He's all right."

"He is very special," she agreed.

"Nice to see you, Carl." Adam guided his grandmother to the glass ice-cream case. Maggie's brother was behind the counter, his back turned. "Hey, Brady."

The other man looked over his shoulder and grinned. "Adam. Good to see you."

"Where's Maggie?"

"In the back feeding Dani."

"Her new baby girl," Adam explained. "This is Brady O'Keefe. Brady, my grandmother."

"A pleasure." She smiled politely. "Eugenia Stone."

"Great to meet you. What'll you two have?" he asked.

She looked over the choices, then said, "A small dish of vanilla with caramel and some of that crushed HEATH Toffee Bar topping."

"The usual for me," Adam said.

"Coming right up." Brady scooped out the ice cream and set their orders on the counter by the cash register.

Adam pulled a twenty-dollar bill from his jeans pocket. "What do I owe you?"

Maggie was just walking out of the back room carrying her sleeping daughter. "It's on the house."

"I was just about to tell him that," Brady added.

"No." Adam shook his head.

"How can I charge the doctor who came through a blizzard to bring my baby into the world?" She smiled down at the little girl in her arms.

"Nice of you, but you're giving up a lot of revenue. I'm here for the long haul and one of your best customers."

"Okay." She swayed gently, rocking the baby as she thought it over. "How about a six-month cap on freebies?"

"Fair enough. And thanks." He handed over the vanilla, then picked up his own sundae. "This is my grandmother, Eugenia Stone."

"It's really nice to meet you," Maggie said. "Adam has your eyes."

"What a lovely thing to say." There was a soft expression on his grandmother's face as her gaze settled on the baby. "She's beautiful. What's her name?"

"Danielle Maureen, after my husband and my mother."

"Lovely."

"I think so. Now eat your ice cream before it melts," she teased.

"Will do." Adam grabbed some napkins from the dispenser on the counter and headed for a corner table. They sat across from each other and ate in silence for several moments.

"She's quite a beautiful young woman. Maggie," his grandmother clarified.

"She is." Adam wasn't sure if that was an observation or a comparison with Jill. "And courageous. Her husband was killed in Afghanistan before the baby was born."

"That's dreadful." Eugenia sadly shook her head. "I can't imagine how she carries on."

"Family. Her mom helps." Adam nodded toward the counter. "That's her brother picking up the slack. The people in town pitch in. Jill is her best friend and worked a regular shift when Maggie's obstetrician ordered bed rest at the end of her pregnancy. And that's on top of raising her son and running her own business by herself."

Eugenia took a bite of ice cream and chewed thoughtfully. "Speaking of that, what is the nature of your relationship with Jill?"

Mental head slap for bringing up Jill. He really didn't want to talk about her or try to define what was between them. He just wanted things to *be*. "What makes you think there is one?"

Adam had expected the question and should have had an answer ready but didn't. It would have been easy enough to say they were just friends or she was nothing more than his landlady, but he couldn't. Neither was the complete truth, but he didn't know what the truth was.

"Really, Adam, I wasn't born yesterday. Remember that life experience I mentioned?"

"What does that mean?" He hadn't been this uncomfortable since he'd been a boy trying to hide the expensive vase he'd broken.

"It means I could see the way she looked at you."

"How was that?" This was something he really wanted to know.

"Like a woman in love, or very close to it." She took a napkin and wiped her mouth. "And I saw the way you looked at her."

He didn't want to know that. Thoughts of his soul had run through his mind earlier and it was said the eyes were a window to what was inside. His grandmother probably saw that he wanted Jill. He had from the very beginning. He liked and respected her and wanted her more than any woman he'd ever met in his life. That's all it was and putting a label on it just made everything more complicated than necessary.

"Grandmother, leave it alone."

"I can't." She jammed the plastic spoon into her half-eaten ice cream. "I hate that you're here in this place without a life."

"On the contrary, I've made a life. These people are the salt of the earth. I'm proud to say they're my friends."

"You have friends in Dallas. Think about your career. You can't reach your potential here. Without a medical center and access to state-of-the-art equipment and treatment options, there's no way to make your mark and rise to the top of your field."

"If I cared about that," he countered, "I'd have chosen a more high-profile specialty. All I ever wanted was to help people. And these people need me."

"What about your needs?"

"They are what I need. There's no doubt in my mind that if I had a personal crisis they would be there for me, just like they were for Maggie Potter."

"You have family for that."

"And everyone in my family has a demanding career.

I like living in a community where neighbors look out for each other."

"Your parents and siblings love you." She folded her arms over her chest.

"And I love them. Living in Blackwater Lake doesn't change that."

"What about the Stone family legacy?" she asked quietly.

"I'm going to assume that's your way of saying that you love and miss me, too. That you wish I lived closer."

Tears filled her eyes. "Come home to Dallas, Adam. You don't belong here."

This woman had a spine of steel, or stone. He had never seen her cry, which was the only reason he didn't let his anger show. Actually, not the only reason. There was that whole wanting your family's good opinion thing.

"Grandmother, I don't want to hurt you, but not only have I found the place where I *do* belong. I finally am home."

"And Ms. Beck?"

"What about her?"

"How does she factor into your decision to bring your career to a screeching halt?"

"First of all, I haven't done that. And second—Jill is none of your business."

He was mature enough now to put the need for family approval into perspective in a way he couldn't when he was younger. That didn't mean anyone could tell him what to do. He'd make his own personal choices—as soon as he knew what they were.

Just because a woman made you feel as if you'd been struck by lightning every time she walked into the room, that didn't mean you were the man who could make her happy. Even though he was at ease and more content than he'd ever been, he didn't want to do anything to upset Jill's world. And he especially didn't want to hurt C.J. He loved that kid.

It was so much simpler with children.

Understanding women hadn't been a class offered in med school, and even if it had been available, he doubted any man could have passed the course. He only knew that since meeting Jill, it was more important than ever to get things right and not screw up.

Chapter Fourteen

Jill put out the store's Closed sign, then walked back to where C.J. was helping Brewster tally receipts for the previous month. Actually, her son had paper, something to write with and a really big imagination that kept him occupied while the older man worked.

"What's your total, son?" Brew asked him.

The little boy chewed on the pencil for a moment as he thought. "Four billion, five hundred thousand million," he said with complete conviction.

"Exactly what I got." The older man smiled down, then looked at her and simply said, "When I get all the figures and you plug 'em into that fancy spreadsheet, I'm betting you'll have black-and-white proof that profit is better than this same time last year."

"I'm glad to hear that and I hope you're right."

Improvement in business was good, but the news didn't lift her spirits as much as it once might have. Before Adam she'd have been doing cartwheels down the dock. Now? She was upset because of what his grandmother had said. It shouldn't bother her so much that the Stone family spokesperson had told her she wasn't good enough for Adam. The woman only said out loud what Jill already knew, but somehow hearing the words had been a blow to her soul.

A person could only take so many blows to the soul before it imploded.

"You okay, Jill?"

She focused her gaze on Brewster. "Hmm?"

"Looks like you're a million miles away."

"Sorry. Just thinking about something else."

"The doc's grandma?"

She could ask how he knew but in a town the size of Blackwater Lake news of Adam's grandmother arriving in a hired car was big and spread fast. Jill could deny that the unexpected visit had bothered her, but this man would just see right through the lie.

"Yeah," she finally admitted.

"That old lady didn't smile much," C.J. commented without looking up from his drawing. "Her eyes were kinda mean."

Adam's eyes, Jill remembered, but his weren't filled with disapproval. Desire maybe. Warmth and humor certainly. But did either mean anything? Eugenia Stone had warned her not to count on marriage. Marry Adam? That was jumping the gun. First, she had to be in love with him. She seriously liked him but wasn't sure what the two of them had could actually be more.

"You're awful quiet." Brewster frowned at her. "What did the woman say?"

"It was nothing."

"Meaning you don't want to talk about it." He glanced down at the redheaded child doodling on the paper.

She met his gaze and nodded. "Pretty much. Adam's family misses him" was all she said. "And I can understand that."

"Me, too. But a grown man makes his own way and everyone has to live with it."

Jill liked to think that if her son moved far away she would gracefully accept the decision and try to become part of his new life instead of alienating his friends. But… There was always a but. She wasn't walking in Eugenia Stone's shoes and didn't know what her own reaction would be.

"Well," she said, "it's none of my business."

"Maybe not." He studied her and there was understanding in his gaze. "But that doesn't stop you from thinking about it."

She would have to work this through and with all the practice she'd had that should be easy. Time to change the subject. "Thanks for staying overtime to get last month's numbers. But I've kept you too long. Hildie must be expecting you for dinner."

"Yeah."

"How is she?"

"Doin' fine thanks to your Dr. Stone."

"He's not mine," she protested.

"I'd feel a whole lot better if he was." Brewster grinned. "I think my wife has a little doctor crush going on. She's looking forward to her appointment tomorrow just a little too much."

"I'm going to tell her you said that," Jill warned.

"I'll deny it."

"But she'll believe me. Hildie only has eyes for you and it's been that way since she was fifteen."

"I know. But like she always says, old doesn't mean deaf, dumb and blind."

"Mommy, I'm hungry." C.J. put down his pencil and gave her the pathetic starving look.

"Then let's get you something to eat."

"I'm outta here." Brewster grabbed his backpack from under the counter.

Jill shut off all but one light. Then they went outside and she locked the door. "Night, Brew."

He waved and headed to his truck while Jill and C.J. walked up the path to the house. The upstairs unit was dark compared to hers with the lamp lit in the front window. A cold wind was blowing out of the north and made her shiver. Earlier Brewster had warned that a storm was coming. More often than not he was right and she didn't know how he knew. She couldn't help thinking her personal life was its own storm and she'd get dumped on soon enough.

"What are we havin' for dinner?" C.J. asked.

"I'm thinking chicken nuggets, green beans and rice."

"French fries," he said.

"We don't have any."

"Then mashed potatoes."

"They take too long to make."

"What about the dry ones?" he asked.

She knew he meant the instant kind that came in a box. "We're out of those, too."

"How come?"

"Because I haven't had time to grocery shop." Too busy hanging out doing chores with Adam on Saturday, then a visit from his grandmother today. The man had turned her routine upside down and somehow she had to find a way to make it stop.

"Do we have ice cream?"

"Yes."

"If I eat four chicken nuggets, rice and green beans, can I have dessert?"

"Yes."

"Awesome."

She breathed a sigh of relief at the successful child/parent negotiation that hadn't ended with her pulling rank. They walked into the house and she hung up their jackets on the coatrack just inside the door. She heard Adam's car coming up the drive, and her heart jolted as if defibrillator paddles had sent electricity to it.

After a couple of cleansing breaths, she walked into the kitchen and flipped on the light, then grabbed a cookie sheet from the drawer underneath the oven. Just as she reached to open the freezer she heard a knock on the door. More electric shocks and that slowed down her timing.

"I'll get it, Mommy."

"C.J., wait," she called out, but heard the sound of him running.

When Jill got there she saw Adam standing in the doorway, scooping up her son in one arm. That was because his other arm was holding a big bouquet of flowers. Her heart did another quivery little jump.

C.J. settled his small arm comfortably on that broad shoulder. "Did you bring those for Mommy?"

"Yes." He handed the cellophane-wrapped daisies, yellow-colored mums and baby's breath to her. "Beautiful flowers for a beautiful lady."

"Yuk." C.J. wiggled until Adam put him down. "Can I watch TV?"

"Until dinner's ready." Needing her distance, Jill turned and left the room.

Adam followed her into the kitchen. "What are you having?"

"Frozen chicken nuggets."

"Are you heating them up first?"

She smiled in spite of her resolve not to. Ignoring the teasing she said, "Rice and green beans round out the menu."

"Can I stay?"

"Why?" She set the flowers on the counter and finally met his gaze.

"Because I want to."

Negotiating with a grown-up man was very different from the back-and-forth with her child. "What about your grandmother?"

"I took her to dinner at the lodge restaurant and she went to her room because she's got a car coming early tomorrow to take her to the airport."

"It's very far away she pointed out." Jill met his gaze. "If you already had dinner, there's no reason for you to stay."

"Yes, there is." He brushed his finger over her cheek and tucked a stray strand of hair behind her ear.

Jill recognized desire in his eyes, and her whole body flooded with liquid heat. The vision of Adam Stone holding flowers in one arm and her child in the other had sent her straight over the edge of the cliff and into love. She hated being so damaged that her very first reaction was to pull back from something that should be joyous.

"Why do you want frozen chicken nuggets?" she asked, her voice a little breathless.

"Because," he answered, "I really want to hang out with you and C.J."

"Okay." She had to set the rules. "On one condition."

"Name it."

"Promise not to bring me flowers again."

"Are you allergic?"

Only emotionally, she thought. Even though she'd defended his small-town choice to his grandmother, she protected herself by not letting herself believe completely that he'd stay. "No. But it makes a statement and..."

"You don't trust me." He put a hand on the counter and looked down for a moment. When he met her gaze his own was dark with irritation. "I've already promised everything

I can. One of the most important things you have to learn in medical school is that healing takes time. I'm willing to wait until your doubts are gone." He nodded emphatically. "Now I'm going to see C.J."

Jill wasn't quite sure what to make of that. He wasn't the only one irritated, but she was mad at herself. She'd let her guard down long enough to fall in love and that scared her so much. It wasn't about the flowers; they were just the focus of her fear.

Seeing her little boy run into Adam's arms was a glimpse of what could be and what she'd lose if he let her down. It was always better not to look and hope and have your dream taken away.

The first ring of the phone woke Adam, a side effect of being a doctor. He automatically looked at the bedside digital clock, which read 2:30 a.m. That was never a good thing and he was on call.

He grabbed the receiver and hit Talk. "Dr. Stone."

"Adam? It's Becky."

His sister. This was *really* not a good sign. Adrenaline punched through him and instantly he was alert. He sat up and swung his legs over the side of the bed. "What's wrong?"

"It's Dad. He had chest pain and Mom took him to the E.R. at Mercy Medical Center Dallas."

"How is he?"

"I don't know."

"Did you call Spencer?" Chest pain was his brother's specialty.

"Yes. He's catching the first flight out of Las Vegas. Probably in the morning."

"And Grandmother? You know she's here in Blackwater Lake." And had just told him his father refused to slow down. Damn it.

"I didn't know that." Relief cut through the strain in Becky's voice. "Thank God. I've been trying to reach her on her cell and the calls kept going to voice mail."

"Cell reception is spotty here in the mountains. I'll call the lodge where she's staying."

"Adam, I'm so glad you're there with her. This will be a shock. She puts on a tough face, but she's not getting any younger and is pretty fragile."

"I'll bring her home," he vowed.

"I was hoping you'd say that."

He turned on the table lamp and blinked at the sudden light. "Who's with Mom?"

"I don't think anyone is. I'm driving up from Houston and will be there in a little while."

He knew the drive took a few hours and wondered why she'd waited so long to notify him. "Why didn't you call me sooner?"

"Mom wanted to wait until there was news and I finally overruled her. I needed to hear your voice."

He stood and walked to the bedroom closet, then pulled out a carry-on suitcase. "Is there any information on Dad's condition yet?"

"They're still doing tests and evaluating him. That's all I know—" Her voice caught.

Adam's concern shifted to his sister. "Are you okay?"

"Hanging in there."

"Is Dan with you?"

"No. We couldn't both leave the twins or yank them out of bed and drag them to Dallas. If—"

"Becky?" *Come on,* he thought, *keep it together while you're driving.* The line cut out and crackled with static. "Becky?"

"I'm here. Sorry. The connection isn't great. Dan will

come with the kids when there's more information. He wanted to be with me, but it was best that I go alone for now."

"You two doing okay?"

"Yeah." She didn't ask what he meant. "Counseling is helping. We're both working at the marriage and things are better. Good, in fact."

"You'll be glad to know Grandmother tortured me relentlessly but I didn't spill my guts or your secret. It's driving her nuts."

She laughed as he'd hoped. "I owe you—"

There was a crackle in his ear and he wasn't sure if the call had dropped or not. But he said anyway, "Gotta go, Becks. See you soon."

He hung up and called the Blackwater Lake Lodge, then asked for Eugenia Stone's room. The phone was picked up on the first ring.

"Hello?" The single word was laced with hesitation, fear and dread, just like anyone who received a call at two-forty-five in the morning.

"Grandmother, it's Adam. Sorry to wake you."

"You didn't. What's wrong?"

As a doctor he'd delivered bad news before but never to family. There was no easy way to say this, so he did it quick. "Dad's in the E.R. with chest pain. They're doing tests."

"Oh, Adam—" Emotion choked off her words.

"Cancel your car. I'll drive you and we'll go to the airport together."

"Thank you."

"He's going to be fine, Gram. Probably just high gas pain. But I'll get you to him." He looked at the clock again. "Pick you up in thirty minutes."

"I'll be waiting in the lobby." She hung up.

Adam made a couple more phone calls, one to arrange for another doctor to take calls and one to the Mercy Medical Clinic manager to cancel his appointments that week. He started to dial Jill's number because he badly needed to talk to her. Then he realized that he'd jar her out of a sound sleep and probably C.J., too. As much as he wanted to hear reassurance in that smoky voice of hers, he just couldn't wake her. She needed her rest. He decided to call later when she'd be awake and let her know what was going on.

Twenty minutes later Adam was showered and packed. He left his apartment and walked down the stairs. Jill's porch was at the bottom and he stared at her dark windows and front door, unable to move past. It wasn't only her voice he needed. The hunger to hold her cut through him like a knife, and the thought of not seeing her left an ache in his heart.

Leaving her was like ripping out his soul and when he got back, the two of them needed to have a long talk.

Jill wasn't sure when she first realized something was off but it began to sink in when she and C.J. walked outside to go to school. That was when she recognized that the pattern of sounds signaling Adam's presence was off.

"Dr. Adam's car is gone." Her son opened the rear passenger door and climbed into his booster seat before buckling himself in.

"He must have had a patient emergency," she said, sliding behind the steering wheel.

It wasn't unusual for him to meet someone early at the clinic, but usually it was close to regular operating hours and she heard his footsteps on the front porch when he was on his way. If he'd gotten a call and left in the middle of the night, that meant someone was really sick and she didn't want to think about who it might be and what was wrong.

A short time later she pulled up in front of Blackwater Lake Elementary and put the car in Park. "Do you have your lunch?"

"Yup." C.J. nodded emphatically as he unbuckled his seat belt and slid down from his perch. Then he opened the back door. "We need to remind Dr. Adam that my birthday party is the day after tomorrow."

"Okay, kiddo. I'll do that when I see him."

"I love you, Mommy."

"Love you, too, baby. Zip up your jacket. It's freezing outside."

"I'm not a baby. I'm almost seven." He slammed the door.

Jill smiled as she watched her little man trudge up the sidewalk to where his class lined up, dragging his backpack behind him. It was almost as big as he was, proving that he was still her little man. And he'd grown very attached to Adam, in spite of her efforts to prevent that very thing from happening. C.J. wasn't the only one.

She'd grown accustomed to having the handsome doctor around, listening for the sound of him leaving in the morning and coming home at night, staying for dinner. Making love. And now she wanted to kick herself for being such a witch when he brought her flowers. He'd promised to wait until she trusted, but a part of her believed that she was just too much trouble and it was only a matter of time before he stopped waiting and moved on.

But she didn't want him to give up on her and she'd tell him so when he got home that night.

Since the school was halfway between home and town, she continued on to the grocery store. The weather forecast had a storm moving in and a lot of snow and she decided to stock up on food and get everything for C.J.'s birthday dinner now. Lasagna was his favorite and easily served a lot of people who'd been invited to the party.

After shopping, she drove home and parked the car in the usual spot. A longing swelled inside her to see Adam's SUV in his usual spot beside it. As soon as possible, she would admit to him that she was an idiot, possibly a tad paranoid, and graciously thank him for bringing her flowers.

With a happy smile, she carried her groceries inside, put the cold items in the refrigerator, then left the rest on the counter to deal with later. Then she headed for the marina store to check on things. Brew always had the situation under control, but there was a lot to do with winter coming on.

When she opened the door, the bell over it tinkled. The older man was standing by the cash register and looked up. "Mornin', Jill."

"Hi." She closed out the freezing air. "It's really cold outside."

"Yeah. Can't say I'm lookin' forward to winter. It's harder as a body gets older." He counted the bills in the money drawer that were used to make change if necessary. "This time of year Hildie always threatens to move to Las Vegas where it's warm."

Her chest tightened at the words, a reaction from the part of her that feared being left behind. Then she remembered that Hildie said the same thing every year right around now.

"What did you tell her?"

"That I'd miss her a lot." He grinned.

"You're bad. And a liar." But she smiled at him. "You'd be so lost without her."

"I know it." He shook a finger at her. "But that's just between us. Don't you ever tell her I said that."

"My lips are sealed." Jill looked around the store's interior. Shelves were neat and fully stocked. Displays were in order and sale signs clearly posted on summer merchandise that needed to be gotten rid of. "What's your plan for the day?"

"Got a fishing party comin' in at ten. The same four idiots come every year at this time. A last hurrah, they call it." He shook his head. "I'll get them outfitted and on the way, and then I thought I'd do some work on Adam's boat."

She glanced through the window and saw it under a tarp. He'd be using it when spring came, and the thought made her insides go all gooey and giddy. "Good idea. But maybe you should bring it into the back room and work there. Out of the cold."

"I'll do that." He closed the cash drawer. "Speaking of Adam, what's up with him?"

"Nothing that I know of." Except his pattern was off this morning. Suddenly her glass-is-half-empty attitude punched a hole in her happy balloon. "Why?"

"Hildie had an appointment today at the clinic, but they called to cancel it."

Now the feeling got really bad. As C.J. had pointed out, his car was gone. If he wasn't at the clinic... "Did they say why?"

"No. And when she asked about rescheduling, the girl said she couldn't do that until they heard from him."

"I saw him last night and he didn't say a word about going anywhere." She met the older man's gaze. "He's gone."

"Sounds like it." It was a toss-up whether his voice was more grim or more angry.

Contrary to what he'd promised, he wasn't willing to wait even twenty-four hours for her trust to heal. Self-fulfilling prophecy. He was going to leave anyway, so she'd driven him away. She'd fallen for him and he left without a word, just like everyone else she'd loved. But she'd been so sure he was committed to the community of Blackwater Lake.

"Well," she said, "I guess that's it."

"I know it's hard, but don't jump to conclusions," Brew warned.

That was a tall order. First his grandmother arrives and all but says she's not good enough and then he disappears. What conclusion was she supposed to jump to?

Fear of abandonment was threatening to swamp her like a tsunami. When that first wave rolled back, there was nothing left but a hurt that stole the breath from her lungs. And then something else pressed down on her heart.

C.J. had fallen for him, too. What was she going to tell her little boy? On top of that there was this stupid storm coming and if it was as bad as predicted, his birthday party would be ruined.

When things went bad, they all went bad.

Chapter Fifteen

Two days later the mouthwatering aroma of lasagna and garlic bread filled the house. A few hardy friends who'd braved the still-falling snow had come in Cabot Dixon's multi-passenger, all-wheel drive vehicle to bring birthday presents. The Adam rumor, pieced together from Liz at the clinic and Blackwater Lake Lodge night staff, was that he was visiting his family. Jill had jumped to every possible conclusion but settled on the one that made sense. His grandmother had convinced him to go home.

She hadn't said as much to C.J., just gave him the facts as she knew them. Dr. Adam canceled his clinic appointments and they weren't scheduling any more until hearing from him. So far no one had heard from him. Her son had taken the news well, reminding her that the doctor had promised to be here. But for the last two nights when she'd tucked him in he'd asked about Dr. Adam.

Baking the birthday cake and getting food on the table for

a buffet-style meal had kept Jill busy and she was grateful. At least for a little while there was something to distract her from the pain she knew would only get worse.

She moved to the kitchen doorway and said to the small gathering, "It's on the table. Come get it while it's hot."

"I love lasagna," C.J. yelled at the top of his lungs. With Tyler Dixon behind him he came running down the hall from his bedroom, then navigated a path through the adults who were standing around talking.

Cabot Dixon was in deep conversation with Brady O'Keefe. He was there because Maggie hadn't wanted to take the baby out in the storm. Jill completely understood the need to protect your child. Hildie and Brew sat on the sofa chatting with Ginny Irwin, the nurse at Mercy Medical Clinic. The people C.J. cared about most were in this room. All except Adam Stone.

Jill stood aside while her friends filed past the food arranged on the table. The two boys took their plates, then sat on the living room floor in front of the fireplace and started eating. She was last in line behind Mayor Loretta Goodson. After getting food, they stood together by the front door as all the seating in the small room was already taken.

Loretta took a bite of the layered pasta, meat sauce and cheese. "Mmm. Really good, Jill. I think it's the best one ever."

"Thanks." That was a relief. She wasn't at her best when she'd thrown this together. When your heart was broken, cooking could be risky.

"So," her friend said, mixing dressing into the salad on her plate, "nothing from Adam?"

"No."

"That's just weird."

"Not in my world."

That was a pitiful attempt to make light of what happened

and fell way short of the mark. Jill couldn't believe it had happened to her again and that this time was so much worse. Her heart ached in places she hadn't even known were there. His leaving had left a big hole in her life. And she was so tired from waking at night and feeling the emptiness chase sleep away for good as reality set in.

"I know you've had a string of bad luck," Loretta said sympathetically, "but I really thought he was one of the good guys."

"Me, too." Ginny Irwin moved closer to join them. "Took me a while to warm up to him, but he finally won me over. I'm usually a good judge of character and I was convinced he was here for the long haul."

"I wish I could say it was some comfort not to be the only one fooled." Jill shrugged. "But it's not."

"You talking about Adam?" Brady O'Keefe moved closer.

"What was your first clue?" Ginny's voice was teasing.

"Besides the fact that you three are looking awfully serious?" Brady's brown eyes tracked from one woman to the next. "It stands to reason you're talking about the guy who isn't here. And for what it's worth, I think there's a perfectly reasonable explanation."

"For disappearing?" Ginny sniffed. "I'd like to hear it. The connection was bad when he called to say he wouldn't be in and we expected more information would be forthcoming. It hasn't been."

Brady grinned. "Don't look at me like that. I don't know what the reason is, just said there probably is one."

"He's right," Mayor Goodson said. "Adam has a home here. A medical practice. Neighbors and patients he worked damn hard to become friends with."

Jill listened to them debate the issue. She didn't have the emotional reserves to be on the pro or con side. From her perspective hope only prolonged the pain until she crawled into the acceptance stage where numbness was a welcome relief.

By the time the adults had finally finished eating, she noticed that the boys were horsing around and getting restless. "C.J., why don't you and Tyler put your plates in the kitchen?"

"Okay, Mom." When the errand was finished, he came back into the room and stood beside her.

She put her hand on his shoulder. "I think it's time to open presents and have cake."

He shook his head. "I wanna wait for Dr. Adam."

Jill's stomach knotted and she was afraid she'd lose the little bit of dinner she'd been able to choke down. "Sweetie, I don't think we can wait any longer."

"I know everyone thinks he just left, but he'll be here." The young voice was filled with the will to make it so. "He promised."

"I don't think he's coming," she said quietly. But gentling a blow like that by softening your voice simply wasn't possible.

"You're wrong." The quickness to anger wasn't like C.J. "Dr. Adam said nothing could keep him away from my party."

Jill saw tears gather in his eyes and wanted to cry, too. The hope on her son's little face just made her heart hurt more. She'd wanted so much for his birthday to be perfect and simply couldn't pull that miracle off. It made her unspeakably sad that betrayal would always be the reason C.J. remembered the birthday he turned seven.

She'd remember it, too, because of how hard she'd worked to keep from falling for Adam only to realize it was the forever-after kind of love. But, darn it all, grieving was for tomorrow because neither rain, nor sleet, nor dark of night, nor snow was going to keep her son from having the best birthday she could give him.

"Okay, kiddo. I have an idea. Maybe we can—" Standing by the door, she heard the sound of an engine, but not a car engine. She listened for a few seconds. "Is that a motorcycle? What kind of idiot would ride something like that in weather like this?"

Brady moved to the window beside her. "It's not a motorcycle. That looks like Carl Hayes on a snowmobile. And there's someone on the back."

"Dr. Adam!"

Jill was right behind C.J. when he yanked open the front door. She grabbed his shoulder to keep him from running out into the snow. It looked as though the flurry was letting up, but she didn't want him getting wet and cold. His hopes were already in the stratosphere, but she'd be there to catch him when he dropped to earth. Life wasn't a Hollywood movie where the hero swooped in at the last minute on the back of a snowmobile. Except...

A man swung his leg over the back of the machine. He said something to the driver, who nodded, waved and gunned the motor before moving away. There was something familiar about the bundled-up figure walking up the path. If that wasn't Adam's winter jacket, this guy had one exactly like it.

All his life, Adam hadn't known how lonely loneliness could be until he saw Jill and C.J. silhouetted in the doorway. It was snowy and dark; he was cold and wet. In fact, he'd never been colder or wetter, but the sight of them made it all go away and filled up the big empty place inside that he'd carried around for years.

By the time he got to the porch where they were standing, he couldn't feel his feet. But the smile on C.J.'s face made everything he'd been through to get here worth it.

"Dr. Adam, you came!"

Adam dropped to one knee as the boy moved close and launched into his arms. "I told you nothing would keep me away, champ."

"I missed you so much."

"I missed you, too." *And your mom.* He met Jill's gaze, and the bruised look in her eyes told him she had not believed he would be here.

He had some explaining to do, but before a word passed his lips, she turned and pushed past the people gathered in the doorway. One of those people was Brewster Smith and Adam guessed this wasn't the time to ask the man how his boat was coming along. The scowl was a big clue.

"I thought this was a party." Adam stood, but kept his hand on C.J.'s shoulder. "You don't look happy."

If anything Brew scowled harder. "I told you the first time we met that this is the face you'd get if you hurt my girl."

"I didn't mean—" The tugging on his jacket made him look down.

"Dr. Adam? Did you get me a present?" There was nothing but eager anticipation in C.J.'s expression.

It was nice that at least one person wasn't staring at him as if they'd like to lynch him from the nearest tree. "I didn't have a chance to shop, C.J. But I will. In the meantime I found this for you at DFW."

"What's that?"

"Dallas/Fort Worth Airport." He unzipped his jacket and pulled out a small bag.

The boy opened it and a wide smile split his face. "Oh, boy!" He put the Texas Rangers World Series 2011 baseball hat on his head. "Awesome. Thanks, Dr. Adam."

"You're welcome."

"That was quite an entrance, Doc." Virginia Irwin was on the porch.

"Yeah." He shrugged. "What can I say?"

"You can start explaining. Your only message was to cancel your clinic patients because you were going to Dallas." She folded her arms over her chest.

"Urgent family matter." He was starting to shiver badly.

"And about that entrance you just made? A snowmobile? Carl Hayes?"

"My car got stuck about a mile from his house and I walked there. Carl offered to give me a lift when I told him that I had a very important date." He glanced down at the birthday boy proudly showing off his new hat. "I can explain, Virginia—"

"Call me Ginny," she said. "That was good enough for me. Now, I'm no doctor, but you should probably get out of those wet things and take a hot shower before you catch your death."

"You don't get sick from being cold. Viruses are transmitted in other ways—"

"Spare me the medical lecture."

"I have to talk to Jill first," he insisted.

"I'll let her know. Now march." She pointed at the stairway leading up to his place.

"Yes, ma'am."

"Because I'm feeling charitable toward you, I'm going to pretend you didn't just call me ma'am."

"Understood."

His legs felt stiff and heavy as he walked up the stairs and his hands were shaking badly as he fitted his key into the lock. Inside, he dropped his jacket over a kitchen chair and then went to the bathroom and stripped off his cold, wet clothes. He tried to move faster and was only more frustrated when he couldn't. He was desperate to talk to Jill, to explain what had happened and hope she'd understand. The devastated look on her face was tearing him apart.

When the shower water was hot, he stepped into it. Every instinct urged him to hurry, but he forced himself to stand under the warm spray until the pins and needles feeling in his extremities let up. After that, he quickly washed away the grime from the airport and a long tense day on the road. Ten minutes later he was dried off and his hair was neatly combed. He was warmly dressed in jeans, a long-sleeved shirt and a pullover sweater.

"Hopefully she'll give me bonus points for appearance," he said to his reflection.

It was time to make her understand and he hoped her past wouldn't make her not want to listen.

Adam jogged downstairs and let himself into the house. Everyone stopped talking and stared at him. He raised a hand in acknowledgment. "Hi."

A chorus of greetings followed and he scanned the room for the one person in the world he most wanted to see. She wasn't there and by process of elimination and skilled deductive reasoning, he narrowed down her whereabouts. Without another word to anyone, he went in the kitchen.

Jill was bending over the dishwasher. Any other time it would have been a spectacular view, but not now. Not when everything he'd ever wanted was at risk.

"Jill—"

She straightened and her whole body tensed, but she didn't turn or say a word.

"Ginny said she'd explain that she bullied me into changing into dry clothes." Still nothing. He walked behind her and gently turned her toward him. "Say something. Even if it's to tell me to go to hell. I really need to hear the sound of your voice."

She burst into tears and buried her face in her hands. His heart squeezed painfully at her distress and he gathered her trembling body against his own.

"Don't cry. Please don't. I can't stand it."

"I'm s-sorry. It's just—" After several moments she drew in a shuddering breath, then lifted her tear-streaked face. "No one I love has ever come back."

"Oh, sweetheart—" A lump of emotion choked off his words. He'd put her through hell. It wasn't his fault, but he still hated that she was upset because of him. "Damn it."

"What?"

"I got a call in the middle of the night about my father. There was chest pain and I suspected he'd had a heart attack. I had to go."

"Oh, Adam—of course you did."

"I had to go and didn't want to wake you. In the morning I planned to call from the airport and explain. But men plan and Mother Nature laughs. There was no cell reception. And in Dallas my sister was waiting at DFW. I had to get to the hospital."

"Is your dad okay?"

"Yes, thank God. The attack was mild and there was no permanent muscle damage. It was more of a warning to slow down and take better care of himself. My brother Spencer is on top of that."

"Isn't he the heart doctor?"

Adam nodded. "He's running point on the recovery including diet, exercise, medication and cardiac rehabilitation."

"You should have stayed," she protested.

"They threw me out."

Her eyes went wide. "Why would they do that? I thought they were on a mission to get you back home."

"That's true," he confirmed. "But I was home and acutely crabby."

"You? Mr. Sunshine?"

He loosened his hold but didn't let her go. "There were storms all the way from Montana to the Gulf and I couldn't get through to you. I needed to talk to you, to hear your voice. When that wasn't possible, I pretty much ticked off everyone with my bad attitude. Dad was out of the woods and I was told in no uncertain terms to go back where I belonged."

"Here?" The shadows started to lift from her eyes even though tears still clung to her lashes. "Blackwater Lake?"

"Yeah." He couldn't look at her hard enough. "So I grabbed the next flight out and managed to get in before the storm closed the airport. Although cell reception was still impossible. So I drove through a blizzard. Almost made it, too, until I got stuck in the snow."

"Near Carl Hayes's place, Ginny said."

"That's right." He let out a breath. "He gave me a ride."

"So, like the hero in a Hollywood movie you fought your way through a snowstorm for C.J.'s party?" Her mouth curved up at the corners.

"Letting him down wasn't an option." He willed her to believe his next words. "Or you either. I love you, Jill."

"You do?"

He nodded. "More than I can say. I love C.J., too. Being with you guys is the most important thing in my life."

"I thought you didn't want a commitment."

"When I moved here that was the last thing on my mind and I said some stupid, macho things. I knew you'd been badly hurt and I have a bad track record. I didn't want to promise anything and be another guy on the list of men who let you down. But going to Dallas made me realize something."

"What?"

"I didn't know it when I made the decision to move, but coming to Blackwater Lake was all about finding family. I didn't understand that until meeting you and C.J."

"Oh, Adam—" Her voice caught and she blinked furiously.

"I hope those are happy tears because more than anything in the world I want to make you happy."

"I confess, when you were gone without a word I went to the bad place because it's just where I've lived for so long. A habit." She met his gaze and her own was clear and bright. "I trust you, Adam. I'll never doubt you again."

"Prove it. Marry me and I swear to you that I'll be the best husband and father on the planet. I will never leave you."

"I believe you." She smiled. "Before I give you an answer, there's something you should know."

"Okay."

"Your grandmother told me that I shouldn't be picking out wedding patterns and monogramming towels. She said that Dallas was your home and you'd be returning to it soon."

"Then apparently my bad attitude while away from you changed her mind." He grinned. "She's the one who told me to leave."

"Really?"

"I couldn't make that stuff up." He met her gaze. "I'm waiting for an answer. Please don't keep me in suspense."

"Yes. Yes. Yes." She rose on tiptoe and touched her lips to his. "More than anything I want to be your wife."

Adam returned the kiss until her eyes crossed and her toes curled. He finally came up for air and said, "Blackwater Lake is where I live, but being in your arms is and always will be home to me."

"Dr. Adam? Why are you kissin' Mommy?" C.J. moved closer and looked up.

Adam went down on one knee and Jill nodded her approval to share the news. "Champ, if it's okay with you, I'm going to marry your mom."

"And live with us forever?" His eyes opened wider.

"Yes," Adam said. "What do you think?"

"I think that's the best birthday present ever, Dr. Adam."

"Good. And maybe you should call me Adam?"

"Maybe I could call you Daddy?" The child looked at him, then his mother. "Would that be okay?"

"More than okay—" Jill's voice caught when a speechless

Adam pulled C.J. into his arms. She swallowed hard, then said, "I know it's your birthday, kiddo, but I just got the best present ever. Not only are my single-mom days over, but the three of us together are the family I always wanted."

* * * * *

A sneaky peek at next month...

Cherish™

ROMANCE TO MELT THE HEART EVERY TIME

My wish list for next month's titles...

In stores from 19th July 2013:

❏ How to Melt a Frozen Heart – Cara Colter

& A Weaver Vow – Allison Leigh

❏ The Cattleman's Ready-Made Family – Michelle Douglas

& Rancher to the Rescue – Jennifer Faye

In stores from 2nd August 2013:

❏ The Maverick's Summer Love – Christyne Butler

& His Long-Lost Family – Brenda Harlen

❏ A Cowboy To Come Home To – Donna Alward

& The Doctor's Dating Bargain – Teresa Southwick

Available at WHSmith, Tesco, Asda, Eason, Amazon and Apple

Just can't wait?

0713/23

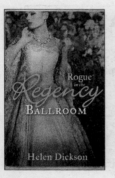